RANDOM
HOUSE
LARGE
PRINT

Also by Fannie Flagg
available from Random House Large Print

**Fried Green Tomatoes at the
Whistle Stop Café**

Welcome to the World, Baby Girl!

The All-Girl Filling Station's Last Reunion

THE
WHOLE TOWN'S
TALKING

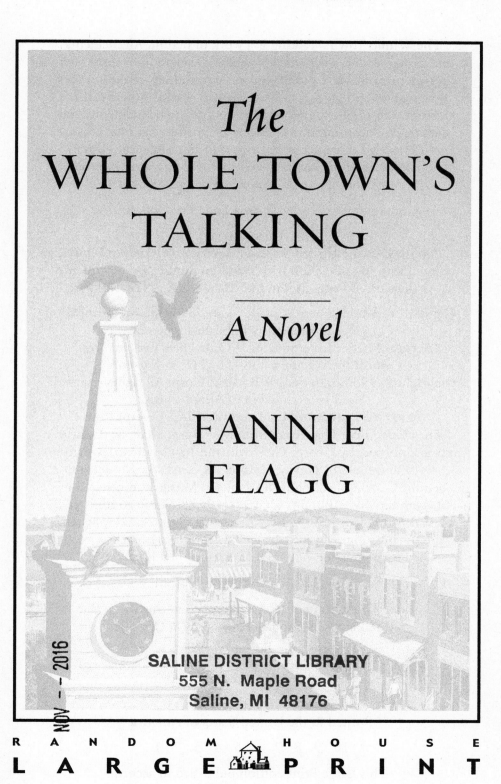

The
WHOLE TOWN'S TALKING

A Novel

FANNIE FLAGG

R A N D O M H O U S E
L A R G E P R I N T

Published in the United States of America by Random House Large Print, in association with Random House, an imprint and division of Penguin Random House LLC, New York.

Grateful acknowledgment is made to the following for permission to reprint previously published material:
ALFRED MUSIC: Excerpt from "I Only Have Eyes for You," words by Al Dubin, music by Harry Warren, copyright © 1934 (renewed) WB Music Corp. All rights reserved. Used by permission of Alfred Music.
ALFRED MUSIC AND HAL LEONARD LLC: Excerpt from "They Can't Take That Away from Me" (from **Shall We Dance**), music and lyrics by George Gershwin and Ira Gershwin, copyright © 1936 (renewed) Nokawi Music, Ira Gershwin Music, and Frankie G. Songs. All rights for Nokawi Music administered by Imagem Sounds. All rights for Ira Gershwin Music administered by WB Music Corp. All rights for Frankie G. Songs administered by Songs Music Publishing. All rights reserved. Used by permission of Alfred Music and Hal Leonard LLC.

Cover illustration: Peter Malone

The Library of Congress has established a Cataloging-in-Publication record for this title.

ISBN: 978-0-7393-2737-1
www.randomhouse.com/largeprint
FIRST LARGE PRINT EDITION
Printed in the United States of America

10 9 8 7 6 5 4 3 2 1

This Large Print edition published in accord with the standards of the N.A.V.H.

For Cluny Brown,
who can fix anything

What the Crow Knows

——

They rise early, in the country and in cities, eager to start their serious crow business. They gather in large groups or, sometimes, just one or two. All day long, they soar high and low, calling out to the busy people below. They shout from the trees, rooftops, and telephone wires . . .

"Now! Now! Live now!"

Poor old crows. They think they are talking, but the only thing the people hear is . . .

"Caw! Caw! Caw!"

Prologue

What can I tell you about the town? I suppose if you had driven through it back then, it might have looked like just another ordinary small town . . . but it wasn't. I was born and raised there, so I know exactly what I am talking about. It wasn't a wealthy town, either, but we all stuck together. And when we heard what had happened to Hanna Marie, everybody was upset. We all talked about it. Everybody vowed to do something about it. But never, in our wildest dreams, would anybody have guessed who would actually be the one to do it. Or, more importantly, how they would do it. But to tell you any more at this point might spoil the surprise. And who doesn't like a good surprise? I know I do.

A Friend

And So It Begins. . . .

Lordor Nordstrom

1889

—

Missouri, USA

At age twenty-eight, Lordor Nordstrom had left his home in Sweden for America, looking for land to buy. Months later, while crossing down through southern Missouri, he found a large tract of good, rich land with plenty of natural springs, just right for a dairy farm. After he had cleared an area for his farm, he placed an ad in the Swedish-American newspapers for young farmers to come and start a new community and soon others joined him, bringing their families and farm animals with them. By 1880, a small farming community had formed that other people in the area called Swede Town, in spite of the fact that two Germans and one Norwegian (who was suspected of being Finnish) now lived there.

Today, Lordor Nordstrom stood on the top of a small hill looking over the long expanse of rolling green meadows and little white farmhouses below. It was so quiet and peaceful up here, nothing but the sound of birds and distant cowbells. He could see there was a most pleasant view from every angle. Exactly what he had been looking for.

He would donate this land to the community and name it Still Meadows. Walking back down the hill, Lordor felt very pleased with himself. As the original settler, he felt a great responsibility to the settlers who had come after him. And he had just found the perfect spot for their final resting place in the upcoming years.

In the following weeks, Lordor and all the local men cleared the land on the hill and began measuring and blocking out rows of burial plots. Each plot was given a number, written out in both Swedish and English, so there would be no confusion. They built a nice wooden arch as an entrance that was carved with flowers and read STILL MEADOWS CEMETERY, ESTAB. 1889.

After all the landscaping was complete, Lordor called a meeting out at his farm, and announced that since they were all first settlers, their plots would be free, first come, first served, which seemed to Lordor the only fair way to do it. In the future, any newcomers would be charged fifty cents a plot.

The following Sunday, all the families packed up their wagons and went up the hill to stake their claim with small sticks. Some, like the Swensens, who hoped to start a large family, staked out an entire row of twenty or more plots to provide for the ones already here and those yet to come.

Birdie Swensen was very happy with their choice.

She was quite musical and liked hearing the birds and cowbells in the distance. She liked the view as well. She said to her husband, "Look, Lars, you can see our farm and the windmill from here. It will be so nice for the children when they come to visit." Mr. and Mrs. Henry Knott wanted to look back at the cornfields.

Although the flat area on the top of the hill was rather large, and they could have spread around, most people are creatures of habit. They all tended to pick out spots right next to their neighbors, much as they lived below, Lordor in the middle, under the big oak tree, and everyone else around him. Everybody, that is, except Old Man Hendersen, who marched way over to the other side and stuck his stick there. Someone once said that Eustus Hendersen liked his mules better than he did people, and he had agreed.

"Mules are mean, but at least they don't talk your head off when you see them."

Later, after everyone had chosen a plot, they sat down for a picnic lunch. Blueberries were in season, so the ladies had made pies. Mr. Lindquist played his fiddle, and Mrs. Knott played her accordion. All in all, it was a fun afternoon.

Of course, at the time, none of them knew about all the strange and mysterious events that would take place on that hill. And even if you had told them, they wouldn't have believed you in a million years.

Love and Marriage

LORDOR GUESSED THAT PREPARING A PLACE TO spend eternity and trying to figure out how many plots to set aside for himself was what made him think about his future. At the ripe old age of thirty-seven, he was still one of the many bachelor farmers living in the area. He hadn't meant to be. He'd just been busy trying to turn a no place into a someplace. There were five married ladies, who were always at him to find a nice woman and settle down, but finding a wife was not an easy thing to do.

Lordor wasn't against the idea. A few years earlier, and at their insistence, he had tried to meet someone. That spring, he'd had his hair cut by a real barber, purchased a brand-new pair of shoes out of a catalog, and traveled all the way over to the Swedish community of Lindsborg, Kansas. But when he got there, he found out that all the good women were already taken. So Lordor had come back home empty-handed with nothing but the same new shoes and a good haircut.

Swede Town really was in dire need of more women. As it stood now, they couldn't even throw a decent square dance. When they did, all the men had to take turns wearing a white handkerchief tied around their arms to signify that they were now assuming the role of a female partner. And having to dance and hold hands with another grizzly, callused, hard-skinned farmer had a way of making the real women seem a lot more beautiful, softer, and much more delicate than they really were. Their lack of ladies was causing them to lose good workers as well. After dancing with five-foot-tall, three-feet-wide Nancy Knott, one young farmhand later told Lordor, "When Mrs. Knott starts to look good to you, it's time to move on." And he did.

Lordor figured if he was ever going to make another attempt at finding a nice lady, the time was now. He had a new contract to sell milk and cheese to the railroad workers, and his financial future was now secure enough to support a wife. Besides, he was lonely. He wanted someone to share the new house he had just built. But courting a lady properly was a time-consuming proposition, and at present, he didn't have enough of it. He was short on help, and his dairy farm required him to be there full-time.

AT THE NEXT BARN RAISING, as everyone was sitting at a long wooden table having lunch, Lordor talked the situation over with his neighbors. Henry Knott, a bandy-legged little hog farmer seated down at the other end, called out, "Hey, Lordor . . . why don't you advertise for one of them mail-order brides? That way, she comes to you, and no work time's lost."

All the women jumped on that notion in a hurry. "Oh, Lordor," said Mrs. Eggstrom, "that's exactly what you should do."

Lordor pulled a skeptical face at the idea, but Mrs. Lindquist, waving a spoon at him, said, "I know what you're thinking, Lordor, but there's no shame to it. A lot of men out west are doing it, and there must be plenty of nice Swedish girls out there looking to marry."

"She's right," added Birdie Swensen, who had just placed another piece of fried chicken in front of him. "And if the girl is interested, she sends you her photograph. That way, we can all get a look at her and help you decide."

Lordor still felt reluctant. He was a little bit shy around women anyway, and the idea of marrying a total stranger made him feel uneasy. But in the end, Mrs. Knott summed it up for him. "You're getting old, Lordor. Get to it!" He guessed it wouldn't hurt anything to at least try. So a week later, a small ad appeared in a Swedish-American newspaper in Chicago.

SWEDISH MAN OF 37 YEARS LOOKING FOR
SWEDISH LADY FOR MARRIAGE.
I HAVE A HOUSE AND COWS.

—LORDOR NORDSTROM
SWEDE TOWN, MISSOURI

A Swedish Lady

1889

—

CHICAGO

KATRINA OLSEN, ONLY FIVE YEARS FROM SWEDEN, was a domestic servant in a large household in Chicago. She had been helping clean the kitchen that morning and had noticed Lordor's ad in a newspaper. She carefully tore it out and put it in her apron pocket. That night, when she and her friend and coworker Anna Lee were upstairs in their room, Katrina showed her the ad.

"Do you think I should answer it?"

Anna Lee looked at the ad with some alarm. "Oh, Katrina . . . Missouri? We don't even know where that is. There could be wild Indians or bears even. And this Lordor Nordstrom might be mean and ugly."

Katrina sighed. "I know, but I don't want to be a servant all my life."

"No, me either, but I don't see much difference in being a servant and being some old cow-farmer's wife. Besides, it's too much hard work with no pay.

No, I'd rather stay in the city and take my chances with the boys here."

Being a pretty girl, Katrina had gone out with a few Chicago boys, friends of Anna Lee's, but they'd been too slick and fast-talking for her taste. And, somehow, the idea of working hard on your own land did not seem that daunting to her. But what Anna Lee had said about bears and wild Indians was a real concern. When they had been learning English, they had read all the popular American dime novels, like **Trapper Bess** and **Mountain Kate,** that told of all the many perils women faced living out in the wilderness.

But the more Katrina thought about the ad, the more it intrigued her. She knew going all the way to Missouri would be a risky venture. She could be eaten by a mountain lion or worse. But the ad said the man had a house. When she had left Sweden, she had made certain promises, and she desperately wanted to keep them. So it might be worth taking a chance, but she had waited so long to respond, she was sure Mr. Nordstrom had found someone by now. Still, she guessed it couldn't hurt to write and see.

Dear Sir,

A 24-year-old Swedish lady of the Lutheran faith with skills of cooking, sewing, and gardening and a good nature is answering your

advertisement. Enclosed is my photograph. If you are so inclined and not already taken, please send your photograph.

Sincerely,
Katrina Olsen

It had been weeks, and Lordor Nordstrom had not yet received one reply to his ad. A lot of girls had seen the ad, but most Swedish girls in Chicago were like Anna Lee. They had left farms in Sweden and had no desire to go back to one. Lordor had almost given up hope when Miss Olsen's reply arrived.

The Verdict

THE DAY THE LETTER ARRIVED, LORDOR BROUGHT Miss Olsen's photograph over to the women as promised. They had all gathered in Mrs. Knott's kitchen for the occasion. After Lordor handed it over, he was told to wait outside so they could speak freely.

Lordor wandered out to the barn and had a smoke with Mr. Knott, who had also been banned from the kitchen. He had no more than finished his smoke when the kitchen door flew open and Mrs. Knott called out, "Lordor, come on in. . . . Henry, you stay out there. I'll get your lunch in a minute." Mr. Knott nodded. He hoped it would be sausage and potatoes today. His wife wasn't much to look at, but oh, her steaming sauerkraut, her Wiener schnitzel, her piping-hot pot roast, creamed noodles, and apple dumplings.

Lordor walked slowly up the stairs to receive his verdict. He took his hat off, stepped inside, and was told to have a seat while five ladies stared at him. He suddenly felt himself start to sweat under the pressure when Birdie Swensen, the gentlest of the five women, spoke.

"Now, Lordor . . . a girl can be pretty and fool a man, but she can't fool another woman. Yes, this girl is pretty, but for a wife, you want someone of good character as well."

Lordor cleared his throat. "Yes, I suppose so."

"Trust us, you do. And so, after careful study, we all agree. This girl has character." They all nodded as she continued. "We think you need to answer her letter right now, before somebody else grabs her."

Mrs. Lindquist jumped in. "Besides, she's a Lutheran, Lordor. What else do you need to know?"

Lordor was awfully glad to hear the ladies' opinion. He cared very much about what they thought, but in this case, he hadn't needed much prompting. The moment he had seen the girl's photograph, he had been smitten. She was Swedish all right, with her blond braids arranged so neatly across her head and wearing her high-necked white lace blouse with a cameo. And she was very pretty. But it was something else that had captured his attention right away. It was a look in her eye that certain immigrants recognized in one another. A look of hope and determination, almost as if she was gazing past him, far into the future. The day the photograph had arrived, he'd stared at it for so long that when he closed his eyes that night, he could still see her face. He figured that must mean something, but he stopped himself from going too far. First, he needed to have his picture taken and give the girl a chance to get a good look at him.

Oh, Lord. Just the thought of her seeing his photograph filled him with dread. Now he knew how that poor horse he'd just bought must have felt when he had examined every inch of him and looked at all of his teeth before putting his money down. Tomorrow, he was going to give that horse some extra hay as a way of an apology.

Katrina Olsen

November 1865

VIKEN, SWEDEN

THE BABY HAD COME MUCH TOO EARLY. A WOMAN named Ingrid Olsen had just given birth beside a lake next to the potato field where she worked. She guessed, by the weight of the potatoes, that the baby girl weighed no more than five pounds. A friend helped Ingrid wrap her up in a torn burlap sack.

Ingrid had already lost two babies, but if by some miracle this baby should live, she would name her Katrina. She knew that winter was coming. And with so little food and a house with such poor heat, she did not hold out much hope.

Ingrid looked down at the squirming little five pounds of blue-eyed life she held in her arms and cried for the child's future.

IN 1865, SWEDEN WAS A LAND with strict class divisions, with no middle ground. If you did not own land, you worked it for the ones who did, with no hope for a different future for you or your children.

But something had happened. Something called America. And there was now hope in the world. A place where if you worked hard, you had at least a chance for something better. But at that moment, Ingrid's baby girl was only forty-two minutes old and already hungry.

Katrina had lived, but she had been frail and sickly all her life. When she was seven, she contracted measles that settled in her eyes and caused her to go temporarily blind. Gradually, over the next few years, her eyesight slowly came back, but it was never good after that. When her father died, Katrina had stayed home to tend to her younger brother and sister as her mother continued to work in the fields.

As Katrina got older, she was able to help with the cooking and the baking. Before she married, her mother had worked in the city as a pastry cook for a wealthy family. But that was before she had fallen in love with a tenant farmer.

Luckily, Ingrid still baked with a light touch. And later, when she could no longer work in the potato fields, she was able to sell her pastries to the family who owned the farm for special occasions. But there was never enough money. Many nights, they went to bed hungry. Their only hope of survival was one of them somehow getting to America and finding work. They all thought it would be Katrina's brother, Olaf, who would go, but Olaf was still too young. Katrina had not wanted to leave home, but she felt she had no choice.

The day she left, Katrina tried not to cry. She wanted to be strong for her mother. They walked to the nearest town and stood waiting for the wagon that would take Katrina to catch a train to Bremen, Germany, where she could take a steamer to Liverpool, then board a huge ship headed to America.

As the wagon approached, her mother reached into her apron pocket and quietly pressed something into Katrina's hand. It was a small white handkerchief, embroidered in red and blue flowers, a gift from one of the wealthy ladies she had worked for in the city. When Katrina saw what it was, she said, "Oh, Momma . . . are you sure? You love this handkerchief." Her mother nodded and held her daughter one last time.

The trip across the sea in steerage had almost killed her. Katrina hadn't had much money for food, and by the time the ship docked in New York, she was so thin, she could barely stand up.

When the inspector at the immigration depot noticed she was not well, he almost sent her back to Sweden, but he could see she was fighting with all her might to look strong and healthy. The inspector was a tough man and used to having to reject people every day, but he didn't have the heart to send this girl with the shining eyes back home, so he passed her through.

Katrina had arrived in America and was given a

job in Chicago right away. At the time, Swedish housemaids were in high demand, and even preferred. They were known for their cleanliness, honesty, and ability to learn the language. Also, in the newly forming wealthy upper-class society of Chicago, a Swedish servant in the home meant something. The beautiful four-story brick home in Lincoln Park where Katrina was employed had five girls in service.

Four months later, Katrina's mother in Sweden was handed a letter, and she could finally sleep without worry.

To My Dearest Mother,

I made it across the sea, Momma. I am in America. I have a job in a place called Chicago. I am working in the day, and my friend Anna Lee and I are learning our English at night. The lady of the house told me I do very well in speaking it. I am hoping the money I am sending will help. I do not spend any on trinkets. Oh, Momma, I miss you. I sleep with your handkerchief. I see your face when you waved me goodbye.

Kiss the little ones for me,
Katrina

Springfield, Missouri

POOR LORDOR. GOING TO SPRINGFIELD AND HAVing his photograph made had been traumatic to say the least. He had seen his face in the looking glass when he shaved, but he'd never paid any attention to what he looked like. But now that he had seen the photograph of himself, he did nothing but stare at it and moan, "God, those ears." Why had he let Mrs. Knott cut his hair with a bowl? He should have gone to a real barber. Nancy Knott had a limp and had walked around his head with the scissors, and the cut was uneven. He was also disappointed in his overall appearance. He had thought that by now, he would look more American, but the man in the photograph looked like a big raw-boned dumb Swede right off the boat. Even in fancy borrowed clothes, he looked like the rube farmer he was. All he needed to complete the picture was a piece of straw sticking out of his mouth. He placed the photograph of Miss Olsen on the kitchen table beside his and stared at them. No. It would never work. She was so refined, so delicate.

He had never been vain, but the stakes were so high. He'd even thought about taking some ink to try and make his ears look a little smaller. But it wouldn't be fair, and he couldn't cheat that sweet girl. He guessed he would have to send the picture as is, ears and all. He had put off sending the letter and photograph, even though the ladies had been after him every day to do it. Finally, they had sent Henry Knott over to his house to pick it up and mail it for him. "Sorry, Lordor, but Nancy said for me to come or she and the ladies would."

Lordor stood on his front porch and watched Henry ride away, and he suddenly felt very sad. He was sure he would never hear from Miss Olsen again. He had tried not to get his hopes up, but in spite of himself, he had started dreaming about having someone to spoil, to work for, to come home to at night. But he knew it had been just a pipe dream. Miss Olsen would look at his picture and wonder how he'd ever had the nerve to think she would consider him for a husband.

The Man in the Derby

WHEN LORDOR'S LETTER FINALLY ARRIVED, KATRINA rushed out of the large dining room where she had been setting the table and ran upstairs to her room. She quickly opened it and looked at the photograph. The tall blond man was sitting in a chair in a stiff studio pose. His clear blue eyes were staring straight ahead, and he was not smiling, but she did notice that his hands looked very clean. Katrina liked that. She had come from a family of farmers with dirty hands.

Dear Miss Olsen,

Your letter and enclosed photograph has caused much excitement in our small community. To me, you look like an angel, and others who have seen your picture say you may be far too pretty for this poor dairy farmer. This may be true. However, I am sending my photograph anyway, and if by some stroke of good luck, my ugly face does not scare you off, I am enclosing some words about myself. I am not good at pleading my own case, but I have friends who have offered to speak on my behalf.

Sincerely yours,
Lordor Nordstrom

Katrina read the three other letters inside.

Dear Miss Olsen,

I am writing to confirm that the photograph enclosed is of the same Lordor Nordstrom who is writing to you at present. It is recent and a true likeness. My husband and I have known Lordor Nordstrom for many years. We knew his family in Sweden. He is a good man, tried and true, and would make you a fine husband. He is shy of nature, but big of heart. Come to Missouri, and give him a chance at the happiness of home and family.

Sincerely, I am
Mrs. Svar Lindquist

Miss Olsen,

Lordor Nordstrom needs a wife. His house is sturdy and has a porch with shade you will like. He is a God-fearing man and can calculate numbers very good. It is pleasant here, with lots of water and good loamy soil for growing. We have pigs. You may expect one as a wedding present. Lordor is a good eater and has all his teeth.

Mrs. H. Knott
Late of Hamburg, Germany

My Dearest Miss Olsen,

I am adding my name to this letter in hopes you will consider our friend Lordor Nordstrom for a husband. He has a fine dairy farm across the field from us and is a hard worker, but he is in dire need of a wife and healthy sons to help. I liked your photograph very much. I can tell that you are a lady of high quality. You look like my cousins back in Stockholm. My husband is enclosing a map of our state, so you can see where we are located.

We have a piano in our home. Do you play? If not, I can teach you. We all await your answer in excited anticipation that you will say yes. Miss Olsen, do come to Missouri and marry Lordor. I promise we will welcome you most heartily and will see that you are treated well. It is not like Sweden here. We

do not let the men rule with an iron hand.
We are all free American women in Missouri.

Most sincerely,
Mrs. Birdie Swensen

Katrina looked at his picture again. He looked like
a kind man, but very uncomfortable. What she didn't
know was that the photographer in Springfield always loaned men looking for wives a special suit of
clothes to help them look more dignified and respectable. But the largest suit the man had was two
sizes too small for Lordor, as was the black derby
sitting on top of his head, and he **had** been uncomfortable. He could barely breathe.

Missouri

My Dear Miss Olsen,

I was so happy to hear from you again. My neighbors say they heard my loud "Whoop!" five miles away. I do hope your sweet reply means that I have jumped the first of the many hurdles yet to come and passed. I am most relieved you did not find my looks too repellant, at least not enough to refrain from writing again.

As you can see, I am not much in the looks department, but you make it up for the both of us. I was most taken with the information you sent along about yourself and find it to be compatible in every way possible.

And yes, I will answer what you ask with pleasure. I have never been married. I have no children, and I do not smoke or drink, except on a special occasion. I am not a card gambler, but I have been known to place a wager on a game of horseshoes. No more than a quarter. I progressed to fifth grade, but not beyond, and as a result, I know all there is to know about cows, but am short on vocabulary. Luckily for me, cows have only a one-word vocabulary and don't care much.

I, too, believe that cleanliness is next to Godliness and appreciate a clean home, but being a man, often fail in that department.

I am mostly Lutheran, but have dabbled in the Methodist church from time to time. However, in that matter, and on the subject of progressive education, I am more than willing to be led anywhere you see fit.

Your devoted servant,
Lordor Nordstrom

Lordor liked that Katrina appreciated a clean home. When he first arrived in America, he'd noticed that cleanliness was not a top priority. He had stayed overnight in a hotel in Dodge City, Kansas, and when he asked for a clean towel, the hotel clerk had been put out. "You're the twenty-sixth man to use that towel and the first to complain."

OVER THE NEXT FEW weeks, whenever anyone saw Lordor, it was always the same greeting. "Has Miss Olsen made up her mind yet?"

Several more letters were exchanged. But Katrina guessed it was the last letter that caused her to make up her mind.

My Dear Miss Olsen,

I write to tell you that last year, my neighbor Lars Swensen and I ordered four big red Swedish cows from home, and they have arrived safe and sound. Everyone says they are very pretty. I am hoping you will approve of the purchase, as the farm is already half yours. All you have to do is come and claim it and the not-so-pretty farmer that goes with it.

Lordor Nordstrom

That night she told Anna Lee what she had decided, but she was a little reluctant to send the letter and say yes. There was still something about herself she had not told Lordor yet. Anna Lee had insisted that she keep it a secret. But later, as she was writing to Lordor, she asked her again.

"Anna Lee, are you absolutely sure I shouldn't tell him?"

"No. Don't you dare. You don't know men like I do. They want their wives to be perfect, so if you want this man, you get him first . . . then tell him."

—

THE MORNING KATRINA'S LATEST letter arrived, Lordor ran to the pump, washed his hands and face, and
combed his hair like he always did when he received
a letter from her. He then sat down on his front porch
stairs to read it. Dear God in heaven, she was **coming**! He jumped up and ran over to the big fire bell in
the yard. Before long, everybody within five miles
knew. When they heard the bell, the Knotts came
over to the house with a wagonload of their homemade German beer and, as always, any excuse for
Mr. Lindquist to play his fiddle was a good one in his
book.

Later that afternoon, after the celebration was
over, Birdie Swensen was up at the new cemetery,
busy watering and pruning the four small willow
trees her husband, Lars, had planted near the Swensen family plot. Still in a festive mood, Birdie began
to hum a little Swedish tune as she moved from tree
to tree. She had no idea that she was being observed.

Chicago Razzle-Dazzle

April 1890

IT WAS THEIR DAY OFF. KATRINA AND ANNA LEE were running across the heavy traffic on State Street, dodging in and out between the rushing horse-drawn trolleys and wagons as they whizzed by at breakneck speed. And, as usual, Katrina was terrified and was holding on to the back of Anna Lee's jacket for dear life.

From the beginning, Katrina had been overwhelmed by the noise and the busy hustle and bustle of the city: the long, wide avenues lined with tall buildings; the smell of the stockyards; the loud rattle and bang that was Chicago. She had grown weary of the constant night and day loud clitter-clatter of wheels and the loud clip-clop of hooves galloping across the cobblestone streets. Everybody was in a hurry to get somewhere.

But her friend Anna Lee had taken to the city like a fish does to water. She loved the excitement in the air, the nightlife, the beer gardens, the hurly-burleys, dance halls, theaters, and twenty-four-hour entertainments, all the razzle-dazzle. Anna Lee had even smoked a cigarette once, and wore only the very latest style clothes.

Today, she was dragging a reluctant Katrina to a ladies' clothing store to pick out a proper traveling outfit. "Do we have to go?" asked Katrina.

Anna Lee shouted over the noise of the street. "Yes, we do. You can't go to Missouri looking like a parlor maid. It might not make any difference to the cows, but it will to him." Suddenly, the driver of a trolley car coming up fast behind them clanged his bell so loudly that Katrina almost jumped out of her skin. Anna Lee just turned and blew the driver a kiss as he passed by. A lot of the men on the trolley car, who were wearing straw boater hats, leaned out of the windows and whistled at her as she lifted her skirt and showed them a tiny bit of her ankle. But that was Anna Lee.

Once inside Anna Lee's favorite ladies' dry goods store and after an hour of trying on clothes, Katrina was finally outfitted from head to toe in the latest fashion, including a brand-new fancy hat. And before she knew it, it was all wrapped up, and they were out the door and headed over to meet one of Anna Lee's many boyfriends at the amusement park for a boat ride.

Although they were the exact same age, Katrina and Anna Lee were as different as night and day. Katrina was small and neat and quiet. Anna Lee was a big-busted gal with a head full of messy blond curls and red lips who loved to laugh and have fun. And, of course, Katrina adored her and would miss her terribly.

Missouri

May 1890

My Dearest Miss Olsen,

We are pleased you will be staying with us. We have a nice upstairs bedroom, light and airy, with a mirror and a chest of drawers. You have my word that your privacy will be respected while you are here. My children have been instructed to never, under any circumstances, enter your room. My oldest girl has seen your photograph and does not believe that someone so pretty is coming to our home.

Miss Olsen, I hope I am not taking liberties, but I have heard that in Chicago, they are putting herrings in a tin can. If this is true and it is not too much of an inconvenience, could you please bring us one? I have enclosed one dollar to cover the cost, and I hope it is sufficient. We are inland here, and my husband and I miss our herring. But if there is no such thing as herring in a tin can, please use the dollar for a box of face powder or maybe a fashion magazine. I am looking so forward to having another lady to talk to. My closest neighbor, Mrs. Knott, is very nice, but is German and very brief in conversation.

Yours truly,
Mrs. Birdie Swensen

The Adventure

THREE WEEKS LATER, MISS KATRINA OLSEN, ALONG with all of her earthly possessions plus one tin can of herring, was sitting on a train headed down to southern Missouri. It was one thing to plan the trip, but to do it was another. After all the excitement of packing and saying goodbye, and now that she was actually on her way, the stark reality of what she was doing suddenly hit her. She wanted to get up, jump off the train, run back to Chicago, and beg for her old job back. Why had she quit? That was so foolish. Yes, she had made promises, and she desperately wanted to keep them, but this man who would be meeting the train was a complete stranger. What had she been thinking? How could she possibly do the things that Anna Lee said were expected of a wife?

And if she did run away, would Mr. Nordstrom make her pay all the money for the train ticket back? Oh, God, what had she done? And why hadn't she written and told Mr. Nordstrom the whole truth about herself?

Now it was too late. Katrina stared out the train

window at the dark gray skies and pouring rain. She had never felt so alone and desolate in her life. She took out her mother's handkerchief and buried her face in it. She missed her mother. She missed Sweden.

The next morning, after a tear-filled and fitful night, she pulled up the shade of her compartment window and was greeted by a big, bright yellow sun. As the morning progressed, the train rattled through the farmlands and on down into Missouri. They passed fields of sunflowers, wheat, and rows of new corn as far as the eye could see.

As the day went on, the sunflowers seemed to be smiling right at her, and she found to her surprise that she was somehow cheered. She was, after all, a true farm girl. This vast open space with the golden wheat blowing in the wind, blue skies, and white puffy clouds seemed more like home to her. And later, as they passed by the small clusters of farmhouses along the way, she began to wonder about Lordor Nordstrom's house. Would it have a real kitchen? Some land for a garden? She liked cows. Maybe he would let her keep some chickens, and if it worked out, Mrs. Knott had promised a pig. She loved little baby pigs.

By that night, Katrina was plagued with a new set of worries. What if Lordor Nordstrom didn't like her at all and sent her back? What if she wasn't as pretty as he had hoped or if he didn't think she was strong enough to make a good farm wife? Now the thought of having to go back to Chicago seemed as scary as leaving had once been. She calmed herself by reading Lordor's last two letters over and over again.

Dear Miss Olsen,

I am pleased the ticket and travel money arrived. I worry, now that plans have been made, you may be having some concern for what to expect of Missouri and me. I beg of you, please do not expect too much or you will surely be disappointed. I am just a simple farmer, and this is a simple place. I live in dread that you will find me and the life here too dull after the time you spent in Chicago. I am suddenly getting cold feet for you. But please be assured that if that does turn out to be true, you are under no obligation on my part to stay. I will respect your wishes in every way.

As for myself, I am pleased beyond belief that you will come at all. I have been reading as many books as I can and trying my best to generally improve myself before your arrival here. Please hurry. All the ladies around here are busy trying to improve me as well. By the time you get here, I may be over-improved and not much good for anything.

Your faithful servant,
Lordor Nordstrom

P.S. Don't be surprised if those same ladies throw a square dance and box supper to try and impress you. They have been pulling me around the dance floor for weeks, polishing me up for that big occasion. How well I will do remains to be seen. Please let me know the exact time and date of your arrival.

Dear Miss Olsen,

I will be there to meet your train on June 16th and deliver you to the Swensen home. I will be wearing a red flower in my hat so you will not miss me on the platform. Also, I am enclosing Mrs. Henry Knott's late mother's wedding ring that she insists you wear on the train. She tells me that because of tinkers, hawkers, slick fancy-pants traveling salesmen, and such, it is not safe for a single lady to travel alone. I am not happy to hear that news. Try not to look too pretty, if you can help it, which I doubt. Our whole community, as Mrs. Swensen says, is "atwitter" with excitement. I am mostly numb to think that you are actually coming.

Yours truly,
Lordor Nordstrom

In his letters, Mr. Nordstrom seemed so sure of his feelings, so kind and caring. It made her feel better just to read them. What Lordor had not mentioned in his last letter was that a few days after he sent the money and the ticket, he, too, had awakened in the middle of the night in a cold sweat, thinking, "My God, what have I done?" He had been so caught up in the community's excitement, and he had suddenly realized that he was asking this pretty young girl to give up everything and come to a place where she knew no one, and to spend the rest of her life with him. What had he been thinking? Miss Olsen lived in Chicago, a big city, with big-city people. What if she didn't like him? What if she hated Missouri? Was she expecting his house to be bigger and grander than it was? She was not a new cow or horse he had ordered. This was a live human being with feelings. And this brave girl was taking a chance on him. He had never felt so scared in his life. Then something occurred to him. He got up and knelt down beside the bed. He was not a praying man, but that night, he prayed that he had not made a mistake. He prayed the poor girl would not be disappointed and turn around and leave.

The Girl on the Platform

Springfield, Missouri

WHEN THE TRAIN ARRIVED, KATRINA LOOKED DOWN the long railroad platform and squinted in the bright morning sun. She could see the outline of a big, tall blond man, dressed in a new black suit, with a red flower in his hat. He was flanked by two married ladies who had accompanied him to pick her up, as was the custom. "It made the first meeting easier for the bride," they said. The truth was that Lordor was the one who needed them. He was afraid he wouldn't recognize her, but the moment she stepped down from the train, he knew it was her. He had studied her photograph for months now, but he was still not prepared for what Katrina looked like in person.

The girl who stood waiting on the platform was small in stature and had the tiniest, most delicate feet he had ever seen. With her white porcelain complexion, pink cheeks, and blue eyes she looked just like the Swedish doll his mother had kept on top of her bedroom chest. The two ladies were so excited to see her that they rushed ahead and left Lordor standing in the dust. After they had hugged her and told her how happy they were to see her and how pretty she was, they began feeling the material on the smart stylish Chicago clothes she was wearing. They examined with delight the fancy little buttons on her leather gloves and the charming feather on her hat and acted for all the world as if she was there just for them, as their brand-new plaything.

After they had examined Katrina from head to toe, Birdie Swensen finally turned around and motioned to Lordor and said to Katrina, "Here he is, Miss Olsen, for better or worse . . . your betrothed!" Lordor shyly stepped up, bowed, and tipped his hat.

Mrs. Knott said impatiently, "Well, say hello, Lordor, don't just stand there! The poor girl has come halfway around the world to see you." But all Lordor could manage to do was tip his hat and bow again.

LORDOR DROVE THEM BACK HOME to the Swensen house and gave Katrina time to get settled in and rest. Doing what he had been told to do, he stayed away until the next day when, as planned, he picked up Katrina and Birdie Swensen and drove them to see his dairy farm and the house. It was a beautiful morning, and the ride over was so lovely. The rolling hills in the background were a bright summer green. As they passed by the other farms, people waved at them. When they drove up to Lordor's house, Katrina thought she could see a side yard full of sunflowers, just like the ones she had seen from the train.

And it cheered her as it had then. She took this as a good omen.

When the horses came to a full stop, Lordor cleared his throat and said, "This is the house." From what Katrina could see, it was just as Mrs. Knott had described it: a large two-story farmhouse with a wraparound porch and lovely wisteria vines growing on the side. "Oh, Mr. Nordstrom, it looks like a very nice house," she said.

As they got down from the wagon, Lordor could hear his heart pounding. This was the moment he had dreaded and looked forward to at the same time. He was also feeling quite guilty. Right after sunup that morning, Nancy Knott had come over and had practically thrown him out of bed. Then she'd started cleaning and scrubbing the house from top to bottom. Lordor thought the house had been clean already, but evidently not. When she finished, the place was spotless. Lordor appreciated it, but he was a little concerned. "Isn't this cheating?" he asked.

"Yah, a little," Mrs. Knott said, laughing.

When they walked up onto the front porch, Lordor opened the door for the two ladies to enter. Inside was a long hall and a living room with a fireplace on one side and a parlor on the other. At the back of the house was a large kitchen with a beautiful shiny black wood-burning stove and a back porch. Because the rooms upstairs were all bedrooms, Lordor had been instructed to remain downstairs when Mrs. Swensen and Katrina went upstairs to see them.

It was a delicate situation, and Birdie knew it. She quickly opened the door to the master bedroom to let Katrina look in for a moment, then closed it again. Even so, Katrina had blushed at the sight of the big four-poster double bed standing in the middle of the room. Then they moved on to the other rooms and back down the stairs.

Next, Lordor drove them to see his dairy farm. It was quite impressive, with two long red barns and three silos. But Katrina's mind was still on the house. It was obviously a man's house, rather bare with little furniture, but Katrina was already envisioning it with rugs on the floor, frilly white curtains in every window, and a pretty picture over the fireplace. She also thought the cows she had petted were very lovely, and told him so. Lordor nodded and said, "Good," but he had yet to smile.

After all the worrying, Katrina found out that Missouri was not the Wild West depicted in the dime novels. In fact, it was so like the farmlands of home. From the moment she arrived, she'd felt safe and comfortable. From Birdie Swensen's cooking to the soft sound of cowbells in the pastures, it was almost as if she had never left Sweden.

My Dear Momma,

I have arrived safely, and I do not want you to worry. There are no wild Indians, bears, or mountain lions here, only cows, goats, chick-

ens, and pigs. I brought your pastry recipes with me and have already prepared several for the family here. They say they taste like home. I am hoping to make an impression on Mr. Nordstrom with your almond tart and cinnamon buns. Tell everyone hello for me.

Your loving daughter,
Katrina

P.S. Oh, Mother, there is plenty of food for everybody here. If I can save enough money, will you come?

The Box Social

As Lordor had warned her, that first Saturday night, there was to be a square dance and box supper social at the Lindquist barn in her honor. She was told that on these occasions, part of the evening was an auction. The women prepared a supper for two and packed it in a shoebox, on which the men could bid. The highest bidder would win both the supper and the lady as a dinner companion. The men were not supposed to know whose shoebox they were bidding on, but by Wednesday morning, every woman in town and Lordor's best friend, Lars Swensen, had secretly clued Lordor that Katrina's would be the one tied with a big blue ribbon.

That night, when the bidding began and the box with the large blue ribbon came up for auction, all eyes turned to Lordor. Mr. Lindquist, who was holding it up in the air, called out, "Come on, boys, what do you bid for this pretty little box? It smells mighty good."

Lordor quickly raised his hand and bid an entire quarter, prepared to win it at first bid, considering that most boxes went for a dime. But to his surprise, suddenly all the other men started bidding against him. Even little eight-year-old Willem Eggstrom with a missing tooth bid fifty cents.

Lordor didn't know it, but they had all gotten together and decided to have a little fun with him. They were all half in love with Katrina by now, and they could hardly contain themselves as they watched him begin to sweat as he bid higher and higher, in a panic that he would be outbid.

By the time poor Lordor made his last bid, it was up to ten dollars and sixty-five cents. The minute Mr. Lindquist said, "Sold to Lordor Nordstrom," everybody in the room burst into laughter. When Lordor realized what had happened, it was the first time Katrina saw him smile. It was a very nice smile. He seemed happy that he had won the bidding. But even so, as they walked over to the table in the corner set aside for the couple, and even all through supper, he barely spoke to her. She had tried to start a conversation. "So, Mr. Nordstrom, how do you find the weather in Missouri?"

"Fine," he said, spooning up a large helping of her potato salad.

"Are the red Swedish cows in your pasture the ones you had sent from home?"

"Oh, yes," he said, nodding as he took another bite of potato salad. And so it went. He never asked her anything, and she wound up having to do all the talking. Even more disappointing, he hadn't said a word about her almond tart.

Afterward, when the dancing started, and everyone started spinning and twirling all around the floor, Katrina couldn't help but laugh in spite of herself at the way the six-foot-two Lordor looked as he lifted his knees high up in the air in his funny stiff way.

But as more days went by, Katrina realized that something was not quite right. Lordor was perfectly nice and polite, but nothing else. She confided to Birdie Swensen that she was concerned. Birdie told her not to worry, that Lordor was just shy, but Katrina sensed that it was more than that. When they were out together, he seemed to just be going through the motions of courting. She had been there almost three weeks now and not once had he mentioned the word "marriage." At this point, she didn't know if she was going to be sent back to Chicago or asked to stay. And now, more than ever, she did not want to leave.

It hadn't been the pretty house or the dairy farm or how he had bowed and tipped his hat or the funny way he danced that made her want to stay. It was something else, something totally unexpected.

She had fallen in love with Lordor Nordstrom on that very first day at the train station. After he had collected and loaded all her baggage, and when he reached for her elbow to help her into the wagon, she could feel that his hands were trembling. It touched her so, it almost broke her heart. There was something so sweet and endearing about this big, strong man caring so much.

But now she'd begun to suspect he did not feel the same way about her. He was not the same man who had written her such wonderful letters. This man hardly ever said a word. And the more she talked, the more silent he became.

One afternoon, when they were out for their afternoon ride in his wagon, she finally gathered up all her courage to ask him, even though she was afraid of the answer. "Mr. Nordstrom, have I done something wrong? Are you not pleased with me?"

Lordor's big blue eyes flew open. "Not pleased?" He pulled back on the reins and called out, "Whoa!" And when the wagon came to a full stop, he turned to her. "Miss Olsen, I am most pleased. Why do you not think it?"

"You don't talk to me. When we are together, you barely say a word. I never know what you're thinking, and it scares me."

Lordor said, "Oh, I see." He then looked down at his hands, took a deep breath, but still said nothing.

"Is it me?" she asked. "Tell me, what have I done?"

He shook his head. "No, no . . . it's not you."

"What is it, Mr. Nordstrom? You have to tell me. I've come all this way."

Lordor seemed to be struggling for words, then he

blurted it out. "I am afraid for my bad grammar. I knew you were pretty, but I didn't know how good with words you would be. I don't talk much because I don't want you to find out how dumb I am. You might go back to Chicago."

Katrina was never so relieved to hear anything in her life, and tears sprang to her eyes. "Oh, Lordor," she said, surprising herself. "I don't care about that. I just need for you to talk. It's not how you say anything that matters to me."

"Wait. Wait," he said, putting up his hands. "There is more you should know. I don't spell so good, neither. Them letters I sent? Mrs. Swensen helped me and spelled out the big words for me."

Katrina smiled and shook her head. "I don't care."

Lordor looked at her in disbelief. "For sure?"

"For sure."

"Then you will stay?"

Katrina started to reply, but then she felt a sudden pang of guilt. He had just been so honest with her. She had to tell him. "Lordor, before I answer, there's something about me . . . you need to know. Something I haven't told you."

He seemed surprised. "What?"

Katrina bit her lip, then slowly opened her purse and took something out of it. "The truth is, Lordor, I don't see very well . . . and you might as well know it now." She then pulled a pair of round black-rimmed glasses out of a velvet pouch, put them on, and turned and faced him. "I wear spectacles. . . . I know how ugly I look, but without them, everything is fuzzy." She sat and waited for his response.

Lordor blinked and looked at her. After a long moment of studying her face he said, "Oh no, Katrina, you are wrong. You look very pretty in spectacles . . . and very smart. I like them." He then smiled at her. "I like them very much."

"You don't mind?"

"No. It's good for a man to have a smart wife."

"I'm sorry I didn't tell you sooner, but Anna Lee . . ."

He didn't let her finish. "Katrina, answer me this."

"Yes?"

"Will you stay?"

"Yes."

"Forever?"

"Oh, yes."

Lordor smiled. "Good."

As they drove off, both were smiling. That day, Katrina saw Lordor's face clearly for the first time, and he was even more handsome than she had thought.

FROM THAT DAY ON, Katrina wore her glasses, and Lordor just about talked her ear off telling her of all his plans for the town, for them, and for their future. Katrina continued to live with the Swensens, and joined in on Birdie's knitting circle with the other ladies. She was a fast learner and soon was knitting with the best of them.

After a respectable three months' time, the Swensens drove with them to the big Lutheran church in Springfield for Katrina and Lordor to get married. When the ceremony was over, Birdie cried, but both Katrina and Lordor breathed a big sigh of relief. After all that waiting, they couldn't wait to get home and finally begin their new life as man and wife. But things don't always go as planned.

THAT NIGHT, WHEN THEY arrived back at their house, it was surrounded by dozens of wagons, mules, and horses, and ablaze with light. The ladies had planned a huge surprise wedding celebration supper and had laid out enough food to feed an army. It was a wonderful party with music and dancing that went on until at least four o'clock in the morning. It was almost daybreak when the last of the hangers-on left. The fiddle player had had too much of Mr. and Mrs. Knott's beer and had passed out cold. Lordor and Lars had to carry him out to his wagon. Finally, they could begin their first night as man and wife.

They went upstairs, and Katrina went into the bedroom and changed from her wedding dress into her nightgown while Lordor went into the room down the hall. He changed out of his new black suit with the velvet bow tie and hung it up in the wardrobe. He put on his new cotton blue-striped nightshirt and walked over to the mirror and combed his hair, then sat down and waited for Katrina to invite him to join her. A few minutes later, he heard, "You can come in now." He walked down the hall and opened the door. She was sitting up in bed, looking so beautiful. They tried acting as calm as possible. Both were nervous.

Just as Lordor climbed into the large feather bed to join his bride, they heard the front door suddenly crash open with a loud bang. Then they heard the sound of heavy footsteps running through the house and the sound of tables and chairs being violently turned over and the loud clatter of glass breaking, pots and pans crashing to the floor. Whoever it was, was now downstairs in their kitchen going on some sort of mad rampage.

Lordor grabbed the shotgun he kept by his bed, ready to defend their life against a gang of bandits or worse. Despite his command to Katrina to stay there and lock the bedroom door behind him, she grabbed her glasses and followed him down the stairs, carrying her new silver-handled mirror as a weapon.

When they reached the kitchen, Lordor kicked the door open and stood ready to fire. But what they saw standing in the middle of all the clutter wasn't a gang of bandits, or even one bandit. It was the 350-pound pig named Sweet Potato that Henry and Nancy Knott had given them as a wedding present. The pig had managed to break out of her pen, had come up the front stairs, and snouted her way into the house. Sweet Potato, who evidently had no fear of guns or humans, glanced up at the two of them, was not impressed, and continued eating all of the leftover food from the party. She seemed to particularly enjoy the leftover wedding cake and her snout was smeared with white frosting.

What a colossal mess. She had knocked over everything there was to knock over, rooting around for food. There were broken dishes, chairs, pots and pans everywhere. All of Katrina's new china and lovely wedding presents that had been on display in the kitchen, including her new white bedsheets and quilts, were now on the floor and covered with food and small pig hoofprints. It took the two of them more than thirty minutes to get Sweet Potato back outside, down the steps, and over to her pen.

The sun was up by the time she had been safely locked in. When the ordeal was finally over, and after they had both tried so hard to look nice on their wedding night, they were covered from head to toe in mud and cake. It was so funny, and they laughed so hard, they finally had to sit down on the ground. Every time one would stop laughing for a moment, the other would start again.

About five minutes later, Ollie Bersen, the hired hand, was on his way to work and saw the two of them, still in their nightclothes, sitting in the front yard, laughing their heads off. Ollie didn't say anything, but he figured it must have been one wingdinger of a wedding night.

They must not have seen him, because all of a sudden Lordor leaned in and kissed her right on the lips. The bride must have liked it, because she threw her arms around him and kissed him right back. And in broad daylight, too. From the look of it, things were going well—so well, in fact, that Ollie was afraid to look, for fear of what they might be up to next.

But being human, once Ollie got safely inside the barn, he couldn't help but turn and look back just in time to see Lordor scoop Katrina up off the ground and carry her up the front stairs and into the house. Oh, mercy! He figured he wouldn't see Lordor down at the barn anytime soon, not that day at least.

EVEN THOUGH SWEET POTATO had almost ruined their wedding night, they had both learned a valuable lesson. No matter how hard you push, cajole, shove, beg, kick, or plead . . . pigs will not be rushed. Especially while they are eating leftover wedding cake. They also learned that the very best way to start a marriage was with a good laugh. Particularly when the children start coming.

Missouri

1890

Dear Anna Lee,

I think of you so often. How are you? I write
to tell you that I am now a married lady and
very happy. Lordor is more than I could have
hoped for in a husband and so kind and gentle. Our house is not grand, but the sur-
roundings are so lovely. The back of the
house overlooks fields of wheat, barley, and
clover. From my front porch, I can see the red
barns of the dairy standing on the hills to the
left. Every morning, the cows pass by on their
way to the fields and back home that way at
dusk. Oh, Anna Lee, if you could only see it,
you would think you were home again.

   Tell that boyfriend of yours that once
called me a country mouse, that he was right.
It is so quiet here on the farm. Lordor and I
are asleep at dark and up at daybreak. But I
love it.

I do hope you are happy and well, dear friend. Write and tell me so.

Love,
Katrina

P.S. Lordor likes my glasses. Isn't that wonderful?

A Daughter's Promise

LORDOR AND KATRINA HAD BEEN LUCKY. OVER THE years, the mail-order bride business had been fraught with pitfalls and disappointments. Some women traveled all the way from Europe, then spent months in a covered wagon, only to find that the man who met them at the other end was not the same man in the photograph sent, nor did he own a house and land as he had claimed.

Conversely, some men sent all their money to purchase the pretty young bride in the photograph, only to have the lady arrive months later, weighing many more pounds and years older than the photograph sent would suggest.

On both sides, it was a desperate game of chance. But, surprisingly, many marriages did work out, and the results helped populate the country with a hardy and adventurous stock. People were willing to travel anywhere, sacrifice anything, to own their own land, to be free and be independent.

—

KATRINA AND LORDOR'S FIRST YEAR together flew by. The house was becoming a real home, with white frilly curtains in the windows, rugs on the floor, and pictures on the wall. But most of all, Lordor and Katrina were happy together. She couldn't wait for him to come home from work, and he couldn't wait to get there. When they were out in public, he sat and stared at her with a stupid grin on his face. As Mrs. Tildholme said, "I've never seen two people act so silly over each other in all my life."

And Lordor had been right about Katrina. From the start, Katrina wasn't very strong physically, but she was brave and determined. The money she sent home had not been much, but it had kept her family from starving. Now, thankfully, her younger brother Olaf was old enough to get a farm job. Her next step was to try and get them all to America. She had promised her mother she would if she possibly could.

1891

My Dearest Momma,

Thank you so much for your last letter. I am so glad the presents reached you in time. I am sure that little Brigette made a very lovely St. Lucia for the Christmas celebration. Tell her how proud I am that she was chosen.

We had a wonderful Christmas here as well. It was almost like being home. We even had a little snow. Mrs. Eggstrom and several of the other ladies prepared the Christmas Eve julbord over at the meeting hall. I brought lussekatters and your gingerbread cookies. Lordor and the men found the most beautiful big cedar Christmas tree and decorated it with candles and flags and little straw animals. At midnight, we lit all the candles and sang Swedish Christmas carols and fed the birds on Christmas Day, so I know we will have good luck all year round.

Oh, Momma, there is a part of me that misses home so much. We are all so very far away. But as you can see, Sweden is still in my heart, as are you.

> Your loving daughter,
> Katrina

P.S. My neighbor, Birdie Swensen, is teaching me how to knit. Hopefully, I will be able to send you a warm sweater next year.

Chicago

Dear Katrina,

Thank you for your letter. I was beginning to think a bear had eaten you or that you had forgotten old Chicago and me. Now I know why you don't write. Hard to believe my little friend is now a mother. Congratulations to you. I know your husband must be happy it is a boy. I do like the name of Lordor Theodore Nordstrom. It is a good one.

We all sure miss you.

The new girl they hired to take your place is Dagmar Jensen from Gutenberg, and she looks it! She sits and eats and cries all night because her husband don't write. I saw his photograph. Ah! Such a big fat block of cheese.

All the boys here still ask where'd you go, and I tell them you are an old farmer's wife now. Not much news here, except that I have the keenest new boyfriend. His name is Hector, and he works as a ticket taker at the new Hippodrome. Me and all my friends get in free. He doesn't have much money, but he has dash and is a real snappy dresser. Write to me again, will you? And come visit me sometime, before you get old and gray. Ha. Ha.

Anna Lee

Neighbors

IN BIG CITIES, NEIGHBORS ARE NICE TO SAY HELLO to or maybe socialize with once in a while, but in small Missouri farming communities, neighbors were much more important than that. You depended on them for your very survival. It didn't matter if you liked some more than others. They were your neighbors. And in Lordor's community, considering they had all come from different places, and even the Swedish had come from different parts of Sweden, they were a pretty harmonious group.

Women as neighbors depended on each other for advice in cooking and raising children and for conversation. The men didn't need much conversation, but they did need help from one another. In the beginning, if money was scarce, they swapped crops, and Lordor provided free milk for the children and cheese and butter for the adults in exchange for hay and wheat to feed his horses and cows.

In 1895, when the Swensens' barn burned, the men all pulled together and had another one up in less than a week. And the next winter, when Katrina was so sick with childbed fever, Lars Swensen had ridden all night in a snowstorm to bring the doctor and, according to him, had saved her life. And no thanks were needed or expected. He knew Lordor would have done the same for him. And when they gave a dinner to raise money to build a silo, the Knotts donated a pig to be roasted, Birdie Swensen gave twenty of her chickens, and Mrs. Lindquist made the pies. Katrina baked the bread and the almond tart and brought cheese and coffee. It was a good dinner. Katrina loved the fried chicken. But since the pig had been a close relative of Sweet Potato's, she passed on the roasted pork dish. It was a friendly and welcoming community, but there came a time when that was sorely put to the test.

In May 1897, a certain Mr. and Mrs. Elmer Mims came and settled in on a plot of land and then proceeded to borrow money from just about everyone to build their house. As time went by, it became clear the man was a drunk and of as low a moral character as they had ever seen. The wife was no better. When Henry Knott came to their house to inquire about a payment on a loan, she informed him she had ways to repay the debt, other than money, and nearly scared him to death. He ran out of the house so fast, he tripped over his own shoes trying to get back home to Mrs. Knott. They gave the couple another year, but no crops were planted nor debts paid. Lordor called a meeting.

One night, a few weeks later, while the couple was

enjoying an unexpected invitation for a free supper at the Knott farm, their entire house was quietly being taken apart, board by board, nail by nail, and neatly packed in a wagon, along with all their belongings. By the time they got home, there was nothing but a packed wagon sitting in the middle of an empty lot. They got the hint and took off and never came back.

Nobody talked about it. It wasn't anything they were proud of, but as Lars Swensen said to his wife, "Sometimes, Birdie, you just have to take the worm out of the apple."

The 1900s

A New Era

The Town

KATRINA NOT ONLY MADE LORDOR A GOOD WIFE and everyone a kind and dependable neighbor, she also helped grow the community with their own two children, first Teddy and then a little girl named Ingrid, in honor of Katrina's mother.

In 1890, the U.S. Census had reported a population of seventy-four people resided in the community of Swede Town. By 1900, it had more than doubled.

LONG BEFORE KATRINA HAD left Chicago, she had grown tired of the dirt and soot and the rush of city life. She truly loved the fresh air and the quiet of the country. But after giving birth to their first child, Katrina had found out firsthand what a hardship it was to be so far away from a doctor and to have to travel so far to the nearest store to buy the things required to run a proper home.

One day, she said, "Lordor, we need a real town here . . . with our own stores." Lordor realized she was right. More and more farm families were moving there, and it was hard on the women to have to travel so far, especially in the winter.

That night, Lordor sat down at the kitchen table with pencil and paper and a ruler and drew up a rough set of plans for a downtown area. After they had brought in the crops that year, the men got busy and laid out four neat, wide streets, then planted elm trees on each side for shade. That completed, they sent off to Chicago for a Lyman-Bridges architecture catalog. When it came, they picked out some mail-order ready-made prefabricated stores, a church, a meeting hall, and a few houses for the merchants to live in. They felt that they were getting a good price. You could get a store for under eight hundred dollars and a church building with pews and a meeting hall all for around five thousand dollars, so they pooled their money and had it all shipped by rail.

Three months later, Lordor and some of the men met the train in Springfield, loaded their new downtown stores in wagons, and brought them home. After they had put up the new church, the stores, and everything they had ordered, they realized it would be good if they came up with a new name for their brand-new town.

A meeting was held in their new meeting hall, and some suggested calling it Nordstrom, Missouri, since Lordor had founded it, but he was against it. "No," he said. "This is everybody's town now." One man said they should name it Brand New, Missouri. The

Norwegian suggested Fiddletown, and after much discussion of fancier names such as Athens, Paris, Gastonia, and Utopia, Lordor suggested that maybe they should pick a more honest and simpler name. "We don't want to mislead people," he said.

A few hours later, they finally decided on Elmwood Springs, Missouri. "That's not misleading," said Mr. Knott. "We've got the elms and the springs. Now let's vote, so I can go home and eat." A vote was taken, and the name was passed with only one holdout for Paris, Missouri, from Birdie Swensen. At that same meeting, Lordor Nordstrom was unanimously voted in as their first mayor, and then Henry Knott went home and had cream noodles and apple dumplings for dinner.

With a new mayor, a new name, and new buildings, the next step for Elmwood Springs was to run an advertisement in the newspapers back east.

ATTENTION: PROFESSIONAL MEN!

We implore those who are contemplating traveling west to engage in business of any kind to come to Elmwood Springs, Missouri. No better or more desirable place can be found in the entire state. Situated in a green valley with some of the most beautiful freshwater springs, on as pretty a site as could be selected, and composed of a class of people who for energy and enterprise are not excelled.

We need a doctor, a dentist, and a storekeeper to carry farm goods, medicines, ready-made overalls, and bonnets and notions for the ladies. Also, one Lutheran preacher. Not too fiery.

Lordor read the advertisement Birdie Swensen had written and thought it might have been gilding the lily just a bit, but sent it anyway. They needed all the help they could get to lure professional men to move there.

All over the West and Midwest, small communities once called Little Poland or Little Italy or German Town were changing their names, becoming more American, and hoping to grow. Elmwood Springs was lucky. Within the year, they had a doctor, a barber who could pull teeth if necessary, and one Lutheran preacher named Edwin Wimsbly. Not too fiery, as requested.

Miss Lucille Beemer

1901

IN THE PAST, ALL THE FARM CHILDREN HAD BEEN taught at home. But soon, the ladies in town felt it was time to think about providing them with something better. Katrina, for one, wanted Teddy and Ingrid to have the advantage of a formal education. As usual, Lordor agreed.

A few months later, a charming little red schoolhouse was built. That fall, they hired Miss Lucille Beemer, an eighteen-year-old schoolteacher from Philadelphia, to teach grades one through eight.

She was young, but what the committee liked about Miss Beemer's particular job application was her special interest in literature and English, so important to their community. As recent immigrants, they wanted their children to speak and read English well.

Miss Beemer's first few years were not easy. Most of the schoolbooks she was given to work with were in Swedish, and nobody had any idea what grade to put what child in. Her oldest student was Gustav Tildholme, a sixteen-and-a-half-year-old eighth grader.

Her youngest child was six-year-old Ander Swensen, and she had fifteen other students of all sizes and grades—all being taught in the same room. It was quite a job. Miss Beemer was so glad to have Gustav in the class that first year. On cold winter mornings, he rode his mule to school early, brought in the wood, and started the fire in the potbellied stove. As he was over six feet tall, he also helped her control some of the younger boys when they got too rowdy. Gustav was more of an outdoor boy and not a very attentive student, but he was a treasure as a helpmate. Like the other children, he loved Miss Beemer.

Dearest Parents,

I am writing to inform you that your daughter is now a real teacher. I have seventeen pupils who call me Miss Beemer, and I am feeling quite the grown-up. The family I am living with is a Swedish couple, Mr. and Mrs. Lordor Nordstrom. He is tall and nice, and she is not tall, but very pretty and sweet and wears a gingham bonnet. Their two children, Teddy and little Ingrid, are darling and very well behaved. Mr. Nordstrom has a dairy farm with many cows, chickens, and one pig. I do not like the pig. I went close to the pen, and it tried to bite me, and I about had a jiminy fit! Mrs. Nordstrom said she was sorry it

had tried to bite me, but the pig thought I had something to eat.

Mother, would you please send me my good blue dress? I did not think I would need it, but the people here are very social and put on many dances and get-togethers. I am putting on a little weight. Mrs. Nordstrom makes a lot of pies and sweet pastries, and I find it hard to say no. Do write and tell me the news of home.

>With love and affection,
>Lucille

Chicago

Hi-Ho, Katrina,

I am so glad to hear from you again. A mother with two children now! I can't believe it. I am still playing the field. You have the babies, and I'll have the fun. You always were the mother type, not me. Anyhow, the kiddies sound swell.

Not much news here at the house, except that Dagmar Jensen's husband has come to join her. He has been hired on, so I now have my own room. It's that cubbyhole up on the fourth floor, where we used to hide our books, but it will do for the meantime.

I am now stepping out with a baseball player. He plays with the Chicago Cubs and oh boy, how that boy can bat. And what parties! They sure know how to have a good time. I'll say they do. Last night, I didn't get home until 4 a.m.

Say, how is that pig you wrote me about?
She sounds like a gal after my own heart.
Gotta run. The old lady is up and ringing
her bell.

Anna Lee

Sweet Potato had been trouble from the beginning. She was never what you would call well behaved. Whenever Katrina or Lordor or the children tried to pet her, she made it quite clear she didn't particularly care for any of them. "Feed me, but don't bother me" was her motto. And she would eat anything. She once ate a pair of Lordor's long red underwear that had blown off the clothesline, buttons and all, plus an entire Sears, Roebuck catalog and a leather shoe.

She was truly a disgusting, gluttonous creature with, evidently, the digestion of a goat. "That pig is such a pig," said Katrina. But as much trouble as she was, Katrina and Lordor could never bring themselves to sell her, nor certainly to eat her for dinner. To them, Sweet Potato had one big saving grace. She was so content in her grotesqueness, so completely oblivious to what others thought, that she made them laugh. Of course, being a pig, Sweet Potato never understood her good fortune.

It was also fortunate that she couldn't understand English. Mrs. Knott had often announced in a rather loud voice, "Katrina, if this was my pig, she'd be in a pot today and sausage in the morning." Sweet Potato just snorted and kept on eating. They said she was the only pig in the state of Missouri that ever died of old age. Sweet Potato would not understand the irony, but she would even outlive Mrs. Knott.

The Neighbor Boy

LITTLE ANDER SWENSEN, BIRDIE AND LARS SWEN-sen's now seven-year-old son, was a cute red-haired boy who looked just like someone had picked up a large bucket of freckles and thrown them at him. He must have had over a thousand freckles on his face and ears alone. But what endeared him to everyone was his sweet nature and silly giggle.

Being such a close neighbor, he spent a lot of time over at the Nordstrom house. He loved Mrs. Nordstrom's cooking and clearly had a crush on Ingrid. And he let her boss him around without mercy.

Ingrid loved to play tricks on her father. One day, she even made Ander help her dress up one of Lordor's favorite cows.

That morning when Lordor went in the barn for the milking, there stood Sally, his prize heifer, wearing one of Katrina's big straw bonnets and a red checked apron. Lordor heard the muffled giggles coming from the hayloft and pretended to be very upset. "Oh . . . my poor Sally. When I find out who did this, I'm going to throw them in the pen with Sweet Potato, and then they'll be sorry!"

Of course Lordor knew who had done it. He had seen the two children sneaking the hat and the apron out of the house earlier that morning.

Later, at the lunch table, when Lordor was telling Katrina and Miss Beemer what had happened, Ander's big brown eyes opened wide, and, being the sincere and truthful boy he was, he immediately broke down and confessed. "I did it, Mr. Nordstrom. It was my idea. You can throw me in the pen if you want to."

It was all the adults could do not to laugh. Lordor said, "What do you think, Miss Beemer? You're his teacher. Should I throw him in the pen or not?"

Ander looked over at Miss Beemer in terror, awaiting his fate.

"No, Mr. Nordstrom. I think the fact he told the truth is very admirable. I believe he deserves to be saved."

Ander breathed a big sigh of relief. "Oh, thank you, Miss Beemer. I'm scared of that pig."

Katrina said, "I agree, Miss Beemer. In fact, for being so truthful, I think Ander deserves a second piece of cake."

Ingrid piped up and said, "I want one, too."

"Sorry, Ingrid, too late. You missed your chance," said Teddy.

Ingrid glared at Ander. "I was going to confess, but you beat me to it."

Ingrid was a little troublemaker all right. One night at dinner she looked over and asked Miss Beemer right out, "Is that big tall Gustav who walks you home from school every day your boyfriend?" Teddy kicked her under the table.

Katrina quickly said, "Ingrid! Don't be so silly. How rude."

"But what's wrong with having a boyfriend? Ander said he was my boyfriend, and Teddy likes Elsa Bergsen."

"I do not!" said Teddy, quickly defending himself. "Miss Beemer, she's lying. Don't you believe her."

Miss Beemer smiled. "Why, Teddy, I think Elsa is a very lovely little girl."

Katrina had been terribly embarrassed that Ingrid had asked Lucille that question, but on the other hand she had wondered about Lucille. She was so fond of her, and was concerned that she didn't seem to have any friends her own age.

Later that night, when the two of them were in the kitchen washing the dinner dishes, Katrina said, "I'm sorry Ingrid was so fresh, Lucille."

"Oh, that's all right, Mrs. Nordstrom. She just has a curious mind."

"But do you have a young man you like, Lucille? I only ask because, if so, I want you to feel free to invite him here to visit anytime."

"Oh no . . . there's no one," Lucille said, taking another plate to dry.

"Well, I'm sure there will be very soon. You're so

good with children I think you will make someone a wonderful wife and mother someday."

"Really? How kind of you to say so, but no. I doubt if I'll ever marry."

"But why?"

Miss Beemer sighed. "Oh, it's just a feeling I have."

"I wouldn't be too sure. I used to think that, and now look at me."

Just then they heard the most awful yelling. "Help, help!" Ingrid yelled as she came running through the kitchen, knocking over a chair, with Teddy not far behind her, knocking over another as he chased her around the table.

He yelled, "Mother, she stole my notebook."

"I did not!" screamed Ingrid as she headed out the other door.

Katrina called out after them. "Children, stop that racket! Right now. Your father is trying to read."

Then Katrina looked at Lucille and laughed. "Of course, I suppose there is something to be said for being single. At least it would be quiet."

IT WASN'T ANY QUIETER over at the Swensens' farm either. For the past few months, Birdie Swensen had been trying her best to knit her boy Ander a new sweater for his upcoming birthday. But it had been difficult with Ander always running in and out of her sewing room, interrupting her. And if it wasn't Ander, it was Lars or one of the farmhands wanting something. So lately, when she went up to the cemetery with her basket of gardening tools, she had brought her knitting things with her. And after she finished her watering and pruning, she would turn the basket over, sit on it, and knit. It was so nice to be out of the house, sitting in nature all alone up on the hill, just her and the birds.

As she sat and knitted, Birdie often thought about the time when someone would be buried up on this hill. They had been lucky so far, other than a few scares—one with Katrina's childbed fever. But everybody was still pretty healthy, and so far, they had not lost anyone. But they were all fairly young yet.

It was on these days that Birdie first began to notice something strange. She suspected it was just her silly imagination playing tricks on her. It had to be. But she continued to have the oddest feeling that someone was watching her. And, of course, Birdie was right. There was.

The Telegram

1902

IN THE NEW LITTLE TOWN OF ELMWOOD SPRINGS, Missouri, wooden sidewalks had replaced the dirt paths, and a real downtown business area started to develop. First, a farm supply store opened, then a blacksmith shop, a drugstore, a general merchandise store, and a grocery store, where you could buy crackers and cheese and a pickle for a nickel.

On Saturday mornings, Main Street was packed with farm wagons and people walking up and down, shopping and visiting, women buying material for clothes, men looking at farm supplies. Kids were eating ice cream cones in the front of the drugstore, and the men (except Reverend Edwin Wimsbly) enjoyed a small shot of whiskey in the back. For medicinal purposes only. But mostly, they just visited up and down the street with neighbors they hadn't seen all week. The men, sitting on the benches in front of the drugstore, feeling warm and rosy after their drugstore medicine, would marvel at how much the women loved to talk. They didn't understand how lonely farm living could be for their wives. Unlike the men, they needed the company of other women.

Katrina loved her lady neighbors and enjoyed the knitting class that Birdie Swensen held in her home every Thursday afternoon. Birdie and the rest of the ladies had been so kind to her, especially when the babies came. But she still missed her own mother so much. Too many years of missing her had passed by. One day, Lordor came in from the farm and found her crying, and when she told him how much she wanted to see her mother again, Lordor took her in his arms. "You write and tell her to come. The whole family belongs here with us."

Soon a telegram arrived saying that Katrina's mother, her sister, Brigette, and her brother, Olaf, would come. Katrina was overjoyed.

Less than three months later, Katrina was smiling as she took her bread out of the oven. So many letters and documents had gone back and forth, and it had taken a lot of time and work, but Lordor had made all the arrangements. At last, her mother would live in a home with heat and running water. Katrina couldn't wait for her to arrive. She and Lordor had saved money in a coffee tin from the profits on the dairy, and some had just been sent to Sweden to buy the tickets. It made Lordor happy to see Katrina so happy.

A few weeks later, a letter came.

My Dear Daughter,

Please forgive me, but the doctor comes and
tells me my old body will not make the trip
to America or live to finish it. But don't be
sad for me. America is for the young, for ones
with prayers yet to be answered. All my
prayers have been answered. Because of you
and Lordor, my children and grandchildren
will never be hungry. Thank you for the
pictures of Ingrid and Teddy. So pretty.
So handsome like his poppa. I think of you
every day.

Love forever,
Ingrid Olsen, Your Momma

Not long after that day, word came by telegram
that her mother had died.

As word spread around town about Katrina's
mother, one by one, the ladies came to the house and
sat with her. They didn't say much. They just didn't
want her to be alone.

Six months later, when her brother and sister arrived from Sweden, Katrina was so happy to see
them, but it was a bittersweet reunion without her
mother there as well. Katrina's sister, Brigette, now
a girl of eighteen, was happily welcomed by the local
boys and quickly married one of the Eggstroms'

sons. Her brother, Olaf, now almost a grown man, went to work immediately at the dry goods store and saved his money. A year later, with a little secret help from Lordor, he sent for Helga, his young wife in Sweden.

Spring Has Sprung, and So Has a Young Man's Fancy

BY THE SPRING OF 1903, A SITUATION HAD DEVELoped between Miss Beemer and her student Gustav Tildholme. She knew Gustav had failed the eighth grade twice on purpose. And she knew why. He had sat in class and stared at her with his big brown eyes full of pure, unadulterated adoration.

Gustav had even written her love notes telling her how much he wanted to marry her one day. It was her fault, she guessed. She had grown to depend on him so much. She might have been too friendly with him.

But even though she was only one and a half years older than Gustav, there was a certain code of ethics, a line she could never cross. And, besides, she was a Quaker, for heaven's sake. Marrying her student would cause a scandal. The very idea of such a thing.

When she finally told Gustav he could not come back to class the following year, and he couldn't walk her home anymore, it broke his heart. She tried to reason with him and explain that what he was feeling was just a schoolboy crush. She assured him that he would outgrow it. "No, I won't," he said. "I'll die first. See if I don't." Then he ran out of the room and into the woods behind the schoolhouse, and he never came back to school again. His family told her later that he had gone to California, but they didn't know where. She always wondered where he was, and whether he would ever come back. That first year, he had carved a little wooden flower out of pine knot and had left it on her desk as a present. She still kept it on her dresser.

Just the other day, someone said that they might have seen Gustav Tildholme down by Elmwood Springs Lake. But it must not have been true. Surely, he would have come to see her, if it had been him.

In the meantime, Elmwood Springs continued to expand. A brand-new Rexall drugstore opened up on the corner with a real pharmacist named Robert Smith, and a real dentist opened a practice upstairs over the Western Union office. Soon tracks were laid, and they had a trolley that ran all the way to the lake and back.

And out in the world at large, it seemed new inventions were happening every day. One day in December, Lordor was in town having his hair cut, when Mr. Goodnight, the telegraph operator, came running into the barbershop, his face all red and excited.

"My God, boys . . . it just came over the telegraph. In North Carolina people are flying up in the air in automobiles! Automobiles that fly!"

The barber stopped mid-shave and said, "What?"

"These two Wright boys from over in Ohio built it, and it has long wings on both sides. They drive it as fast as they can, and pretty soon, it starts lifting up off the ground, and the next thing, it's flying like a bird."

"How can that be?"

"I don't know . . . but that's what it said. They invented some kind of motor that can fly is all I know. I don't know how they did it. They said they have a picture of it, so you know it's true."

"A man flying in the air in a car with wings . . . are you sure?"

"Yes. I'm telling you the news just came in, not more than a minute ago."

"I think there's some serious leg-pulling going on here. Are you making this up?"

"No, I swear it's the truth. You just wait. One day, one of those machines will fly right over us, and you'll see for yourself!"

"Now, George, how could something that weighs as much as an automobile lift up off the ground?"

"How does the moon rise every night? I don't know, but it does. I need a drink," said Mr. Goodnight. "Where is it?"

The barber opened the cabinet and brought out

the bottle. "Hell . . . if this is true, we all need a drink."

Word spread fast, and the next morning, everybody gathered and waited for the newspaper to arrive. After they had all read about the flying machine and seen the photograph for themselves, Svar Lindquist asked a question that, in the coming years, would be asked over and over again. "What in the world will they come up with next?"

Meet Me at the Fair

1904

St. Louis

Although Lordor was not well educated in a formal way, he was very forward thinking and always looked for ways to improve himself and others. One morning, Lordor sat on the side of the bed at the hotel where they were staying. He looked at his wife and said with a serious expression on his face, "I suppose this might be the greatest thing that ever happened." He was talking about the 1904 World's Fair in St. Louis, Missouri.

As mayor, he had arranged for everyone in Elmwood Springs who could afford it to travel to St. Louis. And those who couldn't afford it and wanted to go, he paid for out of his own pocket. Miss Beemer was there with those of her students who were old enough to travel.

From what he had read, Lordor knew the fair would be interesting and informative, but no one could have dreamed about all the wonders, the spectaculars, and the attractions. People had come to St.

Louis from all over the world. The first time they had seen the huge Palace of Electricity lit up with thousands of lights, the sight of it was so totally overwhelming, most people couldn't speak.

Lordor was right. People had never seen anything like it. And the size of the fair; the Palace of Agriculture alone covered twenty-three acres. In just two days, they had seen a real live Chinese man, a real Eskimo, an elephant, moving pictures, and babies in incubators—things and people Lordor never imagined he would see in his lifetime. He looked over at his exhausted sleeping children and smiled. "Oh, what a future they will have, Katrina. So many wonderful things are coming."

GOING TO THE FAIR changed everyone. Before the fair, the people in Elmwood Springs had been mostly small-town farmers, living in their small world, but now, having seen all they had seen, they would never be the same. And they couldn't help but be optimistic.

At the first council meeting after Lordor got home, he said, "My dream is to light up our town, so nobody has to live in the dark anymore." And he did. Thanks to his many visits to the Missouri Electric Light and Power Company, the stores and houses on Main Street—and later, as promised, every building in town—had electricity. In 1906, when the new streetlights came on, they had a party, and everyone dressed up in their best clothes. Ingrid Nordstrom wore one of her mother's hats, and her brother, Teddy, as a prank, wore a pair of his father's big shoes.

Lordor adored his children and, as far as he was concerned, they could do no wrong. Especially Ingrid. Unlike her brother, she liked cows and was already helping with the milking. In the summers, Katrina would stand looking through the kitchen window and watch as Lordor headed out to the pasture with little Ingrid marching along right beside him. Oh, how she loved her daddy.

Lordor indulged her, of course. He even bought her a pair of boys' overalls and rubber boots. "I want to look like Daddy," she said.

As the children grew, so did the little town. By 1907, mostly due to the prodding of Birdie Swensen and the other ladies, they had built a small opera house to accommodate traveling theatrical groups and local plays. As Birdie said, "We may be living in the country, but that's no excuse for us not to be exposed to a bit of culture now and then." Although as everyone agreed, the last Shakespearean Acting Company's presentation had been a letdown. The actor with the spindly legs who played Hamlet had been at least seventy.

More Than Meets the Eye

DUE TO THE INCREASE IN THE NUMBER OF HER students, Miss Lucille Beemer had moved from the Nordstrom home and into town, to be a little closer to school. She was now living at Mrs. Molly Ballantine's Boardinghouse, which catered to single ladies and gents and the occasional traveling salesman passing through. Tonight, Miss Beemer sat in her small room on the second floor, correcting papers. But somehow her heart wasn't in it.

She walked over and opened her window and looked out. Such a warm beautiful summer night. She could smell the honeysuckle blooming on the large veranda downstairs and hear the faint faraway sound of music. Someone in the house next door was playing a song on the Victrola.

It was on nights like these when she would think of Gustav and wonder where he was.

Even though everybody in town, adults and children alike, always addressed her as Miss Beemer, she was still hardly more than a girl herself. She had

barely turned eighteen when she had accepted her
first teaching position.

But as a certain married lady said after Lucille
stepped off the train a few years back, "No need to
worry about her stealing our husbands, ladies. She
has 'Old Maid Schoolteacher' written across her
forehead in large, bold letters." Lucille Beemer had
long black hair that she wore pulled up tight in a
high bun, and a slightly long thin nose. And she did
appear to be a serious and extremely proper person.
But she wasn't quite what she appeared to be. Because of her position and responsibility at such a
young age, she had carefully hidden the part of herself that was still a romantic young girl, full of dreams
of romance and adventure.

Even her father, a minister in Philadelphia, would
have been surprised at his daughter's secret dreams—
dreams of a handsome stranger riding into her life and
sweeping her away. Now, more often than not, the
handsome stranger looked just like Gustav Tildholme.

A few of the old bachelors in town had asked her
out, as well as Mr. Glen Early, a tenor who sang in
the church choir. But she had no interest. The longer
Gustav stayed away, the more she realized her heart
was somewhere else. Lately, she had begun to question why she had cared so much about what people
would have thought if she had run off with him.

Just then, she heard one of the male boarders
downstairs on the veranda laugh in a loud, crude
way, and she slowly closed the window.

Elmwood Springs, Missouri

Dear Anna Lee,

Thank you for your last letter. I write to tell you that I am still happy and well. I wish you could come and see me. There are so many daffodils here this year.

The children are growing like weeds. My boy is so sweet, and Ingrid continues to amaze me. I tell you, Anna Lee, she is not like us. She is a true American girl. In summer, she gets as brown as a berry and runs around barefooted, just like the boys. Lordor says she rides the mules even better than the boys do. And he is so proud of her. Last week, he took her with him to the big cattle sale in Kansas City. He said she already knows more about cows than most of the men.

Anyhow, I miss you and often think of our time in Chicago. What would I have done without you, dear friend?

I close now to go feed the chickens. Yes, we

have many chickens now, including one very big and pretty fluffy white hen I have named Anna Lee, in your honor. You would be proud of her. She lays a lot of eggs, and all the big red roosters are in love with her.

Love,
Katrina

P.S. I am enclosing pictures of Teddy and Ingrid.

Chicago

Dear Katrina,

Sorry I haven't written sooner. Thanks so much for your last letter and pictures of the kiddies. Ingrid looks more like you every day.

    I am in the pink here . . . and speaking of roosters, boy oh boy, do I have a live one on the line. He is an Italian and a little rough, but he has big, dreamy eyes. And does he like blondes. I'll say! Don't be surprised if I don't wind up rich one of these days. He makes his own liquor and sells it for a fortune. Whoo whoo! Just got a swell white fur piece from the lad. Who knows? Next time I write, I could be signing it Mrs. Johnny Zenella. Wish me luck, and pat that chicken on the head for me.

                      Anna Lee

    P.S. WHEN ARE YOU COMING TO SEE ME?!

Is It You?

1908

IT WAS WELL AFTER NINE O'CLOCK WHEN LUCILLE Beemer heard a knock on her door. It was her landlady, Mrs. Ballantine. "Miss Beemer, you have a long-distance phone call. It's a man." Lucille was already in bed with her hair pinned up, but she quickly jumped up, threw on her robe and slippers, and ran downstairs to the phone in the hall. Mrs. Ballantine was waiting and handed her the receiver, then stepped back into her room to give her some privacy.

"Hello, this is Lucille Beemer," she said, almost out of breath. "Hello?" Lucille could hear music in the background, but nobody spoke. "Hello," she said again. "Gustav . . . Is it you? Hello? I'm here. . . ." Again, there was no answer on the other end, and then whoever it was hung up.

Mrs. Ballantine came back out of her room. "Who was it?"

"I don't know. Did he say where he was calling from?"

"No, he just asked to speak to you. But whoever it was sounded a little drunk to me."

"Maybe he'll call back."

"Well, if he does, I hope it will be at a decent hour the next time."

Miss Beemer waited by the phone, hoping he would call back, but he never did.

In the Glove Department

SHE CERTAINLY HADN'T PLANNED IT. MISS BEEMER
ran into Gustav's mother quite by accident. They
just happened to be in Springfield shopping on the
same day. After a few minutes of small talk and trying on several pairs of gloves, Miss Beemer asked the
question as casually as she possibly could, being careful to place the inquiry in an unobtrusive position in
the conversation as a way to make it seem less important than it was.

Before she spoke, Miss Beemer reached over and
put on a pair of gray kid gloves, and while looking at
them, she held them up and asked, "What do you
think of these, Mrs. Tildholme? I'm not so sure about
the buttons. Oh, and how is Gustav? Have you heard
from him lately?" She looked at her gloves again.
"No, these are far too fancy," she said, and took them
off again, her heart pounding, waiting for her answer.

Mrs. Tildholme studied the gloves and said, "Yes,
I agree . . . too many buttons. Oh, Gustav." Then
she sighed and shook her head. "That boy. Now he's
gone all the way up to Oregon, lumberjacking for

some big outfit. He says he's making a lot of money, but I wish he'd come home, even for a visit." Suddenly, Mrs. Tildholme's eyes lit up with an idea. "Oh, Miss Beemer, would you do me a huge favor? Gustav thought the world of you. Could you write him and tell him to come home? He'd probably listen to you. Young people have a mind of their own these days. They don't listen to their parents, but they might listen to their teacher. Would you? I have his address."

The very next morning, Lucille sat down at the small desk in her room and, after a moment, picked up the pen, dipped it in the ink bottle, and began to write.

Dear Gustav,

Hello from Elmwood Springs. I hope you are well. Your mother tells me that you are now a lumberjack. It sounds so wonderfully like a Jack London novel. You have such a good mind. I do hope you are keeping up with your reading. . . .

She crumpled the page and started again.

My Dear Gustav,

Hello from an old friend. Your mother and father miss you terribly and so do . . .

Dearest Gustav,

This letter is a much-belated hello from your old teacher, Lucille Beemer. . . .

Dear Gustav,

I know it has been a long time since we last spoke, but I think of you so often and always with great affection. I wonder if . . .

Dear Gustav,

I am so sorry that our last meeting was such an upsetting one. But you must understand that my position as . . .

She suddenly stopped writing. Oh, Lord. What was she doing? Gustav was not a child. He was a grown man now. She couldn't write to a grown man and tell him that his mother wants him to come home. And with the new, exciting life he was living now, he might not even remember who she was. Writing to an ex-student of hers in such an intimate way was most inappropriate. It would probably embarrass him to receive such a letter from some silly old maid teacher he once knew. He might even laugh and show it around.

Trying to set her feelings down in words and then seeing them on paper in black and white made her realize how utterly hopeless the situation was. Gustav had obviously gone on with his life. There was nothing she could do, short of making a complete fool of herself. She could see now that she had been living with some made-up dream that, one day, Gustav would come home and tell her that he still loved her.

Just then, she heard a knock on her door. "Miss Beemer, it's Sonia, the housekeeper, ma'am. Do you have any trash to be taken downstairs?"

"Oh, yes, Sonia. Just a minute . . . come on in." Miss Beemer crumpled up the last sheet of paper she had written on, dropped it into her almost-full small wicker wastepaper basket, and handed it to her. "Here you go."

As Sonia was emptying Miss Beemer's discarded papers into a larger waste can, she asked, "Busy grading papers?"

"What? Oh, yes."

"Ah. Well, as they say, a teacher's work is never done. People just keep having babies, don't they? But God bless you for what you do. My little one will be with you next year."

"Yes, I know, and I'm looking forward to meeting her."

"See you tomorrow," said Sonia, as she closed the door behind her, leaving Miss Beemer sitting alone at her desk with her empty wastebasket, looking out the window, facing reality. Facing the lonely life ahead of her. But at least she had her students to keep her busy.

July Fourth

1909

AS USUAL, ON THE FOURTH OF JULY, WHILE THE ladies were busy setting out the food for the big picnic, all the men and boys were heavily engaged in a serious game of horseshoes. Suddenly, there was a great roar from the men. Katrina stopped and watched in amazement. Her daughter, Ingrid, the only girl in the game, had just pitched another perfect shot.

Ingrid was so different than she had been at that age. So independent. There was no telling what she was going to do with her life. Ingrid was a first-generation American girl, and the world was changing. There were even rumbles about women getting the vote, something Lordor was all for. He said, "If any addle-brained drunken bum off the street could vote, why not the ladies?"

While Lordor loved having a daughter, his neighbor, Henry Knott, was not happy that he only had girls. He often told Lordor that he wished he had a boy to take over the farm someday.

Lordor agreed that it would be nice to have his son take over the business, but Teddy did not want to be a dairy farmer. He was more like his mother and loved to bake. His dream was to own his own bakery one day. And Lordor didn't mind at all. Some of the best bakers in Sweden were men. He even bought Teddy a white baker's hat. He just wanted his children to be happy. And as he once told Katrina, "You either love cows or you don't."

As the years went by, the dairy farm continued to do well. So well, in fact, that they sent off for even more cows and built four new barns. They didn't know what had caused it. It could have been something in the soil in this part of Missouri or in the clover they ate. Or it could have been the special cows that Lordor was breeding. But everyone around agreed. The milk and cheese that Lordor's cows produced was the sweetest. So, they decided to name the farm Sweet Clover Dairy.

While Teddy did not show any interest in the dairy business, their neighbor boy, fifteen-year-old Ander Swensen, did. And he absolutely idolized Lordor. According to some, Lordor was the best dairyman in the state, and Ander wanted to grow up and be a dairyman just like him.

Since Lordor was his best friend, Lars Swensen asked him if he would take Ander under his wing and teach him the dairy business from the ground up. Lordor was more than happy to do it. He liked Ander. He was a sincere boy, a fast learner, and a good worker. And so Ander moved in with the Nordstroms and did not mind a bit. He loved working with Lordor every day. And there was another reason. A pretty girl named Ingrid.

Chicago

The next letter Katrina received from her friend Anna Lee contained surprising news—something that Katrina would never have expected to hear.

Dear Katrina,

I am writing with news. I met a man named Karl Johanssen. He is a big, dumb Swede and owns a wheat farm in Wisconsin. Of all the swell fellows I've known in Chicago, why did I have to go and fall for him? You can laugh if you want. I wouldn't blame you for all my big talk about farmers.

    Anyhow, he asked me to marry him, and I said yes. Your big-city girlfriend is headed to Wisconsin at the end of the month.

Love,
Anna Lee

Oregon

A TALL, GOOD-LOOKING MAN OF ABOUT TWENTY-five working in a lumber camp somewhere outside of Portland had just been handed a letter from his mother. It had taken the letter almost a month to reach him so far back up in the woods.

Dear Gustav,

Your father and I thank you so much for your last money order. You are very kind to your old mom and dad. We still miss you here, Son. I wish you could see how the town has changed. Downtown is almost one block long, and there is talk of a Masonic Lodge and a new Methodist church being built soon.

We are having a really nice summer. We just got another calf, and we are happy about that. That old Lindquist farm you asked about is still for sale. I am glad you are liking your job and doing so well. Everybody here still asks about you. All your cousins, even your old teacher, Miss Beemer, the one you liked so much, still asks about you whenever I see her. Birdie Swensen told me the other day that Miss Beemer is engaged to be married, and I was glad to hear it. She was always so sweet. There is also talk in town about building a new school, but I will miss the old one. Do come home soon. We are not getting any younger.

> Love,
> Mother

P.S. We got the roof fixed.

Later that night, one of the men in camp asked the guy in the next bunk, "What's the matter with Tildholme? He keeps reading that same letter over and over."

Birdie Swensen was not a gossip. She'd just overheard the wrong information about Miss Beemer. It had only been a rumor started by a jeweler in town who had seen bachelor Glen Early looking at engagement rings. Later, Molly Ballantine had set Birdie straight on the matter. "No, Birdie," she said. "Lucille's not engaged. I know for a fact she turned Mr. Early down flat, not once, but twice."

Birdie was sorry to hear it. "Oh, that's too bad. I guess it's just wishful thinking on my part." Mr.

Early went on to marry his sixth cousin, Iris Loveless, and they moved to Summit Falls, Missouri, and both became Unity ministers.

Mrs. Tildholme never thought to write and tell Gustav any different. She didn't know it mattered.

A Sad Time

IT WAS SAID BY ALL WHO KNEW HIM THAT LORDOR Nordstrom had a heart of gold. He had almost lost the farm twice, because he had often paid other people's debts when they had been in trouble. But according to the doctor's latest report, that same heart was slowly failing. Katrina was devastated to think she might be losing him, and she almost never left his side. They tried to keep it from the children, but as the weeks went by, Lordor became weaker and could no longer go to work. Soon, he was mostly bedridden.

Lordor knew his time was short, and he wanted to leave his family well provided for. The dairy had grown far too large for either Katrina or Teddy to run, and Ingrid had her heart set on going to college. He talked it over with the family, and they made the decision to sell the farm.

Soon after word got out in the dairy industry that Sweet Clover Dairy was for sale, people came from far and wide with more than generous offers.

Closer to home, young Ander Swensen had borrowed all the money he possibly could from his father and the bank, and made an offer. It was far less than the others and he knew it, but it was the best he could do.

Day after day, Lordor listened to men's ideas about how they would run the dairy. They explained in great detail how they would add new ways to produce more milk from each cow.

One morning, Lordor called out from his bedroom to Teddy, who had been in the kitchen, and he came to the door. "Son, I want you to run over to the dairy and get Ander for me."

"Yes, sir."

Teddy rode over to the dairy and found Ander and told him that Lordor wanted to see him right away. Ander dropped what he was doing and asked Teddy if he knew what his father wanted to see him about.

"I don't know."

Ander arrived at the house five minutes later, still in his rubber boots and not very clean. He removed his hat and knocked on Lordor's bedroom door.

"Come in, and shut the door behind you."

"Yes, sir." Ander then went over and sat in the chair beside the bed. He could see how pale Lordor had become.

Lordor pulled himself up and said, "Ander, I see how people run their farms now, and I don't like it. It's not so good."

Ander nodded. "No, sir."

"I want my cows to be treated well."

"Yes, sir."

Lordor then looked at the boy and said, "This is why I take your offer and sell the farm to you."

A startled Ander couldn't believe it. "What? But Mr. Nordstrom—"

Lordor put up his hand. "No . . . no arguments. You are the only one I trust to run it like it should be run. And you earned it."

"But, Mr. Nordstrom. You taught me everything I know—"

"That's fine, but, Ander, I want you to give me your word on something. Just between the two of us . . . You understand?"

"Yes, sir?"

"You promise me that the farm and the cows will always stay in our families. You don't never sell it to nobody else. You agree?"

"I do."

"You will put this in your will someday . . . for even after you are gone?"

A solemn Ander answered, "I swear it on my life, sir."

Lordor smiled and leaned back on the bed. "Good. Now go tell the others."

THE FAMILY WAS GLAD Lordor had chosen Ander to take over the farm. Birdie and Lars Swensen were their best friends, and Ander was like a brother to Teddy and Ingrid, and another son to Katrina.

Later, when the town heard about it, they were relieved as well. They couldn't bear to think of strangers taking over Lordor's dairy. He had worked too hard to make it what it was. Over the years, the Sweet Clover Dairy had become a part of all of them.

TWO WEEKS LATER, as only fitting, Lordor Nordstrom became the first soul laid to rest at Still Meadows. And, as planned so many years ago, he was placed right in the middle, under the big oak tree.

LORDOR NORDSTROM

1852–1911

A Good and Honest Man
Blessings on His Way

A Change of Address

His family missed Lordor terribly, and his passing left a huge void in the community. Lordor had always been their mayor, and the town felt lost without him. Most communities would hold an election to determine who the next mayor would be. But the people in Elmwood Springs all got together and asked "Why bother with an election?" They just informed Lordor's son, Teddy, who had recently turned twenty, that he was now the new mayor. They had all gotten used to saying Mayor Nordstrom, and they did not want a change. Losing him had been hard enough. They had all been at Lordor's funeral, but they still couldn't believe that he was actually gone. And in a way, they were right.

Shortly after the funeral, the strangest thing happened. Lordor Nordstrom woke up. And he knew exactly who he was. He could still think and remember. He could see the blue sky and the clouds above him and hear birds singing. Not only that, he felt as light as a feather, and he could breathe again without any effort or pain. And everything smelled so fresh. The earth, the grass, the flowers. He felt so calm and peaceful.

But where was he? Was he in heaven? Was he dead or alive? Then Lordor looked up again and saw the old oak tree standing above him and suddenly he knew exactly where he was. He was right up the hill in his own plot at Still Meadows. He was dead all right. But he was still here.

What a pleasant surprise. If someone had told him this was going to happen, he wouldn't have believed them, and yet, here he was. He had no idea how or why it had happened. All he knew was that he'd never felt better in his life. Lordor took in another deep breath, then drifted off into another long, relaxing nap.

AFTER LORDOR PASSED AWAY, Ander asked the Nordstrom family to stay on the farm. But Katrina and the children decided to use the money from the sale of the farm to buy a new house in town. Katrina's eyesight was worsening and, without Lordor, the farm was no longer the same for her or Ingrid or Teddy. They missed him too much. Especially Katrina. There were too many memories on the farm. There was a part of her that half-expected Lordor to walk in the back door at the end of the day. And every day that he hadn't was painful. Losing Lordor prompted Katrina to sit down and write her daughter a letter while she could still see well enough to do it.

My Darling Ingrid,

If something should happen to me, I want you to have this handkerchief. It belonged to your grandmother, and it comes to you from so far away, so do take care of it. We have so few things left from the old country. I hope someday you will go and visit the place where I grew up.

I am leaving Momma's recipes to your brother. I think you will not mind. As your father said, "You either like to bake or you don't," and Teddy does.

Do you know how proud you made your father and how proud I am of you? You are my very own American girl. Also, I am enclosing some baby things that Birdie Swensen knitted for you and your brother. They are so dear, and I could never bear to give them away.

Love forever,
Mother

After she finished, she wrapped everything up and put it in a safe place.

—

WHEN LORDOR HAD BEEN up at Still Meadows for a while, he became even more pleased with himself than he had been before. From his new vantage point, he could see that there was a lovely view. He had indeed chosen the perfect place to be, and he could hardly wait for others to join him and tell him so. Of course, being older, Lordor thought he might have to wait awhile for Katrina, but in the meantime, he could hear the sound of the faraway cows in the pasture, roosters crowing, the soft whir of the tractors in the fields below, and church bells ringing on Sunday. All the sounds of home.

He found that it was a relief not to have to worry about the farm anymore, and he liked having time to just rest and think. And he wasn't lonesome. He had plenty of visitors on all the holidays. He loved having Katrina, Ingrid, and Teddy come up and seeing how tall Ingrid was growing. At first, he had tried to talk to them, but he realized they couldn't hear him. But the good news was that he could hear them, and they always brought such interesting news. And it was nice to know that people had not forgotten him.

Just last week, Ander Swensen had come up to see him and sat and talked about all the new things he was doing at the dairy now and said he hoped that Lordor would have approved. He had approved. Ander was a good man.

Life Moves On

1915

DOWNTOWN ELMWOOD SPRINGS CONTINUED TO flourish. Two Greek brothers named Morgan opened up a real department store that carried all the latest men's and ladies' fashions. Katrina's brother, Olaf, was hired to work in the shoe department.

And also keeping up with the modern world, the old opera house had been converted into a moving picture theater. A projectionist was hired, a stand-up piano was brought in, and Birdie Swensen, the church organist, supplied the background music for all the different silent films, romance and chase music being her specialties.

Moving pictures opened up a whole new world of imagination. Soon, all the young girls either wanted to be Mary Pickford or the vamp, Theda Bara. When **The Perils of Pauline,** starring Pearl White, came to town, Ingrid Nordstrom begged her mother for a pair of jodhpurs and boots, just like Pauline's.

Boys, enthralled with the adventures of silent screen star Tom Mix, "the king of cowboys," started riding their fathers' mules around the farm, pretending they were Tom Mix astride Tony the Wonder Horse, riding the range in search of bad guys.

After the initial excitement of the movies was over, everything went on pretty much the same. Kids graduated from grammar school and high school, people got married, and babies were born.

Elner Knott and Katrina's niece Beatrice Olsen had just entered the first grade. Elner, the eldest Knott girl, already large for her age, was a good-natured, happy girl. She showed up for her first day of school wearing a homemade feed-sack dress and carrying a very large white tin lunch pail.

Beatrice was small and delicate and had on a brand-new store-bought dress with a lace collar and white patent leather button-up shoes. Olaf had walked her to school that morning and handed her over to Miss Beemer personally. But Beatrice was still scared and nervous, being away from home for the first time.

At the lunch recess, Beatrice ran over to a wooden bench and sat by herself crying. She wanted to go home. When Elner saw her sitting all alone, she picked up her lunch pail and went over and sat down by her. After a moment Elner said, "If you won't tell on me, I'll show you a secret . . . and it will be just between us. But you have to stop crying first."

"What is it?" said Beatrice through her tears.

"You have to promise me you won't tell," said Elner.

Beatrice sniffed and shook her head. "I won't tell."

Then Elner slowly opened the lid of her lunch pail with small holes in it and said, "Look."

Beatrice leaned over and looked inside and saw a fluffy little yellow baby duck sitting in a small blue bowl.

"His name is Pete, and you can pet him if you like."

Beatrice reached in and petted its soft downy head. "Ooh, he's so cute," she said.

Elner said, "We've got lots more ducks and chickens at home. And some baby rabbits too."

"Really?"

"Un-huh. Do you want a biscuit? I've got five of them under the towel. I'm German; we like to eat a lot." She then reached under and pulled one out and handed it to Beatrice. "Here, eat this. I've got some jam, too."

After they had eaten all the biscuits, and petted the little duck some more, Elner said, "I can do a somersault. Do you want to see it?"

"Yes."

She did. And when her dress went up over her head and Beatrice saw her long white bloomers, it made her laugh.

Later, when Miss Beemer rang the school bell, they went back in together, and Beatrice wasn't scared anymore. They didn't know it yet, but from that day on, they would be friends forever.

—

THINGS WENT ON PRETTY MUCH as usual, but then, in the spring of 1916, the men in Elmwood Springs began to feel very uneasy, and they weren't sure why. It seemed their wives had begun to look at them in a strange way. They also noticed a lot of whispering going on among the ladies.

Soon women began to attend secret meetings held in the middle of the day in the back room of the pharmacy, and after they all arrived for the meeting, they would lock the door. Hattie Smith, the pharmacist's wife, stood guard outside. When her husband, Robert, politely inquired what they were doing in there, Hattie would only reply, "That's for me to know."

The men didn't know it, yet, but inside the room was a meeting of the brand-new Elmwood Springs Suffragette Club.

Birdie Swensen, a subscriber to **The Missouri Woman** magazine, had passed an article regarding the subject of the vote to all the other ladies for them to read and discuss. There was a struggle going on, and even though Elmwood Springs was just a small town, they wanted to be a part of it.

Birdie had been corresponding with the president of the St. Louis Woman's Suffrage Association, and she told Birdie that something very important was going to happen in June. She warned them that it could be dangerous, but to a woman, they vowed to stand together shoulder to shoulder when the call to arms came. They might be a small group, but they were determined to take their place in history, no matter what the consequences.

As the days went by, men would come home from work only to find their wives, still locked in their sewing rooms, working away on what, they did not know or care. They just knew there was no supper on the table, and Henry Knott, for one, was not happy about it. He wanted his creamed noodles and schnitzel at six o'clock on the dot.

ON JUNE 14, 1916, the Democratic National Convention was to take place at the St. Louis Coliseum, the largest convention hall in the county. St. Louis was in a festive mood, with each building colorfully decorated with bunting of red, white, and blue. The town was packed with delegates from all over the country.

On the first morning of the convention, as all the male delegates poured out of their hotels and began marching down the middle of Locust Street, toward the convention hall, they were in for a big surprise. Both sides of the street were lined with hundreds of women, young and old, each holding a yellow parasol and wearing a long white dress with a bright yellow sash that read VOTES FOR WOMEN. As far as the eye could see, women from all over the country stood together in silent protest in what they called a walk-less, talkless demonstration of solidarity.

The sight was very effective. By the time the men

reached the St. Louis Coliseum, they had passed by many ladies who, by the look of them, could have been their own wives or mothers. Some delegates had been swayed to reconsider their position on the matter of votes for women. And it had been done without making a sound.

That day, twelve Elmwood Springs women stood proudly on the Golden Lane alongside women from all over the world, holding their homemade yellow parasols and wearing yellow sashes over their long white dresses.

Birdie Swensen, Nancy Knott, and Nancy's little girl, Elner, were there. And although her eyesight had worsened, and she had to be led, Katrina Nordstrom and her daughter, Ingrid, were there, too. She knew Lordor would have been proud.

Yes, their cause was noble, but the Elmwood Springs ladies were not averse to having a little fun while they were in St. Louis. After the demonstration, they all went to the movies and saw Irene and Vernon Castle in **The Whirl of Life** and went wild over Irene Castle's short hairdo. The next morning, six of them went downstairs to the hotel barbershop and had their hair cut in an Irene Castle bob. Nancy Knott went first, then Ingrid, followed by Lily Tildholme's seventy-two-year-old mother, who said she was just dying to learn to do the turkey trot.

When Nancy Knott came home from St. Louis with her new short bob, her husband, Henry, about fainted. "Momma, where's your bun?"

"Up in St. Louis, with everybody else's. Why?"

By the look in her eye, he knew not to push the issue. "Just wondered," he said.

As Henry opined to the men at the barbershop the next day, "We're doomed, boys. The women have all gone as wild as heifers in a snowstorm. No telling what they'll be up to next. Hell, I'm living with four of them. I'm liable to be killed in my bed, just for the gold in my teeth."

Of course, Henry didn't have any gold in his teeth. He just liked to embellish a bit.

Reunited

KATRINA NORDSTROM, WHO SADLY HAD COM-
pletely lost her sight in the last few months of her
life, succumbed to a sudden consumption, and in
December 1916, was laid to rest beside her husband.

KATRINA OLSEN NORDSTROM
1865–1916
**She Arrived a Stranger
and Died Among Friends**

When Katrina opened her eyes, she heard her hus-
band's voice saying, "Katrina? Can you hear me?"
"Lordor? Am I dreaming?"
"No, darling. It's me."

AFTER THEIR LONG-AWAITED AND happy reunion,
Katrina sighed and said, "Oh, Lordor, I can hardly
believe it. It's so wonderful up here. . . . I can see
again . . . and everything is so beautiful, the sky, the

clouds, the stars. Even more beautiful than I remembered."

He said, "So I made the right decision? This is a nice spot?"

"Oh, yes," she said.

"Good, but I'm so glad you're here with me now."

"Me too."

"I miss the children, but you know what I missed the most, Katrina?" asked Lordor.

"No, what?"

"Listening to you talk. I could listen to you talk forever."

It was a lovely moment. Just the two of them, so happy and content to be together again. Then, suddenly, someone said, "Hello there, folks!"

A startled Lordor asked, "Who the hell is that?"

A gravelly man's voice answered, "A deceased man by the name of Evander J. Chapman."

"Where are you?" asked Lordor.

"Acrost the way . . . up to your left."

"My God, how long have you been there?"

"June of 1854. How long's that?"

"A long time. Why didn't you say nothing before?"

"Well, mister, you hain't said nothing, so I hain't said nothing. Truth to tell, twern't aware I could . . . tilt I heared you greet your missus here. How do, ma'am," he said politely.

"Hello, Mr. Chapman," said Katrina. "My name is Katrina Nordstrom, and this is my husband, Lordor."

"How do, Mr. Nordstrom. Pleased, I'm sure."

"Hello."

"Yes, sir. I was passing through here in '54, trapping beaver and muskrat, when an Injun got me! Been here ever since and sure am glad to have the company. What brings you folks out here? I wuz shot with an arrow myself, clean through my liver."

"Oh, no, Mr. Chapman," said Katrina. "That must have been awful."

"Yessum, twas. That Injun snucked up on me, and after he donest shot me and left me afoot, this ole Canook out of Quebec I was trapping with come up apon me and sees me a-laying here, shot and scalped, and says he'd come back through in a day or two, after I wuz fully dead, and bury me. So's I let off a right mean volley of cussing at him. I figgered he wuz a-turn-tailing and runnin' off, leaving me to the buzzards. Afore that, I hain't never put much stock in him. He was a bad one to swill corn liquor. But in the end, that old Canook done me fair and Christian. True to his word, he come back and buried me on this hill good and proper-like, even said words over me. The words wuz French Canook, so I don't knowed what he said, but . . . I sure wisht I hain't a-cussed him like that."

After Lordor and Katrina had recovered from the shock of discovering they weren't alone, they learned that Mr. Chapman was originally from Kentucky and a distant cousin of John Chapman, better known as Johnny Appleseed. He also told them more about his trapping days and said that in 1854, the year he had passed through this part of Missouri, the woods had been so thick, you had to cut a path with a knife.

Katrina asked, "Did you see any bears?"

"Why, missus, I musta seed two a day!"

"Mountain lions?"

"Had one jump at me onest, but I rolled in a ball and confused him. He gimme a bad bite and a scratch before he left, though."

"Were there lots of Indians living around here?"

"Couldn't say for sure, missus. I just seed the one who absconded with my pelts, my horse, and half my scalp."

Some time later, Lordor said, "Mr. Chapman, I think I owe an apology to you. I didn't know someone was already buried here. I might have given your plot away. I'm not sure, but you could be in the Lindquist family plot."

"Oh, don't give it no nevermine, Mr. Nordstrom. I'm glad more folks is a-comin'. Jus' hope they be some females amunst 'em. I seed one smart-lookin' gal up on this hill afore. Comes up pretty regular like, a-prunin' them willer trees."

Katrina said, "Oh, that was Birdie Swensen you saw."

"Well, I always did like the ladies. I sorely do miss 'em."

Lordor asked, "How old a man were you when you got shot?"

"Well, lemme see . . . I weren't no young man, so

I reckon I go back over a hundred years or more by now."

Later, when Lordor and Katrina told him about present-day Missouri, Mr. Chapman could hardly believe it. "Horseless carriages that you can drive for miles and light you turn on pulling a switch? You're a-funnin' with me, ain't you, Mr. Nordstrom?"

"No, sir."

"And them carriages goes without pull of horse, mule, or oxen?"

"Yes, sir."

"Well, what do they feed the critters?"

"Gasoline."

Mr. Chapman thought for a while, then said, "Don't know it."

Lordor tried his best to explain how electricity worked, but it was no use.

"I heared what you tell me. . . . I jus' cain't get a good handle on it. It's too ahead of me."

Lordor decided he wouldn't even attempt to tell Mr. Chapman about airplanes. It would probably scare him to death.

Katrina felt sorry for the man and jumped in. "Oh, Mr. Chapman, don't feel bad. I feel the same way about electricity. I can't understand how it works, either."

"Who's the president now?" asked Mr. Chapman, changing the subject.

Lordor said, "I don't know. I forgot to ask. Who is it?"

Katrina answered, "Woodrow Wilson."

"Is he a good one?" asked Mr. Chapman.

"I guess just like all of them, time will tell, sir. Time will tell."

Mr. Chapman said, "Ol' Franklin Pierce was the last president I voted for. . . . How did he fare?"

"I couldn't say. He was before my time."

"Ah."

The three of them didn't know it, but there were actually four people out at Still Meadows. Across and up was an elderly Osage Indian, who had washed up on the other side of the hill during the flood of 1715. When the old Osage heard the three of them talking, he didn't recognize it as language. He thought it must be some kind of birds having a fight, and rolled over and went back to sleep.

OVER THE NEXT FEW MONTHS, the three of them would visit and chat often, and Katrina and Lordor so enjoyed hearing about Mr. Chapman's trapping and scouting days. They didn't know if he was just a master spinner of tall tales or if he really had seen and done all the things he said, but either way, he was very entertaining. One day, he said, "You'll not believe it, but I scouted with ol' Kit Carson hisself. He twern't no taller than my nose, but a better man wuddn't ever borned." Then, as was his habit, Mr. Chapman switched subjects and said, "Hey, I'll tell you a good one. You folks is Swedish, ain't ya?"

"Yes, both of us."

"Well, like I say. I seed a awful lot in my day. But folks, I hain't never seed nor heared anything so beautiful as when the Swedish songbird, Miss Jenny Lind herself, alive and in the flesh, come to Tennessee. I remember it like daylight. It was April of '52, and all the mens come from miles around to see her. Why, I had to shoot a man in the big toe jest to get a ticket, but I got it. My seat wuz way back up in the balcony, but there twern't no disappointment to it. She sunged like a bird . . . and them golden curls. Why, she was so purty, it hurt you to look at her. It wuz like seein' an angel from heaven, and I hain't got over it yet. Yes, sir, seeing her wuz the best night of my life. And I'll tell you somethin' else. . . . It eased off my dying just a-recalling it."

Katrina often wondered if Mr. Chapman really had seen Jenny Lind and how she would have felt if she had known that a man in the audience that night, almost seventy years later, thought seeing her had been the highlight of his life.

And then one day, without a warning or even a goodbye, he wasn't there anymore. They called to him over and over again, "Mr. Chapman? Mr. Chapman?" But he never answered. He was gone, leaving Katrina and Lordor wondering what had happened to him.

Nancy Knott

BEING OF A CERTAIN AGE, LORDOR AND KATRINA weren't alone long. In 1918, they were joined by other original settlers. Nancy Knott arrived first, and, as usual, she got right to the point.

"Since you two died, we had a war."

"Oh, no, Nancy," said Katrina. "I was afraid of that."

"Yah, but it was over soon. The Yanks went over there and come right back home."

A concerned Lordor jumped in. "Did we lose any Elmwood Springs boys?"

"Oh, no. The Eggstrom boy went, but he come home safe and sound. Oh, and your boy, Ted? He still don't marry, but if I know men, not for too much longer."

"Oh, I hope not, Nancy."

"Me, too. Gerta, my middle girl, has her eye on him."

"And Ingrid? Does she have a young man?" asked Katrina.

"Ah . . . that one's too smart for them boys that

live around here, but everybody says she looks more like you every day now."

"Really?" asked Katrina.

"That's good," said Lordor, "better than looking like me. And everybody else is good?"

Nancy said, "Oh, sure. But my Henry? He's not so good. He don't walk good anymore, and he coughs and he coughs. It's a surprise I'm here first."

Katrina said, "Yes, it really is. What happened to you, Nancy?"

There was a long pause, then Nancy said, "Too much beer."

Katrina wondered if she had heard correctly. "Too much beer?"

"Yah."

They waited for her to elaborate, but she didn't. They didn't want to pry. It would be rude, but they did wonder how too much beer could kill you.

A little while later, Katrina said, "I hate to ask, Nancy, but how is Sweet Potato?"

"Ack! That pig. What a waste of good sausage, but she is still herself." Katrina was relieved to hear it.

As expected, right after New Year's, Henry Knott came up to Still Meadows and joined his wife. One of the first things he said to Katrina and Lordor was, "Hey, did Momma tell you how she got drunk and fell out of the back of the wagon coming home from the dance?"

"Hush your mouth, Henry," Nancy said.

"We found her the next day, in the ditch by the old Tildholme farm, frozen solid."

"Henry!" shouted Nancy. "Hush up!"

"Oh."

Then, by way of explanation, Nancy said to Katrina, "I told him a hundred times that old board was loose, but he don't listen."

Lordor and Katrina were very happy to have their old friends join them, but there was still the matter of Evander Chapman's sudden and mysterious disappearance. They decided not to mention meeting Mr. Chapman to Henry and Nancy or tell them what had transpired. It might be too upsetting for them. They were also not sure if it would ever happen again. They still wondered where he had gone and whether he would ever come back.

The Dating Game

YOUNG TED NORDSTROM, THE NEW MAYOR OF Elmwood Springs, had good common business sense like his father. With his share of the money from the sale of the dairy farm, he purchased several downtown buildings. And as there was still a large number of Swedish in the area, he opened Nordstrom's Swedish Bakery, using a lot of his mother's recipes, the same ones she had brought with her from the old country so many years ago. Needless to say, it was successful. Swedish or not, who doesn't love a good bakery?

After his mother died, Ted had gone out with a few girls. One from Joplin, Missouri, and, later, with the new dental assistant who had just moved to town. However, as Nancy Knott had guessed, he eventually wound up marrying Gerta Knott. Everyone said it was a perfect match. Ted loved to bake, and Gerta, a sweet, plump girl, like all the other Knotts, just loved to eat. They were as happy as two peas in a pod.

But the dating and marriage situation with Ted's

sister, Ingrid, was an entirely different situation. People had hoped that she and Ander Swensen would marry someday, but they had grown up together and were too much like brother and sister.

Although she was a pretty girl like her mother, and many boys asked her out, she simply wasn't interested and would turn them down.

When she was not in school, she either had her face in a book studying or else she was busy at her job working for the local veterinarian. People began to wonder if Ingrid would ever make a wife. She seemed to like animals more than boys.

In fact, once, when a boy named Morris Shingle was not treating his horse the way she thought he should, she'd punched him in the nose.

More Good Friends

1919

THE NEXT TO ARRIVE UP AT STILL MEADOWS WAS Mr. Lindquist, who had been buried with his fiddle, and the first thing he said was, "Well, hell, if I had known I was just heading up the hill, I'd have told them not to get me so dressed up. So, Lordor, what's it like being out here?"

"It's, well, I don't know exactly how to describe it. Oh, it's just . . . Katrina, you're so good with the words. You tell him."

"Oh my, thank you, Lordor, but I'm afraid this is just one of those times when mere words are just not adequate. It's certainly beyond beautiful or euphoric. I would say 'sublime' is the only word that comes close, and even that doesn't capture it. All I can say is it's a feeling you never dreamed existed, and it just keeps going."

Lordor said, "Exactly!"

A few months later, when Birdie Swensen arrived at Still Meadows, just like everyone else, she was amazed. One would have thought, aside from the usual misconceptions about being deceased, that if anything, it would certainly be boring, but it was not. Everyone said that no matter how long they had been at Still Meadows, they had not been bored for one second. True, they couldn't move around like before, but they could talk to anyone there at will. All they had to do was call out their name. And no matter what time of day it was, there was always someone to converse with.

But, most importantly, without all the distractions of everyday life, there was the endless panorama of nature to enjoy. Sunrises, sunsets, rain, snow, cloudy days, and sunny days, plus many unexpected and thrilling events: a shooting star, a sudden glorious ray of sunshine after a storm, rainbows, silver light-ning bolts flashing across the sky. And the moon. Just the moon alone was a show unto itself. Some nights, it was big and orange, sometimes a half moon, a big white moon, or just a little white fingernail of a moon. And each season brought its own special joys. Endless flocks of ducks and geese flying overhead in the fall; the trees blossoming in the spring. In the summer, on warm, balmy nights, the air was full of the fragrance of honeysuckle and wisteria. And in the winter, when the air was full of wood smoke, some of the older men could name the type of wood being burned, and they would call out cedar, oak, or hickory. Winter was so lovely. Sometimes Still Mead-ows would be covered with snow, but they always felt cozy and warm. Bored? Good heavens, no. Birdie said to Katrina, "Why, I can hardly wait to wake up and see all the wonderful things the day has in store."

The Twenties

All the Wonderful Things in Store

Elmwood Springs
Is Looking Up

THANKS TO THE EFFORTS OF THEIR YOUNG MAYOR and his city council, and much to the delight of everyone in town, a huge water tower was built with ELMWOOD SPRINGS, MISSOURI written on it in big black letters. You could see it from miles away. Nobody knew why, but it made them feel important to look up and see it.

As more and more people from the younger generation moved from the farms and into town, a lot of new businesses began opening. The Trolley Car Diner opened next to the movie theater, and in 1920, a Miss Dixie Cahill rented the large room upstairs over the drugstore and opened the Dixie Cahill School of Tap and Twirl. And shortly thereafter, a lot of little girls and a few unhappy boys were immediately signed up.

Over at the picture show, Charlie Chaplin and Buster Keaton were making them laugh. And all the boys and girls in town had each fallen madly in love with their own special movie star. Mrs. Eggstrom even showed up at the box office and claimed that Greta Garbo was her second cousin on her father's side by marriage. It was a long shot, but she did get a free ticket and a bag of popcorn.

ELMWOOD SPRINGS CONTINUED TO miss Lordor Nordstrom. May 22, the date the town had been incorporated, had been officially named Founder's Day. Every year on that date, the city council and the entire grammar school and high school came up to Still Meadows and placed a huge bouquet on Lordor Nordstrom's grave. Later, everyone in town would gather at the outdoor stage in the park for the annual pageant.

Lucille Beemer wrote, directed, and produced a musical pageant:

FROM SWEDEN TO MISSOURI: THE SAGA OF LORDOR NORDSTROM

The inspiring story told in song and dance of how in 1880, the twenty-eight-year-old Swedish pioneer left his homeland, traveled to the area, and cleared the land now called Elmwood Springs.

The pageant depicted Lordor and all the other early pioneer families arriving in the area one by one, each bringing farm animals and farm tools with them. Men were dressed in overalls, ladies in long dresses and gingham bonnets.

The pageant, first staged and performed in 1920, went off very well, except that some of the farm animals that had been cast as farm animals had misbehaved. In later years, they used large cardboard cutouts of sheep, pigs, cows, and mules instead. Not nearly as authentic, but as Lucille Beemer said, "Better safe than sorry."

The Shoe Department

SINCE KATRINA'S YOUNGER BROTHER, OLAF OLSEN, had taken over the shoe department at the Morgan Brothers Department Store, it had become very busy. All the children in town loved to come in and have him measure their feet with the silver and black steel sliding measuring device. After he measured their feet, he would always act surprised and kid them about how big their feet were, tell them that they were going to grow up and be a ten-foot giant, and then give them a stick of peppermint candy. Besides being a friendly type of person, Olaf also had the kind of looks and manners that all the ladies and girls appreciated: hair slicked back, and always wearing a nice, neat white collar. Naturally, he had a lot of female customers who would come in at least once a week and spend an hour or so trying on shoes. He didn't mind. He knew they would eventually buy a pair.

IT WAS A SATURDAY in May of 1921, and Olaf was, at present, waiting on three ladies who were busy discussing their favorite topic, Ingrid Nordstrom. As Olaf was removing the eighth pair of shoes from a box for Mrs. Bell to try on, she said, "Oh, and Olaf, how is that darling little daughter of yours . . . little Bertha?"

He smiled. "You mean Beatrice?"

"That's right, Beatrice."

"She is just fine, Mrs. Bell. She and her school friend Elner Knott are at the movies. They should be here any minute now."

"How old is she now?"

"Ten, almost eleven."

"Ah, well, you won't have to worry about finding her a husband for a while, yet."

When Olaf left to go into the back room and bring out more shoes, the ladies continued their conversation about Ingrid Nordstrom. "She was such a daddy's girl. I don't think she'll ever find anybody who could live up to Lordor Nordstrom," said Mrs. Bell.

"No, he was one of a kind. They just don't make men like that anymore," Mabel Whooten said, weighing in on the subject. "Well, even if she **doesn't** find a man, Miss Beemer never married, and she seems happy enough."

"Of course, she **seems** happy, Mabel," said Mrs. Gumms, "but you know, no woman is really happy without a home and children."

Mrs. Bell said, "I'm not so sure about that. Oh, not that I don't love Lloyd and the children, but still . . . it might be nice to have a little time to myself every once in a while." She sighed. "But even so, I just hope, for Ingrid's sake, she finds somebody nice."

Finally, after six more pairs of shoes were trotted out, Mrs. Bell tried on a pair that felt comfortable. But when she took them off and looked at the size, she was alarmed. "Olaf, I wear a size five. These are size seven!"

Olaf looked at the shoe and said, "Oh, Mrs. Bell, you're right. This brand always runs exactly two sizes too small. It's really a five."

"Oh, I see. . . . Well, in that case, I'll take them."

After the two ladies left and Olaf was gathering up all the boxes of rejects, he had to smile. They had forgotten that Ingrid Nordstrom was his niece. He'd known Ingrid all her life. He wasn't worried about her one bit.

Just then, his daughter, Beatrice, came running through the store and back to the shoe department, dragging her friend Elner Knott by the hand. "Daddy, Elner wants you to measure her feet!"

He laughed. "Okay . . . come here, honey. Take off your shoes and put your foot right here." Elner took off her shoes and placed her foot on the machine. "Stand up straight now, and don't move." Olaf pulled the lever back until it touched her toes and noted the size. Elner had rather large feet for a girl her age. But he didn't tell her that. He feigned surprise and said, "Oh, my . . . look at that. Why, Elner, you have the exact same size feet as Princess

Margaret of Sweden. You must have royal blood."
Then he looked at Beatrice with mock solemnness.
"Beatrice, we have to do exactly what she tells us to
do from now on."

Beatrice giggled and said, "Now do my feet,
Daddy."

ELNER, AS SHE OFTEN DID, spent that night in town
with Beatrice. Later, when they were in bed, as young
girls do, they talked about what they wanted to be
when they grew up. Beatrice was very specific. She
said, "I want to marry a handsome man and have
three children, two boys and one little girl, and I'm
going to name her Hanna Marie, after my grandmother in Sweden. What about you, Elner? How
many children do you want?"

Elner thought about it, then said, "Oh, I don't
know, Beatrice. Momma said having babies is awful
painful. I think I'd just as soon have a litter of kittens
myself."

Beatrice laughed and said, "You can't have kittens,
silly!"

"Why not?"

"Because you're a person. You have to have babies."

"I do?"

"Yes."

"Well, that's too bad. I'd rather have kittens."

Ingrid Nordstrom

1922

To everyone's surprise, Lordor and Katrina's daughter, Ingrid, became the very first female to attend the famous Iowa State College of Veterinary Medicine. But it had not been easy.

Although she had scored the highest of anyone on her entrance exam, when first-year student I. Nordstrom turned out to be a female, Mr. Richard Livermore, the faculty administrator, had been thunderstruck.

This had never happened before. He quickly called a meeting of the faculty and the dean of admissions to figure out how best to handle the mistake and get rid of her as gracefully as possible. But when Mr. Livermore's wife heard about Ingrid showing up for school, she marched into the meeting and addressed her husband. "You'd better accept that girl in this school, Mr. Livermore, or you will hear from every woman in Iowa . . . starting with me!"

Nobody wanted to cross Mrs. Livermore. And, as the dean said, "If we keep her out, there will be hell to pay." So they let her in.

Ingrid knew the next years of study would be a lot of hard work and that she would face a lot of opposition from the male students who were not happy about her being there. But she was a lot like her mother, brave and determined. And, thankfully, there was at least one young male student who was awfully glad she was there.

THERE WAS ANOTHER SURPRISE that year, only this time, it was up at Still Meadows. Late one afternoon, Nancy Knott was singing one of her favorite German drinking songs when suddenly, right in the middle of the tune, she stopped. They all waited for her to pick up the tune again, but they heard nothing but silence. After calling to her for some time and receiving no reply, it was clear to them that Nancy was definitely not there. It had happened again.

When Lordor and Katrina then explained to the others about Mr. Chapman's earlier disappearance, a somewhat irritated Henry Knott said, "Well, ain't that just like Nancy to up and disappear on me right in the middle of a song. I tell you, that woman always did have a mind of her own. And now she's flew the coop without a goodbye or nothing. Well, dang."

Fun at Still Meadows

EVEN THOUGH SOME SAID HE WAS TOO MEAN TO DIE, Old Man Hendersen finally expired and came up to Still Meadows. And, as expected, after the folks on the hill had all greeted him, he let them know that he had no interest in conversation. He said, "I'm glad you're glad I'm here, but how in the hell can I rest in peace if all of you keep nattering at me? I need my sleep. Good night!"

Lordor laughed. "I guess it's nice to know some things never change. Let the old boy sleep." So they did.

Over the next couple of years or so, old Mrs. Tildholme; Birdie's husband, Lars; Mrs. Lindquist; and the Eggstroms came up to Still Meadows. It was so good to be with them again.

And it was nice to know they all could still laugh. There were a lot of things to laugh at up at Still Meadows. Every Halloween, invariably, some boys in town would dare one another to go out and spend the night at the cemetery to prove how brave they were.

Last Halloween, around midnight, after two little boys had just finished rolling out their sleeping bags, a huge owl hooted and flew out of a tree, and the two boys screamed like little girls and ran home. They never did come back for their sleeping bags. And, of course, there was the water tower. Boys were always trying to climb up to the top, but most got scared and stopped halfway up. The men up at Still Meadows would watch and make bets on who would make it.

IN SEPTEMBER 1923, Mrs. Hattie Smith became the very last of the old settlers to join her old friends, and she could hardly wait to tell Katrina the good news. "We got the vote! The bill passed!"

"Oh, Hattie! How wonderful. Did you hear that, Lordor? Women can vote."

Before he could respond, Hattie continued. "And that's not all. Hold on to your hat. You and Lordor are now two old grandparents. A big, fine boy named Gene Lordor Nordstrom, after his grandpa."

Katrina was thrilled. "Oh, Lordor, we have a grandson."

"A boy? What does he look like? Have you seen him?"

"What do you think? He looks just like you, Lordor. Blond, blue eyes . . . you just wait. They'll surely be up to visit at Christmas. You'll see for yourself."

Hattie Smith had been right. That Christmas, when Ted and his wife, Gerta, came out and decorated their grave, Katrina and Lordor saw their new grandbaby, nine-month-old Gene Lordor, for the first time, and just as Hattie said, he was a blond boy with blue eyes, and he did look like his grandfather.

In Elmwood Springs, as everywhere, the last generation moved on, and the next one was coming up right behind it. Besides Lordor and Katrina's new grandson, one of the Lindquist girls, Hazel, had married Clarence Goodnight, and they now had eight-year-old twin girls named Bess and Ada and a little one on the way.

The Wedding

IN 1927, CHARLES LINDBERGH THRILLED THE world with his flight over the Atlantic, and everyone was singing and dancing to the new tune "Lucky Lindy."

In Elmwood Springs, the whole town was abuzz about the upcoming wedding of Ingrid Nordstrom. As Hazel Goodnight said to Gerta over at the bakery, "We don't hear from her for years, and now she's coming home and marrying a total stranger."

"Not only that," said Gerta, handing Hazel a large cream puff in a small pink box, "he's from Texas!"

Ingrid's young man, Ray Wallace, was a lot like her father. He loved a smart woman, and he had been mad for Ingrid the first day he met her. He pursued her all through the first two years of school, mostly being turned down. But one day, while they were in the middle of a class, and out of the clear blue sky, she decided she loved him and told him she would marry him right after graduation. He had nearly fainted, and Ingrid continued dissecting the large bull cadaver on the table. She was fascinated with its reproductive system, in comparison to that of the equine family.

The couple, along with his parents and brothers and sisters, arrived in town the day before the big ceremony. The wedding party was mostly a family affair. Ingrid's brother, Ted, baked the wedding cake and also walked her down the aisle. Her sister-in-law Gerta was matron of honor, and her cousin, seventeen-year-old Beatrice Olsen, was a bridesmaid. And last, but not least, Katrina and Lordor's grandson, little four-year-old Gene Nordstrom, who was the ring bearer. They all talked about how sad it was that Lordor and Katrina had not lived to see this day.

Everyone in town came, except Morris Shingle. He was still afraid of Ingrid, after she'd socked him in the nose that time, so he just skulked in the bushes, watching through the window. However, he did send his little boy, Lester, into the reception to steal a piece of cake.

EARLY THE NEXT MORNING, before the couple left for their honeymoon, Lordor Nordstrom looked up and was surprised to see their daughter, Ingrid, standing above them. "Katrina, wake up!" he said.

After Ingrid had placed her wedding bouquet on their grave, she began to speak. "Momma, Daddy. This is Dr. Ray Wallace, my husband. We just got married, and I wanted you to meet him." She motioned for him to step up. "And he has something he wants to say."

The young man in the new blue suit cleared his throat and began. "Uh, hello, I'm awfully sorry we didn't have a chance to meet, but I just wanted you to know how much I love your daughter. Ingrid is the grandest girl in the world, and I want to thank you for having her . . . and to tell you that you don't have to worry about her. I'm going to take very good care of her for you from now on."

Ingrid stepped up and took his hand and said, "He will, too. Guess where he's taking me on our honeymoon? Sweden! And we are going to see where you and Uncle Olaf grew up. I still have the handkerchief you left me, Momma. I had it with me at the wedding as something old. Well . . . goodbye for now. I love you."

After they left, Katrina said, "Oh, Lordor, just think, our baby is married. And didn't she just look beautiful? I can tell she's happy. And the boy seemed very sincere, don't you think?"

"He seemed all right, I guess."

It was a typical reaction. Katrina knew that daddies never think anybody is good enough for their daughters, and a little while later, she said, "You know, Lordor, there was something about that young man that reminded me of you."

"You think so?" asked Lordor, brightening up a bit.

"Oh, yes. He seems very strong and steady, and very smart. Just like you."

Lordor didn't say anything more, but he did feel a little better. If Katrina liked him, he couldn't be all that bad.

ANDER SWENSEN NOT ONLY owned the Nordstrom dairy, he had inherited his family's adjoining farm, and was now in charge of a very large dairy operation. He rarely had time to go anywhere, but, of course, he had attended his friend Ingrid's wedding.

Romance must have been in the air that year. Ander had known Beatrice Olsen since she was a little girl, but somehow that day, when he saw a very much grown-up Beatrice walk down the aisle in her pretty pink bridesmaid dress, something happened. Cupid shot an arrow that hit poor Ander right between the eyes, because all at once, he was in love. Weddings have a way of doing that.

As for Ingrid, right after the honeymoon, she and Ray moved to his hometown of Mansfield, Texas, right outside of Dallas, and started a veterinary practice together. Although they treated all animals, Ingrid, not so surprisingly, had a special interest in cows. And she loved the wide open spaces of Texas and got to wear cowboy boots every day.

The Little White Box

VERY SOON AFTER ANDER SWENSEN HAD SEEN BEA-trice Olsen at Ingrid's wedding, he began asking her out. Ander realized that at age thirty-two he was a little older than most of her other boyfriends, and she might be uncomfortable about it. So he always made it a point to include her friend Elner in all of his invitations. And that suited Elner just fine. That summer she got to go for a lot of rides in Ander's new car, eat in several fancy restaurants, and see a lot of good movies. The three friends had a lot of fun together that summer. As it turned out, Ander could be as silly as Elner. One time he picked them up wearing a blond curly wig. Another time he drove them all the way to Springfield and back with the top down.

On the afternoon of August the twelfth, at Bea-trice's big eighteenth birthday party in the town park, people were squealing with laughter, watching all the ladies and young girls running in the "egg in spoon" footrace. The object was to see who could reach the finish line without dropping the egg. And as usual, Elner won. She ran in her bare feet, holding up her dress with one hand and the spoon and egg with the other. For a big girl, she could move fast.

Later Ander and Beatrice entered the sack race together but two eight-year-olds beat them by more than five feet. Ander supplied all the food and the ice cream for the party, and as a special treat, had brought in a barbershop quartet from Joplin to serenade the birthday girl. After the birthday cake was cut, Beatrice opened all her presents. Ander had given her a nice ladies' leather traveling case she had admired in Springfield. And even though it wasn't her birthday, Elner got one too. After the party was over, Ander quietly handed Beatrice a small white box, and said, "Don't open it until you get home, all right?"

Elner was staying in town with Beatrice that night, and after they got back to Beatrice's room Beatrice sat down on her bed and shook Ander's present. "I wonder what it is?"

"Well, open it up, Silly."

When she did, to her surprise, inside was a large diamond engagement ring, with a note that read "I adore you. Will you marry me?"

"Elner, look! Ander wants to marry me. Oh no. I knew he liked me, but I didn't realize . . . I mean I like him a lot . . . but . . . what am I going to do?"

"Well, you could marry him."

"But, Elner, he has that red hair and all those

freckles. What if I had children with freckles all over them?"

"I wouldn't let freckles stop me. I had a speckled hen once, and she was my favorite. But you know me. I like Ander."

Beatrice smiled and nodded. "He is awful cute . . . isn't he?"

"Cute as a bug in a rug."

"I sure would hate for some other girl to get him. I don't think I want to say no, but I'm not ready to say yes. I want to go to college."

"Then maybe you can just tell him that. But in the meantime, I'd hang on to the ring."

"Oh, I couldn't," said Beatrice. "It wouldn't be right."

"Well, he won't take it back. I know that."

"How do you know?"

Elner looked up to the ceiling. "A little red birdie told me."

"Oh, you devil, you knew about this all along, didn't you?" Beatrice said, hitting Elner with a pillow.

Elner laughed and covered her head. "I'm not saying I did, and I'm not saying I didn't." But she had known. She had helped Ander pick out the ring.

Beatrice took Elner's advice and told Ander the truth—that she really wasn't ready to commit to anybody yet. She asked how long he was willing to wait for an answer.

Ander thought about it for a moment, then said, "Oh, just a lifetime. How long is that?"

In September, as planned, Beatrice went off to St. Louis to a two-year girls' college, but at Ander's insistence, she kept the ring.

Ander knew when she left that he might lose her for good, but he also wanted her to be happy.

Missing Mrs. Knott

AFTER HIS WIFE, NANCY, HAD SUDDENLY DISAP-
peared from Still Meadows, Henry Knott was feeling
very lonesome. But thankfully, their three daughters,
Elner, Gerta, and Ida, came out to visit often. The
last time Elner had come to Still Meadows, she had
Will Shimfissle with her. Henry had laughed and
said to Katrina, "I wonder what she's doing with that
little peanut. I hope she ain't thinking of marrying
him."

Katrina said, "But Will's a very nice boy and a very
good worker, Henry."

"That's true. Oh, well. Whoever marries Elner is
getting themselves a mighty fine gal."

AND SURE ENOUGH, LATER that year, Elner, a big, tall
girl at five foot ten, surprised everyone in town by
marrying the little skinny hardscrabble farmhand
named Will Shimfissle, who stood only five foot five
in his stocking feet. But as someone said, "Every sock
has its mate, and little Will Shimfissle is Elner's."

—

THAT NEXT CHRISTMAS, TO everyone's delight, when Beatrice came home for the holidays, she agreed to marry Ander Swensen in the spring.

When the time came, Elner was her matron of honor, and as such, Elner had to come to town and was outfitted from head to toe for the big occasion.

The wedding was lovely, marred only by the fact that the groom embarrassed himself by sobbing his way through the vows.

Later, at the reception, wearing her new high heels, Elner hobbled over to Ander and Beatrice and said, "Now that the big shindig is finally over, you two have to promise me to stay together because I can't go through this torture again. I've never felt so trussed up and gussied up in all my born life. My feet are killing me. I can't wait to get back to the farm and jerk this girdle off. Then I'm going to have Will take it out to the yard and shoot it to death."

They both laughed. And Beatrice said, "Oh, Elner . . . what would I do if I didn't have you to make me laugh?"

"You'd have to go through life being miserable, I guess."

THAT SAME YEAR, SOMETHING so sweet and unexpected happened. A brand-new grammar school was built on the Still Meadows side of town, and on days when the wind was blowing just right, everyone up at Still Meadows could hear Miss Beemer ringing the school bell and the voices of children laughing and playing in the schoolyard. It was such a happy, cheerful sound.

Many summers had passed since the day Katrina joined her husband, and she knew that one of the children she heard playing must be their own grandson, Gene. On one such day, she turned and said, "Oh, Lordor, is this heaven? Surely, it must be."

Lordor smiled. "Well, if it's not, it'll sure do until the real thing comes along."

The Thirties

The Show Must Go On

Dancing Cows

By 1930, THE GREAT DEPRESSION HAD HIT THE country hard. Elmwood Springs, still being somewhat of a rural town, survived it better than most. Because of the Swensen dairy, the children had milk, and they had plenty of corn, wheat, and alfalfa to feed the cows and pigs. They grew their own vegetables, and a lot of people had fruit trees in their yards. Figs and apple trees did very well, and almost everybody kept chickens. They knew they were lucky. They were spared the hunger that a lot of the rest of the country suffered. The dance school still held their recitals, and Lucille Beemer saw that the town's annual Founder's Day pageant honoring Lordor Nordstrom continued as well. "Tradition is the hallmark of a civilized society," she said.

As usual, in Elmwood Springs, there were more weddings and more babies born; thankfully, in that order. In 1930, the Warrens, who ran the hardware store, had a baby boy they named Macky. And in 1931, Beatrice and Ander Swensen moved into a brand-new house in town and planned to start a family as soon as possible.

That same year, Elner's sister, Ida, married Herbert Jenkins, the banker's son, and Ida moved from the Knott farm into town. A respectable eleven months later, she gave birth to a baby girl she named Norma.

Ida, who was prone to putting on airs since birth, had informed everyone that she had named her daughter Norma not after the popular movie star Norma Shearer, but after the lead character in the opera **Norma.** Ever since she married the banker's son, she had aspired to join the highbrow set she read about in magazines.

To Ida's everlasting dismay, her sister Elner listened to **The Grand Ole Opry** radio show out of Nashville. Elner still lived out in the country, which suited her just fine. Unlike Ida, Elner enjoyed herself, no matter where she was.

Thanks to her own good cooking, Elner was now a large, soft young farm woman who wore her hair swept up in a bun, and although she was a grown woman, she still had the sweet, open face of a child. She loved all animals and people. "I like anything that is living," she said.

When Lucille Beemer died of breast cancer in December of 1932, it was a great loss for the town and the annual musical pageant. Luckily, Dixie Cahill was able to step in and take over the reins of the pageant. She added a lot more dancing, and the following year, the cardboard farm animals held by her students danced as well in the big finale. The founder's grandson, ten-year-old Gene Nordstrom, wearing Swedish clothes and a large round black hat, was cast as his own grandfather. Everyone said that with his blond hair and blue eyes, he looked very much the part.

Later that year, when the "all-singing, all-dancing" film **42nd Street,** starring Ruby Keeler, came to the Elmwood Springs Theater, it seemed the whole town suddenly went tap dance crazy.

That was the year Dixie Cahill first formed the Tappettes, a group of young girls who would dress in their signature blue spangled outfits, march in every parade, perform at any local county fair, attend any special occasion, and welcome any dignitary. So far, no dignitaries to speak of had shown up, yet. But they were hopeful.

It seemed that movies were getting better than ever. Every Thursday night was dish night at the theater, and popcorn was only a nickel. And with her snappy way of talking and her bleached platinum-blond hair, Jean Harlow was the new swoon girl at the movies among the younger set.

WHEN TWO OF THE older, more staid ladies in town, Mrs. Bell and her friend Mrs. Hazel Goodnight, attended a matinee featuring Miss Harlow, they had been shocked. When the blond bombshell, originally from Kansas City, sashayed across the screen in her long white satin gown, Mrs. Bell gasped and whispered so loudly that everyone in the theater heard her. "My God, Hazel . . . the girl's not wearing underwear!"

Later, while they were sitting at the Rexall drugstore counter having their weekly hot fudge sundae, Mrs. Bell was still in a state of shock. "And she's a Missouri girl, too. What will people think? I wouldn't be caught dead going out in public without my girdle and bra, would you? Much less parade around on the screen for the whole world to see. I tell you, Hazel, if our morals slip any lower . . . I just don't know what. Whatever happened to modesty? Why, to this day, Mr. Bell has never seen me in the altogether."

The seventeen-year-old soda jerk who overheard her couldn't help but wince a little. It was much more than he wanted to know.

Unexpected Visitors

April 1933

THIS MORNING, ELNER SHIMFISSLE WAS WANDERing around her backyard in her pink floral cotton housedress, carrying a blue and white speckled pan full of Purina chicken feed, throwing it out to her chickens and singing, "Ooohhh, in your beautiful Alice Blue gown, you're the prettiest gal in the town . . ."

Elner always sang to her chickens. She believed it made them lay bigger eggs. And besides, she liked to sing. Unfortunately, she sometimes didn't know the words and was always just a hair off-key, but the chickens didn't seem to mind.

A few minutes later, Elner spied her husband, Will, way out in the back field on his tractor. She waved and called out to him. "Whoo! Whoo!" He saw her and waved back.

After she finished feeding the chickens, Elner walked over and hung her pan up on a nail on the side of the house, and then she heard a car drive up to the front of the house. She thought that maybe it was Ida or her friend Beatrice who had come to visit.

She quickly wiped her hands on her blue-checked apron and walked around to see who it was. It was a man she had never seen before, sitting in a big black dusty car, and he was looking at a map.

"Hey, there," she said. "Can I help you?"

The man looked up, startled to see her standing there. "Oh, hello. We seem to be lost. Is this the way to Joplin?"

She laughed. "Oh lands, no, honey." She went over and put her foot up on the running board and leaned in and pointed down the road. "You need to turn around and head back the other way, then turn right on the highway, at your first crossroad."

"Oh, I see," said the man.

Elner then noticed the girl sitting in the front seat beside him. She was wearing a cute little tam. By the look of them, Elner figured them for newlyweds and said, "I'm sorry you're lost, but now that you're here, come on in. Let me fix you a nice glass of iced tea or a cup of coffee before you head out again."

The couple looked at each other quizzically, then the girl shrugged. The young man said, "That sounds awful good. We've been driving for quite a while, so . . . if it's not too much trouble. . . ."

"Oh lands, no. Glad to have the company. We don't get many visitors this far out." She walked up and opened the front door and said, "Come on in. Hope you don't mind cats. I'm Elner Shimfissle. My husband, Will, is out in the back field plowing, and he's gonna be sorry he missed meeting you. What's your name?"

"Clyde. This here's Bonnie."

"Nice to meet you."

As they went through the house and back to a big kitchen that smelled of bacon, about six cats scattered everywhere. Elner pointed to a white enamel table with four wooden chairs. "Have a seat. Hey, I'll bet you kids are hungry. Have you had your breakfast, yet?"

"Well, no," said the man, "not yet. We were thinking to have it in Joplin."

Elner looked over at the girl. "You're just a teeny little thing. You need to eat something or you're liable to fall out in a faint, and I'm not going to let you leave until you do. I'll call you when it's ready. In the meanwhile, you two just make yourselves to home." She looked at the girl. "I know you probably have to use the bathroom, so just help yourself, honey. I've even got a bar of store-bought soap in there. I used to make my own, but I got too lazy."

ABOUT TEN MINUTES LATER, the couple sat down to a huge plate of bacon and eggs, freshly made hot-buttered buttermilk biscuits, and homemade preserves. "Be sure to eat them while they're hot," Elner said. Just as the couple sat down, a big, fat raccoon, obviously a pet, slowly waddled into the kitchen and toward the screen door and without saying a word, Elner got up from the table and held the door open while it waddled out. "See you later, Richard," she said, then sat back down. "So you folks are headed to Joplin? I know it's not too far, but you know, I've never been to Joplin. My daddy was a pig farmer, so I'm kinda scared of big cities. My sister Ida's been there and said it was real nice."

Between bites of the delicious biscuits and bacon, the young man became rather talkative. At first, the girl said very little, but pretty soon, she joined in the conversation. She told Elner that she had once worked as a hairdresser back home in Texas. Elner was impressed. "Oh, you don't say? Well, that takes a lot of skill . . . and you're smart to have that in your background. No matter what, you've always got that to fall back on. There's a young gal in town named Tot that Ida and Beatrice go to, who does hair out on her back porch, but I don't think she's licensed. What kind of business are you in, Clyde?"

"Uhhh . . . the bank business," he said, as he buttered another biscuit.

"Oh, my, what a coincidence. My sister Ida, the one I was telling you about, is married to a banker by the name of Herbert Jenkins. Do you know him?"

Clyde shook his head. "No . . . I don't believe I do."

"Well, anyway, his daddy owns the Elmwood Springs bank. You need to go in and say hello to him. You're gonna pass right by Elmwood Springs on your way to Joplin. It's a real nice little town. My sister Gerta and her husband, Ted, run the bakery. My friend Beatrice and her husband, Ander, live there, too. Ander owns that big dairy farm you passed by."

AFTER HEARING ALL ABOUT her ten-year-old nephew, Gene, the Cub Scout with all the badges, they were shown an old photograph of Elner's parents, Nancy and Henry Knott, standing beside their prize-winning pig, Dumpling No. 3. "They're both gone now," she said. "Both up at Still Meadows. Momma fell off the back of a wagon and froze solid, and Daddy got TB. I sure do miss 'em."

Almost forty-five minutes later, when the couple stood up to leave, Elner said, "Wait. I've got a little something for you to take with you." She went to her pantry and pulled out two jars of her homemade fig preserves from a shelf full of jars. She handed them to the girl. "Here you go, honey. Made fresh yesterday, right off my tree. I hope you enjoy them."

The girl took them and said, "Thank you," as they walked to the door.

"Well, listen, good luck to you two. And if you're ever anywhere around here again, stop by and see me again, will you?"

"We sure will," they said.

"Oh, and don't forget to stop by the bank on your way out. You can't miss it. It's right there on Main Street. Be sure and tell them Elner sent you." As she washed the breakfast dishes, Elner was so happy to have had such a pleasant visit with such a nice young couple.

Elner had no idea until she saw their picture in the paper that the couple were the famous criminals Clyde Barrow and Bonnie Parker.

After the police raid of their hideout in Joplin, they'd managed to escape, but a camera with undeveloped film was found, and photos of the notorious couple brandishing guns were published by **The Joplin Globe**. Bonnie was shown holding a gun and smoking a cigar. Elner's husband, Will, had been horrified when she told him that they were the same two people she had made breakfast for.

"Honey, couldn't you tell they were cold-blooded killers?"

"Well, no, I didn't even know she smoked. They just looked like a nice couple to me, and what I don't understand is why would that girl want to rob and kill people when she could have made a good living fixing hair?" Then Elner had an alarming thought and looked at her husband. "Oh, Lord, Will, you don't think the police will trace those fig preserves back to me and think I was one of their accomplices, do you?"

"Well, I don't know, Elner. Nobody makes fig preserves like you do. They could."

Elner's eyes got wide.

"Just kidding, Elner. Of course not."

The other thing Elner hadn't known about was

that the day the two had stopped at her house, they'd planned to rob the bank in Elmwood Springs on their way to Joplin to meet up with Clyde's brother, Buck. But after meeting Elner, they had changed their minds.

Another thing she didn't know was that Bonnie had lied about having been a hairdresser. It was Buck's wife, Blanche, who was the hairdresser. And although it was never reported, the police had found a half-eaten jar of fig preserves at their hideout in Joplin. Elner was lucky they hadn't checked it for fingerprints, or she would have had a visit from the sheriff for sure.

Things Are Looking Up

1934

IN 1934, THANKS MOSTLY TO THE CONTINUED growth of the Sweet Clover Dairy, Elmwood Springs got its own train station. The train came through once a day, and its long, sweet whistle was so pleasant to hear. It stirred up memories of the past for some up on the hill. The first time she heard it, Katrina said to Birdie Swensen, "I still remember that first day when you and Lordor met me at the station in Springfield."

"I remember it, too. Just like it was yesterday," said Birdie. "You were so stylish. I never dreamed that we would turn out to be lifelong friends."

"And even after," Katrina said.

Birdie laughed. "That's right . . . and even after."

ALSO THAT YEAR, KATRINA'S GRANDSON, Gene Nordstrom, and his friend, Cooter Calvert, on a dare, were determined to climb to the top of the water tower. Gene, with a pocket full of red balloons, went first. He didn't let on to Cooter that he was scared to death, and since it was July, the higher they went, the hotter it got. By the time they reached the landing, they were both exhausted, red, and sweaty, but triumphant. After they blew up the balloons and tied them to the railing to prove they'd been there, they stood up and surveyed the land and the town, full of the hopes and dreams of a glorious future, laid out before them.

Gene said, "I'll tell you what I want to do when I grow up. I'm gonna be a newspaper reporter and travel all over the world." He was presently reading the book **Billy Banyon, Cub Reporter.**

Cooter was impressed. "Wow . . . can I come?"

"Sure. Then I'll start my own newspaper, like **The Joplin Globe,** only bigger! I might even get to interview Babe Ruth . . . or the president. Won't it be great?"

Cooter said, "You know, Gene, when you think about it, you're already in the newspaper business in a way, ain't you?"

Gene, who had a newspaper route at the time, looked at his friend and said, "Yeah, Cooter, you're right. I am. I never thought of it that way. I'm kinda a newspaperman already."

AT STILL MEADOWS, OLD Man Hendersen, the first to see the red balloons dancing in the wind, announced, "Look at that. Some idiot gal-darned fool's climbed the water tower again."

—

THAT NIGHT, GENE AND Cooter both had blisters on their hands and were so sunburned they could hardly move. Gene, the fairest of the two, was so sunburned, he couldn't wear clothes and had to stay in his soft cotton pajamas for two days. But he was happy. He and Cooter had passed the bravery test, and the balloons were still flying.

Later that year, when Hazel Goodnight found out that her daughter Ada had just climbed all the way to the top of the water tower, she had been appalled. She told Ada that it was "a disgrace" that a girl would do something so dangerous and unladylike. But Ada's grandmother said, "Oh, horsefeathers, Hazel! If my mother could give birth in the back of a covered wagon in the morning and fix dinner for ten men that night, Ada ought to be able to do anything she wants to."

This daredevil action only portended what was to come. Ada would go on to do many more dangerous and unladylike things, just like her idol, Amelia Earhart. Ada's identical twin sister, Bess, had other ideas. She wanted to grow up, marry Tarzan, and live in a tree.

Problem Solving

By 1936, A LOT OF NEW BUSINESSES HAD OPENED, and, as someone said, Elmwood Springs was "getting to be a regular metropolis." While the statement was a slight exaggeration, the downtown area was now almost two blocks long and growing. Merle and Verbena Wheeler opened the Blue Ribbon Dry Cleaners next door to the post office, and a new brick Masonic Lodge that doubled as an Odd Fellows meeting hall had been built on the corner. A brand-new swimming pool named Cascade Plunge had opened in the spring, and, last but not least, there was now a Cat's Paw shoe-repair shop across the street from Nordstrom's Swedish Bakery that had a pink neon shoe in the window.

Ted and Gerta's Swedish bakery had now expanded to include the room next door. Their thirteen-year-old son, Gene, had just received his junior lifeguard badge, and he and his friend Cooter would be working at the pool that summer. All in all, people seemed happy and content. Except, that is, for those up at Still Meadows.

In the past months, an unforeseen problem had developed. Counting the original settlers, and with the usual number of heart attacks, cancer, deaths of old age, accident victims, and so forth, the place was filling up fast . . . and it was becoming sheer chaos.

At present, when a new resident arrived, everybody started talking to them all at once. Some got so excited to say hello that they talked over the others to be heard. And for the poor newcomer, waking up at Still Meadows was confusing enough, and all the people talking were just too much.

Finally, Lordor Nordstrom addressed the problem at hand. He said, "Now, folks, I know you're happy to see your loved ones, but just because we're deceased is no reason not to have a few rules."

And so a resolution was put forth. They would pick just one person to speak to the new arrival first and act as the official greeter. Everyone agreed that Miss Beemer, who had recently joined her friends on the hill and was used to controlling unruly children, was the obvious choice for the position. Lucille had taught sixth-grade English for years and she had a particular interest in elocution. She also had a lovely manner and a soothing speaking voice.

The procedure decided upon was that Lucille would welcome the newcomer and explain the situation. They'd let them rest awhile if needed, and then, one by one, the others would speak in an orderly fashion. Close relatives first: mothers, fathers, grandparents, and so forth, then husbands, wives, and children, if any. Next, neighbors and friends, and then passing acquaintances who wanted to say hello. Those wishing to be introduced to the newcomer would speak last.

Of course, the plan was not foolproof. They knew some might not wish to speak to their relatives first, but it seemed to be the only way to keep some kind of order. Thankfully, the system worked perfectly well, except for Old Man Hendersen, who jumped in and talked whenever he pleased.

The Trap

ALTHOUGH THEY READ ABOUT CRIME IN KANSAS City and elsewhere, Elmwood Springs did not have a police department. Luckily, other than a few minor offenses, they had never had any serious crime problems until 1937, when a Peeping Tom was spotted. Within a day, word spread through the town, like wildfire, and everyone in Elmwood Springs was alarmed. The peeper had been seen hiding in the bushes at several houses where young girls lived. It was always dark when they saw him, and he quickly ran away, so they could not see his face. It was nerve-racking for the parents in town to know that someone was out there lurking around in the dark, peeping in at their daughters. Some men would even walk around their houses at night carrying a shotgun, hoping to be seen and scare him off.

On July Fourth, he was spotted in broad daylight peeping in the school window at the Tappettes when they were changing clothes after marching in the parade. Mary Childress, who had seen his silhouette, had screamed. But he had gotten away.

After almost a year of putting up with it, Hazel Goodnight put forth a plan at the next city council meeting. She said that she suspected the peeper had been at her house several times, looking in her girls' bedroom window, and as bold as he was there was no reason to think he wouldn't show up again. And so Hazel proposed that they set up a trap for him. The idea was to plant a brand-new shiny quarter on the ground by the window and hope he would pick it up.

The quarter, unbeknownst to him, but known to the storekeepers in town, would have a small dab of red fingernail polish on it. They all agreed this was a fine plan. The quarter was planted, and the whole town held its breath in anticipation of catching him.

Several weeks went by, and nothing happened. Then one Saturday morning, fifteen-year-old Lester Shingle walked into the bakery and plopped the quarter with the red fingernail polish down on the counter to pay for a dozen doughnuts. Gerta picked it up, noticed the dab of fingernail polish, and yelled, "It's the quarter!"

Suddenly and within a flash, their son, fourteen-year-old Gene, came flying out of the back room where he had been working with his dad, ran after the fleeing Lester, and tackled him in front of the dry cleaners. When they heard all the commotion, people up and down the street came out of the stores, just in time to see Gene pick up the screaming and kicking Lester and punch him in the nose. Gene was mad. His girlfriend had been one of the Tappettes changing clothes that day, and he didn't like the fact that Lester had spied on her one bit.

Once caught, Lester Shingle said he'd found the quarter by the post office earlier that morning. They couldn't prove he hadn't, but nobody believed him. The good news was that they were all pretty sure they had caught the Peeping Tom.

Elner's Dream

ALTHOUGH THE PEEPER HAD BEEN CAUGHT, THERE
was also some sad news. Beatrice Swensen, after trying for so long, was finally expecting. But a month
later, she suffered a miscarriage and lost the baby.

After it happened, Ander was heartbroken, but
Beatrice was almost inconsolable, to the point that
Ander asked Elner to come and stay with her when
he had to go work at the dairy.

Every day, Elner sat in Beatrice's room by the bed
and held her hand while Beatrice cried. "Oh, Elner . . . I wanted that baby so much."

"I know you did, honey. I know you did," said
Elner, patting her hand.

"Why did it happen, Elner? I was so careful."

"We don't know why, but you're young yet.
There's plenty of time for you and Ander to have lots
more babies."

"I don't think so. The doctor said that I—"

Elner stopped her midsentence. "Oh, pooh on
that old doctor, Beatrice. He doesn't know everything. Besides, I had a dream last night. I was in my

kitchen out at the farm, peeling potatoes, and you called me up on the phone all excited and said, 'Guess what, Elner? I'm expecting again.'"

"You did?"

"Yes! And you know me, Beatrice, my dreams always come true. Why, didn't I dream that you and Ander would get married, and didn't I tell you so?"

"Yes . . . I remember," said Beatrice.

"So, you mustn't lose heart. Just have a little faith. You just wait and see."

THE NEXT MORNING, A very grateful Ander Swensen met Elner at the front door. "I don't know what you said, but last night, she seemed a little better."

"Well, good," she said. "I'm glad." As Elner headed upstairs carrying the tiny black-and-white kitten she had brought for Beatrice, she called out, "Yoo-hoo . . . I have a little friend who's come to see you."

She never talked about it, but Elner believed that sometimes, something living to take care of was the best medicine for a broken heart.

It Don't Mean a Thing If It Ain't Got That Swing

Swing music was sweeping the land, and by popular demand, Mayor Ted Nordstrom had an outdoor dance pavilion built out at Elmwood Springs Lake for the younger set.

Mr. Warren from the hardware store came out and strung up lights all around and set up four loudspeakers. The first night it opened, the place was packed with people. As it turned out, everybody young and old loved dancing and jitterbugging to the big band records by Glenn Miller, Benny Goodman, Tommy Dorsey, and others. Ted and Gerta were town chaperones, and sixteen-year-old Gene set up a refreshment stand and sold ice-cold drinks to the thirsty dancers. Old Mrs. Gravely got so whipped up and excited, she threw her hip out the first night.

Up at Still Meadows, when some of the old-timers first heard the music coming from the pavilion, they were concerned about the loud beat of the drums. But most of the others came to enjoy listening to the music on the long summer nights while they looked up at the stars.

Lordor and Katrina had laughed the first time they heard Glenn Miller's "Little Brown Jug," and almost everybody out there loved the Andrews Sisters. Birdie Swensen admired their brilliant harmony when singing "Bei Mir Bist Du Schön." "Those girls have perfect pitch," she said.

Lucille Beemer particularly enjoyed Tommy Dorsey's "I'm Getting Sentimental Over You." It always made her think of Gustav.

IN 1939, THE HUGE blockbuster **Gone with the Wind** had all the girls doe-eyed over Clark Gable. Twenty-two-year-old Tot Hagood, the hairdresser, had even married James Dwayne Whooten (a would-be housepainter), because she thought he looked just like Clark Gable. Her mother said that James Whooten looked as much like Clark Gable as a squirrel looked like an elephant. But Tot could not be deterred. She was in love.

It was a nice wedding, except that Tot's daddy got drunk and passed out in the vestibule and couldn't walk her down the aisle, and James got a piece of rice stuck in his ear, so they spent their first night in the hospital. But other than that and a few other ups and downs it had been a pretty good decade.

The Forties

The World Speeds Up

Good News

1940

IT SEEMED TO THE OLDER GENERATION THAT THE world was speeding up at an alarming rate. The new jitterbug dance the kids were doing was far too frantic to suit them. As old Mrs. Childress said, "I'm afraid to cross the street, with all these teen-agers racing around in their hopped-up hot-rod jalopies."

But in general, people were in a good mood. Franklin Delano Roosevelt was on his way to being elected to an unprecedented third term, and the Depression was finally turning around, and they were beginning to feel hopeful again.

Elmwood Springs had just gotten its own official Greyhound bus stop, with a sign on a pole and everything. A brand-new bowling alley had been built, too. Warrens' Hardware now had a layaway plan, and by summer, almost every child in town had a pair of roller skates and a new blue-and-white Schwinn bicycle. In June, the Warrens' ten-year-old son, Macky, had climbed to the top of the water tower and had scared his mother, Ola, half to death. Macky survived the climb with flying colors, only to almost drown a week later over at the swimming pool, when he knocked himself out on the diving board. Luckily, Gene Nordstrom, who was the life-guard, saw him and reached down and pulled him out of the pool by his hair just in time.

Also, surprisingly enough, that June, the town hairdresser, Tot Hagood Whooten, without any collateral to speak of, was able to get a loan from the bank and open her own beauty shop. Tot didn't know it, but Ida Knott Jenkins, the banker's wife, had helped Tot get the loan. Ida was a client of Tot's, and she didn't think that having her hair done on the Whootens' back porch was in keeping with her new social standing. One night, over din-ner, she had pointed a celery stick at her husband and said, "Herbert, I don't care about any bottom line, you men have a barber shop, so there's no rea-son in the world that our town shouldn't have a beauty salon." Herbert knew he would have to give Tot the loan, or he would never hear the end of it. Whenever Ida pointed celery at him, she meant business.

TWO WEEKS LATER, IDA Jenkins, her hair in pin curls, was at the beauty shop, sitting under a brand-new hair dryer, engrossed in a magazine article:

Do You Suffer from Perfectionism?

1. Are you a fussbudget?
2. High-strung or nervous?
3. Impatient?
4. Critical of others?
5. Ill at ease among disorder?
6. Worried about future events?

The list went on and on from there. After she had finished reading, Ida hadn't found one single description that had not applied to her, and she was thrilled. Who would not want to be perfect?

"After all, you don't walk into a jewelry store and say, 'I'm looking for an imperfect diamond,' or go to the eye doctor and say, 'Oh, I'll just settle for imperfect vision, thank you,'" she said. From the time she was a child, she had never understood why anybody wouldn't try and strive for perfection.

Ida had always been different. At school, when all the kids used to play church, and one would be the preacher, another the preacher's wife, a deacon, and the choir leader, and some would be the parishioners who had come to the church, Ida said she wanted to be God, because she was the only one who knew how to do it.

Of course, Ida's strong standards were already taking a toll on her daughter, Norma. That same year, Norma Jenkins had been cast as one of the dancing tulips in Dixie Cahill's spring dance recital. And on the night of the performance, when she had missed a step, she had run off the stage in tears. As her aunt Elner Shimfissle, who was in the audience that night, said to Gerta, "Poor little Norma—only nine years old and already a nervous wreck."

Norma had two aunts: Gene's mother, Gerta, and her aunt Elner. They were as different from Norma's mother as night and day.

Ida had been the prettiest of the Knott sisters, and the problem was that she knew it. She had been determined from the get-go to marry the banker's son and move up in the world. And she had. Her sister Elner was just a simple farm lady who still wore old-lady tie-up shoes: black in the winter, white in the summer.

Ida aspired to be a trendsetter, and she read all the fashion magazines. She wanted to dress like the ladies in **McCall's** and **Glamour.** She had made friends with Miss Howard, head buyer in Ladies' Better Wear at the Morgan Brothers Department Store, who kept her supplied with all the latest fashions.

Norma never thought her mother had ever been very nice to Aunt Elner. Ida would often say, "I just wish she wasn't so country. She lets chickens walk in and out of her house, Norma!"

Ida was ashamed of her farm background and took it out on poor Elner. Although their parents, Henry and Nancy Knott, had owned a pig farm, Ida would spend the rest of her life pretending it wasn't so.

Norma had never seen a photograph of her grandparents. Ida had hidden them, along with the family Bible that had everyone's date of birth listed. The little fat German farm woman in an apron and the skinny man in overalls standing in front of a fence with pigs in the background was not the family portrait Ida had in mind. She often complained to Elner about having that photograph out in plain view. "If they couldn't have dressed up, why did they have to have pigs in the picture? It's so embarrassing."

Elner said, "Maybe so, Ida, but those pigs paid for your wedding." As Elner later told her niece, "Now, Norma, I love Ida . . . but Lord, she's bad to put on airs."

And it was true. Ida's ideal woman at the time was Eleanor Roosevelt. True, the woman had absolutely no sense of style, her clothes were atrocious, her hair a disgrace. But she had spunk. She was a real go-getter, with agendas of her own, a real no-nonsense person who did not sit around in the background. Much like herself, Ida thought.

Ida had her own political aspirations for her husband: first become governor of the state, and then later sweep on into the White House. But, sadly, Herbert Jenkins was perfectly content to be just a banker and live in Elmwood Springs, and it upset Ida to no end. "If I thought a woman could get elected, I'd run myself," she said. Poor Ida. She was born ahead of her time.

It seemed as if summer flew by that year. The

movies continued to inspire fashions and hairstyles, and everybody wanted a figure like Claudette Colbert's.

Especially Gerta Nordstrom. She attended the county fair in October and made the mistake of stopping at the "Guess Your Weight" booth. The man had been right on the nose and announced it in a loud voice for all the world to hear: "The little lady weighs one hundred and seventy-nine pounds!"

The fair was fun for all the 4-H kids, who won lots of blue ribbons. Elner Shimfissle took first place in Preserves and Jellies. And Merle Wheeler had the largest tomato.

On November 16, Gerta and Ted's son, Gene Nordstrom, now a junior at Elmwood High School, threw the winning touchdown pass, and they finished the season as tri-county champions. Then, before they knew it, it was December.

The Morgan Brothers Department Store had their usual big, beautiful Christmas display in the window, this year with moving parts. Seeing Santa's reindeer bob up and down thrilled everyone. Little Norma Jenkins got a Sparkle Plenty doll, and her mother, Ida, received the fox fur she had wanted, with plastic eyes and nose.

On Christmas Eve, Tot's husband, James Whooten, got drunk on eggnog and fell into the Christmas tree, but other than that, everybody had a great Christmas.

A New Year

Now that the Depression was ending, the bakery was back in full swing: the long glass cases lined with cinnamon buns, cream puffs, and cupcakes, all looking wonderful. Everybody loved to go into the bakery. It had such a sweet smell and a pretty shiny black-and-white-tile floor that Ted and Gerta kept so clean, you could eat off it. And a lot of children did. If they dropped a pastry, they'd pick it right up and continue eating it, and their parents didn't mind.

At the movies, Clark Gable had been replaced by the new heartthrob of the moment, Tyrone Power, and all the boys wanted to be John Wayne. But as it turned out, not all the women in town still wanted to be Claudette Colbert. One afternoon in May of 1941, when the newly formed Elmwood Springs Ladies' Bowling Team had been on their way out to the new Blue Star Bowling Alley to practice, Ada Goodnight, the larger twin, announced that she wanted to become an actress just like her idol, Joan Crawford. Her youngest sister, Irene, made fun of her, but as their mother said later, "Who knows, Irene? Ada may not have the acting talent, but she certainly has the shoulders for it."

The weekend dances continued out at the lake, and as Birdie Swensen noted up at Still Meadows, "There seem to be more fireflies than ever this summer."

September came around again. And, as usual, over at the high school, the seniors were very happy to be seniors, the freshmen were nervous, and the sophomores and juniors felt like they were in limbo and just slogged through the long days. At the end of November, Irene Goodnight, who was a junior, came home and fell onto the living room couch and sighed, "I'm so bored with home economics, I don't know what to do. If I have to bake another angel food cake, I'll throw up."

Then on December 7, the Japanese attacked Pearl Harbor and, suddenly, everybody's world was turned upside down.

THE VERY NEXT DAY, all the senior boys at Elmwood High School drove to Springfield and signed up for military service, including eighteen-year-old Gene Nordstrom, who joined the marines. Emotions were running high everywhere. People couldn't believe that the Japanese had attacked us and killed so many of our boys. "I don't understand it—what did we ever do to them?" asked Gerta. Everyone agreed. Verbena Wheeler said she would never eat another can of chicken chow mein as long as she lived. James Whooten was so mad about the attack that he sobered up for three days and tried to join the army, but failed the physical.

People remained in shock for quite a while. It seemed that overnight, the whole town had suddenly focused on the war. But as the weeks went by and after all the boys had gone off to their different training camps, they all got busy doing what they could to help.

Hazel Goodnight organized groups of ladies and high school girls to drive over to Springfield and meet the troop trains they knew would be passing through. They would set up a stand and serve the boys hot coffee and sandwiches through the train windows. Scared soldiers on their way to who-knows-where threw pieces of paper with their names and addresses on them, hoping to get a girl to write to them. Some did and always sealed their letters with a kiss.

Within six months, Ander Swensen had the Sweet Clover Dairy operating close to twenty-four hours a day, busy shipping milk and cheese for the boys at all the training camps close by.

The poor cows had no way of knowing there was a war going on. All they knew was that people seemed to be in a hurry.

Schoolchildren were busy collecting rubber and scrap. In June 1942, Beatrice Swensen agreed to be head of the local Red Cross. She was in charge of the ladies rolling bandages and packing up boxes to be shipped overseas, and Elner agreed to help her. Because of the mandatory blackouts, all the streetlights in town were painted blue. It made all the little white houses look like something on the moon. But as Ruby Robinson said, "It must be working. We haven't been bombed yet."

People on the home front were kept as informed as possible. News of the war was broadcast over the radio three times a day, and three times a day, everyone stopped what they were doing and listened. And every Sunday night, they all tuned in to FDR's fireside chat.

By the end of 1943, everybody had a ration book. Sugar rationing was hard on the bakery business, and most of the sugar Ted and Gerta were allowed went into the baking of cakes and cookies that they mailed to their son, Gene, his best friend, Cooter Calvert, and all the other hometown boys all over the country. Cooter Calvert was all the way up in New Jersey, and Billy Eggstrom was stationed at Scott Field in Illinois.

Ida Jenkins, who had always prided herself on her yard and beautiful camellias and boxwoods, suddenly appointed herself chief inspector of all the town's Victory gardens. She even had a green uniform made and a cap with a gold star on the brim. It meant nothing, but she so enjoyed wearing it as she marched through people's gardens, barking orders.

She was good at her job, and for the duration of the war, the town did have excellent produce. As Verbena Wheeler said, "Ida can be a real pill sometimes . . . but she does know her squash." Someone else remarked, "By God, if Ida had been a man, she would have made general by now."

Ada Goodnight, thanks to an old boyfriend who had been a crop duster, knew how to fly a plane and went to Texas to join up with the newly formed group of women fliers known as the WASPs. Female pilots were desperately needed to ferry planes and supplies around the United States and free up the men for combat duty.

Letters were so important. After a long wait, one mother in town danced with joy when she received a one-word message from her son, who had been in the Battle of Midway. The word was "Okay."

The next day, Hazel Goodnight was happy to get a letter from her daughter Ada.

Sweetwater, Texas

Dear Mother,

Sorry to be so long in writing. We've been in flight training 24 hours a day, it seems. Did you know that Texas was HOT? I am nearly burning up here . . . but have met a swell bunch of gals. My roommate is a real corker from Wisconsin, named Fritzi Jurdabralinski.

She is the best flier here. Me second, I think. Will let you know after the next test flight. Send all my love to Bess and Irene. Please write news of home.

Love,
Ada

ELMWOOD SPRINGS, MISSOURI

Dearest Daughter,

The biggest news from home is we continue to miss you. We are doing everything we can here. You would be proud of your sister Irene. She is working part-time at the dairy, and your sister Bess is doing fine over at the Western Union office.

Mr. Ericksen fell off his bike and broke his leg, so Macky Warren is now delivering telegrams. Elner Shimfissle brought us two dozen eggs and asked about you, as does everybody. Oh, and I almost forgot, last week, I caught that rotten Lester Shingle in the bushes outside Irene's window again. Chased him, but he got away, dammit.

Love from,
Mother

San Francisco, California

1943

THE BOYS DIDN'T KNOW EXACTLY WHERE THEY were going, but they all had a general idea. It was their last three weeks in San Francisco, and the town was swarming with servicemen like them, looking for dates. The USO dances were so crowded that there were about ten soldiers to every one girl, so Gene had more or less given up.

That afternoon, he was just hanging around with his friend Beamis outside a big department store in Union Square. Lucky Beamis had a date that night with a girl who worked there, and he was waiting for her to get off.

As they were standing there shooting the breeze, someone came out of the revolving glass door, and Gene caught a quick glimpse of the girl behind the perfume counter. "See you later, Beamis," he said, as he went in to buy a bottle of perfume for his mother.

In the next few weeks first his mother, then his aunt Ida and aunt Elner, and even his little cousin, Norma, each received a beautifully wrapped bottle of perfume from the I. Magnin department store in

San Francisco. It took a while, but he finally got a date. Her name was Marion.

For their first date, he wanted to impress her, so he took her for dinner and dancing at the Top of the Mark, the glamorous supper club in the sky overlooking the city. He had on his dress blue uniform, and she wore a lavender dress and had a white gardenia in her hair. Anyone who saw the couple that night sitting at the small round table by the window could see that the boy was in love.

San Francisco

Dear Folks,

By the time you get this, I will have shipped out. I am sorry there was not time for you to get here for the wedding. It was just a quick courthouse affair. But don't worry, when I get back, we will come home and do it up right. I can't wait for you to meet Marion. You won't believe how beautiful she is. Also, sorry I haven't written sooner, but these last two weeks I have been busy dealing with stuff, making sure Marion gets my allotments from the government, etc. Gosh, life sure changes when you are a married man. I'm so happy I don't think I'll ever climb off this pink cloud.

Love from your lovesick son

P.S. Tell Aunt Elner thanks for the preserves.

The War

IN LATE 1943, THE WAR WAS HEATING UP, AND BESS Goodnight relieved a man who had been drafted and she was now running the Western Union office.

The army needed all the men it could get. Even thirty-two-year-old Snooky Pickens, the movie projectionist who was terribly nearsighted, was drafted and ordered to report to training camp in two weeks. He quickly trained James Whooten to take over his job at the theater, but it was always hit or miss. With James working the projector, sometimes the picture was on the screen, and sometimes it was on the side wall.

That summer, the weekend dances at the lake were canceled. There was nobody left to dance with, except Lester Shingle and a few old men.

At around ten A.M., the names of the boys from Missouri who had been killed in action were posted on the Western Union office front window. Bud Eggstrom, who had served in World War I, had a son who was somewhere in the Pacific, but he didn't know where. Every day, he would get up and walk downtown to look at the list, along with all the families whose sons were serving. And every day, they all held their breath. Every day that Billy Eggstrom's name did not appear on the dead or missing-in-action list, Bud would stop by the church and say thank you.

By 1944, Hollywood had gone to war full-time. Even cartoon characters Bugs Bunny and Daffy Duck were reminding people not to waste precious gasoline, so needed for the war effort. Film stars such as Jimmy Stewart and Henry Fonda had entered the service, and others were kept busy entertaining the troops. Suddenly, big Hollywood stars were criss-crossing the country, selling war bonds.

In May 1944, movie star and Missouri native Ginger Rogers went on a tour of the Midwest selling war bonds, and when they found out that she would be stopping in Elmwood Springs, the whole town went crazy. Mr. Warren and a few of the other men helped set up a platform in front of the theater for the occasion.

On the day Miss Rogers was to appear, everybody within miles around was there and crowded the street, so excited they could hardly stand it.

At around three o'clock, she arrived looking exactly like herself, only better. People screamed and cheered as the high school band played "Hooray for Hollywood." Mayor Ted Nordstrom proudly presented her with a key to the city. Immediately after the presentation, the Tappettes dance troupe, under the leadership of Dixie Cahill, came running out of the theater and up onto the stage to perform a special dance number in her honor to the tune of "Isn't It a Lovely Day."

Thirteen-year-old Tappette Norma Jenkins had been nervous to begin with, and Ginger Rogers was her very favorite movie star in the entire world. So when she looked up and saw her in person for the first time, she fainted halfway through the number. A distraught Dixie Cahill had to run out and drag her off to the side. As Norma's aunt Elner said later, "Being in such close proximity to greatness had just been too much for her."

V-J Mail

1945

Dear Mom and Dad,

I'm sure Marion wrote to you about the baby. You are now the grandparents of an 8-pound, 7-ounce, 22-inch-long baby girl. Her name is Dena Katrina Nordstrom. Can you believe I am a father? Have you gotten her photo yet? What a beauty. I am convinced that she will be Miss America 1965. All the more reason to get this rotten mess over with soon. All the married guys with kids feel the same way, and it makes us fight even harder.

Gene

P.S. Lost my friend Beamis last week.

Iwo Jima, Japan

1945

SPORADIC GUNFIRE COULD STILL BE HEARD AS THE medic slowly crawled toward the soldier. When he reached him, he quickly removed the chain around his neck, shoved the metal dog tag up between his two front teeth as hard as he could . . . and moved on.

It was a brutal job. He had sometimes cracked a tooth or split a lip in the process, but with so many bodies blown apart, guts, brains, arms, and legs everywhere, mistakes could be made. In the rush to get the dead and wounded off the battlefield as soon as possible, dog tags had fallen off or were lost, and mix-ups had occurred. This was the only way they knew to try to get the right soldier shipped back to the right place. With so many casualties, too many families had been sent the wrong body.

As the medic crawled over to the next one, he hoped the boy he had just left would make it home okay. He looked like a nice kid. Probably came from a nice family.

Elmwood Springs

ALL THROUGH THE WAR, THE TOWN HAD CONDUCTED the required blackout drills and elected neighborhood fire wardens, but nobody really believed that Elmwood Springs would be attacked. They heard about the war, saw it in the newsreels, read about it in the paper, but the war was so far away, most felt that it couldn't possibly reach them.

Then on a Sunday in 1945, fifteen-year-old Macky Warren, who was working for Bess at the Western Union office, would get on his bicycle and deliver a telegram that would change a family's lives forever. Why did it have to be on a Sunday?

San Francisco, California

WHEN HE WOKE UP, IT WAS DARK, AND HE COULD hear a loud clacking noise rumbling underneath him. From the vibration, he had the strange sensation that he was moving. But where was he? . . . In a hospital? . . . Still on the beach?

Twenty-two-year-old Private First Class Gene Lordor Nordstrom lay there trying to figure out what was going on. The last thing he remembered was being scared, running up the beach, then nothing. It wasn't until he felt the dog tag that had been shoved in between his two front teeth that he knew where he was. Oh, shit . . . he was dead. He was dead on a train going home.

Well, that part was good, he guessed. He knew some of the boys never made it out of there. Then he suddenly panicked. "Wait a minute. I'm married. I have a little girl. What's going to happen to her? Oh, God. I hope my GI insurance will be enough." Then he thought about his wife, Marion. "Oh, Marion, I didn't have nearly enough time with you."

Two days later, when the train screeched to a slow stop, a man's voice called out, "Elmwood Springs!" It was still dark, but soon Gene heard the sound of boxcar doors being slid open all the way down the line, and he began to get a little impatient. "Come on . . . here I am." Finally, they were at his boxcar. He heard the loud scraping sound of a metal door being slid open, and bright sunshine suddenly filled the car. Two men climbed in and walked over to him.

One man said, "Are you sure this is the right one?" The other answered, "Yeah, it says right here on the tag: Nordstrom, Elmwood Springs, Missouri, but Ed said not to move him until the family gets here."

While they waited, one of the men lit a cigarette. "God," thought Gene, "that cigarette smells good." Then he heard more footsteps and someone said, "Okay, boys, bring him on out." Gene suddenly felt himself being lifted up, then lowered down onto something flat. That's when he looked over and saw his parents and his aunt Elner standing there. He was so happy to see them, he wanted to shout a great big hello, but they were so quiet, so still, as they walked along beside him. As he was wheeled down the platform, he thought, "Say something, some-body. . . . It's me. I'm home." But there was nothing but the sound of footsteps and the creaking of the wheels beneath him. Everyone they passed stood still and silent. Men had taken off their hats, and Hazel

Goodnight stood with her hand over her mouth, then reached out and touched his mother's arm as she went by.

It had been a military funeral, and he was proud when the soldier took the American flag off of his coffin, folded it, and handed it to his mother, but then he had to look away. The look on his mother's face hurt him too much. He must have drifted off again because when he woke up, he felt himself being lowered into the ground. After a moment, he heard a very familiar voice say, "Hello there, young man. Welcome to Still Meadows."

"Miss Beemer? Is that you? Do you remember me? It's Gene Nordstrom. I had you in the sixth grade."

"Little Gene. **Of course**, I remember you . . . but what in the world are you doing here?"

"I got killed in the war, Miss Beemer."

"Oh, you don't mean it. Well, bless your heart. Oh, I know your parents must be so upset."

"Yes, ma'am, they are."

"Of course, they would be. I remember when you were in my class, I told your mother . . . I said, 'Mrs. Nordstrom, Gene is one of the sweetest boys I have ever taught.' Well, I sure am sorry."

"Thank you, ma'am. I appreciate it."

"What happened, honey?"

"I got shot, but it didn't hurt or anything."

"Well, I'll be. You just never know in this world, do you?"

"No, ma'am. You sure don't."

Gene heard someone snoring. "Miss Beemer, who's that over there?"

"That's Eustus Percy Hendersen. He's awake a lot more than he pretends to be." Then she asked in a loud voice, "Are you awake, Mr. Hendersen?"

"Well, I am now," said the old man.

"Mr. Hendersen, this is Gene Nordstrom. He used to be one of my students."

Gene said, "How do you do."

Mr. Hendersen nodded. "What's that uniform?"

"I'm in the marine corps. Or I used to be."

Lucille said, "He got killed in the war, Mr. Hendersen."

"What war?"

"The Second World War."

"The second? You mean there was another one? Who are we fighting this time?"

"Germany and Japan," answered Lucille.

Mr. Hendersen said, "Germany? Hell. We licked them once. What the hell are we doing fighting them again? It figures. . . . That's the most ornery bunch that ever was. Who else did you say?"

"Japan, Mr. Hendersen," said Lucille. "Haven't you heard us all talking about it?"

"No, I don't listen to all that yimmer yammering. Japan . . . huh . . . well, that's nothing to worry about. Hell, they ain't no bigger than a minute."

Gene said, "Yes, sir . . . but there's an awful lot of them."

Lucille decided to change the subject. "I was telling Gene a little while ago that he was one of the sweetest boys I ever taught, but then his mother and daddy are sweet people. I taught his aunt Elner, too."

Mr. Hendersen grunted. "You're not going to have a whole bunch of relatives stomping around here, are you?"

"Mr. Hendersen, let's just let the boy rest for now. He just got here."

A FEW MINUTES WENT BY, and Gene said, "Miss Beemer?"

"Yes, honey?"

"Did you know I got married?"

"No, I didn't. Is she an Elmwood Springs girl? Do I know her?"

"No, ma'am, she's not from here. But you'd like her. I have a little girl, too. I haven't seen her yet, but I'm sure they'll come to visit pretty soon."

"Well, that will give you something to look forward to, won't it?"

"Yes, ma'am."

"Why don't you try and see if you can't get a little sleep. I know you must be worn out."

"Yes, ma'am, I am."

"I'll wake you up if anybody comes to visit."

"Thank you. Like I say, I am expecting my wife and little girl, so if you could . . ."

"Don't worry, I'm a light sleeper. I promise. I'll let you know the minute they get here."

"Thank you."

Gene closed his eyes, but before he drifted off to sleep, he thought that if somebody had told him he would wind up buried next to his sixth-grade teacher, he wouldn't have believed them in a million years.

GENE'S DEATH HIT the town hard. Nordstrom's Bakery closed, and the town's flag flew at half-mast. Gene was the first boy they had ever lost in a war, and it had an effect on almost every person there. They had all watched him grow up. He had mowed their lawns, delivered their papers, and quarterbacked their football team. Even the younger people who had never met him had seen his picture in the bakery window and felt the sadness that was everywhere. People didn't know what to say to Gerta and Ted. So they mostly just left little notes on their porch to let them know they were thinking about them. Elner sensed that it was best not to say anything. What could you possibly say?

After Gene had gone off to training camp, Gerta had kept his room exactly as it was the day he left. Same pictures on the wall, same bedspread. It was almost as if the room didn't know he was not coming back and was expecting him to walk in at any moment.

Gerta now sat in his bedroom every day, looking at all the things he had collected over the years. The little metal car on his desk, the model airplane hanging from the ceiling, a box of marbles, an old broken yo-yo. She realized the items could not bring Gene back, but they reminded her of when he was still there.

HERBERT JENKINS, THE PRESIDENT of the bank, waited a few weeks, then one day walked over to his sister-in-law's house to have the talk he hated to have. The one he knew would be so painful for Ted and Gerta.

He wasn't supposed to, but he had taken the liberty of closing down Gene's savings account that he had started when he was twelve. Gene had been saving all the money he had earned during the summers and after school, and it came up to almost eight hundred dollars. Herbert sat them both down, then handed them the check.

"I thought you might want this to . . . well . . . do whatever."

Ted looked at it. "I had no idea. Are you sure this was all Gene's? It seems like so much."

"Oh, yes. Don't forget, it's been collecting interest all these years."

Gerta looked at Ted and said, "This should go to Marion. We'll give it to her when she gets here."

"Is she coming to town?"

"Yes, just as soon as the baby is old enough to travel."

"Good, that should help a little with expenses and all."

"Well . . . we sure do thank you, Herbert, for coming over."

"Oh, you're so welcome. Anytime you need anything, just call us. Ida sends her love."

HE DIDN'T TELL THEM, but he and Ida had added an extra two hundred dollars to the account. Most people didn't know it, but even with all of her airs, Ida could be almost human at times.

Saying Hello

WHEN GENE NORDSTROM WOKE UP AGAIN, LUCILLE Beemer greeted him cheerfully. "Good morning. How are you feeling? A little more rested?"

"Yes, ma'am."

"Well . . . quite a few people have been waiting to talk to you."

"Oh?"

"Yes. Go ahead, Lordor."

"Hello, Gene. I'm your grandfather Nordstrom. You didn't know me. I died before you were born, but welcome home, son."

Gene was astonished. "Oh, wow . . . Well . . . hello, sir. Nice to meet you. I played you in the Founder's Day pageant."

"Miss Beemer told me. You did a fine job, too, I hear."

"I've heard so many great things about you from Dad. . . . Mother, too. She said you were such a nice man. They still have your picture hanging in the living room."

"Oh, really, which one?" asked Lordor.

"I don't know, sir. You were wearing a dark suit . . . and a derby hat?"

Gene suddenly heard a woman laugh. "How well I remember that photo. Hello, Gene, dear, it's your grandmother."

"Grandmother Katrina?"

"Yes."

"Really? I can't believe it. I never thought I'd actually meet you."

"I know. Isn't it wonderful?"

"It sure is. So, umm, Grandmother . . . would you mind if I asked you a question about something I've always wondered about?"

"Not at all."

"Were you really a mail-order bride, or did Dad just make that story up?"

"No, it's true. I was."

"She's telling you the truth, Gene," said Lordor.

"Wow . . . what was that like?"

"Well, back then, we had to do our courting by mail. And when I saw your grandmother's photograph, that was it."

"I see. Well, no wonder. I saw an old-timey picture of you, Grandmother, and you were a real knockout. What did you think of his picture?"

"I thought he was very clean looking."

"So did you get married right away?"

Lordor answered, "No, it took some time . . . to get to know each other."

"Too long," Katrina said with a laugh.

Gene spent the rest of the day meeting other relatives and having people say hello. Because he was such a young man, most of the people who spoke to him were older, including his old high school football coach. "Hey, boy. Welcome back. It's Coach Cready here."

"Coach? I didn't know you were up here. Nobody told me. . . ."

"Yeah, well, the old ticker up and quit on me. Just happened a year ago."

"Oh, I'm sorry, Coach."

"Thanks. . . . But listen, boy, I'm mighty proud of you. A marine. Semper fidelis. I was there the day you got on the bus to go to Quantico for training."

"Yes, sir, I remember."

"How was it? Tough?"

"Yes, sir."

"But you could take it."

"Yes, sir."

"Did you go down fighting?"

"Yes, sir."

"Good boy. So, Gene . . . what do you think? Do you reckon we'll win this thing?"

"Yes, sir. I know we will."

"That's the spirit." Then the coach proudly made an announcement. "Folks, I just want you to know this boy here was the best damn quarterback Elmwood Springs ever had, and he made a damn good marine, too."

—

GENE WAS AMAZED AT all the people who remembered him and that he had actually met his grandparents. He had heard so many stories about them, but to be able to meet them was something he had never expected. Who would have? Another thing surprised him as well. Nobody had ever told him they both had Swedish accents.

AS THEY WERE SAYING good night, Lucille Beemer said, "Wasn't that just wonderful? All these people so happy to see you."

"Yes, ma'am, it was. But I still don't quite understand what happened. I mean, I got killed. Why am I still here? Why is everybody still here? I'm a little confused."

"Of course you are, honey. We all were. I suppose the best way to explain it is that your body is dead, but you, Gene, are still alive. Does that make sense?"

"Some . . . I guess."

"I used to question it," said Lucille, "but not anymore. Nobody really knows how we got here. But I'm just glad we did. But, Gene, dear . . . now that you're one of us, there's a little something else I need to tell you about Still Meadows."

"Yes, ma'am?"

"And again, we don't know why it happens, but

after they have been here for a while, some of our residents have left . . . quite unexpectedly."

"I'm not sure what you mean."

"Well, one day they are here, and the next, they're not. They just seem to disappear into thin air . . . and they never come back. At least, none have, yet."

"Wow . . . that's weird," said Gene.

"I don't want to upset you. I'm only telling you this, so you won't be caught off guard, if it happens. Good night, Gene, dear."

"Good night."

Gene was tired, but he did not go right to sleep. That last piece of information about people disappearing was a bit unsettling. At this point, Gene didn't know if this was good news or bad news. But either way, there was a lot more to being dead than he'd thought.

The Baby

A FEW MONTHS LATER, GENE'S WIFE, MARION, and their baby boarded a train in San Francisco, headed to Elmwood Springs, Missouri. At last, they were coming.

Gerta and Ted, Elner and Ida, and Ida's daughter, Norma, were all to be a part of the welcoming committee meeting the train. They had seen photographs of them but they were anxious to finally get the chance to see them in person.

Marion was not even Ida Jenkins's daughter-in-law, but Ida used the occasion to purchase a new outfit for herself and for Norma. She told her husband, "It's important we make a good first impression on her. After all, she's from San Francisco. I just hope and pray Elner doesn't show up in that old cotton housedress and tie-up shoes." And, of course, Elner did.

It was a long trip with two train changes along the way, but they finally arrived. The first thing Elner said when she saw the baby was, "Oh my, look at those blue eyes and that blond hair. If she's not the spitting image of Gene, then I don't know who is!" Marion was as pretty as Gene had described her and almost as shy. During the ride back to the house, she hardly said a word, but just smiled as they all took turns holding the baby. Gene had told her all about his family, and it was amazing how right he had been in describing them. They all were as nice and as friendly as he had said. Gene had also told her about his aunt Ida Jenkins. At the time, she had thought he'd been kidding, but as it turned out, he hadn't been. Ida never stopped talking the entire way home.

The following Sunday, they all went up to Still Meadows to show Marion where Gene was buried. Elner led the way, and when they got to Gene's grave site, she said, "Here he is, honey." Then she said, "Here's your wife and baby . . . come all the way from San Francisco to see you!" Gene heard her just as plain as day and looked up and saw his baby for the first time.

Little eleven-month-old Dena Katrina Nordstrom was far too young to know it, but when Gerta and Ted took their new grandbaby all over town and showed her to everyone, people started to feel better, knowing there was a part of Gene that was still here. Pretty soon, the bakery opened up again.

August 1945

THE PEOPLE OUT AT STILL MEADOWS HEARD THE commotion going on down in the town, horns blowing, church bells ringing, but they didn't know why. Things were quiet for a while, and just like everybody, they were concerned about the war. But as luck would have it, just a few days after V-J Day, Mr. Albert Snavely, by way of a burst appendix, came in with the latest news. When he told them what had happened, everyone was stunned.

"A **what**?" they asked.

"An atomic bomb . . . the biggest bomb that was ever made. Germany surrendered, but not the Japs. They just kept on fighting, so we dropped one bomb. And they still wouldn't surrender, so old Harry Truman says, 'Oh, yeah? Well, we'll see about that.' He dropped another one . . . and **wham** . . . we had ourselves a surrender in no time, signed, sealed, and delivered."

"So the war's over? We won?"

"Yes!"

You could hear everybody all over Still Meadows

breathing a sigh of relief. Then Katrina said, "And the boys are coming home?"

"Any day now."

"What about Ada Goodnight?" someone asked. "Is she still flying planes?"

"She's already back, and she brought a new husband with her."

"You don't mean it? Oh, my stars . . ."

Coach Cready called out, "Hey, Gene . . . you were right, boy! We won. By God, we won!"

A FEW WEEKS LATER, Gene Nordstrom had a visitor. He had first met Cooter T. Calvert in the fifth grade, when Cooter's parents had moved to town. And today, a tall and lanky twenty-two-year-old Cooter, still in his army uniform, had come out to see him.

Cooter walked up to the grave, stood there for a while, then squatted down on his haunches, pushed his hat back, and said, "Hi, buddy. I just got back, and your mom told me you were out here. Damn, Gene . . . of all the guys to get it, why did it have to be you? The best of the best. Everybody is still real upset. Your mom still has your picture in the window down at the bakery with the gold star. Anyhow . . . I just wanted to come out and thank you for being such a good friend. I mean, of all the guys, it's hard to think about you not being here anymore. Shit . . . it should have been me. I'm just a screwup. But you . . . we all figured you'd come home and . . .

anyhow . . . if you hadn't let me tag along with you all those years and keep me out of trouble, I don't know . . . but I'll tell you what, Gene, I'm gonna do better. I owe that to you. I'm gonna try to live the best life possible . . . just for you. Your dad says you're getting a medal—how about that, Kemosabe? I heard you got married and that she's a real looker, too. You always did get the pretty ones. Anyhow . . . I don't know what else to say. Except don't worry about your folks. I'll keep an eye on them for you." He sighed and shook his head. "Oh, man, I just hope this war was worth it. You . . . of all the guys in the world . . . why did it have to be you?" Then Cooter, thinking he was alone, broke down and sobbed like a little kid.

AFTER COOTER LEFT, GENE thought about what he had said. "Was the war worth it?" Gene wondered. If he had to do it all over again, would he still do it? He couldn't sugarcoat it. He would've loved to have had more time. To have had a chance to be a husband, a father to his little girl. He wished like hell he hadn't been killed, but would he do it all over again? And the answer was yes, he would. He wasn't a historian or a philosopher, but he knew there had to be at least some free countries left in the world or else there would be no point in living. He was surprised to hear he was getting a medal, though. He wondered what kind of medal and what for? He didn't remember doing anything heroic.

Good News

1946

THE SWEET CLOVER DAIRY HAD ALMOST TRIPLED its production during the war and was now the largest dairy in the area. Ander Swensen owned thirty-eight delivery trucks and employed more than one hundred people, and the dairy was still growing. Ander and his wife, Beatrice, had just bought a brand-new two-story brick house and a new car. They now had everything a couple could want, except a child.

IN LATE SEPTEMBER, Elner Shimfissle was at the kitchen sink, running cold water over her string beans, when the phone rang.

"Hello?"

It was Beatrice, who said, "Elner, are you peeling potatoes?"

"No, I just finished stringing some beans. Why?"

"Do you remember that dream you had?"

Elner had to think a minute . . . then she remembered. "Oh, no, Beatrice . . . you don't mean it!"

"Yes, I do. I just got home from the doctor."

Elner was so happy for her friend, she danced a little jig around her kitchen.

Beatrice and Ander had given up hope of having a child long ago, so when out of the blue, the doctor had informed Beatrice that she was pregnant at almost thirty-six years old, she and Ander were overjoyed.

A week later, the happy couple flew to Chicago and went to Marshall Field's department store to shop for their new baby. They bought all the latest baby clothes, a bassinet and a Mother Goose baby bed, and almost cleaned out the toy department. The salespeople got a kick out of the joyful couple, who were obviously from a small town. Ander handed out cigars to the salesmen and a "bouquet of roses" pin to all the salesladies. They bought two of everything, one in pink and one in blue. This child would be loved and raised as a prince or a princess. They didn't know which yet. They didn't care. All they knew was a baby was coming.

That same day in Chicago, in a tenement apartment building with gray rickety wooden stairs in the back, another woman was expecting a child, her sixth. But there was no joy in it, only despair.

She was so tired. But there was no way to stop the babies from coming year after year. And her priest said it was a sin to try. As she stood looking out at the clothesline full of wet sheets and diapers strung between the buildings, she suddenly winced in pain. This one would be a boy. She could tell by the way he kicked at her. He wasn't due for a month, but he was already like his father. He would come out like the rest of the boys had, hungry and angry, wanting to kick someone.

Two different babies were coming. Two different lives. The chances of their ever meeting one another would be slim to none.

It's a Girl!

AFTER SOME DELIVERY DIFFICULTIES, THE LONG-awaited Swensen baby was born. She was a beautiful little brown-eyed girl they named Hanna Marie. Both Ander and Beatrice were over the moon with joy. Ander gave all of his employees at the dairy a fifty-dollar baby bonus, and a huge party was planned in her honor.

As someone said, "My Lord, you would think that they were the first people in the world to ever have a baby." The party was held at the house, and everyone in town was sent a pink invitation tied with a white ribbon.

Come say hello to
MISS HANNA MARIE SWENSEN
Tuesday afternoon, 2 to 5

One year later, pink cards were sent out to every child in town that read:

You are cordially invited to a celebration
in honor of
MISS HANNA MARIE SWENSEN'S
First Birthday
Favors, entertainment, and all the ice cream
you can eat!

Every child in town came. They didn't care so much about seeing the baby, but all the ice cream you could eat was a once-in-a-lifetime treat. And their parents were only too glad to take them. They all liked the Swensens and loved to visit their home. It was beautifully decorated with the finest furniture that could be bought and had a magnificent grand staircase leading up to the second floor. Ida Jenkins marched through each room and exclaimed, "I swear, Beatrice and I have the **exact** same taste." When Ida got home that night, she asked her husband, Herbert, why they couldn't have a grand staircase like the Swensens.

"Because, Ida, we live in a one-story house."

"Couldn't we add an upstairs?"

"We could, if we were made of money. Just because I work at the bank doesn't mean I own it."

"Well, you're the president. Couldn't you give yourself a loan?"

Herbert sighed. He loved her, but the woman just didn't understand finance.

—

By the time Hanna Marie was a year old, her smiling picture was on the side of all the Swensens' milk delivery trucks. Everybody in town waited for their invitation to her second birthday party. But it never came.

Other people had noticed it first. Some even whispered about it. They couldn't quite put their finger on it, but Hanna Marie was not like the other children her age.

At first, her parents tried to ignore it, to pretend everything was all right, but soon it became very clear. There was something wrong with their little girl.

Mayo Clinic

OF COURSE, THEY HAD SUSPECTED IT. A LOCAL doctor had told them as much, but the words were still hard to hear. The specialist at the Mayo Clinic sat down across from Ander and Beatrice Swensen. "Your little girl is completely deaf."

This was devastating news. They had been hoping it had just been a hearing impairment and that she could possibly get help.

Ander said, "Money's not a problem, Doctor. Isn't there anything . . . an operation or something?"

He shook his head. "No. I'm sorry."

The little girl could see her parents were upset, and she kept stroking her mother's face. "Will she ever be able to speak?" asked Ander.

"No, when children are deaf from birth, they don't know what speech sounds like. They see our lips moving, but it's a silent world for them. But as you can see, she is very bright. Her cognitive tests are perfectly normal. And, my God . . . just look at her. She's the prettiest little child with that smile, and there are plenty of schools for the deaf. She can be taught sign language, lip reading . . . with some special training, she should be able to live a completely normal life . . . get married, have children . . . a lot of deaf people do."

Beatrice asked, "Do you really think she could get married?"

"I don't see any reason why not," said the doctor with a smile. "We'll just have to wait and see and hope for the best."

All the News
That's Fit to Print

A FEW MONTHS AFTER COOTER CALVERT GOT HOME from the army, he married his old girlfriend and later, with a little help from his father-in-law, he started a local newspaper.

After mulling it over, they named it **The Elmwood Springs News.** It was not very original, but the town was excited to have its own paper at last, and all promised to buy advertisements.

The first day Cooter opened his door for business, Ida Jenkins appeared in his office and said, "Well, Cooter, you'll need a society columnist, and I'm here to volunteer my services."

Cooter was not aware that there was any society in Elmwood Springs, but you did not say no to Ida Jenkins. Besides, she had already written her first column and had supplied her photo to be used at the top.

THE WHOLE TOWN'S TALKING

by Mrs. Ida Jenkins

Greetings to all! This week, the whole town's talking about the magnificent soiree thrown by Mr. and Mrs. Swensen, owners of our very own Sweet Clover Dairy. The festive affair was in celebration of the third birthday of their lovely daughter, Miss Hanna Marie Swensen. When it comes to fashion and style, none can hold a candle to the Swensen mother-daughter duo. Hanna Marie was a perfect picture of "What does the well-dressed little girl wear?" in her darling frilly pink dress. Mother Beatrice was also lovely in a pale aqua knit frock, so flattering to her slim figure. Never saw such a proud poppa. As usual at any of the Swensens' delightful get-togethers, anybody who was anybody was there. Elner Shimfissle, longtime friend of Mrs. Swensen's, was also in attendance.

Memorial Day

1949

AT AROUND SIX A.M., J. J. BALLANTINE, THE CARE-taker, walked around the cemetery and placed an American flag on each veteran's grave. It was only a small flag, but it meant a lot, especially to the boys who had been killed. They considered themselves to be grown men, but most were still young enough to enjoy the special attention.

Gene woke up early that day and was starting to get a little fidgety waiting for his family to arrive. He could tell by the sun that it must be around nine-thirty. Last year, they had brought his little girl, Dena, with them. He hoped they would bring her again.

Pretty soon, he began to hear cars driving into the cemetery, and he immediately recognized the sound of his father's car, the same big black 1936 Plymouth he had driven forever. Gene heard it pull up to the curb and stop and then the sound of all the doors opening and slamming shut, and here they were. As always, his mother came first. His father held the rest back for a moment while she walked right to him and placed her hand on the white cross that stood above his head and said, "Here's my baby."

Gene could almost feel her hand as he had so many times as a boy. That cool hand that had soothed away his fears or made him feel better when he was sick, that hand like no other that told him that everything was all right. "I miss you, son," she said. "I miss you, too, Momma."

Now came Dad, looking a little older this year. Gene noticed a little potbelly starting, but he owned a bakery, so who could blame him?

And there was Aunt Elner. But where was Dena? He knew she always spent the summer with her grandparents. He was starting to worry, when he saw her come running from around the other side of the car, pulling his cousin, Norma, behind her. Norma was busy talking to some sandy-haired athletic-looking boy he did not recognize, when the little girl broke loose from Norma and ran toward him. He was surprised to see how tall she was getting. He figured she must have grown an inch since last year, and he was amazed at how much she looked like pictures of him at that age—the same white blond hair and blue eyes. Aunt Elner walked up behind her and said, "Here's your daddy, honey. You can talk to him if you want to." The little girl looked where Aunt Elner was pointing and seemed puzzled.

"Where do I look?"

"It doesn't matter. He'll hear you."

She stood there while Gene tried his best to help. "Come on, honey," he thought. "Say something. I can hear you, sweetheart."

"Go ahead, honey, tell your daddy what a big girl you are," urged Aunt Elner.

The little girl looked down at the grave, held out four fingers, and said, "I'm this many." And it tickled Gene. Then she said, "I've got a kitten," and then, "Why don't you come home?"

Aunt Elner petted her head. "He would if he could, baby girl. But he loves you and watches over you every day."

"That's right," Gene thought. "Tell her I **wanted** to come home."

"Dena, don't you want to tell your daddy you love him, too?"

"Yes, ma'am."

"Go ahead. Tell him."

The little girl then leaned over and shouted into the grave as loud as she could, "I love you, Daddy!"

Gene had to laugh. He then heard his mother call out from the car for them to come help with the flowers and the rest of the things.

Katrina, who was enjoying seeing everyone, said, "Oh, Gene . . . she is so pretty."

"Isn't she? She's going to be very tall, I think."

"Yes, I can see that."

Gene was pleased to see that the basket of flowers they placed at the head of his grave was even larger than last year's. They were not getting smaller, at least. His only fear was that he would be forgotten.

Suddenly, he noticed what a pretty girl his cousin, Norma, had turned out to be. After a moment, he recognized the boy Norma had brought with her. It was Macky Warren, whose daddy ran the hardware store, all grown up. Gene had taught him to swim when Macky was such a skinny little kid that he could hardly keep his swimming trunks on. Gene guessed Macky must be "the boyfriend" because Norma was gazing at him like a lovesick calf.

Gene dozed in the warm sun for a few minutes, but awoke again when he heard the trunk of his father's car open. Then he saw his dad coming toward him, walking around with the picnic blanket, looking for a place to set it down, and finally choosing more or less the same spot he always did, just to the right of his son's grave.

It was a perfect spot for Gene. He was downwind and could smell the food as each basket was uncovered. First the potato salad . . . good and tart, bread and butter pickles, olives, hot fresh corn on the cob. And then . . . oh, here it comes. Just as the white towel was lifted, a gentle breeze caught the familiar aroma of his mother's golden fried chicken, and, what's that? Oh, Aunt Elner's fresh buttermilk biscuits. Someone was buttering one right now. Then he heard a jar of Aunt Elner's fig preserves pop open.

He was happy to see the family seeming more talkative. For the first two or three years, they had been so quiet. But this time, they weren't, and he was enjoying listening to them. He found out that Tot Whooten had thrown her husband, James, out of the house again, and his aunt Ida, Norma's mother, was in St. Louis at one of her many garden club conventions. And according to Elner, she was still busy putting on airs, which made him smile. Nothing much changes.

After the meal was over, Aunt Elner stood up and poured out what was left of the iced tea close to his feet, and he laughed as the cold liquid cooled the ground. Had he really felt it? Or had he just imagined it? Oh, well, it didn't matter; it felt good. After they had cleared off the blanket, and his father had folded it back up, Gene heard the trunk open and close again. That was always a signal they were getting ready to leave. He hated to see them go, but the sun was about to go down, and he knew the mosquitos were bad at this time of day, and they should get Dena on home. It was probably a long day for such a little girl.

After they all got back in the car, they waited as they did every year, as his father made the solitary trek back to his son's grave, removed his hat, stood perfectly still, then saluted his son. As Gene heard the car turn around and drive away, he called out, "Goodbye, everybody. Don't forget me."

At sundown, a group from the VFW came out, and Bobby Smith, a Boy Scout, played taps as they lowered the flag. Later, after everyone had driven away, the cemetery was quiet again. The fireflies had just started to twinkle, and a half moon was beginning to show itself, when Mr. Hendersen, who had said nothing all day, commented, "Hey, Marine, your old man's getting a little fat."

Gene smiled. "He's getting a belly, all right." Gene figured that, had he lived to be his dad's age, he probably would have looked a lot like him, and that was fine with him. Mrs. Lindquist called over, "Gene, I swear, Gerta and Elner look the same as they did the day I died, still just as chubby and cute."

Mary Childress said, "All the Knott girls are heavy-set, except for Ida, and she starves herself."

After a moment, his grandfather called over to Gene. "It was good to see everybody looking so well today, wasn't it, son?"

"Yes, sir, it was."

Lucille said, "All in all, I think it was just a lovely day."

The Boyfriend

MACKY WARREN AND NORMA HAD BEEN DATING each other since high school. He had never even looked at another girl. But as he walked home from Norma's house that Memorial Day night, a question kept going back and forth in his mind. Should he and Norma get married now or wait? She wanted to. So did he. But somehow, going out to the cemetery that day with the Nordstroms had started him thinking. Even though he had been the one who had delivered the telegram about Gene four years ago, it was still hard to believe that Gene Nordstrom was really dead.

Gene had been a boyhood hero of his and of most of the other boys in town. They had all wanted to grow up and be just like him: play baseball, basketball, and football; be a lifeguard at the pool, just like Gene had.

And it wasn't just the boys who idolized him. All the girls in town hung around the pool all day, staring at him and giggling whenever he said hello, but Gene seemed oblivious to the fact that everybody had a crush on him. The last time Macky had seen him was at the bus station, the day everybody had gone down to see the boys off. That day, Gene had been so alive, so bigger than life. Now all that was left was a photograph in the bakery window.

Gene's death had greatly affected Macky and the other boys his age. Before that, they had all felt so safe and secure. But Gene Nordstrom being killed in the war had changed all that. In the movies, it was always the bad guys that got killed, and the good guys lived happily forever. Gene's death had forced them to face the reality of life. If something like that could happen to Gene Nordstrom, then you could never really be sure of anything ever again.

Life was so unpredictable, and death was so damn final. You didn't get a second chance. This was it. You had to make the most of your life right now.

If he got married now, what would he miss out on? He might wind up like his father, never going anywhere but to work and then home again with a one-week vacation to the same place every year. It was tough to be grown up, to make decisions that would change your life forever. It didn't seem fair that he got only one life. He needed three or four to do all the things he wanted to do: play professional football, go fly-fishing in Alaska, take a year and follow the sun to Australia. He dreamed of a year of two summers. He had even worked at his dad's hardware store after school and saved money for the trip. But if he married Norma now, he would have to use that money for a down payment on a house. He loved Norma, but she was never going to be adventurous and go places with him. She was too nervous to travel too far from home.

But, on the other hand, if he didn't marry Norma, what would he miss out on then? What if Norma married someone else? In the coming months, Macky would change his mind about getting married a hundred more times.

That night up at Still Meadows was the last time Gene ever spoke to his grandfather. The next morning, Lordor was gone. It was quite a shock for everyone. Lordor had been there from the very beginning. The news spread throughout Still Meadows, and there were the usual questions. Where did he go? Would he come back? The same old questions their loved ones had asked about them when they died were now being asked up at Still Meadows . . . questions that nobody had the answer to.

The Fabulous Fifties

—

All This and
Elvis, Too

A Special Day

1950

THAT JULY, THE SUN SEEMED TO KNOW EXACTLY what day it was. Eager and excited to get an early start, it couldn't wait a moment longer and quickly burned through the morning mist and flooded the town with bright clear light. "Get up, everyone, lots to do, fun to be had!"

Up on the hill, Lucille Beemer said, "Good morning, everybody." Two hundred and three people just waking up answered, "Morning," or something similar. Mr. Hendersen just grunted. It was his idea of a reply, and he only did that because, as hard as he tried, he couldn't help but join the human race today.

Today was the Fourth of July, and there were to be big doings all day and fireworks tonight. As old as he was, he still had his childhood July Fourth memories of red, white, and blue, firecrackers, sparklers, whirligigs, watermelons, footraces, parades, and ice cream.

Later that morning, they could smell the hot dogs being grilled over on the outdoor VFW grill. Gene

Nordstrom said, "I could eat about ten of those right now."

It was almost eleven, and from the sound of it, the parade would be starting soon. They could hear the band already gathered in the parking lot, warming up their instruments. The quiet little toots and trills of the trumpets and trombones, the soft rattle of the drums.

Soon they heard the sirens and horns blowing, and they knew the Shriners had arrived in their clown cars. A few minutes later, a loud whistle from the band major, and they were off with a rousing rendition of "Stars and Stripes Forever." All during the parade, they heard people talking on megaphones, shouting orders, and the crowd cheering as the flag went by, applauding the floats that followed. They heard the familiar sound of Dixie Cahill's troupe of tap dancers, the Tappettes, doing their routine down the street.

Everybody enjoyed hearing the music, except Birdie Swensen, who had been the church organist and had perfect pitch. She whispered to her husband, "Dear God, how an entire band can play flat is beyond me. John Philip Sousa must be rolling over in his grave."

But, thankfully, most people down in town were too excited to notice and were having a fine time as the Tappettes danced by. What a sight! Twenty-four girls in short bright blue sequined outfits and white boots with tassels were tapping and twirling batons down the street. It was enough to stop a young boy's heart, and throw a flutter in some of the old men's hearts as well.

Dixie Cahill was marching alongside her girls, keeping an eye out, making sure their line was straight. Glenn Warren, who owned the hardware store, was driving the tractor pulling the Washington Crossing the Delaware float, and his son, Macky, one of the volunteers, was not far behind him, carrying a shovel and a pail, cleaning up after the animals in the parade, which included two goats, four miniature ponies, and all the 4-H Club cows and pigs and sheep, each wearing a big red, white, and blue ribbon.

The Lions Club, the Rotary, the Optimists, and the Chamber of Commerce all had floats this year. The largest was the huge two-hundred-foot chamber float with Hazel Goodnight dressed as Betsy Ross, sitting in a chair, sewing the flag on one end, Uncle Sam in the middle, and Ida Jenkins as the Statue of Liberty on the other end. Two dressed-up dogs riding in decorated baby carriages followed.

AFTER THE PARADE WAS OVER, everyone went over to the big picnic ground out by the grammar school, and up at Still Meadows they could hear all the noise and fun going on, children laughing and chasing each other, and the crack of the bat at the Fourth of July baseball game. But the best was yet to come.

Later, when it got dark, the sky lit up with huge bursts of bright pink, white, red, and green explosions of light that cascaded down to the ground in long streamers, then faded. Then more explosions: a golden one, a purple and gold one, a silver one, each burst bigger and louder than the one before.

Then came the grand finale. Pop! Pop! Pop! Pop! Then one great big boom as the sky lit up with ten bursts shot off all at once. And when they all faded, one last giant fireworks display of the American flag. Wow!

When it was finally over, it was late, and everyone on the hill was tired and happy, including the people who had come out to the cemetery and put down blankets to watch the fireworks from up there.

It really was the very best place to see them. Macky Warren and Norma were one of the couples up on the hill that night. But Macky had more than fireworks on his mind, and he had been planning it for weeks. Right before the big finale, he pulled something out of his pocket, then turned to Norma. "Will you marry me?" he asked. He couldn't hear her answer because of the noise of the fireworks, but he could see the look on her face, and it was a definite "Yes!"

A Happy Time

1950 WAS A HAPPY TIME IN ELMWOOD SPRINGS. Glenn Warren's hardware store now carried Motorola and Sylvania television sets, and almost everyone in town had one. All the kids loved Howdy Doody and Buffalo Bob. Merle Wheeler was hooked on watching wrestling with Gorgeous George, and his wife, Verbena, was hooked on Liberace. And everybody loved watching Uncle Miltie. Tot Whooten said, "There's nothing funnier than a man dressing up like a woman."

Cereal was the breakfast of choice for most American kids. If you didn't eat your Wheaties, you wouldn't grow up and be a famous baseball or football star. Ice cream was the dessert they all screamed for. And both cereal and ice cream required milk, milk, and more milk. Which was good news for the local dairy business.

ANDER AND BEATRICE SWENSEN were still so overjoyed with their little girl, Hanna Marie, and they wanted to do something nice for the town. And so Ander brought in a professional landscape architect and had a lovely city park designed and built with a little lake in the middle, sidewalks, benches, a fountain, and streetlights. He named it Lordor Nordstrom Memorial Park, in memory of his friend and mentor.

The Elmwood Springs Ladies' Bowling Team finished first in their league to become county champions. Over at the picture show, marquees boasted about its brand-new air-conditioning, and on hot, muggy summer days, kids and grown-ups alike spent hours sitting inside the ice-cold theater. It was so cold you could see your breath, and the candy girl in the lobby had to wear gloves and a scarf. One mother complained that her son had come home after a day at the movies, and his lips were still blue.

But that summer, lots of hot-buttered popcorn and hundreds of boxes of Sugar Babies, Raisinets, Goobers, Good & Plenty candy, and Junior Mints were sold, due to the sudden increase in attendance.

ALTHOUGH HER PARENTS WORRIED about her, little Hanna Marie didn't seem to realize yet that she was different and unable to talk. But she was friendly with everyone. She would walk around town with her mother and visit people up and down the street. She was like the town pet, and everybody loved Hanna Marie. All they had to do was hold out their arms and she would run up and give them a big hug. All the merchants in town would give her a candy bar or, in Gerta Nordstrom's case, pastries. They loved to see her smile. But this soon became a problem, and Beatrice had to ask them to please not give her any more sweet things to eat. She said to Gerta, "As it is, with all the ice cream Ander brings her, she won't have a tooth left by the time she's twelve."

Poor Tot

1951

THERE WERE NOW FOUR CHURCHES IN TOWN, AND on Sunday mornings, it was so wonderful up at Still Meadows to hear all the different bells ringing all at once. But other than the church bells and the occasional lawn mower, it was mostly quiet and peaceful up on the hill.

However, down in town, on the afternoon of August 12, that was not the case over at Tot Whooten's house on First Avenue North.

IN EVERY TOWN, THERE SEEMS to be the one who always gets the hard luck. And in Elmwood Springs, that person was poor Tot Whooten. Because of money problems at home, she had started working at sixteen, fixing hair on her back porch. Her father had been a drunk, and she had, like so many, turned around and married an alcoholic just like her father. Her husband, James Dwayne Whooten, was a mess and could not hold a job to save his life.

It wasn't as if Tot had a natural talent for being a

hairdresser. It was just the only way she knew to make a living. And she now had two small children, Dwayne Jr. and Darlene, to support, plus a husband and a mother who was not quite right. Most of the women in town let her fix their hair out of pity for her. Of course, everybody went home afterward and redid it, but they felt it was their Christian duty to help poor Tot. Tot was a skinny redhead who smoked too much, but who could blame her? First she'd had her daddy to deal with, then James, and now her mother was as nutty as a fruitcake.

But she didn't complain. Tot could be pushed and pushed . . . but when she did lose her temper, watch out. The last event even wound up in **The Elmwood Springs News.**

Domestic Dispute

August 14

Deputies arrested a woman who scratched, punched, and threw empty glass whiskey bottles at her husband during an argument on First Avenue North. She also uprooted numerous garden plants and shrubbery, then threw a cement garden gnome at the man as he attempted to flee their home in his car. As he was pulling away, she grabbed onto the car and was dragged several feet and sustained abrasions from the fall. She was later booked at the county jail and charged with aggravated assault after being released from the hospital.

No names were used in the article, but everyone in town knew it was Tot. She had uprooted an awful lot of her bushes, and her yard was just a mess. Upon hearing her charge in court of aggravated assault, Tot had remarked to the judge, "You're damn right I was aggravated. The son of a bitch was cheating on me!" She was let off with a warning.

THE WHOLE TOWN'S TALKING

by Mrs. Ida Jenkins

This week, the whole town's talking about the recent wedding of Miss Norma Jenkins and Mr. Macky Warren. And in case you didn't know, I was the happy mother of the bride! Goodness, I don't know how other mothers can hold up under all the pressure of picking just the right outfit. Miss Howard in Ladies' Better Wear at Morgan Brothers Department Store was a tremendous help to me. And after days, we finally settled on a lace-trimmed dress and jacket in eggshell pink with shoes, hat, and gloves to match. The bride was lovely in white satin. The couple is honeymooning and will return this time next week.

Other topics of conversation this week: Stratford-upon-Avon has nothing on us. Thanks to Ander and Beatrice Swensen, a charming pair of adult swans were purchased and are now happily gliding along in their new home in our own city park. Let's hope they are a married couple. It would be so much fun to see baby swans. I am told they are gray in color, hence the moniker "Ugly Duckling."

Just a reminder, a front lawn says so much about the people who live inside. What does your lawn say? Does your lawn reflect your personality? Hint: Neatly clipped bushes and freshly laundered curtains in the window are always a sign of an orderly home.

Lester Shingle

In April of 1952, when word got out that Lester Shingle was dead, there were at least four women in town who were not too unhappy about it. They never said so out loud, but they thought it. Three of them went to his funeral, but Tot Whooten was not the kind of person who could pretend to be sad when she wasn't. The service was on a Sunday, and her beauty shop was closed, so she went bowling instead. She had a big ladies' tournament coming up, and she liked to get in as much practice as she could.

Last year had been another glorious year for the Elmwood Springs Ladies' Bowling Team. They had taken first place in the state championship.

Both the Goodnight twins and their younger sister, Irene, better known as "Good Night Irene" for her ability to roll so many strikes, were all excellent bowlers. But when it came right down to the wire, they had won mostly because of Tot Whooten, who had been nicknamed by the other teams "Terrible Tot, the Left-Handed Bowler from Hell" for her uncanny talent with a bowling ball. Even though she was a skinny, wiry woman, Tot used a thirteen-pounder and never saw a spare she couldn't hit. Her aim was lethal and legendary in bowling circles. Tot could pick up a spare with a spin that would knock a pin sideways to hell and back. "I got my spin from rolling up hair in pin curls for so many years," she said.

When Lester Shingle woke up at Still Meadows and realized where he was, the very first thing he said to Lucille Beemer was, "Guess what happened to me?"

"I have no idea," she said.

"Well, guess. Guess why I'm here."

"Well, let's see. Were you ill? A bad flu of some sort?"

"No. I was murdered in cold blood."

Lucille was stunned to hear it, and for the first time in her official position as greeter, was almost rendered speechless. She simply couldn't imagine such a thing happening in Elmwood Springs. All she could do was reply, "Oh, dear . . . I'm so sorry. That must have been very upsetting." She knew it was a completely inadequate response, but under the circumstance, what else could someone say?

And, of course, she remembered Lester. He'd always had that bad skin. And now this. She was also aware that he had never been very well liked . . . but even so, this was just shocking news.

She hoped he wouldn't bring it up again. It was just too upsetting to even think about, much less talk about. But, of course, when the very next person came in, a Mrs. Carrie Uptick, by way of a failed liver, Lester immediately grilled her for answers. "Have they arrested the murderess, yet?"

"Excuse me?" said Mrs. Uptick.

"The woman who murdered me."

"Oh, gosh . . . I haven't heard anything about anybody being arrested for murder."

"Damn," thought Lester. Whoever she was, she was still on the loose and could possibly kill again. Law enforcement was certainly not up to snuff in Elmwood Springs. Meanwhile, the woman could flee the state.

There were four women he suspected, but he didn't know which one had done it. For all he knew, they could have been in on it together. They had all threatened his life at one time or another. And all four had been at the Blue Star Bowling Alley that night. He'd seen them.

He had forgotten Wednesday was ladies' night, and when he walked in and saw them, he'd turned around and left as fast as he could, but he figured one of them must have seen him, because the last thing he remembered was one minute being hit in the back of the head with a heavy round object, and the next, waking up at Still Meadows. There was no doubt about it. One of those women had hit him in the head with a bowling ball and killed him deader than a doornail.

A Visit to the Farm

NORMA AND MACKY HAD BEEN MARRIED LESS THAN a year when he was drafted and sent to Korea. A week later, Norma was out at her aunt Elner's farm, sitting on her porch. "I hate changes. I wish everything would stay the same."

"Well, honey, lots of things do," Elner replied. "No matter what little old man does, the sun will come up in the morning, and the moon and the stars will always be there. No matter how many of us humans come and go, nature stays the same. Isn't that some comfort to know you can count on spring every year?"

"I guess."

"You need to get yourself a kitten to keep you company. That will get your mind off your troubles."

"Aunt Elner, if Macky gets killed like Gene did, I swear I won't be able to stand it. I'll . . . well, I don't know what I will do."

"Now you just stop with all that worrying. Little Macky is not going to get killed, and besides, you've got a baby on the way. Don't be thinking sad thoughts. You need to think happy thoughts, so the baby won't be nervous. I told your mother, I said, 'Ida . . . I think your being so nervous is what makes poor Norma nervous.' "

"Well, I know I'm nervous now."

"Oh, honey, you were always nervous. You were a nervous baby. So you'd better watch what you think. You don't want a nervous baby, do you?"

"No."

"Besides, worries will give you wrinkles. Look at me. I'm an old woman, and I don't have any wrinkles. Why? Because I don't worry."

DRIVING BACK INTO TOWN, Norma realized that her cousin Gene had been on her mind a lot lately. His parents had never really gotten over losing him. None of them had. She remembered the time he came to one of her dance recitals. She had been lead tulip and had messed up her steps. Of course, her mother had not been happy about it, but after the show, Gene had put his arms around her, told her she was "the prettiest one up there," and slipped her a Hershey bar on the drive home. When she was six, she'd had such a crush on him and told him she wanted to marry him when she grew up. He had laughed and said, "Cousins can't marry, but you just wait and see. Some boy is going to come along and steal you. And if he isn't good to you, I'll poke him in the nose." She wished he could have lived to see her married. If the baby was a boy, they were going to name him Gene.

Losing Gene had been difficult for everyone. A family is like a puzzle, and now there was a big piece missing. There would always be an empty space.

Seven months later, Norma gave birth to a little girl named Linda. And the good news was the baby wasn't nervous at all, and Macky came home safe and sound.

The Whole Town's Talking
---

by Mrs. Ida Jenkins

The whole town's talking about the attractive new stand-up console television set in the display window at Morgan Brothers.

Also happy to report that the annual Easter egg hunt was made special this year by the personal appearance of the Easter Bunny, who delighted the children.

Thank you to all who came early and hid the eggs. Lots of pretty polka dot and striped pails were supplied by Warrens' Hardware. Don't forget, next week the pony man comes to town, so be sure to get your child's picture taken on the pony. I still have one of Norma and on that very same pony, I believe.

Now that Easter is past, time to gear up for Mother's Day. Next week, the Garden Club is preparing to make corsages for all of our mothers and grandmothers out at Happy Acres Nursing Home.

You know I do not like to be the town naysayer . . . but . . . I saw the new Western movie **High Noon,** starring Gary Cooper as a sheriff, with the beautiful Miss Grace Kelly taking the role of Mr. Cooper's long-suffering wife, while in reality, Miss Kelly should have been cast as his daughter. Here is my question: Who is doing the casting for these films coming out of Hollywood lately? Methinks it must be old men, blinded by a lot of wishful thinking. I do not recommend this film for that reason.

Also hate to end on another sad note, but we lost our beloved citizen Olaf Olsen last Wednesday. Condolences to his wife, Helga Olsen, and his daughter, Beatrice Swensen. Our younger readers may not remember Olaf, but for those of us who grew up seeing his friendly face in Morgan Brothers' shoe department, he will be sorely missed.

Ida failed to mention that the Easter Bunny had been her sister, Elner Shimfissle, dressed in a homemade bunny outfit with big fluffy ears and feet.

The Shoe Salesman Arrives

IN NOVEMBER OF 1952, KATRINA'S YOUNGER brother, Olaf Olsen, came up to Still Meadows and was overjoyed to see Katrina again. He said, "Katrina, you wouldn't recognize the dairy anymore. It's so big."

"How is my darling niece, Beatrice? Still happy?"

"Oh, yes. She and Ander are doing so well and so is the dairy. I think they are the richest people in town. They live in a big two-story brick house. Can you imagine, Katrina? From where we came from, so poor, and now one of our family owns the biggest house in town with heat and hot and cold running water. Wouldn't Momma be so proud? And you won't believe this. . . . After I retired, Helga wanted to move back to the country, so we moved into your old farmhouse."

"Oh, Olaf, I'm so glad. I was afraid somebody might have torn it down."

"Oh, no . . . it can never be torn down. You know

how Ander loved you and Lordor. He pulled a lot of strings and had that house declared a state historical monument. He said, 'I had so many happy times in that house, I couldn't bear to lose it.'"

"Oh, what a sweet boy."

"He is. And did you know that you now have a grandniece named Hanna Marie?"

"Yes, it's wonderful."

"Yes it is. . . . The sad thing is, Katrina, she was born deaf."

"So I was told, the poor angel."

"But I must say, she does very well in spite of it. I know she's my granddaughter, and I'm prejudiced. But Katrina, I think that little girl really is an angel. A real one. There's just something about her. She has this way. You can't help but love her."

Just then, Gene Nordstrom called out, "Hey, Uncle Olaf! Guess who this is."

Olaf called back, "You don't fool me. It's my nephew, Gene Nordstrom, with the big giant feet. . . ."

"That's me. Glad you're here, Uncle Olaf."

AND WHAT OLAF SAID about Ander was true. He had idolized Lordor, and had learned everything he knew from him. One afternoon, when Ander was about sixteen, he and Lordor had been headed over to the barn at milking time, when Lordor said,

"Ander, I'm going to tell you the secret of what makes for a good dairy farmer."

Ander was all ears. "Yes, sir?"

"Are you ready?"

"Yes, sir."

"Keep your cows happy, and they will make you happy."

"Oh . . . but how, Mr. Nordstrom?"

"Just like with women, Ander. Every day, tell them they are beautiful. Watch." Lordor walked over to a big red cow grazing in the meadow. "Ah, there is my beautiful Sally. Ah, you are looking so pretty today, my love." The cow raised her head up, batted her eyes, and followed Lordor right into the barn, swishing her tail as she went. No question. Lordor had a way with cows.

Ander never forgot it. When he took over the dairy, he'd instructed all his workers to name every cow and tell her she was beautiful daily. Even when they had to switch to milking machines, Ander invested in top-of-the-line machines and the most comfortable ones for the cows. He also instructed the workers to stay and talk to the cows while they were being milked. It must have worked, because the dairy's production numbers kept going up.

In 1950, when Ander had a professional logo designed for all the products, it was a colorful portrait of a pretty red cow with long, curly eyelashes wearing a Swedish lace hat. Underneath the picture was a quote:

SALLY THE SWEDISH COW SAYS,
"YA, IT TASTES JUST LIKE FROM
THE OLD COUNTRY."
(Only the finest milk and cheese products provided
directly to you, courtesy of the happy cows
in Elmwood Springs, Missouri.)

Time to Let Go

1952

Robert Smith, the pharmacist at the drugstore, had a young son named Bobby. And Bobby,
along with all the other kids in town it seemed, had
a sweet tooth, so anytime he had a nickel, he would
run into the bakery and get two doughnuts, one
maple and one chocolate-covered with sprinkles.

The bakery was now completely back to normal,
but at home, Gerta Nordstrom still had not moved
Gene's things out of his room. One night that summer, when they were sitting out on the porch after
dinner, Ted said, "You know, little Bobby Smith was
in again this afternoon. He sure is a cute kid."

"Oh, he is. He reminds me of Gene at that age."

"Yeah . . . anyhow . . . I got to thinking that he
might just get some good use out of Gene's old baseball glove, and maybe the basketball. They're just
going to waste, sitting in his closet like that." Tears
sprang to Gerta's eyes at the thought of parting
with any of Gene's things. But her husband reached
over and took her hand and said, "It's time, honey . . .
and I think that's what Gene would have wanted."

She nodded. "All right . . . if that's what you think."

"I do."

THE NEXT MORNING, ON his way to work, Ted walked over to the Smith house with a big cardboard box. When Dorothy Smith came to the door, he said, "I'm leaving a few things I thought Bobby might get some use out of."

Dorothy opened the screen door and called out, "Oh, thank you, Ted. I know he will."

When Bobby saw the box, he was thrilled. He grabbed the metal toy car first. "Wow! Look at this," he said to his mother. "It has real rubber wheels!"

ANOTHER SUMMER ROLLED AROUND, and up at Still Meadows the smell of freshly mowed grass was so pleasant; as Gene Nordstrom noted, "It's especially pleasant when you aren't the one having to mow it." Everybody everywhere, above and below, loved summer. Out on the hill, the clouds were so pretty. They looked like big balls of white cotton floating by.

During these beautiful warm days, Beatrice would often take little Hanna Marie out to the farm to visit with Elner. Elner kept big, fat chickens in her yard that she spoiled by feeding cornbread and milk, so she always had lots of baby chicks on hand for Hanna Marie to see.

Today, when Beatrice and Elner were sitting out on her big screened-in back porch watching Hanna Marie laughing and playing in the yard, Beatrice said, "Oh, Elner, she just breaks my heart. She's so happy out here with you, but when we take her to the park, she tries so hard to talk to the other children, but she can't. After a while, they just move away from her, and she doesn't understand, and I can't even explain to her why."

Welcome Home, Harry

January 1953

DWIGHT D. EISENHOWER HAD JUST BEEN SWORN in as the new president of the United States, and former president Harry S. Truman, and his wife, Bess, were on a train from Washington, D.C., headed back home to Missouri.

Several days later, a group of Elmwood Springs ladies drove up to Independence and were among the fifteen hundred cheering people who stood outside the Truman family home at 219 North Delaware Street to welcome them back.

Although Ida was a Republican and had voted for Thomas E. Dewey, she joined them. She had not appreciated the way people in Washington had called Truman a country bumpkin and made fun of his blunt Missouri accent. "They are the ones with the accents," she said.

As she was standing there in the crowd, waiting for the Trumans to return, Ida thought to herself: "Thank God it's January and Elner is wearing her long winter coat. There's no telling what she is wearing underneath. But she has on that old ratty black hat. **Now** she wears a hat!" Norma's wedding had been a formal afternoon affair, and Elner had been the only lady there without a hat. "Elner never did understand occasion," thought Ida. She often wondered whether blood really was thicker than water . . . or if maybe she had been adopted.

With her fox furs and new alligator purse, snakeskin shoes, and long brown leather gloves, Ida was adorned from top to bottom with the remnants of a number of dead animals, and she felt swell and elegant. Ida, a slave to fashion, would have draped a kangaroo over her shoulders if she had seen it in **Glamour** or **Harper's Bazaar** magazine. Beatrice, on the other hand, who could afford anything she wanted, remained conservative in her dress, in a neat black suit with a white satin collar and had, unlike Ida, let her hair go gray around the temples.

Finally, the long wait was over, and the Trumans arrived. They walked through the cheering crowd up to their front porch and stood there and waved to everyone. Bess Truman shielded her eyes from the flashes going off and squinted over toward the group from Elmwood Springs, then called out, "Is that Elner Shimfissle I see over there?"

Elner called back, "Hi, Bess! Welcome home!"

Bess punched Harry in the ribs. "Look, Harry, it's Elner Shimfissle."

He looked over and saw her and smiled. "Hey, Elner, good to see you."

"You, too, Harry!" yelled Elner. "Welcome back to Missouri!"

Ida was dumbstruck and turned and stared at Elner like she had never seen her before in her life. Finally, when she could speak, she asked, "How do you know Harry and Bess Truman?"

Elner, still waving her white handkerchief in the air, said, "Oh . . . they stopped by the farm once."

"Why? Why would they stop at your farm?"

Elner looked at her and said, "Well, why wouldn't they?"

WHEN THEY GOT BACK into the car, Ida turned to Elner, somewhat irritated. "Elner, why didn't you ever tell me you knew the Trumans?"

Elner shrugged her shoulders and said, "You never asked."

Ida sat in a stunned state of silence all the way home, and it tickled Elner to death. She didn't tell Ida that Harry and Bess had stopped at her farm for the same reason that everybody else had. They had been lost. Thanks to that bad turn on the road to Joplin, she had met some of the nicest people.

The real truth was it had never occurred to Elner that the Trumans would even remember her. It had been years earlier, long before he was president. But Elner had not taken into account how many people in their lifetimes the Trumans would meet who had a blind possum named Calvin Coolidge that ate ice cream out of a dish at the table, and a three-legged banty rooster. And then there were the fig preserves she'd sent them every year. Harry had been a farmer and during those troubled years in the White House, those preserves had made him think of home.

But then, Elner had never told Ida about meeting Bonnie and Clyde, either. Or that she'd given them directions right to Herbert's bank and told them to tell him that Elner sent them. Thank heavens they hadn't gone there and held it up or she would never have heard the end of it.

As upset as Ida was over the Truman affair, her next column had this glowing thing to say:

The Whole Town's Talking

by Mrs. Ida Jenkins

This week, the whole town's talking about our recent motor trip to Independence to welcome home our longtime family friends, former president Harry Truman and his wife, Bess, from his stint in Washington, D.C., and add our "Well done, Harry" sentiments.

In her weekly column, Ida had sounded like everything was hunky-dory, but she was still very upset with Elner. As she told her husband, "My one chance to hobnob with notables, and she doesn't even tell me she knew the Trumans. If I had known that, I would have been sitting up at the White House having tea with them within the week."

Herbert asked, "How would you do that?"

"Easy. You know me. I would have gotten myself up to Washington, D.C., as fast as I could, knocked on the door, and said I was Elner's sister and just dropped by to say hello."

He laughed. "Oh, Ida."

"You may laugh, but I guarantee you that before I left that day, I would have gotten you a high-ranking position with the government, an ambassadorship, if nothing else. But no. All Elner said was, 'You never asked,' and here we sit, stuck in Elmwood Springs, Missouri, when who knows how far we could have gone. I could just strangle her."

Herbert looked at his wife and shook his head in sheer amazement. He smiled and said, "Honey, you're wonderful. Crazy, but wonderful."

Bring Your Child
to Work Day

1954

EIGHT-YEAR-OLD HANNA MARIE SWENSEN WAS taken to Springfield twice a week to learn sign language. Beatrice and Ander would often sit in on the lessons and learn signing as well, so they could talk to their daughter.

Signing was harder for Ander, with his big, beefy hands, but he tried. He'd practiced over and over, and on Hanna Marie's eighth birthday, he surprised her by signing, "You are the most beautiful girl in the world." Ander didn't know it, but he had signed, "You are the most beautiful squirrel in the world." Hanna Marie had giggled at his mistake and hugged his neck. She loved her daddy.

Ander had a particular interest in mentoring young people, as Lordor had before him. Every summer, Ander trained all the young 4-H Club members how to care for and raise cows properly. Many grew up and worked for him at the dairy.

Also years ago, Ander had established a "Bring Your Child to Work Day" on the first Monday in May. He felt it was good, even for the younger children, to see what their parents did to make a living, and he thought that this might help to instill a good work ethic at an early age. But besides the practical side, it was a lot of fun for everyone. The kids loved running all over the dairy, petting all the cows and seeing every aspect of the dairy business, from the milking to the bottling to the making of the cheese to watching the office workers handle the billing and ordering.

Hanna Marie loved going to work with her daddy on this day. And he delighted in taking her around to all the different departments, introducing her to each of his employees. She would shake hands with everyone she met while Ander beamed with pride.

This year, when Hanna Marie saw little Miss Davenport, who worked in the office, Miss Davenport had been surprised at how she had grown. She looked at Ander and said, "Oh my, Hanna Marie is almost as tall as I am now."

At the end of the day, there would be a big outdoor party for everyone, and Hanna Marie and Ander would help scoop ice cream for the children.

Every year, when they would come home, they both would have ice cream all over their good clothes, but Beatrice didn't care. She knew that day meant so much to both of them.

HANNA MARIE WAS UNABLE to attend regular school with the other children in town, but Beatrice and

Ander hired a private teacher who specialized in teaching the deaf to come and live with them. Soon Hanna Marie was learning to read and write, and was quite excited about it.

Several months later, Elner went to her mailbox, and was surprised to see a letter written in childish, but quite readable handwriting, addressed to

AUNT ELNER SHIMFISSLE
COTTONWOOD FARM
RURAL ROUTE 216
ELMWOOD SPRINGS, MISSOURI

Dear Aunt Elner,

This is me, Hanna Marie, writing a letter to say hello to you. I hope you are fine. I am fine. Mother and Daddy say hello to you too. Please write a letter to me sometime too. My teacher said that I can read very well. I am drawing you a picture of my teacher.

**I love you very much,
Hanna Marie Swensen**

Even though Elner was not her real aunt, Hanna Marie did love her. She had known her all of her young life. She had often spent the night with Elner and Will out at the farm. And even now, almost every Saturday morning, Norma would drive Hanna Marie and her own little girl, Linda, out for a weekly visit.

One pretty morning in June, Norma and Elner were sitting on Elner's big screened-in back porch drinking iced tea while the two girls played with a new baby rabbit. Ever since Hanna Marie had learned to read and write she always had a pad and pencil with her, and today, as usual, she was busy writing down another one of her many questions. When she showed her pad to Elner, it said, "Is this a girl bunny?"

Elner took the baby rabbit, examined it, then handed it back to her and nodded yes. Then Hanna Marie quickly wrote down her next question. "How can you tell?"

Elner looked over at Norma for help. "Oh Lord, Norma, I can't write that down."

Norma laughed. "Well, you'd better write something, or else she'll just keep asking."

Elner took the pad and wrote, "Girl bunnies have shorter ears."

It was a lie, of course, but it must have satisfied Hanna Marie, because she was on to the next question.

"Aunt Elner, can we go and see the baby goats now? Please!"

Elner put her tea down and stood up. "Oh, sure, honey. Come on, Norma. Let's go see the goats."

Norma shook her head. "No, you all go. I don't care much for goats. They smell. So if you don't mind, I'll just sit here and observe from afar."

"Well, okay, but hold the fort down till we get back."

As they went down the steps, Norma called out, "Linda, you hold on to Aunt Elner's hand now."

Norma smiled as she watched Hanna Marie and Linda head off to the barnyard with Aunt Elner, so excited. She remembered when she had been that age she had felt the same way, coming out to the farm to visit. So much in her life had changed since then. Everything but Aunt Elner. She was still the same sweet person she always was. She even looked the same.

THE WHOLE TOWN'S TALKING

by Mrs. Ida Jenkins

The whole town's talking about the new pink stoves and refrigerators now offered. What fun. Finally the kitchen doesn't have to be the same old black and white dull affair it was in the past.

Also, there is much excitement about the new planned community being built right off the new interstate highway. As we are so close to Joplin, Husband Herbert tells me that within a year, over 75 affordable brick ranch-style homes will be ready for commuters. So many new young couples are needing housing. Husband Herbert says this will be a real boon to our downtown and schools.

Some say that a weeping willow tree brings bad luck. Well, I have it on good account that under one of the lovely weeping willow trees that line our lake, Miss Edna Bunt said "Yes" to Mr. Ralph Childress. By the way, did you know that the willow's origin is China? We don't agree with their Communist policies, but we do love their trees.

Have you done your Christmas shopping? I haven't. However, downtown is so festive and merry with all the lights strung across Main Street, it makes it all such fun. We love the music piped from the stores now. Have you seen Rudolph the

Red-Nosed Reindeer in the hardware store window? Yes . . . it glows!

By the way, a fresh sprig or two of holly placed upon a mantel or holiday table is so festive . . . don't you think?

The Election

1956

AT THE CITY COUNCIL MEETING THAT MAY, as they discussed whether the town needed its own police department, Merle Wheeler brought up a good point. He said, "I don't think it's good for a town not to have some kind of law and order. It looks like we don't care."

"I agree," added Glenn Warren. "And we don't want to have to call in the Joplin Police every time we have a little problem. Besides, we have to think about the future. I heard this new rock and roll music is a Communist plot to lower the morals of our young people. Have you seen that Elvis Presley guy? Who knows what they will start doing next? We need to be ready." It was put to a vote and passed.

At the same meeting, Mayor Ted Nordstrom brought up another excellent point. "Listen, while we're at this, don't you all think it's time for us to have an election? I've been doing this for a long time, and somebody else might want a chance to run for mayor."

Herbert Jenkins quickly spoke up. "It would just

be a waste of time and money, Ted. Nobody is going to run against you . . . and for God's sake, don't give my wife any ideas about running for mayor. She's never home as it is."

Later, when newspaper owner and editor Cooter Calvert covered the meeting, he reported the yes vote to create a local police department. But he did not include anything about a possible mayoral election. He knew it was withholding information from the public, but Ida Jenkins was already driving everyone in town crazy with all of her hare-brained projects. If she ever became mayor, there'd be no telling what the woman might do.

Is It You?

Lucille Beemer had been at Still Meadows for quite a few years now, and she still loved her job. It was fun to see all the different reactions from people who arrived there, especially the ones who had been so terribly sick, to not have any more pain and to suddenly feel light as a feather. And every day was a surprise. You never knew just who might be coming up next.

Lucille Beemer didn't know it, yet, but in a few days, she was going to be in for a surprise herself.

Lucille had just finished greeting Mrs. Koonitz and welcoming her to Still Meadows. She no sooner had gotten her settled in when another resident arrived. "Good afternoon, and welcome to Still Meadows," Lucille said. "We are so happy you are with us, and we will do everything we can to make you feel at home. May I ask, to whom am I speaking?"

"What?" said a man, who was still clearly a little confused.

"To whom am I speaking?" she repeated.

"Oh. I'm Gustav . . . Gustav Tildholme."

If Lucille hadn't been dead, she would have fainted. This time, she really was speechless.

After a long moment, Gustav said, "Is anybody there? Hello?"

"Gustav, it's Lucille Beemer. Do you remember me? I used to be your teacher?" She waited, but he did not answer. He obviously didn't remember her, so she continued on, trying to hide her disappointment. "Well, there's certainly no reason in the world you should, it was so long ago. I just want to let you know that you are up at Still Meadows, safe and sound, and you have a lot of family and old friends here that will be so happy to say hello. Shall I tell your mother you are here or would you rather rest first? . . . Gustav?"

"Do I remember you? I never forgot you for one minute. I even remember what you were wearing the last time I saw you."

"Oh." Lucille was taken aback. "Do you?"

"My God, yes. Is it really you?"

"Yes, it's me."

Suddenly, a flood of memories came rushing back, and Gustav was once again a big, handsome, strapping boy of sixteen, and she was still the pretty young teacher of eighteen with roses in her cheeks.

Gustav never saw the little spinster with gray hair and glasses she had become. She never met the bald, wrinkled old man that he was today. In each other's eyes, they would always be young.

They both had so many questions they wanted to

ask, but Gustav's parents could not wait another minute and called out, "Hello!" and soon others were joining in to speak to him as well.

Katrina said to Lucille, "It must be so nice for you to have Gustav here. I remember that he was always one of your favorites."

"Oh yes," replied Lucille. "He always was."

The Whole Town's Talking

by Mrs. Ida Jenkins

Criminals, beware! This week, the whole town's talking about our very first officer of the law, Mr. Ralph Childress, a recent graduate of the Police Academy in Kansas City. I am sure with Ralph on the job, we will all feel much safer. So when you see him in his brand-new black-and-white police car, give him a wave.

By the way, Ralph's lovely bride, Edna, is also not unknown in these parts. As you all may recall, last fall, she was a finalist in the Pillsbury Bake-Off contest with her one-of-a-kind sweet-and-sour double cream apple pie. Yum yum. Ralph is the son of Mary and Richard Childress. Edna is the daughter of Mr. and Mrs. J. D. Nobblit of Second Avenue South.

We were saddened to hear of the death of Elmwood Springs native Mr. Gustav Tildholme, who still has several cousins living in the area. Mr. Tildholme was buried here last week. Arvis and Neva Oberg, who own the Rest Assured Funeral Home and were in charge of the interment, said that dozens of condolences came in for Mr. Tildholme from all around the world. I am told that Mr. Tildholme had been quite successful in the import-export business and owned companies in many different countries.

P.S. Make sure your roses are watered. And don't forget to watch out for aphids. Remember, lady-bugs are your roses' best friend.

Catching Up

Some time later, after Gustav had said hello to everyone, he and Lucille continued their conversation where they'd left off.

He said, "I always thought about you, always wondered how you were doing. After I left, I had some crazy notion that I would come back with lots of money, buy the old farm, and—"

"Oh, Gustav, I wish you had written."

"I should have. But then I heard you were engaged to be married, so I just didn't."

"But . . . I was never engaged to anyone."

"You weren't?"

"No, Gustav . . . that was wrong."

"I heard that you were . . . so then I just took off. Jumped on a freighter and just traveled the world. Japan, China, India, South America, you name it."

"Oh my, Gustav, all those exotic places. But then, you always did so well in geography."

"Yes, I guess that was the one subject I really liked. So . . . you never married?"

"No . . . never."

Gustav said, "Good God, all these years, I thought you had. I was a fool to run off like that. Too much pride, I guess. I wasted all that time. Always looking for someone like you. I even married once. A really nice lady in Rio de Janeiro. But she was not you. I should have just come home. . . . How could I have been so damn stupid?"

"Oh, Gustav, it's not your fault. I could have written to you and asked you to come home . . . I suppose I was just too afraid of what people might say. But we can't do anything about the past. You're here now, and that's all that really matters . . . and if you had come back, you might never have seen the world."

"That's probably true . . . but what about you, Lucille?"

"Well . . . I was lonely at times. Luckily, I had my students. And you know, Gustav, to this very day some of my old students still come out and visit me. Can you imagine that?"

"I can. You were a wonderful teacher."

"Oh, thank you, Gustav. It means the world to me that you thought so."

It was true. She had been a wonderful teacher. Lucille's life had been, in some ways, a lonely life, but a fulfilling one. She loved watching all of her students grow into adults. And then teaching their children, and later their grandchildren, had brought her a lot of comfort.

She didn't know it, but she had changed so many

lives just by being there year after year, and by saying the right things at the exact right time.

One student, a frail boy who some of the other boys sometimes made fun of, had gone on to become a very successful playwright in New York and had written to tell her about something she had forgotten:

> Even when I was failing math and everything else and I was feeling so bad about myself, you sat down with me and said, "Honey, there are those who do well at math, and then there are those, like yourself, who have been blessed with a creative mind and a wonderful imagination. I just know you are going on to do great things." You'll never know how you changed my life that day.

Sadly, she had not lived to hear it. But when that same student won the Tony Award for "Best Play of the Year," he had ended his acceptance speech with these words: "Last of all, I'd like to thank my sixth-grade teacher, who believed in me when nobody else did." He then raised the award up in the air, looked up, and said, "This is for you, Miss Beemer."

As LUCILLE BEEMER HAD learned over the years, people may never really know why their lives turn out the way they do, but in the end, they usually turn out exactly the way they're supposed to. She had lost Gustav for a while, and it had been hard, but she had him now forever and just maybe . . . even beyond.

After Gustav had been at Still Meadows for a couple of years, he said to her, "Honey, listen. If one day, I should leave here before you do, remember this: No matter where I go . . . or wherever I am, I'll wait for you. I'm not going to lose you again. No matter what, I'll find you."

Old Man Hendersen suddenly called over. "Good God almighty. How long are you two gonna keep all this love mush up? You're making me sick."

Gustav laughed and yelled back, "Forever, you crazy old coot. Go back to sleep."

DOWN IN ELMWOOD SPRINGS, things continued to run pretty smoothly. People were laughing at **Candid Camera** and **The Red Skelton Show** and enjoying **The Garry Moore Show** with funny girl Carol Burnett. Elner Shimfissle, who had just gotten television out at the farm, never missed **The Lawrence Welk Show**. Her mother had played the accordion, and she liked his playing and loved to watch Lawrence and the "Champagne Lady" dance. And all the young girls were in love with Tab Hunter.

The Sixties

—

Something's Blowing in the Wind . . .

Moving Along

By 1960, Sweet Clover Dairy had expanded its products into six states. It not only was providing a lot of employment for locals, but it had become a real source of pride to the town.

When Glenn Warren attended a dinner for Midwest store owners, held in Cincinnati, he asked Mr. Sockwell of Little Rock, Arkansas, if he had ever heard of Sweet Clover Dairy butter. Mr. Sockwell said, "Sure, they stock their products in all the local markets in my area. The wife buys the milk and cheese, too . . . why?"

"That company was started in my hometown."

"Really . . . Huh . . ."

"Yes, by a Swedish fellow named Nordstrom. My dad was good friends with him."

Ander and Beatrice had done so many things that had endeared them to the community. In 1949, they had started a college scholarship fund and had funded the building of the local hospital.

Ander had also put up the money to bail Tot Whooten's husband, James, out of jail on numerous occasions. When he brought him home for about the fifth time, Tot said, "Ander, thank you, but you ought to just let him sit in jail for a while. . . . He's just gonna do it again." And, of course, he did.

NORMA'S DAUGHTER, LINDA, WAS now attending Dixie Cahill's School of Tap and Twirl. Tot Whooten's daughter, Darlene, had been attending, but Dixie called Tot one day and told her that it was best that Darlene not come back. Dixie said, "Tot . . . Darlene is never going to make a dancer, and I hate to have you spend your hard-earned money on something that is never going to pay off."

IN OCTOBER OF 1963, when Mayor Ted Nordstrom passed away, there were more than two hundred people at his funeral. His sister, Ingrid, was at the graveside service, and it was good for Katrina to see her daughter again. Ted's passing was a great loss for the town, but his transition up to Still Meadows was an easy one. So many people couldn't wait to talk with him, and he felt the same way. The first day, he told his old teacher, "Just think, Miss Beemer, I was able to say hello to my mother and my son on the same day." There was something so comforting about that to Gene. Having his father join him at Still Meadows made him realize he would never be forgotten.

Later, Gene said to Ted, "Hey, Dad. I haven't seen Marion or Dena in a long time. Are they all right?"

"Oh, yes, son. They're fine. The only reason you haven't seen them is that Marion had to go back home for a while. I think somebody in her family was sick. Anyhow, she then went to New York and had a really nice high-paying job in some big fancy department store. I think it's called . . . oh, I forget . . . your mother knows. You wouldn't recognize Dena now. Marion just sent us a picture of her. She had her photograph in **Seventeen** magazine. A regular grown-up girl now."

Gene smiled at the thought of his daughter being a teenager now, busy running around doing teenage things, as he once had.

At the next Elmwood Springs City Council meeting, Glenn Warren was appointed the new mayor. He said, "Geez, fellows, I don't know. Being mayor is a big responsibility. Can't we have an election?"

"Now, Glenn," said Merle Wheeler, "you were Ted's best friend. You need to do this."

Trapped. He finally agreed.

When Glenn went home for lunch to tell his wife, Ola, he was surprised when she met him at the door with a great big "Hello, Mayor Warren."

"How did you know? It just happened."

She laughed. "Verbena Wheeler called me."

"Oh. She couldn't wait to get on the horn and spread the news, could she?"

"No."

It was true. A piece of information like that was like a piece of hot coal to Verbena Wheeler. She just had to get rid of it as fast as she could. By two o'clock that afternoon, everybody in town knew that Glenn Warren was now the mayor of Elmwood Springs.

Up at Still Meadows, nature was putting on a wonderful show. Just last week, a large hawk suddenly flew up out of a tree, and the bright moonlight turned his wings as white as snow as he sailed over the hill and down into the valley.

And when the big jet planes started flying over, they too became part of the big show. It was amazing how many planes they saw flying over at night; big planes, little planes, their red and white lights blinking in the dark night sky.

The first time one old Norwegian farmer saw a jet, he said to his grandson, "You mean to tell me there are real, live people riding in that thing?"

"Yes, sir. I've flown on a jet—went from St. Louis to New York on one."

"And did you feel like you were sitting in a bird?"

"Oh, no. No, it's too noisy for that. And the wings don't flap."

"How does it work?"

"Well . . . you get inside a tube that looks like a long, skinny bus. You find your seat and strap yourself in, and in a few minutes, they turn on these big loud engines. Then they drive down the runway as fast as they can, and before you know it, it lifts up off the ground, and you look down and see the ground way down below, and you are up in the clouds, on your way."

"Wowzer!" said a teenage boy who had passed away in 1923.

"Then a pretty girl brings you a bag of peanuts and a drink and before you know it, you're back down on the ground again, hundreds of miles away from where you started."

"How high do you go?"

"Oh . . . thousands of feet."

"Good Lord. Boy, what will those fools come up with next?"

Leaving Home

TODAY IT WAS JUST BEATRICE WHO CAME OUT TO the farm to visit Elner. And she was upset. Hanna Marie was getting ready to go off to a special college for the deaf in Boston. Beatrice said, "I'm so worried about her, Elner. She's never been away from home before. And Boston is so far away. I'm going to miss her so much."

Elner said, "I know it's hard, honey, and I know you'll miss her. We all will. But look on the bright side, Beatrice. If she has to go, at least you and Ander have the money to send her to the very best school. What if she had been born to a poor family?"

"I know, and I'm grateful. It's just that left to my own devices, I would just keep her home with me forever."

"When does she leave?"

Beatrice sighed. "In a few weeks. . . . And, oh, do I dread that day, but they say that she has to learn to become independent . . . and I know they are right. But I do worry. She's just so trusting and innocent about the ways of the world."

"Well, I think that's a good way to be."

"You think so?"

"I do," said Elner.

Beatrice smiled. "Oh, I know she'll probably do just fine, but it's not only the school that worries me; it's her future. What if she never marries? Ander and I are not young. What if something should happen to us? Who would take care of her?"

"Oh, Beatrice. Nothing is going to happen to you or Ander, my heavens."

"I know," she said. "But promise me, Elner, if anything does, you'll look after her . . . make sure she's all right?"

Elner patted Beatrice's hand. "That's not something you even need ask. You know I would. If anybody ever tried to harm that sweet angel, they wouldn't do it while I was alive and kicking. And don't forget, I'm a big, strong farm woman. Besides, there's not a person in this town that doesn't feel the same way."

September 2, 1965

Dearest Aunt Elner,

Hello from Boston! I'm so sorry I haven't written sooner, but it has been so hectic up here getting settled into the dorm, signing up for classes, etc. Hardly have a moment to myself. I thank you so much for the gift of fig preserves. It will make me think of you whenever I eat them. Aunt Elner, do keep an eye on Mother and Daddy for me, will you? They looked so sad when they left for home.

Please don't tell them, but I miss them both so terribly. Sometimes at night I cry myself to sleep. But I am learning so many new things—math for one. Ugh! But they are things I will need to know to help Daddy with his charities. Bye for now.

Love as always,
Hanna Marie

November 28, 1965

Dear Aunt Elner,

I hope you are well. I am doing so much better. Of course, I still miss home, but I must say there is something really nice about being with people who are just like me. I have made many new friends from all over. One girl is all the way from South America. She signs in Spanish! How hilarious! We are both learning to ice skate at the same time and it is so much fun. When I come home for Christmas, I will show you the photos I took of the snow up here. I am attending church for the deaf every Sunday, and next week in drama class, we are doing the Shakespeare play Romeo and Juliet. And yours truly is playing Juliet. But

please don't tell Mother and Daddy. If I
know them they will want to come and make
me even more nervous than I will be.

Love,
Hanna Marie

P.S. Guess what? Next semester, I will be
taking a class in ballroom dancing!

January 30, 1966

Dear Hanna Marie,

I got your last letter. And, honey, I don't
want you to worry any more about your
mother and daddy. Believe me, they are just
fine. I have talked them out of moving up to
Boston and taking a place near you. So you
just do your lessons, have fun, and leave old
Beatrice and Ander to me. You know me. I
have my wily ways. Norma sends her love,
and so do I. You better be careful up there in
all that snow that you don't catch triple p-
new-monnia . . . or however you spell it.

Aunt Elner

P.S. Is there such a thing as a Boston bean?
Is it different than a regular old bean? If so,
bring me one, will you?

February 18, 1966

Dearest Aunt Elner,

Thank you, thank you, a thousand times thank you! I love them both to pieces, but if they moved here, I know I would spend most of my time worrying whether they had things to do all day. When I get home this summer, I'm coming out to the farm and spending the night with you right away. I have soooo much to tell you. Love to Uncle Will and Norma, and Macky and Linda.

Love,
Me

Hello, Cooter

GENE NORDSTROM'S FRIEND COOTER CALVERT came into Still Meadows at a rather early age, due to prostate cancer.

He was happy to find that Gene was the same great guy, still full of enthusiasm, still interested in hearing all about what he had been up to. A lot had happened in the more than twenty years that Gene had been gone, and so the two of them had a lot of news to catch up on.

"After I got home, I married Thelma, and we have a daughter named Cathy. And, Gene, I started that newspaper, the one we always talked about."

Gene was elated to hear it. "Good for you, Cooter. Good man. Did it do well?"

"Oh, yeah. And Momma is out at Happy Acres Nursing Home now . . . and you know Macky and Norma have a little girl named Linda."

"Yeah, I knew that."

"Let's see . . . who else . . . Oh . . . and your aunt Elner is still going strong. Last I heard, she still had a bunch of cats."

Gene laughed. "That figures. And Aunt Ida?"

"Oh, Lord, what can I say? Ida is Ida." He laughed. "She writes a column for the newspaper now."

"You're kidding. What about?"

"Oh, you know. Just a lot of silly Garden Club stuff."

They spent the rest of the time with just small talk. Gene wanted to know how the football team was doing. Things like that.

Mostly they joked around and talked about all the fun, crazy things they used to do.

Cooter said, "Do you remember all the movies we went to?"

"Oh, yes . . . we must have spent hours in that place."

Cooter kept the conversation as light and as positive as he could. A lot of other things had happened in the world since Gene had been up at Still Meadows. He didn't tell Gene that boys were now burning their draft cards and refusing to serve in the military. How could you tell that to someone who died fighting for his country?

MEANWHILE, LESTER SHINGLE WAS still on the alert for news. He kept waiting for someone to come up to Still Meadows and tell him that they had finally caught his killer, but so far, nobody had. Nobody was even talking about his murder. And in such a small town, you'd have thought it would have been a huge topic of conversation. As time went on, he began to wonder. Was she going to get away with it? Had there been no witnesses to the crime? The bowling alley parking lot was empty that night. Had they checked for blood on all the bowling balls? Had they checked for fingerprints? Of course, with so many people using the same ball, it might have been difficult. But still, she must have slipped up somehow, somewhere. It just didn't seem right. A healthy young man cut down in his prime by a vengeful female, and nothing had been done.

A Special Boy

1967

HANNA MARIE SWENSEN HAD GROWN INTO A LOVELY young lady, slender with beautiful silky brown hair and big brown expressive eyes. She had a naturally sweet personality, had many friends, hearing and non-hearing alike, and was quite social. She had her mother's sense of style and was always dressed in the best clothes. Even so, at the beginning of her senior year, when she wrote to her parents and told them about a wonderful young man she had met, it had come as somewhat of a surprise. Beatrice knew she had made a lot of friends, but she had never before mentioned a special boy. And, of course, Beatrice was excited. But at this point, she didn't know if the young man was a deaf boy or not . . . or anything else really.

My Darling,

So happy to hear you are doing so well and still enjoying college life. Your friend Michael

sounds like a nice person. Not to be a prying mother, but is he a hearing person?

Not that it matters, just wondering. If you like, your father and I would be happy to have him come and visit sometime. Anyhow, sweetie, remember your mother and daddy love you and miss you so much.

Mother

Hanna Marie's father would have worded the letter somewhat differently. He would have said, "Bring this clown home, and let me get a good look at him." Luckily, Beatrice was the one who wrote the letters.

But men are different than women on the subject of their daughters. When Linda Warren had started dating boys, Macky hadn't liked any of them. As he told Norma, "No matter how polite they may seem, I was a boy myself, and I know what the little bastards are up to."

THE WHOLE TOWN'S TALKING

by Mrs. Ida Jenkins

This week, the whole town's talking about what a wonderful job our new mayor Glenn Warren is doing. He had some mighty big shoes to fill. Also, congratulations to the Elmwood Springs High School Mothers' Club. Their bake sale was a marvelous success. I shamelessly confess to buying two of Edna Childress's apple pies and going off my diet, but then, who can blame me? My question is, "How does her husband, Ralph, manage to remain so thin?" Oh, well, it was all for a good cause. I know we will all be happy to have that much-needed tuba replaced. Bandleader Ernest Koonitz said the old one had had it!

By the way, a common problem this time of year is wondering what to take to the cemetery. On Mother's Day, we all know that roses are always a lovely idea. Also, a flowering gardenia is always in style for a mother or grandmother, but here is a question I am often asked: "Ida, what is considered proper for Dad or Granddad on his special day?" I say one can never go wrong with a small potted plant, something that says "I love you," that isn't too feminine. There are many delightful choices. Next time you are stumped, consider a small potted geranium, begonia, or ivy. Also delightful is a multicolored or red or green pepper plant for your male loved ones. Aren't we lucky nature provides us with so many choices?

By the way, has anyone noticed that the tulips the Garden Club planted by the fountain in the park are starting to bloom? Oh, my, take a stroll, and you will think you are in Holland.

Beauty is important, and its cost is so little.

Flowers are nature's way of saying "Cheer up, it's spring!"

_____

The Young Man

HANNA MARIE BROUGHT MICHAEL JAMES VINCENT home to Elmwood Springs to meet her parents, and everyone was charmed by him. A few days later, Beatrice and Ander gave a big house party so Hanna Marie's friends could meet him.

That evening, Ander and Beatrice were sitting in the parlor, watching the young people having a good time, when Beatrice turned to her husband. "Oh, Ander. I'm so happy. He seems like such a nice boy. Don't you think?"

Ander glanced at the boy standing in the other room. "Maybe, but just the same, I think we need to have him checked out."

Beatrice frowned. "What do you mean, 'have him checked out'?"

"Just make a couple of phone calls. We don't know that much about him or what kind of family he comes from."

"Ander Swensen, don't you dare do anything like that. I don't care where he comes from. Hanna Marie loves that boy, and if she ever found out you did such a thing, she would never forgive you . . . and neither would I!"

Ander stared up at the ceiling. Beatrice knew that look. "And, Ander, if you think you can go behind my back and do it anyway, you know I'll find out sooner or later."

Ander sighed and thought, "God, it's hell to be married to someone who knows exactly what you are thinking. Dammit." She was right, of course. She would find out one way or another. The woman was uncanny. Just last week, he'd eaten two Hershey bars on his way home from the office, thinking she would never know, and darned if she didn't find the wrappers in the glove compartment the next day.

The boy seemed all right, but nevertheless, he was glad Lordor had him put that clause in his will. It made him feel good knowing that even after he was gone, nobody would ever be able to take the dairy away from his daughter. He still missed Lordor. More and more, he realized that Lordor was the wisest man he'd ever known.

THAT CHRISTMAS, AS ALMOST an answer to Beatrice's prayers, the young man had proposed, and he and Hanna Marie were to be married in the spring. Elner was the first person Beatrice ran to call, almost beside herself with the good news. "Elner, our girl is engaged!" Everyone in town was so happy for Hanna Marie. The young man was so handsome, with curly black hair and blue eyes, and he was obviously crazy about her. He was a hearing person, but he had learned sign language just for her.

Cinderella and Her
Prince Charming

THE WEDDING WAS THE BIGGEST SOCIAL EVENT
ever held in Elmwood Springs. Hanna Marie had
been the ring bearer at Norma's wedding, and now
Norma was pleased to have been asked to serve as
her matron of honor. Hanna Marie's former sign-
language teacher came to sign the marriage vows to
her as the minister spoke to them. When both the
bride and groom looked at each other and signed, "I
do," there wasn't a dry eye in the church.

At the reception, the couple danced the first dance,
and he was so tender with her. Elner Shimfissle was
sitting with Beatrice and Ander at the bride's table
when Beatrice said, "My poor darling, she can't even
hear the music at her own wedding."

Elner said, "Oh, but look how happy she is. I don't
think I've ever seen a happier bride."

Ander beamed. "You're right, Elner. And that's all
that matters. I want my girl to be happy."

As Ida then reported in her column, "The wedding was like the perfect ending of a fairy tale, where

the princess marries her Prince Charming and they live happily ever after."

RIGHT AFTER THEY WERE MARRIED, and thanks to a generous gift from his new father-in-law, Michael and Hanna Marie sailed to Europe for an extended honeymoon trip. When he purchased the tickets, Ander had thought it was a swell idea for a family trip, but when he told Beatrice, she had not agreed.

"No, Ander, we cannot go on their honeymoon with them."

"Why not? We'd all have our own rooms."

Beatrice had compromised with Ander and agreed that they could at least go as far as New York to see them off. That day, as the large ship's horns blew, preparing to sail, Ander and Beatrice stood on the dock covered with confetti, waving goodbye, and, as usual, it was Ander who became emotional.

ON THE THIRD NIGHT out at sea, in the grand dining room, a wealthy widow and a five-time divorcée who'd made the crossing many times before sat at their usual table observing the view and listening to the orchestra. When she noticed Michael and Hanna Marie, the widow asked her friend, who knew everything about everybody, "Who's that lovely young couple on the dance floor? I've not seen them before."

"No," said her friend. "Me neither. Their name is

Vincent. Word has it that her daddy owns a big dairy somewhere in the Middle West."

"Ahh . . . And who is he?"

"Just her husband is all I know, but someone overheard him telling the purser that his wife is completely deaf and to please address everything to him."

"Oh, no. And such a beautiful girl."

"And evidently such a rich girl," said her friend. She watched for a moment, then said, "Wait a minute, Claudia. How can she dance like that if she's deaf?"

"I don't know. He leads and she follows, I guess. Look at her. She's so graceful, so slender, so stylish. They may be from the Midwest, but that dress definitely is not."

"No, definitely not. Look at the way she looks at him—like he just hung the moon."

The divorcée took another spoonful of her parfait. "She'll get over that in a hurry, trust me. You never know a man until you live with one, and I should know."

Just then a singer in a tuxedo stepped up to the microphone and sang:

"Are the stars out tonight
I don't know if it's cloudy or bright
'cause I only have eyes for you, dear."

TOO BAD ABOUT HANNA Marie's Prince Charming. Had Ander Swensen followed his instincts and made just a few strategic inquiries, he would have found out that Michael Vincent had indeed been raised in Lake Forest, Illinois, and had attended Northwestern University. But the man his daughter had just married wasn't **that** Michael Vincent. In fact, "Michael Vincent" wasn't even his real name. He had picked the name out of a yearbook.

THE WHOLE TOWN'S TALKING

by Mrs. Ida Jenkins

This week, same as last week, the whole town's talking about the big plan to build an indoor shopping center across the highway from the nursing home. The rumor mill has it that several of our downtown businesses have already started making plans to relocate to this new "mall." So many changes are taking place.

And as Elmwood Acres, the new trailer park, is now completed, many worry that it will attract tornadoes to our area. Husband Herbert tells me this belief is just an old wives' tale. I hope he is right. My question is, "Why can't things stay the way they are?" I like our town just the way it is. Husband Herbert says progress is good for everyone, but sometimes I do wonder.

Oh, how we hate these long, cold winter days. Just a reminder, houseplants are such a lovely way to bring nature inside. A begonia, azalea, or hydrangea turns a dark room into a festival of color. And does anyone remember the lovely collection of blue glass violins with blooming ivy that Dorothy Smith displayed in all of her windows? Oh, dear, I must be getting nostalgic in my old age.

Is it my imagination or is time just flying by? It

seems only yesterday that my daughter, Norma, was a baby. Now she is a grown-up young woman with a daughter of her own.

By the way, on our recent trip for husband Herbert to see his heart specialist in Chicago, I was most impressed with the new stylish form-fitting navy-and-white outfits the stewardesses were wearing. **Très chic!**

Ida could not say so in her column, but she was not only concerned about the new trailer park attracting tornadoes to the area. She was also concerned about the certain class of people it had brought. One family in particular. She had seen the mother (who had three front teeth missing) beating the living daylights out of her five-year-old son named Luther. True, he had kicked her in the grocery store when she had tried to take his candy bar away from him, but the language she had used and the names she had called him were not the kinds of things usually heard in Elmwood Springs. Except maybe from Tot Whooten. But Tot's salty language had not been directed at a child. And her use of certain words could be understood and forgiven, under the circumstances.

Poor Tot. After she'd put up with her drunken husband for years, he had finally sobered up, only to run off a year later with a younger woman named Jackie Sue Potts. Tot was in such a rage over it that everyone's hair was a mess for months. She had given Verbena such a tight permanent, Verbena couldn't get a comb through it.

You Must Be Kidding

PEOPLE IN ELMWOOD SPRINGS HAD ALWAYS LOVED a good joke or a tall tale and told a lot of them, so they were always suspicious that someone was pulling their leg.

So in 1969, when Mr. Clayborn came up to Still Meadows and told them that an American named Neil Armstrong had just walked on the moon, almost nobody believed him.

"Sure, Willard, we may be dead, but we ain't stupid," said Old Man Hendersen.

"No, I'm telling you, it really happened. I saw it on television. And he even talked. He said, 'One small step for man, a giant leap for men.' Or was it 'mankind'? Something. But believe me, it's true. I'm not kidding. I swear."

"Oh, sure, Willard. And my grandmother has three heads."

Even though they suspected Willard was kidding with them, they all looked up at the moon that night and wondered if it could really be true that a man could get all the way up there and walk around.

—

A FEW WEEKS LATER, when Jack Look came in by way of a stroke, the first thing they asked him was, "Did a man really go to the moon?"

"Oh, yes, I saw it on television from the moon. Neil Armstrong."

"And he talked up there?"

"He did."

"I told you so, you bozos," said Willard.

When that unbelievable information turned out to be true, the old guys stopped even wondering what they would come up with next. After going to the moon, what else was left?

The Seventies

Saturday Night Fever

Vietnam

HUNDREDS OF BODY BAGS WERE BEING STACKED IN the back of trucks, ready to be shipped home. It was another sweltering day, and some of the soldiers on duty were stoned, and the others making out the tags might as well have been, they were so tired. They had been there far too long, and mistakes were being made.

As usual, Lucille Beemer greeted the newcomer. "Welcome to Still Meadows. I'm Lucille Beemer. What is your name, dear?"

The boy seemed confused. "Uh, Jackson. C.J. Where did you say I was?"

"Still Meadows. Still Meadows Cemetery."

"Am I in New Jersey?"

"No, you are in Missouri."

"You're kidding . . ."

"No."

"Well, I'm not supposed to be. I'm in the wrong damn state. I'm from Elmwood Hills, New Jersey."

"Oh, dear. Well, honey, I just don't know what to

say. But if it makes you feel any better, we are honored that you are here."

Rusty Hagood, another recent arrival, over in plot 431, realized what must have happened and jumped in. "Hi, buddy. I just got back from Nam myself. What happened? Where did you get it?"

"Phnom Penh," said C.J. They had a long chat, and Rusty introduced him around to all the other vets, including Gene Nordstrom.

Later, C.J. was exhausted from talking to so many people and settled down for a nap. Before he went to sleep, he thought about his odd predicament. Oh, well. He hadn't much liked New Jersey—at least not the part he came from. The only relative he had there was an older half sister, and she never liked him much, so he guessed it was all right. These people seemed nice. He figured he might just as well hang out here as any other place. He had always wanted to go to the Midwest. An army nurse from Iowa had been mighty nice to him once. Mighty nice. So what the heck?

Ida Jenkins

1971

THE NEXT ARRIVAL AT STILL MEADOWS DIDN'T wait to be greeted; she just jumped right in. "Hello, everyone. It's Ida Jenkins. I'm here far too early, but that's another story. I just wanted to say that now that I am here, feel free to ask me about our latest project."

"What's she talking about?" asked Bertha Gumms. "What project?"

Mrs. Bell said, "Oh, she was the president of the Garden Club. I guess it's a Garden Club thing."

"I don't even know who she is."

"Well, just be glad you didn't have to deal with her. She ruled that club with an iron thumb, and if she wasn't happy with the way your yard looked, she was known to come to your house and clip your hedges."

"No."

"Oh, yes," said Mrs. Bell. "One time, when I was out of town, she had four of my camellia bushes dug up and replanted where she thought they would look better."

"Did they?"

"Yes, but the point is she didn't ask."

"Ah."

Ida called out, "Is that Mrs. Bell over there?"

"Yes, it is. Hello, Ida."

"Hello, dear . . . I just want you to know that your camellias are holding up very nicely. I had a little talk with your husband's new wife . . . your friend, what's her name? She was not watering properly, but I straightened her out."

"Onzelle Deasen?"

"Yes. Anyhow, your husband is holding up very nicely as well, although, I must say, everyone was just a teeny-tiny bit surprised when Lloyd remarried so soon after you died, but alas . . . you know men. I'm just glad my Herbert went first. I would hate to be in your shoes, having another woman move into my house so soon. Weren't you surprised? Mrs. Bell?"

"I didn't know he **had** remarried, Ida."

"Oh, well . . . good to catch up with you, dear."

After a few moments, Ida's husband, Herbert, who had come up earlier that year, said, "Ida, don't you ever think before you speak? Now you've upset Mrs. Bell."

"Well, I don't know why she would be upset. It's not like he married a **stranger** or anything."

It was true. The woman Mr. Bell had married had not been a stranger. However, when he passed away a few years later and arrived at Still Meadows, he received a very chilly reception from the first Mrs. Bell. He didn't think he would ever see her again, much less have her find out about his second marriage. Oops. And he had bought the plot on the other side of him for Onzelle. This spelled big trouble. When she died, he was going to be stuck in between both wives for eternity. Lord, help him.

LATER THAT NIGHT, Ida said to her husband, "Herbert, you know I'm glad to be with you again, dear, but I am quite worried."

"Ah, about Norma?"

"No. My column. Now that I'm gone, how will people find out the news?"

She needn't have worried. Cooter Calvert's daughter, Cathy, who now ran **The Elmwood Springs News,** had taken over the column, writing under the byline "Chatty Cathy."

Elner Moves to Town

1972

AS AN ONLY CHILD, IT HAD BEEN HARD FOR NORMA to lose both parents. First her father, and now, only a year later, her mother had suddenly succumbed to a rare case of leukemia. She missed her mother very much, even though she had driven her crazy when she was alive.

Now she was just tired. She had been left with the daunting task of having to sell her parents' old house and clear out all four of her mother's storage bins. It had taken forever. Why anyone would want nineteen sets of dishes and seventy-six bird figurines was beyond her.

After her uncle Will Shimfissle passed away, Norma more or less insisted that Aunt Elner sell the farm and move into town. Ida had hidden the family Bible, so nobody really knew how old Elner was, but she was far too old to be living alone. Norma wanted her to move closer to her, so she could keep an eye on her. Aunt Elner finally agreed. "All right, honey, if it will make you feel better."

Elner sold the farm to a friend, but she kept some

of her old furniture, one old orange cat, and a few of her favorite chickens. And Norma **so** wished she hadn't. Nobody in town kept chickens anymore, and she was afraid there might be complaints.

Norma had wanted Elner to buy one of the brick townhomes on the new side of town, closer to the new mall. But Elner bought the Warrens' old house in the older part of town, with a fig tree in the side yard. She said, "I couldn't be happy if I didn't have a front porch to sit on and a nice backyard for my chickens."

As it turned out, her neighbors were not bothered by the chickens at all. In fact, they got a kick out of hearing Elner sing to them. This morning, she had treated them to a rousing rendition of "When You and I Were Young, Maggie," and everyone enjoyed it. Despite their recent move to town, her chickens just kept on laying eggs in remarkable numbers. And thanks to Elner, not one of her neighbors ever had to buy eggs (or fig preserves) again.

It meant a longer ride to Elner's house for Norma, but one of the nice things about Elner moving to the older part of town was that she already knew her neighbors. Merle and Verbena Wheeler, who owned the Blue Ribbon Dry Cleaners, now lived directly across the street from her. And to the right of her was Ruby Robinson, a retired registered nurse, and her husband, John. Tot Whooten and her ninety-two-year-old mother lived on the other side. And they were all quite social. Their houses backed up to a large open cornfield, and when the weather was warm, they would bring their plastic chairs and sit in Elner's yard and watch the sunset together and drink iced tea, or a beer, if you wanted.

They didn't need a NEIGHBORHOOD WATCH sign. Between the fact that Verbena was nosy and that they all kept an eye out for one another, a burglar wouldn't stand a chance in hell on that street. Consequently, Elner never locked her doors, a fact that made Norma somewhat concerned. But Elner said, "Honey, a burglar would be doing me a favor; I have too much stuff as it is." It was true. Her house was a mess, and, of course, she never kept it as clean as Norma would have liked.

One day, shortly after Elner moved in, Norma noticed a large Maxwell House coffee can full of dirt sitting in the middle of Elner's kitchen table. "Aunt Elner, what is this? Did a plant die?"

Aunt Elner laughed. "No, those are my worms. I brought them with me. They're my pets, but they don't know it . . . and they're the cutest things. Every once in a while, one will stick its little head up and wiggle it all around. Oh, they just tickle me to death."

"You have pet worms?"

"Yes, and they're so easy to keep . . . give them some bread crumbs and throw in a few coffee grounds once in a while, and they are happy. Oh, honey, speaking of that . . . guess what I have for you? I found it just this morning in my yard."

"It's not a snail or a worm, is it?"

"No, it's a four-leaf clover. I said to Merle, I said, 'I'm giving that to Norma.' I have it in the icebox."

Norma sat at the table, staring at the can. "Aunt Elner, do those worms ever crawl out?"

"A few times, but I just pick them up and put them back."

"Aren't you worried about germs?"

"Oh, no. The table's clean."

Driving home, all Norma could do was thank God her mother hadn't lived to see it. If Ida knew that her sister had a can of worms sitting out on her kitchen table, she would have been mortified. Norma had been only mildly horrified. But then, Norma was a clean freak. If you were visiting Norma and lit a cigarette, she emptied your ashtray before you finished it. She tried her best not to. She tried not to look; but she couldn't help it. One day, she asked her daughter, "Linda, do you think I have obsessive-compulsive disorder?"

"Oh, I don't know, Mother. Doesn't **everybody** clean their venetian blinds with a Q-tip twice a day? Duh!"

Norma sighed. "Well, it's your grandmother's fault. If my room wasn't just perfect, she would say, 'Do you want people to think you were raised in a pigsty? Only common people live in a dirty home, Norma!'"

Norma had read up on this need for perfection in a **Psychology Today** magazine. Her mother was clearly "shame-based," and had passed it down to her.

She knew exactly where her behavior came from and how silly it was, but, on the other hand, if she didn't clean those blinds, who would? She wasn't drinking or taking drugs or robbing banks; she just had a thing for Clorox.

And at least she could laugh about it . . . sometimes. . . . Well, once in a while . . . maybe. But really, she didn't see a thing funny about a dirty house. Besides, cleaning gave her something to do. She didn't understand why Linda and Macky made such a big deal out of it. Other people had hobbies; hers was cleaning. What's so terrible about that? And why were there fingerprints all over her refrigerator door? As she was wiping the handle for the fourth time that day, it occurred to her she probably did need psychological help, but then, who didn't? Everybody had their little quirks. Aunt Elner had pet worms. Of course, Macky had thought it was the funniest thing he'd ever heard. But Aunt Elner could do no wrong, as far as he was concerned. He just loved her to death. Every morning before he went to work, he stopped by her house and had coffee with her. What the two of them found to talk about was a mystery to Norma, but Aunt Elner was always calling the house night and day, wanting to talk to Macky. And she had no concept of time. Sometimes she would call as early as five-thirty A.M. wanting to ask him something or tell him some stupid joke she'd heard.

Just this morning when she had called at the crack of dawn, Macky had picked up the phone and said,

"I don't know, Aunt Elner. Why did the armadillo cross the road?" Then he laughed and hung up the phone. Of course, Macky could go right back to sleep but she was up for the entire day.

And she didn't care why the armadillo crossed the road.

The Anniversary

1974

MICHAEL J. VINCENT WAS IN CHICAGO FOR A BUSI-
ness meeting with the advertising company that handled his father-in-law's dairy. He was going back to
Elmwood Springs that afternoon, but before he left
town, he had to buy the wife something. Tomorrow was their sixth wedding anniversary, and the old
man would be watching him like a hawk.

Before he married Hanna Marie, he had assumed
her father would build them a home of their own.
But the old man had more or less blackmailed him
into moving into the big house with them. "It will be
yours someday, and her mother and I can spend what
time we have left with our daughter." So now Michael was just biding his time, playing the game, and
waiting. Hanna Marie and the mother were easy.
Pleasing the old man was getting harder and harder.

He walked into the store, brushed the snow off his
shoulders, stopped by a jewelry counter, and motioned to a pretty salesgirl. "Hey, honey, come here.
Pick something out from this group of stuff and wrap
it up."

The saleslady was confused. "But, sir, don't you have a preference? Would you prefer rubies or emeralds or . . . ?"

"It doesn't matter; just pick something. I'll come back and get it. Where are the cuff links?"

"Two counters over."

It really didn't matter what he bought the woman. She mostly stayed alone in her room all day, doing her charity work and fooling with those damn cats the Shimfissle woman had given her. She didn't need anything. He was the one who needed things.

He and Hanna Marie had been born the same year. Her father had given her anything she wanted. He'd been raised across town on the south side of Chicago in a filthy one-bedroom tenement cold-water flat, the sixth of eight screaming and yelling brothers and sisters. The only thing he'd ever received from his father was a smack across the mouth and a kick out the door when he was fifteen. The day he left, he'd vowed two things: One, he'd never have kids, and two, he would never set foot in that apartment again, and he hadn't. A few years earlier, he had driven by the back of the building, looked up at the gray, rickety wooden stairs, and wondered if any of the family was still alive. He hoped not. If they knew he had money, they'd try to get some of it, and that was not going to happen. He'd worked too hard for it.

He had started working at age thirteen, being a lookout for the guys running numbers, making pretty good money, but it wasn't enough. It seemed to him that he had been born with his face pressed to windows, looking inside at how the other half lived. His one burning ambition had always been to get on the other side of one of those windows. And he was determined to do it any way he could. Lie, cheat, steal . . . or even marry a rich girl.

Michael didn't like going back to Chicago. He'd had a bit of a sketchy history there. He'd gotten a job at an advertising agency and was doing well. So when the girl in the office had told him she was pregnant, it had irritated the hell out of him. Then she started making noises about marriage. She was just some secretary. He made a plan to meet her at a little restaurant close to where they worked so they could talk it over.

Two hours later, the girl was sitting alone, looking at a piece of paper with a name and address on it. The address was in a part of town she had never been, and the room was in the back of a discount luggage store. When the girl knocked on the door, a little fat man opened it to see a pretty young blonde standing there, shaking with fear over what was about to happen. She looked very much like the last girl that Sardino guy had sent.

That night around seven-thirty, Hershie Abrams was sweating. He'd been working hard for the last couple of hours. He finally dialed Sardino's number and whispered in the phone, "It's me. . . . She didn't make it."

"What?"

"She's dead. I don't know what happened. I couldn't stop it—"

"Who's dead? Who are you talking about?"

"The girl . . . the girl you sent. She bled out. You've gotta come over and get her out of here."

"I don't know what you are talking about. I didn't send you any girl."

"The blond girl. She said you sent her."

"I don't know any blond girl."

Now sweat was pouring down Abrams's face. "You've gotta help me. The girl is dead."

"Like I said, I don't know any girl."

"What am I gonna do?"

"I don't know, Hershie. I guess you could always call the police," he said. And then he hung up.

Hershie was stunned. He had dealt with a lot of cold-hearted bastards in his day, but this one was scary. Sardino had turned on him in a matter of seconds.

Anthony Sardino was sure there was no way he would be implicated in it, but he decided it was best if he moved on anyway. Stupid women. He decided not to fool with them anymore, unless it could do him some good.

Boston, Massachusetts

1967

ANTHONY PATRICK SARDINO, WHO NOW CALLED himself Michael James Vincent, was half Irish, half Italian, and 100 percent son of a bitch. But he was handsome, and he had charm and drive. He was now living in Boston and working at an advertising firm there.

He'd studied preppy boys—how they walked, how they dressed. It wasn't so hard. He knew how to work people. And today he had wangled his way into a fraternity party where he had a friend. He liked college girls. He was standing looking around the room when he spotted her. He turned to someone and asked who the deaf girl was. The boy glanced over. "Oh, that's the Swensen girl. Her father owns a huge dairy farm somewhere in the Midwest. Missouri, I think."

He knew a little about cows. His father and uncles had worked in the Chicago stockyards. It was a dirty, smelly, filthy job that he would never do. But he wouldn't mind owning a nice, big, clean dairy farm. He looked again. The girl was not bad looking at all.

Kind of pretty really, in a wide-eyed innocent sort of way. So what if she was deaf? It might be nice to be married to a woman who didn't talk. He nodded and smiled at her from across the room. He could see she was shy. She had even blushed. No, the girl was not bad looking at all. He put down his beer and walked over to her.

Mother's Day

Up at Still Meadows, everyone was in a good mood. Spring was always a favorite time of year. First came Easter, which meant lots of visitors, and usually by noon, the entire hill was filled with baskets of Easter lilies.

Now it was Mother's Day. And even if you weren't a mother, everybody there had a mother, and they were thinking about her today. Ted Nordstrom was able to wish his mother Happy Mother's Day in person.

Katrina said, "I'm so happy to have my son with me. This is the best Mother's Day I could have wished for."

That morning, Macky and Norma drove over and picked up Aunt Elner to take her to the cemetery. Aunt Elner had brought roses for her mother as she had for the past sixty-something years. Macky and Norma both brought roses for their mothers, as well.

That night, the fragrance of roses covered the entire hill. Before she went to sleep, Ida said, "Isn't it nice to be remembered?"

"Oh, yes," answered Katrina. "And you were so lucky to have such a sweet daughter."

Ida smiled. "Yes, she was always a sweet girl. Nervous, but sweet."

AT TOT WHOOTEN'S HOUSE, Mother's Day had come and gone without much notice. It had never been a particularly happy day for her. Tot's daughter, Darlene, had worked in the beauty shop with Tot for a while, until she'd dyed the preacher's wife's hair bright orange. Darlene couldn't read a label if it killed her. And then she left a lit cigarette on the shelf with the end papers and set fire to the back room. She was a liability, and Tot'd had to let her go. And then Darlene had the nerve to demand a month's severance pay. From her own mother.

Neither Darlene nor her brother, Dwayne Jr., finished high school. It had been so discouraging when Tot would see cars with bumper stickers that read MY CHILD IS AN HONOR STUDENT AT ELMWOOD HIGH. Her children had been mostly high at Elmwood High. But she guessed it was to be expected. She and their father had not set good examples for them. Looking back now (too late), she would have left James much earlier and not subjected them to seeing all those terrible fights. And she really shouldn't have broken the phone over James's head. The doctor said that if he hadn't been so drunk, it would have killed him. But then there were a lot of things she would have done differently.

First of all, she wouldn't have been born who she was and where she was. She had just read an article claiming that you picked out the parents you needed, to learn what life lessons you had to learn in this life, but she didn't believe it for a minute. If that were true, who in their right mind would pick a drunk father and an insane mother? Her father had been so drunk at her wedding he'd passed out in the vestibule, and she'd had to walk down the aisle by herself, and when the minister asked, "Who giveth this woman?" nobody answered. Her mother had gone around the bend a few years after that. Early dementia, they said, but Tot figured she'd just checked out on purpose, and who could blame her? But still, it was no fun to have to take care of her, a poor old lady who kept wandering off.

The last time it happened, they'd been at the mall. Tot had turned her back for five seconds, and her mother had disappeared into thin air. When she told Grady, the security guard, she had lost her mother, he had said, "Oh, Tot, I'm so sorry, when did she die?" She had to tell him that she wasn't dead—she had really lost her mother somewhere in the mall. Two hours later, and after a long search, she finally showed up. She had wandered into the movie theater, taken a seat, and watched the movie to the end.

After that, Tot put a tag on her that read, "If found, please return to Mrs. Tot Whooten at the beauty shop."

Poor Tot was part of the sandwich generation, long before it had been named that. She had been caught between her kids and her mother. She knew people felt sorry for her, and she also knew a lot of her customers were loyal because of it. She didn't want to be a victim, but she needed the money. Between caring for her mother and the kids, she had never been able to save a dime. At night, when everyone was asleep, she sat in the living room in the dark, smoked cigarettes, and dreamed of being single and childless.

A Final Sale

AFTER IDA JENKINS PASSED AWAY, THE GARDEN
Club sort of disbanded, which was not good news for
Still Meadows. For a while, Norma and her friends
volunteered one day a month to do cleanup, but,
eventually, a lot of people moved away or dropped
out, and people wound up just tending their own
families' graves.

When the local bank closed down, Arvis Oberg,
who owned the Rest Assured Funeral Home, had
been put in charge of the Still Meadows corpora-
tion account, and after twelve years, was tired of
fooling with it. It was a lot of paperwork, and most
of his customers were now going to the new cemetery. He talked it over with his wife, and they decided to just sell off the remaining plots and be done
with it.

When Cathy Calvert came into the newspaper office the next morning, she read the ad Arvis wanted
to run in the Friday edition.

WHERE WILL YOU SPEND ETERNITY?

Wondering what to get Dad on Father's Day?
Mom on her special day?
Stuck with what to buy the spouse for that an-
niversary?
Diamonds are forever, but a burial plot is for
eternity.
Last call for the cemetery plots at Still Mead-
ows.
Hurry . . . Hurry . . . Hurry . . . only 54 left!
This week only, we are offering a his-and-hers
two-for-one sale.
Call or stop by Rest Assured Funeral Home
today!

Cathy did not agree with Arvis's assumption that a cemetery plot would make a good gift, but Arvis was one of her regular advertisers, so what could she do?

Another Anniversary

NORMA AND MACKY WERE COMING UP ON THEIR twenty-fourth wedding anniversary, and Macky was so hard to buy a present for. Most women got something for their husbands at the hardware store, but when your husband owns it, it's a problem. So she wound up buying him a pair of pajamas with fishing lures on them from Sears.

Macky had a similar problem. He never knew what to get Norma, and the date was getting closer and closer, so when he saw the ad in the paper about the cemetery plots on sale out at Still Meadows, it was like an answer to his prayers. He ran over early the next day and was glad he did. He got the last "two-for-one plots" left. Arvis said there had been a run on plots all morning. He said since the minute he opened his office door, plots had been selling like hotcakes.

Norma was still in her housecoat when Aunt Elner called. "Happy anniversary," she said.

"Oh, thank you, Aunt Elner."

"What are you two lovebirds doing to celebrate? Are you going out to eat?"

Norma sighed. "I suppose so."

"Where?"

"I don't know. He said he was going to surprise me."

"What's the matter, honey? You don't sound happy."

"Well . . . I guess I'm not. You won't believe what Macky gave me for our anniversary."

"What?"

"Are you sitting down? A his-and-hers burial plot out at Still Meadows. I said, 'Macky, a burial plot is not exactly romantic.'"

"Awww, I think it was real thoughtful of him."

"Maybe so, but I would rather have had something I can use now. What fun is a burial plot? I won't even be alive to enjoy it."

Aunt Elner laughed.

"You can laugh, but I don't think there is a thing **funny** about death."

"Oh, honey, you mustn't lose your sense of humor. Death is just a part of life."

"It's a serious and horrible part of life, and I hate it."

"Yes, it's serious. Losing our loved ones is the hardest thing we humans will ever have to go through. I think that's why the good Lord gave us a sense of humor. Because if we didn't have that, we would surely all die of grief, don't you think?"

"Well, maybe, but . . . I can't help it. Just thinking about it gives me the willies."

"Well, sweetheart, we're all gonna die one day."

"Yes, but I don't want to. And I don't want to have to think about me or Macky dying, especially on my anniversary."

"Very few people do, but, nevertheless, it's gonna happen, and as for me, I'm ready to go whenever He sees fit."

"Aunt Elner . . . I swear. If you die, after what I went through losing Mother and Daddy, I'll never forgive you. I'll even have Tot Whooten do your hair."

Aunt Elner laughed. "Ohhh, then I'd better hang on. I don't want to wind up looking like Ida." Norma had to laugh in spite of herself.

"Oh, my God, Aunt Elner, will you ever forget how Tot fixed Mother's hair—all poufed up on one side?"

"It's a good thing Ida was dead or else she would have killed both of us."

"Poor Tot. And she thought Mother looked so pretty, too. All through the viewing, I was just horrified. The look on people's faces . . ."

"I know. I was there. But bless her heart. Tot has good points. Unfortunately, doing hair is not one of them."

Norma then screamed with laughter.

"Well, you know it's true."

"Oh, God . . . let's just pray she retires before we die, or we'll wind up with a pouf."

After she hung up, Norma wiped her eyes with a

napkin, and she did feel better. Aunt Elner was right. Macky buying her a burial plot for her anniversary was sweet, and the more she thought about it . . . well, it was pretty funny. Some women get rubies and pearls. **She** got a plot.

Run for Your Life!

1975

IT WAS TWELVE NOON, THE DAY AFTER EASTER, when everyone heard the siren go off. A few minutes later, the clear blue April sky suddenly turned an ugly, sick-looking dark green, and the wind picked up and began whipping around in circles. Merle Wheeler saw the gray spinning cone first and yelled, "Tornado!" Soon they all heard the loud roar as it got closer, twisting and twirling right through town, spewing roof shingles, chicken coops, and lawn chairs in the air, then passed right overhead, taking baskets of Easter lilies and broken parts of the old wooden archway up at the cemetery along with it. An eerie silence followed, then came the sound of fire trucks and news helicopters.

Everybody up at Still Meadows waited, worrying about their friends and family members in town. By the horrible sound of it, they were sure that many people would be coming up in a few days, due to the tornado. Will Shimfissle was especially concerned about his wife, Elner. "God, I hope she reached the cellar." Thankfully, her neighbor Verbena had warned her in time, and she had made it to her cellar along with her cat and a baby squirrel she had in a shoebox.

AFTER A FEW WEEKS, when not one person came in, they were all relieved. Gene said, "I guess nobody was killed. That's good."

He was right. But the tornado had taken down the old wooden water tower and had completely leveled the entire Elmwood Estates Trailer Park. There was nothing left of it now but a vacant lot full of broken and scattered butane tanks and thirty-four cement slabs where mobile homes had once stood.

Many people in town immediately volunteered to take in families rendered homeless by the event. A kind and generous neighborly gesture to be sure, but everyone who signed up made one stipulation. "We will be happy to do it, as long as it isn't the Griggs family."

The parents were one thing, but it was the son they were really leery about. Eleven-year-old Luther Griggs was a hellion on his way to being a fully fledged juvenile delinquent. He had tried to burn the school down twice.

By the following week, all of the families had temporary homes. But only one displaced family remained. Luther's parents decided to go back to West Virginia, but they thought it was best to leave Luther behind to finish out the school year.

"I ain't gonna live with some old lady," he said as

he was being dragged up Elner Shimfissle's front stairs with a paper bag of donated clothes. A frustrated Merle Wheeler, who was in charge of the Placement Committee, said, "Well, Luther, that's too bad, but she's the only one who will take you, so shut up."

Elner was at the front door to greet him. "Well, hey, little Luther. Come on in and welcome."

Luther did not move, so Merle pushed him through the door and said, "Good luck, Elner," and left in a hurry.

Once inside the house, Luther glared at her. "I ain't gonna stay."

"Well, that's fine, honey. But before you take off, let me fix you a little something to eat and maybe wash those clothes for you."

"Well . . . but I ain't gonna stay. And you can't make me."

"I'm sure not."

He looked around. "This is a stupid old house anyway . . . and you're old and ugly." After he said it, he flinched, waiting to be hit, but Elner just agreed with him.

"Yeah, it is pretty stupid. And I am pretty ugly at that," she said, looking in the mirror. "Oh, well. Come on, let me show you what I've got in the kitchen. I've got bacon, hot biscuits, and honey . . . and do you like strawberry ice cream? We can have some of that before you leave, if you want."

He stood there and then, after a moment, followed her to the back of the house.

When Norma heard that Elner had taken in Luther Griggs, she called Elner, almost hysterical. "Oh, my God, Aunt Elner. Why did you let Merle Wheeler talk you into doing such a stupid thing? You should have called me first."

Elner knew Norma and so she had been expecting the call. She said, "I know, but Norma, somebody had to take him in. Besides, it's just for a little while."

"Well, don't be surprised if he burns your house down . . . or murders you in your bed." Norma put the phone down and was still upset. "Good Lord." She was worried enough as it was, with Linda being off at that big college so far away from home, and now this. How could she possibly relax? Her Aunt Elner was in danger of life and limb.

The next day, Mayor Smith came over to Elner's house carrying a box. He said, "Elner, I found this old box of Bobby's things in the closet and thought maybe Luther might get some use out of it."

After Robert left, Luther looked inside the box in the living room and quickly grabbed the metal toy car that had once belonged to Gene Nordstrom, ran to his room with it, and locked the door. It turned out the boy loved anything with wheels.

Four weeks later, when the school year was almost up, Elner and Luther were having breakfast, and

Elner said, "I know you must be missing your parents something awful about right now."

He looked up at her between bites of buttermilk pancakes dripping with maple syrup. "No, I'm not."

"Aren't you getting anxious to see them again, honey?"

"Nope. They didn't never care a thing in the world about me. I'd just as soon stay with you."

"Oh, sweetheart, I'm sure that's not true."

In this case, it was true. He had been unwanted and had been told so many times by his mother. "If it weren't for you, me and your daddy wouldn't have to stay in this rotten town. We could be living in Las Vegas or somewhere where we could have a little fun."

When Elner called Luther's parents and asked if it would be all right to keep Luther a little while longer, his father had said, "Hell, yes. You can keep him as long as you want to." And so she did.

In August, when Hazel Goodnight arrived at Still Meadows, everyone there was anxious to hear about the tornado. "Oh, it was awful," she said. "There was a lot of damage downtown—blew out a lot of windows. The hardware store and the Blue Ribbon Dry Cleaners both lost their signs. But at least they're still standing. The worst-hit area was out past 289. It took out the entire trailer park."

Ida Jenkins immediately said to her husband, "See?

Didn't I tell you? Didn't I say the minute we let it be built, it would attract a tornado? And it did!"

Old Henry Knott, who had died in 1919, asked, "What's a trailer park?"

"Oh, Daddy," answered Ida. "You don't even want to know. People are living in tin cans now."

"Why?"

"You tell me. The world has lost all the graciousness and charm that we knew growing up. I'm just so glad I was raised where I was, when I was." A curious sentiment coming from someone who grew up on a pig farm.

Something Was Bothering Ander

At first, Ander Swensen had been grateful that his son-in-law had agreed to move into the house with them. But now, having lived under the same roof with him for the past years, he wasn't so sure.

Ander was a successful businessman, and had dealt with a lot of people in his day, but he had never encountered anyone quite like Michael Vincent before. No matter what time of night or day, Michael always looked as if he had just stepped out of an Arrow shirt ad. Every hair slicked down, and perfectly cut. The shoes always shined to a high gloss. Everything he wore was crisp and pressed. He even smelled good. And, oh, how he could charm the ladies.

And tonight was no exception. When the family came into the dining room for dinner, Ander watched as Michael pulled Beatrice's chair back for her, did the same thing for Hanna Marie, and then seated himself between the two. And as usual he addressed his next sentence to Beatrice. "You're looking beautiful this evening, Mother. That brooch is very attractive. It brings out the blue in your eyes."

Beatrice fingered the jeweled horn of plenty pin she was wearing and said, "Why, thank you, Michael."

Ander could see that on the surface everything about Michael looked good, but something was bothering him, and he was not quite sure what it was. For some time now he had been torn between being pleased his daughter was still so happy with her husband and wanting to dump a plate of mashed potatoes on the guy's head. Something was not right. He didn't know if Michael was just a little too slick for for his taste or what it was, but every time Michael called him Dad it irritated the hell out of him.

Tonight, after Bridget had served the soup, Michael smiled and said, "Dad," taking Hanna Marie's hand in his and looking right at her. "If you don't mind, I'd like to take our two girls on a picnic this Sunday. Might I borrow the big car?"

Hanna Marie's big brown eyes lit up as she looked hopefully over at her father, waiting for his answer. Ander had already made other plans for the family that Sunday. He could turn down any offer in business he didn't like, but never Hanna Marie. She was still his baby, and anything she wanted she could have.

Later, after dessert, when the cook came back into the room, Michael said, "You can clear now. We'll take our coffee in the living room."

When Michael first started giving orders to the help, Ander didn't like it, but he'd let it pass. Tonight, though, when Bridget reached for his plate, Ander put his hand up and said, "No, not yet, Bridget. I'm not finished."

Michael quickly said, "Oh I'm sorry, Dad, I thought you were."

Ander looked at him and in a tone that almost sounded like a warning said, "No, not yet, Michael. Not quite yet."

Being deaf, Hanna Marie could not hear the slight change in her father's voice, but she knew something had just happened. She felt it. She quickly looked over at her father and then back at Michael, who smiled at her as if nothing was wrong. The subtlety of the exchange went completely over Beatrice's head. She still thought Michael was wonderful. But Michael got the point. He would have to be more careful from now on.

A Visit

1976

LUCILLE BEEMER SAID, "GENE, WAKE UP. SOME-body's here to see you."

Gene looked up to see a beautiful blond woman standing by his grave. He had no idea who she was, but, wow, she sure didn't look like an Elmwood Springs lady. She was wearing a brown suede jacket, a black turtleneck, and black slacks, and looked like someone out of the movies. Just then, his aunt Elner walked up to her and started talking.

"I see you found him."

"Yes."

They both stood there for a moment. Then Aunt Elner said, "Do you remember coming out here to see him when you were little?"

The blond woman seemed surprised. "No. . . . Was I here before?"

"Oh, yes, two or three times. We'd bring you out here on Memorial Day. You used to talk to your daddy and everything."

"I did?"

Aunt Elner nodded. "I wish you could have known

your daddy. He was such a sweet boy . . . and smart. Oh, my, I always thought when he grew up, he might have been a writer."

"Really?"

"Oh, yes, even when he was in grammar school, I'd come over to the house, and he would be up in his room, just typewriting away . . . tap tap tap tippy tat. You used to play with that old typewriter when you were little."

"Huh, I don't remember. Who else is buried out here?" she asked, putting her hands in her jacket pockets.

"Everybody. Your great-grandparents, your grand-mother and granddaddy, and me someday." Then Elner looked at her with concern. "Honey, do you have your plot yet?"

"No."

"Well, I would advise you to get it. I know you're young yet, but it's nice to know where you're going . . . sort of comforting."

After they walked away, Gene was left in a little bit of a state of shock. That beautiful woman was his daughter. The last time he had seen her was almost thirty years ago. And now she was a grown woman, older than he had been when he died. He was sure she didn't know it, but with that blond hair and blue eyes, his daughter looked a lot like the picture he'd seen of his grandmother Katrina.

Dena was going to be in town for only a few days, and so after they left the cemetery, Norma drove them out to the country, so Dena could see the old original Nordstrom farmhouse. As they pulled up, the first thing Dena noticed was the large field of flowers blooming on the side of the house. "Oh, wow. Look at all those sunflowers. I love sunflowers."

Elner laughed. "Well, you should. You come by it naturally. Your great-grandmother planted those almost eighty years ago . . . and they just keep blooming year after year."

"They do?"

"Oh, yes," said Elner. "I remember Momma saying that Katrina Nordstrom always loved her sunflowers. I wish I'd known her, but she died when I was little. But everybody loved her, I can tell you that. I just wish she could see you and how pretty you are. She sure would be proud."

THEY COULDN'T HAVE KNOWN it, but Katrina **had** seen her and was talking to Gene about her at that very moment. "Oh, Gene, she's grown up into such a beautiful young woman."

Gene said, "Hasn't she? I think she looks just like you."

Birdie Swensen, who had been listening, piped up. "Gene's right, Katrina. She is the spitting image of you when you were that age . . . only taller."

"Oh, thank you. But I was never that pretty."

"Yes, you were!" said Birdie.

"But I wore glasses."

"Even with your glasses, you were always pretty. You just didn't know it."

WHEN DENA LEFT TO go back to New York, she was sorry she had not come back to Elmwood Springs sooner. Living in a big city as she had for so many years now, she had almost forgotten where she had come from. She got on the plane with a jar of fig preserves and a four-leaf clover that her great-aunt Elner had found and given her.

She Will Survive

1978

TOT WHOOTEN SEEMED TO BE GETTING OVER HER upset about her husband, James, running off with eighteen-year-old Jackie Sue Potts.

This morning, Norma was at her weekly standing appointment with Tot, having her hair done. In between taking drags off her cigarette, Tot was telling Norma about her new philosophy in life. "You know, Norma," she said. "Everybody's whining about how this is the new 'Me' generation, and how terrible it is, but it suits me just fine. And that's who I'm gonna think about from now on, me. I've had a lifetime of thinking about everybody else, and what has it gotten me? Hell, I spent twenty years taking care of Momma, and she didn't even know who I was. She called me Jeannette for the last five years of her life."

"Who is Jeannette?"

"I have no idea. Now, I'm sorry she died, but it has sure freed up a lot of my time to do what I want for a change."

—

ANOTHER THING THAT HAD cheered Tot up a bit was that the beauty business was good. Thanks to Farrah Fawcett and the television show **Charlie's Angels,** big hair was in. Now, if your hair wasn't stacked, packed, curled, feathered, teased, and sprayed high enough to hide a small child, you just weren't in style. And today, Tot had teased and sprayed poor Norma's hair until it looked at least a foot high.

Ever since Tot had seen the movie **Saturday Night Fever,** a big change had come over her. All of a sudden, she was wearing four-inch platform shoes and polyester pantsuits with bell-bottom pants and going out dancing at Disco City every weekend. She told Verbena, "You know that song 'I Will Survive'? I think that gal wrote that song just for me. Like Mary Tyler Moore says, 'I think I just might make it after all.'"

Tot had thrown herself into the seventies with a vengeance. In 1973, she had put up a Billie Jean King poster in the beauty shop. Now she had a lava lamp in her bedroom, a beanbag chair in the living room, and had even bought a mood ring. As she explained to Norma, "Every morning, when I wake up, I look at my ring, and if it tells me I'm in a bad mood, I just cancel my appointments that day. It saves a lot of wear and tear on me and my customers."

The Eighties

—

The World
Turns

Too Cool for Words

Tot's son, James Dwayne Whooten, Jr., had always hung out with the cool kids. His gang had started smoking pot and drinking beer in the seventh grade.

In high school, they didn't play football or basketball or play in the band, like the jocks and nerds, and they sure didn't study or make good grades.

They also didn't date much, but it didn't matter to them because hot damn, they were "cool to the max, man," with their long, stringy hair and Grateful Dead T-shirts. And if you weren't stoned by eight in the morning, you were "an uptight loser, man." By the eleventh grade, most of his crowd had already dropped out of school or, like Dwayne Jr., been kicked out.

To make beer money, Dwayne Jr. would sweep up his mother's beauty shop at night, and his friends, Weezer and Buck, worked at the car wash during the week. But on the weekends, they partied. And for most, the party never stopped.

At thirty-one, Dwayne Jr. now had three ex-wives

and was living at his mother's house, on probation, with two DUIs and two possession arrests. Weezer was still working at the car wash, and three of his other buddies were in jail for selling crack. His best friend, Buck, was up in Kansas City, sleeping on the streets at night, standing on the side of the highway from eleven to two every day, holding a homemade cardboard sign that read HOMELESS VET, PLEASE HELP. Which wasn't true. He wasn't a vet, but it was good for business. By two P.M., thanks to the nice people who would hand him a dollar bill and sometimes more, he usually had enough to buy drugs to get him through the night. He didn't have to work for "the man" or pay rent. How cool was that?

Secret Dreams

ONE OF THE MOST ENDEARING THINGS ABOUT PEO-
ple is their little secret dreams. Edna Childress,
married to Chief Ralph Childress of the Elmwood
Springs Police Department, dreamed of one day
going to the Mall of America and shopping. Cathy
Calvert, over at the newspaper, dreamed of inter-
viewing someone famous.

Luther Griggs, now seventeen, dreamed that Bobby
Jo Stash, who worked at the Tastee-Freeze out at
the mall, would talk to him. Ernest Koonitz, local
boy and tuba major at the University of Missouri
and now band director at the high school, also had
a dream that one day, his band would be picked
to march in the Macy's Thanksgiving Day Parade in
New York.

Tot Whooten dreamed of the day when her two
children, Dwayne Jr. and Darlene, would leave home
for good and stop coming back.

Even Lester Shingle up at Still Meadows had
dreams of his own. He had given up all hope for any
kind of justice from the Elmwood Springs Police. It

was clear that if someone had not been arrested for his murder by now, there was no case. And whoever it was, was sitting around down there in Elmwood Springs right now, thinking they had committed a perfect crime, probably eating ice cream, too. Oh, well . . . he had plenty of time. He had read a few Perry Mason books in his day, and he had come up with a plan. If the law couldn't catch them, he would. He would wait until all four women were at Still Meadows and then confront them one by one, lay out his case point by point, interrogate them without mercy. Surely, one of them would break . . . or squeal the real killer's name. Or maybe someone who had been at the bowling alley the night he was killed would suddenly remember something, some small detail, and he would catch them red-handed, expose them to the entire Still Meadows community. They may have gotten away with it down there in Elmwood Springs, but not here. He would see to that. In the meantime, he was tired. All the planning had worn him out. He figured he would sleep for a few years. He called out to his neighbor, "Hey, Jake . . . wake me up when any of the Goodnight women or Tot Whooten gets here."

"Okay, will do."

Lester drifted off, dreaming about his day in court to come, when vengeance would be his at last.

A Dream Come True

SOMETIMES IN LIFE, DREAMS DO COME TRUE. IN 1986, after years of trying, the Elmwood Springs High School band won a competition and became the only band in that part of the state to ever be invited to march in the big Macy's Thanksgiving Day Parade in New York. It was a huge honor, and everyone in town was so excited they could hardly stand it.

Everybody agreed that their high school band was a step above all the others in the area. Their rendition of "Brazil" was thrilling, at least to the people in Elmwood Springs. How Brazilians would feel about it was anybody's guess; however, it did get them to the state finals and on their way to national fame.

Norma and Macky's daughter, Linda, had been a majorette, and Norma was still a band mother and in charge of fundraising. All over town, people worked to raise money to buy new band uniforms and majorette outfits and replace some of the old instruments. They had bake sales, chicken dinners, garage sales, book sales. On the weekend, the high school seniors set up a car wash service. Every day after school and on Saturdays, the band practiced marching up and down Main Street. They wanted to look and sound the very best they possibly could. Not knowing what was going on, the people up at Still Meadows were wondering why there was so much practicing.

Merle Wheeler, over at the dry cleaner, said, "I like a good band . . . but, Lord, I'm so tired of hearing 'Brazil,' I don't know what to do."

October

1986

Elner and her neighbors were watching the sunset over the back cornfield when she said, "I love a fall sunset. Sometimes they're prettier than the summer ones."

"They last longer. Then around Thanksgiving, the sun starts to go down fast," said Verbena.

Tot said, "Hey. Isn't it great the kids won that trip to New York?"

"They worked hard for it. . . . They should be very proud of themselves."

Merle said, "I won a prize once."

"You did? What for?" asked Elner.

"I had the largest tomato in the county—weighed over twelve pounds. I think it was a mutant."

Verbena said, "I wonder if Luther Griggs is a mutant? I never saw anybody grow up so fast in my life . . . or eat as much food in one sitting."

Elner laughed. "He's got a good appetite, all right."

Luther had barely graduated from high school. He had made all Ds in every subject but shop, where he excelled and had made all As. And by some rare genetic fluke, it turned out that Luther was some kind of mechanical genius where cars were concerned. He was car crazy and could fix anything with a motor. A lot of boys his age had pictures of girls on their bedroom walls; Luther had pictures of cars and trucks and tanks. He had been working at the local gas station after school since he was twelve, and by age seventeen, was already in charge of auto repair.

Elner was so proud of him, which pleased him. She was the only person in his entire life that he felt cared about him. Who would have guessed that the little scrawny boy who had been as feral as a cat would have grown into a big, burly 230 pounder?

Elner took almost no credit. "He just needed somebody to pay a little attention to him."

Oops

AFTER A PARTICULARLY NICE SUNDAY EVENING AT home, Norma woke up and saw a note Macky had left for her on his pillow.

"Good morning, you good-looking, sexy wench, you. Talk to you later. Have a good day."

Norma smiled. It was amazing that after so many years of marriage Macky still thought she was sexy. She had always assumed when they hit a certain age their romantic life would be over.

Later Norma was in the kitchen having her coffee. When the phone rang, she picked it up and said in her best low voice, "Well, good morning, you great big, sexy, handsome hunk of man, you."

There was a slight pause. "Ah . . . Good morning, Mrs. Warren. This is Emmett down at Olivera Auto Repair, and I'm calling with an estimate."

A horrified Norma desperately tried to recover and said in as normal a voice as she could muster, "Oh, yes, Emmett."

"My boss says we can do the whole thing, fender and top, for seven twenty-five."

"Well, thank you," she said, and hung up.

Emmett put the phone down at the shop and thought, Lord, what was the world coming to? Mrs. Warren was pretty for her age, but he figured she was at least fifty-something. She must be one of those women that go after younger men.

Norma immediately called Macky, hysterical. "Oh, my God. I am so embarrassed. Why didn't you call me?"

"I was just getting ready to. Why?" When Norma told him what she had said, Macky just laughed. "Well, I'm sure you made his day."

"I'm just mortified."

"Oh, honey, don't worry about it. It probably happens all the time."

"Not to me. I want you to call him and tell him that I certainly didn't mean him."

"What do you care what Emmett thinks?"

"What if he tells his wife and it gets all over that I was coming on to her husband?"

"Oh, Norma . . ."

"No, no. You don't understand, Macky. I can't live in this town with people thinking that. You have got to call him, right now!"

"Why don't you call him?"

"I can't. Oh please, Macky. Please!"

As usual Norma was hysterical over nothing. But he would call.

Down at the auto shop, a voice on the intercom said, "Emmett . . . phone call . . . on three."

He wiped his hands and picked up. "Hello."

"Emmett, this is Macky Warren."

"Yes, sir?"

"Are you having an affair with my wife?"

"Ah, oh no, sir. Oh God, no!"

"Just kidding."

"Oh."

"Hey, listen . . . you knew she thought it was me calling her when she picked up the phone, right?"

"Uh, yes, sir."

"Okay. She was just a little embarrassed and I wanted to clear it up. Okay, buddy?"

"No problem . . . done."

"Good. Oh, and that estimate's fine."

"Yes, sir."

When Emmett hung up his heart was still pounding. He knew Macky had been a Green Beret, and it scared the hell out of him.

Two minutes later, Norma was on the line. "Did you call?"

"Yes, no big deal. He laughed about it. So you can go on with your life, okay?"

"Okay, but you'll have to take the car in. I can't face him."

"I figured."

"This is all your fault, you know. You shouldn't be so sexy," she said.

"I'll try not to. Oh, and by the way, Emmett told me I was a lucky man to have such a hot-tamale sex-pot of a wife."

"He did not! Did he really say that?"

"No, but I bet he thought it."

"Oh, Macky!"

"Gotta go. Bye."

Norma hung up and shook her head. Macky could be so silly sometimes.

The Parade

THREE DAYS BEFORE THANKSGIVING, THE ENTIRE town gathered down at the high school to see the big yellow band bus off to New York. Several band mothers were aboard as chaperones, as well as Tot Whooten, who was along to fix the majorettes' hair for the parade. She told Cathy Calvert, "The whole country will be watching us, so I'm doing everybody in a flip and extra-strength hair-spraying them to hell and back, so no matter what the weather is, our girls are gonna look good from start to finish." Luther Griggs went along to help load and unload the bus.

Two days later, the bus full of screaming and excited kids finally arrived at the motel in Newark, New Jersey, where they would be staying. When they walked into the lobby, they were greeted with a big banner across the lobby that the town had ordered: GOOD LUCK TOMORROW. WE ARE SO PROUD.

At around four A.M. early Thanksgiving morning, just a few hours before the Elmwood Springs High School Band was to have their brush with greatness, something happened.

When Luther Griggs went out to the motel parking lot to unlock the bus, it wasn't there. It had been stolen, along with all their uniforms and instruments still inside.

Later, when the kids were told what had happened, they wandered around the hotel in a state of shock. A lot of the girls cried. They couldn't believe it. After the whole town had worked so hard to raise money to get them there, and all their parents and grandparents had been looking so forward to seeing them on television. Some had even bought new television sets just for the occasion. They were not going to be in the parade. The police came and took a report, but said there was nothing they could do for the moment.

Later, the kids sat in the lobby with Mr. Koonitz and the chaperones and watched the parade on television. They had come all that way, worked so hard, all for nothing. That afternoon, the school board had to charter another bus to go up and bring them home.

As Merle Wheeler said to Ernest Koonitz when they came back, "It makes you wonder about people, doesn't it? How can thieves live with themselves? Didn't they think what stealing that bus would do to those poor kids?" Tot Whooten was mad as hell as she stomped off the bus. She said to Verbena, who had come to pick her up, "Can you believe it? They got my hot irons, rollers, and all my gel and spray."

Macky and Norma Warren were there to meet the

bus. They had gone down to the high school to help get the kids home. When Macky saw the stricken looks on the kids' faces, it really got to him.

That night, after they went to bed, he said, "I wish to God I could find the bastards who took that bus. I'd kill them with my bare hands."

Like everybody else in town, Macky was upset about losing the bus, the instruments, and the uniforms, but he knew those things could be replaced. What had made him so mad was how the theft had affected the kids. Having that rotten thing happen had caused them to lose a little bit of the innocence and trust in the world they once had. And that was something they could never get back.

Naturally, in Elmwood Springs, a predominantly Christian community, the following Sunday, most of the sermons had been about forgiveness; the main thrust being "Forgive them, Father, for they know not what they do." But Macky was having none of it. As far as he was concerned, the sorry low-life son of a bitch who took the bus knew exactly what he was doing. Sermon or no, he would have broken his neck if he could have found him.

Bad Karma or
Two Gold Chains

AFTER THEY HAD STASHED ALL THE STUFF FROM the school bus in the basement of a deserted building they used to store things, the two thieves drove the bus across town, stripped it, and dumped it in a parking lot.

When they got back to the building, the mother of one of the thieves and her boyfriend were going through the clothes and had already cut all the buttons off the uniform jackets. All the patches that said ELMWOOD SPRINGS MARCHING BAND had been ripped off and thrown away.

A week later, the buttons, along with the uniforms, white shoes, and majorette boots, were sold to a secondhand shoe store in Secaucus for two hundred bucks.

All the band's drums, trumpets, trombones, saxophones, clarinets, and tubas that the kids had worked so hard to pay for eventually wound up in various pawnshops all over New Jersey and New York. The buyers never knew where the instruments had come from. Most didn't care. All they knew was they had gotten a good deal. The thieves were never caught, and the robbery earned them a lot of street cred and respect in the gang.

Three years later, after things got too hot in Newark, the two moved on to San Francisco, where one had a cousin. In October 1989, the day of a World Series game, they were out at Candlestick Park, but not to see the baseball game. A few minutes later, they sped out of the parking lot in a brand-new red Ferrari they had just stolen. As soon as they hit the freeway, they started high-fiving each other and laughing their heads off. They gunned it as fast as it would go and headed north on the Nimitz Freeway with the music blasting away. A few seconds later, an earthquake shook the entire Bay Area and the top layer of the freeway collapsed onto the lower level, smashing the Ferrari and its two passengers as flat as a pancake.

During the cleanup of the freeway, as the large crane rotated around and lifted what was left of the red Ferrari from the rubble, a bystander remarked, "Shit . . . that car looks like a red Frisbee."

The owner of the stolen Ferrari had filled out a police report. Several weeks later, when the man received a call from the police department, a man's voice said, "Sir, I'm calling about a police report you submitted regarding a stolen car?"

"Yes?"

"I'm calling to inform you that we found your car.

You might want to contact your insurance company."

"Was it wrecked?"

"Yes, sir."

"Where is it? Can I see it?"

"Sir, I wouldn't bother if I were you. There's not much left to see."

"Oh . . . Where did they find it?"

"On the Nimitz Freeway. The suspects appear to have been headed out of town when the earthquake hit, and the bridge collapsed on top of them. Both were killed instantly."

"Oh, I see. Have they been identified?"

"No, sir. Not much left to identify, just two gold chains."

"Oh, so . . . uh . . . can I press charges against them or what?"

The officer, who had a sick sense of humor, paused. He wanted so much to say, "They have already been pressed, sir." But he didn't.

THE ABANDONED BUS HAD been found a week after the theft in the back lot of a warehouse in Newark, stripped down to the bone. They had stolen the motor, the tires, the radio, the leather seats, everything. And someone had painted graffiti all over the sides in black paint.

Cathy Calvert typed up the headline for her column:

New Bus, Uniforms, and Instruments on the Way

by Chatty Cathy

The Elmwood City Council announced today that thanks to a generous donation sent by an anonymous donor, the band bus and its contents will all be replaced by no later than January 15.

Of course, everybody in town knew it had been Hanna Marie who had sent the check. Even though she was now Mrs. Vincent, she was still a Swensen and her father's daughter.

Ander, who was up in years now, had retired a few years earlier. When he did, he appointed Beatrice's nephew, Albert Olsen, to take over operations. Ander had trained the young man and felt he had left the dairy in good hands. But he would still stop by the dairy from time to time just to say hello.

Ander Swensen may have felt good about Albert Olsen taking over as manager, but his son-in-law, who now had to take orders from the nephew, did not. He felt that as Hanna Marie's husband, the position should have been his. But he didn't say anything at the time. He figured he wouldn't have to put up with Albert too much longer. The old man was getting up there, and as soon as he was out of the way, things would change.

Growing Older

AUNT ELNER'S BIRTHDAY WAS COMING UP, SO Norma asked her what she wanted this year. Aunt Elner said, "Oh, honey, I don't need a single thing. I'm trying to get rid of things as it is."

"You have to want something, Aunt Elner."

"I don't."

"No, really. . . . Think, if you could have anything in the world, what would you want?"

"But, honey, I don't want anything."

"Really?"

"Oh, if I was younger, I suppose it would be a litter of kittens. Oh, there's nothing in this world more entertaining than watching a bunch of kittens playing. They are the cutest little things . . . with their little paws, I could just kiss them to death."

"I know, but the problem is they grow up to be big, ugly cats, and you can't get rid of them. Nobody has any use for some old mangy cat."

"Oh, Norma, they can't help it. We all grow up. What if nobody had any use for us when we grew up? Just because they are older doesn't mean they aren't sweet."

AND IT SO HAPPENED, up at Still Meadows, they were talking about the exact same thing. Lucille Beemer had just posed a question. "Mrs. Bell, at what age did you begin to feel old?"

"Well, the last time they took my picture for my driver's license, it nearly scared me to death. 'Mercy,' I thought. 'When did my eyes get so squinty and all those chins show up?' It's best not to have your picture made or hear your voice on a tape machine. It can really depress you. I thought I was still cute, but I was wrong. I was an old lady with an old lady's voice. It sure wrecked my high opinion of myself."

"What about you, Birdie?"

"When I started to look like my grandmother. But the funny thing was I didn't feel old inside. I remember how I used to feel about old people. I could never imagine them as young . . . but it's a different story when you're on the other end."

"Oh, is it ever," said Ola Warren. "At the end, I got to the point where I hated having a body. Everything started going haywire on me, and I started falling apart like an old car. If it wasn't one thing, then it was another. You just get your gallbladder out, then your heart starts acting up, then you need a new hip, and after that, a cataract operation, then you need a hearing aid. Oh, it just goes on and on. You finally get everything fixed, and you think you are ahead, then you come down with the heartbreak of psoriasis. Most of the stuff I got after that, I couldn't even spell."

The Early Bird Special

LORENE GIBBLE WAS AS MUCH OF A PERMANENT fixture at the downtown Main Street Café as the table and chairs. She had worked at the café since she was sixteen, only taking time off to have three babies, and even then only a few weeks. After her kids were grown, she started working the early bird dinner shift. The hours suited her. Check in at three, do her prep work, start serving at four-thirty and home by eight-thirty, just in time to see her television shows, then to bed.

Tonight it was sad for Lorene not to see sweet little Mrs. Floyd sitting at table 4, the same little table by the window she had occupied since 1966. Her friend said that she had passed away the day before. Even though Mrs. Floyd had been unable to speak since her stroke, Lorene still missed her and her sweet, somewhat crooked, little smile. With Mrs. Floyd, it was always the same order: iced tea, baked chicken breast with the green beans and mashed potatoes, and chocolate pudding, if they had it.

Lorene loved all her little early birders, mostly

widows and one or two old widowers. But it was the ladies that touched her. They were all living on fixed incomes, and for most this was their only real meal of the day. After they finished, Lorene would carefully pack up their leftovers and throw in a couple of extra dinner rolls she knew they would probably eat for breakfast. They were all poor as church mice, but still they dug in their change purses to try and leave her a tip, even when they couldn't afford it. Lorene knew the dates of all their birthdays and made sure to make a fuss over them. Free cake and ice cream. It was such a small thing to do, and it meant so much.

For years now, just like clockwork, they all lined up outside the door at four-thirty, dressed in their best, powdered and clean smelling. She knew that most would be going home to an empty house. It just broke her heart to think that these ladies who had taught school, raised children, worked in stores or libraries, and paid their taxes and their mortgages on time, were now having to count their nickels and dimes.

It wasn't fair. All those who had never contributed a thing to society and could work if they wanted, but were instead living off the government, sucking the life out of it. Namely her daughter, who was living on disability, just because she had a little back pain and a doctor that was a fool. Lorene had worked all her life with bunions, a bad knee that gave her fits, and sometimes with a hangover from hell, but she went to work and had a smile and sometimes a little joke to cheer her ladies up.

In this world of spectacular achievements, most would say Lorene never amounted to much. Every day for the past forty-two years, rain or shine, feeling well or not, she made sure her early birders were well taken care of. And for some, Lorene was the only bright spot in their day. She may not have set the world on fire with her brilliance, but when she finally arrived at Still Meadows, a lot of people were very happy to see her. "Our Lorene is here," said Mrs. Floyd, without a hint of the stroke that had silenced her.

The Nineties

Walmart and Supercuts

More Changes

DOWNTOWN ELMWOOD SPRINGS WAS LOOKING A little shabby these days. Ever since the big Walmart opened just north of town, almost nobody shopped downtown. After Dixie Cahill died, there was no one to take over her dance studio, and so it was closed. So was the old Main Street Café and the Trolley Car Diner. The only place you could eat was the coffee shop on the corner, and it closed at three in the afternoon. Hardly anybody went downtown at night.

All the teenagers hung out at the mall, which had just opened a new multiplex movie theater and a food court. Even the Morgan Brothers Department Store had moved its downtown store out to the mall.

There was now a new Ace Hardware store near the Walmart, and Macky was having a hard time competing with their prices. The mall had also affected Tot Whooten's business. As she told Norma, "Ever since they opened that new Supercuts out there, none of the younger set come to me anymore . . . just my old regular customers. I'd relocate to the mall myself, but a lot of my oldsters can't drive that far.

Some of them have been with me for over fifty years, so I'm gonna stick with them to the end." And she did.

On Monday mornings, no matter how tired she was, she got into her car and drove out to the nursing home and did all the ladies' hair for free. Darlene didn't understand her mother. "Why do you fix them old ladies' hair out there? They ain't going nowhere."

"Because, Darlene, it makes them feel like they're still in the game. And they look forward to it . . . and everything is not about money, Darlene."

"Oh, yeah? Then why won't you lend me and Buster any money?"

"So you and Buster can buy more of that white stuff to snort up your nose? I don't think so. You're lucky I don't call Ralph Childress on you."

"You drink beer."

"Yeah, and the last time I looked, it was still legal. I'm not harboring any criminals under my roof."

"We'll just move out then."

"Oh, Darlene, quit flapping your lips. You know as long as there is a free meal to be had, you and Buster ain't going nowhere."

The old adage "Your children will be a comfort to you in your old age" did not ring true to Tot, at any age. Darlene and Dwayne Jr. had married every idiot that came their way. She had paid for seven divorces between them. Tot was not happy with the way the world had changed, either. There was no Disco City anymore. Years ago, it had become the Red Barn, a country-western boot-scootin' line-dancing joint. Even the radio was now "less talk, all country, all the time."

"I miss disco," she said.

In 1990, at age eighty, when Beatrice Swensen came up to Still Meadows, her parents were excited to talk to her. Her father, Olaf, asked right away, "How is my precious grandbaby, Hanna Marie?"

"Oh, Daddy, she's wonderful. She's married to a nice man named Michael. He works at the dairy with Ander. And she's so pretty now. Everybody says she's the most elegant lady in town. I'm so proud of her."

A year later, when her husband, Ander, came to Still Meadows and was asked about his son-in-law, he said very little.

Little Miss Davenport

It's funny, in a small town, how certain people are always referred to in a certain way. All her life, Tot Whooten had had such bad luck that everyone always called her Poor Tot. The same thing was true of Dottie Davenport. She was only five feet tall, and so everyone always referred to her as Little Miss Davenport. She was a dream employee, had worked for Mr. Swensen as his office manager for more than thirty-five years, and was loyal to a fault. Even after Mr. Swensen had retired, she'd stayed on at the office, just to keep an eye on the son-in-law. She didn't trust him.

Michael Vincent had been taken into the company right away and seemed to be doing well. Everybody, including Little Miss Davenport, had been pleased that Hanna Marie had found someone so nice. Her new husband was so loving and so good to his young wife, at least in public. But after a while, some people started seeing right through him. His father-in-law for one. He and Little Miss

Davenport had begun to figure out that he was pilfering money out of the business account. And it was so unnecessary. All he had to do was ask, and he would have been given anything he needed. Ander hadn't said anything to his wife or Hanna Marie. As long as she was happy with him, and he treated her well, whatever else he did didn't really matter.

Then, when Mr. Swensen died, he left his entire company, the house, and the land to Hanna Marie. Pretty soon, people at the dairy began noticing a change in her husband's behavior. Michael Vincent had started barking orders at employees and telling them to forget how Albert Olsen, the dairy manager, wanted it done. He was in charge. Everyone was confused. After the head of the packaging department had a run-in with him, he went into Little Miss Davenport's office. "Dottie, are you **sure** there was no mention of Vincent in the will?"

Little Miss Davenport said, "Absolutely. Mr. Swensen put everything in Hanna Marie's name. So he may be strutting around acting like he owns the place. But on paper, he's still just another employee working under Albert."

"Well, he's causing a lot of trouble, going behind Albert's back, threatening to fire people. Three guys in my department have quit already."

"I know," she said.

"Excuse my French, but it's too bad Hanna Marie

The Sunset Club

1994

LATE SATURDAY AFTERNOON, THE NEIGHBORS WERE all sitting in Elner Shimfissle's backyard, looking at the sunset, discussing life, wondering why some people acted the way they did. Tot said, "Hell, I don't know what it's all about. One day Darlene says she hates life, then she meets another deadbeat to marry and loves it again."

"I think most people are confused about life, because it's not just one thing going on," said Elner. "It's many things going on at the same time. Life is both sad and happy, simple and complex, all at the same time. Take my sister Ida. She was always looking for things to make her feel better . . . the rich husband, the big house, the perfect child, the right garden club, you name it. And by and large, she got them all, but she was never happy. No matter how much she got, it was never enough. She just kept buying more things and putting them in storage. I sat down and figured it out, and I said, 'Ida, did you know that in twenty-five years, you have spent over thirty-two thousand dollars to store things that you don't have room for?' But it didn't stop her. She just kept buying in case she wanted to use something in the future. I tell you that girl had the energy of a chipmunk, always running here, running there. She never gave herself time to feel sad. Even when Herbert died. The day after the funeral, she was already out shopping at the Sit and Sleep store. Ida was a piece of work all right, but with all her faults, I miss her, and I miss my sister Gerta, too."

"Oh, so do I, Elner," said Ruby. "Since the bakery closed, you can't find a good pie anymore. The stuff they sell at the supermarket is terrible. I bought one of their pies, and it was so bad I threw it out to the crows."

Elner said, "I'll tell you who makes the best pie in town is Edna Childress. And she makes it right from scratch. You know me. I love a good apple pie, and you can't beat Edna's apple pie."

"No, you can't," said Verbena. "That's why Ralph's got such a big belly now. Edna said he comes home from the police station every day and has his pie and coffee for lunch."

Tot said, "Can you blame him? If I was married to Edna, I would, too."

"She spoils that man something awful," said Verbena.

Verbena's husband, Merle, looked at her. "Why don't you spoil me a little?"

"Hey, listen, bub. I cook you three hot meals a day, that's enough."

Tot Whooten took a drag off her cigarette and said, "Hey, speaking of missing people, has anybody seen Hanna Marie lately?"

Elner shook her head. "No, not much, not since her daddy passed away, and I worry about her. I hope she's all right."

"Me, too," said Verbena. "Little Miss Davenport told me she used to come down to the office, but now she mostly just stays alone all day in that big old house. But, of course, I see that husband driving around town in Ander's big car all puffed up with himself. I feel sorry for Hanna Marie is all I can say."

Elner said, "You know, it isn't like Hanna Marie to not come and see me or at least drop me a note."

"She's probably just busy with all her charity work," Ruby said. "I'm sure she'll contact you soon."

"I hope so. I'm a little worried about her," Elner said.

"Me, too," said Tot. "And it's not like you can call her on the phone."

"No, you can't," said Ruby.

THE TRUTH WAS THAT Hanna Marie had not been busy, as Ruby had thought. She had been devastated. Almost immediately after her father had died, her husband had told her he didn't want her to come to the dairy anymore, and he hardly ever came home, except to change clothes and go out again. She didn't know what she had done. When she tried to ask him, he told her she was imagining things.

On the rare occasion when someone spotted her in town, she looked so sad. Then in November, the housekeeper happened to mention to Verbena that she had heard Hanna Marie crying up in her room. When Elner heard this, she decided not to stand on ceremony and went over to see her. The maid answered the front door, and Elner went in and walked straight up the grand staircase to Hanna Marie's bedroom, where she found her sitting at her desk. Hanna Marie looked up and was surprised to see her and came around and hugged her.

"I haven't heard from you for a while. How are you?"

Hanna Marie smiled and jotted down on her pad, "Just fine, and you?"

"Oh, you know me. Same as ever."

Elner noticed for the first time that Hanna Marie had aged. Her brown hair that she wore pulled back from her face was now peppered with gray, and the youthful sparkle in her eyes had begun to fade. Elner said, "Are you sure you are all right?"

Hanna nodded that she was.

Elner then looked around the room. "Hey . . . where's your kitty?"

Hanna made a sad face and wrote, "He ran away."

"Oh, that's too bad. Well, honey, I know you are a grown woman. But just the same, I promised your mother I would look out for you, and if you ever need anything, you send somebody to get me. I'll be mad if you don't."

Hanna Marie smiled and nodded and hugged her goodbye.

Just as Elner was leaving, Michael Vincent was coming in the door. When he saw her, he was taken aback. "What are you doing here?"

"Just visiting a friend," Elner said, and walked down the stairs.

He called after her, "You better not have brought another damn cat."

The Milkman

VERBENA'S COUSIN VIRGIL A. NEWTON HAD BEEN with the dairy for more than forty years. He'd been up every morning at 3 A.M., dressed in his starched white uniform, black leather bow tie, and cap, and was out at the dairy loading his truck by 3:40 and in town by 4:15. As he drove through the empty streets, the whole town would be sleeping. It was Virgil's own private world, a world before the town woke up and all the clatter of cars, machines, and people began. A few dogs barked, and a couple of roosters crowed now and then, but mostly, it was quiet, and Virgil went out of his way not to disturb the silence of the dawn. At each house, he would ease his truck up to the curb as quietly as he could and stop, then carry the wire basket of milk up on the porch and place it down as softly as he could. He even wore black leather shoes with double thick soles. When he picked up the empty bottles, he tried not to have them rattle too loudly.

Later that morning, people all over town would

open their doors, pick up the milk he had left, and never give him a thought. But Virgil had been there every day, rain or shine, in the heat or freezing cold of winter, long before the paperboy, the bread truck, and the mailman arrived.

But the years had gone by, and his route became smaller and smaller. The A&P grocery store started selling milk and cream in cardboard cartons, and people didn't want to fool with bottles anymore. And then one day, the dairy stopped home deliveries all together, and he was put to work counting inventory. His new hours were from 8 to 4, but still, he could never sleep past 3 A.M. And sometimes when he woke up, he would get in his car and drive around town before dawn, remembering a time when he was still delivering milk.

He would drive his old route and watch the older people's lights come on at around 5 A.M. Elner Shimfissle was usually in her kitchen by 5:15, and her neighbors by at least 5:30. Elner was like him. She never wanted to miss a sunrise. He remembered when Glenn Warren and his family used to live in that house. There used to be around seventy-five houses in this part of town. Now there were only a few of the older houses left, but he could still remember each one and who had lived there.

Sometimes while driving around in the early mornings, Virgil, who could whistle, would start whistling one of his favorite tunes.

The way you wear your hat,
The way you sip your tea,
The memory of all that . . .
No, no, they can't take that away from me.

Virgil had loved being a milkman. Old Mr. Swensen had been such a nice man to work for. But he had died, and the son-in-law had pretty much taken over, and a few weeks ago, Little Miss Davenport had died. Nothing stays the same. Life for him had been just a series of transitions. From glass bottles to cardboard cartons, driving a truck to counting inventory at the plant. Working for a nice man, then working for a bastard. The dairy had always been a local family business before that guy wangled his way in.

Nobody liked working at the dairy anymore. It used to be a happy place. Not now. What did that sweet lady see in that guy? He heard things from the girls who worked in the office, things Vincent had done. Somebody should tell her.

Achy Breaky Heart

1998

ALMOST EVERYBODY HAS A SECRET THEY TAKE TO their grave, and Bonnie Gumms, a recent arrival at Still Meadows, was no exception.

Bonnie had taught line dancing out at the Red Barn for years, and being a professional of sorts, considered herself to be in show business. She had once met Tammy Wynette, and she certainly knew all the country-western songs. Although she had reached a level of local semi-celebrity, she was restless and not satisfied with her lot in life. Bonnie was always waiting for something exciting, always looking for a new face, craving some unknown thrill.

And then one night, it happened. As she was showing her class a new move, she'd looked up and thought she spotted the famous singer Willie Nelson quietly slip in the back door of the Red Barn. And he was now sitting alone at the bar. She had heard that he sometimes did that; just sneaked in and out of a place, not telling anyone who he was. Between sets, her heart started to pound as she casually walked over to get a closer look. It was him all right. The same old, wizened face, the scraggly hair and beard, the telltale red bandana wrapped around his head. Bonnie tried her best to just leave him alone, let him have a little incognito, but her proximity to greatness was just too much to handle. Finally, she could no longer contain herself, and she sidled up beside him at the bar as quietly as she could, hoping he would appreciate that she was professional enough not to blow his cover. Besides, if she had, he would have been mobbed, and she would miss her chance at rubbing elbows with the great Willie Nelson. After a moment, she leaned in and said in a low voice while looking the other way, "By the way, I know who you are. But don't worry, I won't say anything. Just wanted you to know I'm a big fan."

He looked at her, somewhat taken aback, but answered in the same low tone, "Thank you, honey, I really appreciate that."

"Just passing through?" she said, glancing up at the ceiling.

"Yep," he nodded. "Nice place you got here. And those are some pretty fancy moves you have out there on that dance floor, young lady," he said with a dangerous twinkle in his blue eyes. "Whatcha drinking, sweetheart?"

The next morning, Bonnie woke up at the motel with the world's worst hangover, and Willie was gone, obviously on the road again.

It was bad enough that she'd had sex with Willie Nelson, a man twice her age, but then later she found out that the man wasn't even Willie Nelson. How horrifying. Now, some twenty-four years later, when she was actually in her grave, Bonnie still kept her mouth shut.

THE NEXT PERSON TO ARRIVE at Still Meadows was none other than Bess Goodnight, and Lester Shingle's friend, as promised, immediately called out, "Hey, Lester . . . wake up! One of the Goodnight women is here." Bess had been one of the four women out at the Blue Star Bowling Alley the night he had been murdered and was a prime suspect.

Then, as fate would have it, only six months later, Bess's twin, Ada Goodnight, joined her sister up on the hill. Now two prime suspects had arrived!

From then on, Lester Shingle was wide awake and carefully listening for clues. He was on the alert to hear if he was mentioned in any of their conversations. So far, nothing. Just a bunch of chatter about births and weddings and crap like that.

A New Millennium

—

The End of
an Era

Elner Moves On

2006

A COUPLE OF YEARS EARLIER, ELNER SHIMFISSLE had fallen out of her fig tree and been taken to the hospital. Her neighbor Verbena Wheeler immediately spread word all over town that Elner was dead. Which had not been exactly true but Cathy Calvert didn't find out until after she had written Elner's obituary. When Elner came home from the hospital she had gotten a big kick out of reading it. Sadly, this time when word got out that Elner Shimfissle had passed away in her sleep, it had been true. Cathy printed the same obituary that Elner had liked so much. And because Elner had been such a strong presence in everyone's lives for so long, Cathy decided to ask people in town to give her a one- or two-word description to add.

She got "funny," "sweet," "childlike," "wise," "good cook," "generous," "hilarious," "wonderful neighbor," "best fig preserves I ever ate," "one of a kind," "loved animals," "loved bugs," "true Christian," "unique," and two "irreplaceables." You can't do any better than that.

Although Elner Shimfissle's death was a sad occasion in town, it was a happy time at Still Meadows. Word spread quickly. "Elner Shimfissle is here! Elner is here!" Lucille Beemer was particularly delighted.

She knew that Elner would be such fun for people to chat with. She always had such interesting opinions on things.

But then, everybody liked Elner, and being so old, Elner knew an awful lot of people and had quite a few relatives out there. It took almost an entire week for her to say hello to everybody. And after she had been thoroughly greeted, she said, "Well, you can't imagine how surprised I am. I just couldn't wait to see everybody again, but I thought I'd be traveling way up in the clouds, way up to heaven, and all the time, you were just right up the street!"

Her husband, Will, laughed, "What I want to know, woman, is what took you so long to get here? I've been waiting for you."

"I know you have, honey. I wasn't trying to live so long. Just too healthy, I guess."

Her nephew, Gene, was so glad Aunt Elner had arrived. The first thing he asked about was Dena and whether she was okay. "Oh, yes, honey. She's married to the nicest doctor and so happy."

"Really?"

"Oh, yes, Norma just got a letter from her last week."

"Well, that's good news. Thanks for telling me. How is Norma?"

Aunt Elner laughed. "Still jumpy as a cat, sweet as ever. I'm gonna miss that gal. Little Macky, too." Elner was sorry that by the time she arrived on the hill, most of the old-timers had already left, but she sure was enjoying the ones who were still there and all the conversations going on. Before people got up to Still Meadows, they just loved to talk about their operations. Now they just loved to talk about how they'd gotten there.

This morning, Mrs. Bell was telling her story again, for at least the tenth time since she'd been there. "So, the doctor calls me in and says, 'I'm sorry to tell you this, Mrs. Bell, but you have cancer, and I need to start setting up your treatments right away.' So I said, 'Don't be bothering me with all that. I don't have time to fool with cancer. I've got too much to do.' So I walked out of there and lived another five years. But you know when it's your time, it's your time, and it was mine, so I have no complaints, but here's the funny part. I died of a heart attack."

Gustav said, "I don't know if you know this, Elner, but a tick got me."

"Oh, no, where did you get a tick?"

"Alaska. Got it off a moose I shot. The bite got infected, and I was gone in a week."

"That old moose certainly got even."

He laughed. "Yeah, now that I think of it, he did."

The Kid

MACKY WAS SITTING IN THE WINDOW OF THE coffee shop having his lunch when Tommy Lindquist, Jr., the new high school football hero of the hour, strolled by. Macky watched as everyone went out of their way to smile and wave at him.

Macky had once been The Kid, the town's fair-haired boy who had thrown the winning touchdown and married Norma, the prettiest girl in town. He had been the one who was going to set the world on fire. The one everybody waved to and smiled at. And then one day, he wasn't.

After he came back from Korea, he had to help his father run the hardware store. He never did try for that professional football career everybody thought he would have.

Now he was going a little bald, his knees were bad, and somebody else was The Kid. He and his contemporaries had been pushed aside to make room for the next wet-behind-the-ears gang coming up behind them. Now he was just another aging nobody sitting around watching the new kid strut around town, so sure of himself, so sure life would stay this way forever. It wouldn't do any good to tell him how fast his big-shot days would be over, how soon he would find himself wondering what had happened, still thinking he was just getting started in life, then having to realize it was almost over. What was that song? "Is That All There Is?" Surely there must be more to life than this.

God, he usually wasn't this maudlin. He missed Aunt Elner, he guessed. It was hard to realize he would never see her again. He had known her since he was a boy. His parents used to buy eggs from her, and then he married her niece. And up until the day she died, she had called him "Little Macky" and had always made him feel young. Jesus Christ, what the hell was the matter with him? He was sitting in the window feeling sorry for himself, he guessed. God . . . life gets away from you so fast. Stupid things distract you, and by the time you realize it, it's too late, and you wind up some old fart whose time has passed, being jealous of some kid.

When the young waitress walked by, she noticed he was wiping his eyes and blowing his nose on a napkin. "Mr. Warren, are you okay?"

"Oh, yeah." Macky sniffed. "I'm just fighting a cold."

"More coffee?"

"Sure. So, Becky, are you still planning to take off in the fall and go to community college?"

Verbena's Unfortunate Trip to the Ladies' Room

BESIDES BEING WITH HER BELOVED WILL AND SO many friends and family again, what made coming up to Still Meadows especially nice for Elner was that within a few years, the last of her old neighbors would be joining her. Verbena, Ruby, and Tot had all bought their plots around the same time and, happily, they were in the same area. It was just like old times. Same people, different address. Verbena came first, and she came up with a bang, literally.

When word got out at Still Meadows that Verbena Wheeler had arrived, Elner Shimfissle in particular was happy to have her old friend back. After Verbena said hello to her relatives, Elner was the next to greet her.

"Hey, Verbena, I'm so glad you're here, I missed you."

"I missed you, too, I went to your funeral and sent you flowers."

"Thank you. I'm sorry I wasn't able to reciprocate."

"That's all right. You know, Elner, Luther Griggs bought your old house."

"Yes, I know. How do you feel, honey?"

"Well, I feel good. My hip doesn't hurt anymore, but I don't mind telling you, Elner, I'm not happy."

Elner was surprised to hear it. "Oh? Why not, hon?"

"I hate that I'm dead, that's why. I've been saving for ten years to be able to make that trip to California, and now I'm not ever going, and the ticket was nonrefundable."

"Oh, I'm sorry. How did it happen—were you sick?"

"That's the other thing. All my life, I just knew I'd die funny. Here I lived my whole life trying to be a lady. I never cussed, I never smoked in public. You know, Elner, I always carried a clean handkerchief, never missed a Sunday service, and then at the end, my damn toilet exploded and shot me right through the ceiling."

"Oh, no!"

"Oh, yes. I hope to God they kept it out of my obit. And I'll tell you something else. Justin Klump has no more business calling himself a plumber than a chicken does an ice-skater. When the thing first started acting up, I told Merle to call O'Dell Plumbing. But no, he said they were too expensive. You know what a cheapskate he is. Remember when he bought all that surplus artificial grass? None of it was the same color. And that secondhand walk-in tub?

The thing never did work. Always penny-wise and pound-foolish. And I hope he enjoys that extra ten dollars he saved. Now I'm dead, and he's a widower."

"I'm so sorry you missed your trip to California, but try to look on the bright side. At least you didn't die young."

ELNER WAS SO GLAD Luther had bought her old house. He had practically been raised there.

Luther had done so poorly in high school that he had almost been ready to give up, but Elner had kept saying to him, "Honey, everybody is good at something. The trick is to find out what it is." And thankfully, he had. Right after high school, he got a job through Ander over at the dairy, driving a fourteen-wheeler truck. And for a boy who had a D average, he made very good money and had been able to marry his girlfriend, Bobby Jo.

Unfortunately for Bobby Jo, Luther's idea of a good time was to pack up and drag her to every auto, truck, and recreational vehicle show within five hundred miles. He said, "It's business, honey. In my line of work, I have to keep up with all the latest automotive innovations." Of course, that was a bald-faced lie. He just loved cars and trucks.

All the News Fit to Print

CATHY CALVERT WAS IN A REAL DILEMMA OVER how to word Verbena Wheeler's obit. Her father, who had started the newspaper, had always stated cause of death, and now her readers had a flying fit if she didn't include it.

She had tried leaving it out once when old Mrs. Speir had eaten a bad oyster at Arnold's Seafood Restaurant (Arnold was one of her biggest advertisers, and Mrs. Speir was 102), but her subscribers had burned up the phone lines.

"Why did she die?"

"I want to know what killed her!"

"Don't just say she died. We want details."

She learned the hard way to never withhold pertinent information, and Arnold's went out of business anyway. But this was different. Verbena Wheeler's demise was an extremely delicate situation that walked the line between the public's right to know and a titillating invasion of privacy. And so, after wrestling with just exactly how to word it, Cathy skimmed over the specific details with the phrase "fluke and tragic household accident."

But even though she tried her best to protect Verbena, word spread, and everyone found out exactly what had happened, especially after Merle sued Klump Plumbing, and the details came out. And yes, some insensitive people did have to suppress the tendency to laugh at the thought that someone flushing their toilet had caused it to explode, sending it and its occupant straight up through the ceiling.

However, the real tragedy of Verbena's demise was that on the day in question, Verbena hadn't really needed to use the bathroom. She was on her way out to the store and sat down, just in case. A completely preemptive gesture on her part. And when nothing happened, she'd flushed the toilet only out of habit. Of course, this was something only Verbena knew and did not share.

THREE MONTHS LATER, VERBENA's husband, Merle, arrived. After he had been greeted by Lucille Beemer, he said, "So, this is the hereafter . . . the great by and by I've heard so much about."

"That's correct, Merle."

"Well, thanks for your welcome and all the information, Lucille. But let me get this straight. You say that sometimes people up here just disappear?"

"Yes."

"And nobody has ever come back?"

"No, and until one does, I'm afraid it remains a mystery."

Elner Shimfissle, as was her habit, suddenly started singing, "Ah, sweet mystery of life, at last I've found you."

Birdie Swensen whispered to her husband, "Why is it that the ones who can't carry a tune are always the ones singing?"

A Blue Christmas

NORMA WAS FEELING BLUE. THIS WAS HER FIRST Christmas without Aunt Elner, and to make things worse, when she woke up on Christmas morning, Macky was gone. That was not like him. And on Christmas, too, when he knew darn well she was depressed. She got up, put on her robe and slippers, and went down to the kitchen. The coffee was on, but Macky and his car were gone, and there was no note. He usually left a note. What in the world? She called his cellphone number, and, after a long time he picked up.

"Where are you?"

"Sorry. I had to run out a minute, but I'm on my way home." And then he hung up. She fixed herself a cup of coffee and went back upstairs. Now she was irritated. He knew it scared her to wake up alone with no note or anything. About five minutes later, she heard the front door.

When she came back downstairs, he was sitting in the living room grinning from ear to ear, and she saw that there was now a large package under the tree.

She sighed. "Oh, Macky. I told you not to get me anything. We promised no presents this year."

"Open it," he said.

"All right . . . but I hope you didn't go and spend a lot of money. Let me get some more coffee."

"No, I want you to open it now."

As she walked over, she heard some strange sounds coming from the package. "What in the world?" When she pulled the paper off the top and looked inside, there was a litter of six gray striped kittens all mewing at the same time.

"Oh, my God. Macky, have you lost your mind? Where did you get these cats?"

"Santa Claus left them," he said.

"I can't believe you have brought these things in the house. What are they?" As she was talking, one of the kittens climbed up out of the box. When Norma picked it up, it started to purr like a little motor.

"Oh, Macky," she said, glaring at him. "I could just kill you. That's all I need is a bunch of ugly smelly stray cats to take care of."

THEY SPENT THE NEXT few days buying toys, kitty litter, cat food, and playing with the kittens. It was the best Christmas they had spent in a long time.

A few months later, they found homes for three of the kittens and kept the rest. All girls. The one they named Elner ripped up Norma's good curtains, but somehow, she didn't care.

Howdy, Neighbor

IT WAS A HAPPY DAY FOR ELNER AND VERBENA. Their old friend Ruby arrived and was pleased about it as well. "Oh, I just feel so at home up here, with all my old neighbors beside me. After you two gals left, I broke my hip and wound up in a wheelchair. I couldn't go anywhere, do anything. And there wasn't a thing good on television anymore. I was getting bored out of my gourd."

"So nothing exciting has happened since we left?" asked Verbena.

"No, not a thing. Oh, except that Dr. Orr got himself all embroiled in a scandal."

"Who?" asked Elner.

"Dr. Orr, the dentist. The one that was a dentist by day and Elvis impersonator at night. He used to go over to the Red Barn and perform sometimes. He said he preferred being called a 'tribute artist,' but he was an Elvis impersonator, no matter what he called himself."

"What happened to him?"

"Oh, well, he got caught with his dental assistant

out at some motel . . . and he had to skedaddle out of town in a hurry. Her husband said he'd shoot him on sight if he ever saw him again."

"Well, I guess that's the end of his performing days, don't you reckon?" said Elner.

"I would say so."

Verbena said, "Well, shoot. I'm kinda sorry I missed that."

Elner then said, "Hey, Ruby, have you heard anything about Hanna Marie?"

"No, honey, nobody has. She's just become a regular recluse."

Verbena jumped in. "How is that crazy Tot doing?"

Ruby laughed. "Oh, you know Tot. Same as ever, drinking coffee, still smoking cigarettes. I'm sure she'll be up here pretty soon."

The ladies had not been aware of it, but Beatrice and Ander had heard the conversation about Hanna Marie. Beatrice said, "That's not like her, Ander. Something must be wrong."

Happy Birthday

2008

NORMA WALKED UP THE WOODEN STAIRS TO AUNT Elner's old house and looked around. It didn't look the same. The old fig tree in the side yard that Aunt Elner had fallen out of looked a little weary. And the dark green plastic chairs from Walmart that Luther and Bobby Jo Griggs had out on the porch did not lend themselves to the charm of the house. Aunt Elner had had a white iron glider swing with yellow and white polka-dotted cushions and two white chairs on the porch, and it had looked so cheery. Oh, well, it's their house now. Norma knocked on the screen door, but nobody was home. She saw through the door that the cat cage sitting in the hall had a note attached. Sonny, Aunt Elner's orange cat, was inside the cage. She went in and read the note:

Had to run, Norma. Here he is.
—**Bobby Jo**

Norma picked up the cat and drove over to the cemetery. When she reached Aunt Elner's grave, she noticed a new pot of plastic yellow flowers someone had left. She knew it must have been Tot. She meant well, but Lord, they were ugly. She moved them just a little to the side and said, "Hello, Aunt Elner, it's Norma. I don't know if you remember or not, but today is your birthday. So happy birthday! Macky and Linda send you their best wishes. I've brought you some fresh flowers, and I also brought Sonny out here to see you. I knew you'd like that." She put the cat down on the grave, facing the tombstone. Sonny seemed only somewhat interested in where he was.

Norma then pulled a small tin container out of the ground, walked over to the faucet, and filled it with water. As she was arranging the flowers, she continued talking. "You know, Aunt Elner, when you were still alive, you used to get on my nerves so bad calling night and day, asking all your crazy questions, but now that you're gone, you have no idea how much I miss you. I must go to the phone ten times a day to call you. And when our phone rings, my first thought is, 'Oh, that's Aunt Elner calling,' but, of course, it isn't." She sighed. "I knew I'd miss you. I just didn't know how much. Macky, too . . . he misses not having coffee with you every morning. . . . Well, I'm going to run over to Mother and Daddy's plot and say hello, but I'm going to leave Sonny to visit with you for a while."

Every time Norma came out to the cemetery, she was appalled at how the look of it had changed and not for the better. The beautiful wooden arch with the carved flowers had been knocked down by the tornado and had never been replaced. The roads needed repaving, and the grass was getting spotty. She remembered when it was all lush green grass, and the whole cemetery was full of fresh flowers, neatly arranged. Today she saw that somebody had left their old potato chip bag on the ground.

And the headstones! Norma knew that men sometimes included a small Masonic symbol on their gravestones or a small insignia of a military branch they'd served in, but since when was a carving of an eighteen-wheeler truck or a motorcycle considered a proper gravestone motif? There were just no guidelines or rules anymore or any kind of cohesive look to the place. It was all a mishmash. A bench here, a round ball here, a new, large shiny black headstone next to a small cement sheep from the twenties. It was like putting a McDonald's next to a lovely home.

She really was not a snob. Norma understood not being able to afford things, but it was getting harder every day to hold on to whatever semblance of decorum and civility was left in the world, especially with all the insane things going on on the TV all day. And now the one place you'd think you could depend on for peace and quiet and beauty was not the same. But what could she do? People had even started putting snapshots of themselves on their gravestones. It was so unnerving to walk by and see dead people smiling at you. How did they do it? She wouldn't know how to begin to pick out a picture of herself that she would want people to see forever.

And then, of course, there was Harold Wiggler's gravestone inscription that read "Hey, it's dark in here. Somebody switch on the light." It was so horrible in so many ways; she couldn't even begin to think about it. She always avoided row 12, if she could possibly help it. She did not find the inscription the least bit funny. To Norma, death was not a joke, and in Harold's case, it wasn't even a funny joke.

After she had visited her parents' graves, Norma came back, picked up Sonny, said goodbye to Aunt Elner, and went on her way.

After Norma left, Elner said to her neighbor Ruby Robinson, "Old Sonny looked good, didn't he?"

"He did, if you like cats, I guess. But wasn't it sweet of Norma to remember your birthday?"

"It was."

"She really misses you."

"And I miss her. She's a sweet girl. She tries so hard, but sometimes her nerves just run away with her."

"Oh, I know. I think she's the one person who taking a little drink once in a while might help."

Hello, Tot!

As predicted, Tot Whooten arrived at Still Meadows not too long after Ruby. As soon as she had been greeted by Miss Beemer, a voice said, "Hello, Tot. It's Mother."

Tot was stunned to hear her mother's voice sounding so young and vital. "Mother? Is that you?"

"Yes, honey, it's me."

"Do you know who I am?"

"Of course I do."

"You don't have Alzheimer's anymore?"

"No . . . my mind came to me the minute I passed away. It's going to be like old times having my little girl back with me."

Tot never dreamed that she would ever be able to talk to her mother again, much less have her back in her right mind. Her mother had not recognized Tot for the last sixteen years of her life.

Later, she spoke with her grandparents, her old neighbors, and many of her old clients from the beauty shop. Verbena called out, "I'll bet you won't miss having to go to work every day, will you, Tot?"

"You got that right, honey," Tot said, and turned to Elner. "The thought that I will never have to tease another head of hair makes me want to jump for joy."

Ruby said, "You're just gonna love it here, Tot. Just think, all your troubles are over . . . no more cares or woes. Nothing but smooth sailing from now on."

"Well, hooray. I wouldn't go back and do that life I had over again if they paid me. What about you, Elner? Weren't you glad when it was over?"

"Oh, I don't know, Tot. Even with all the little worriments of life, I enjoyed it."

"Easy for you to say, Elner," said Tot. "You weren't married to a fool."

A male voice interrupted. "Hello, Tot."

Tot was taken by surprise. "Is that **you**, James? Where are you?"

"Six rows back."

"Oh, that's right. We put you in the old Whooten plot."

"How are you, dear?" asked James timidly.

"Well, other than being dead and buried, I'm just fine." Tot turned to Elner. "Good Lord, I forgot he was out here. I'm just glad he's way back there and not next to me. I don't need to have that new wife of his stepping over me every time she comes to visit, thank you very much."

James heard what she said. "She doesn't come out here much, Tot."

"Ah, well . . . I could have told you that."

"Yeah, she ran out on me."

"So I heard." After a moment, she said, "You broke my heart, James."

"I'm sorry. Do you still hate me?"

"I never hated you, James. I was just frustrated. If you had just stopped drinking sooner, we could have made it. I needed you, and your kids needed a father. And God knows I certainly didn't turn out to be much of a mother, working at the beauty shop all day, but what could I do? Somebody had to make a living. Anyhow, both the kids are a mess. I don't know how many generations it's going to take to undo the damage we caused them. Dwayne Jr. keeps marrying all these idiot women who think they can save him; Darlene has had three no-account husbands and is working on her fourth. You've got one granddaughter who's hooked on crack cocaine and been arrested twice, and another who's a pole dancer up in Kansas City, full of tattoos and nose rings. And the worst part of it is, she thinks she looks good." She sighed. "I don't know, James, I tried, but I failed. I was just telling Elner I'm glad I'm dead."

"Oh, honey, now don't say that. . . ."

"It's true. I was awfully tired. I just couldn't do it anymore. You have no idea what a relief it is going to be not to have to jump every time the phone rings, wondering which grandchild has been arrested now and for what."

"I'm sorry, Tot. I always loved you. I just didn't know it."

"I'm sorry, too, James. I guess I didn't make it any easier on you. I shouldn't have thrown that cement gnome at you."

"That's all right, honey."

"But in your defense, I don't think you were ever the same after you got that piece of rice stuck in your ear at the wedding."

"Maybe," said James. "But still, it was no excuse for me to act the way I did."

There was another long silence, then Tot said, "James, we can't go back and undo all the hurts, but I would like to be friends. Can we do that?"

"Tot, you don't know how long I've prayed about that."

"Good. Now that we are friends, could you please tell me what in the hell you ever saw in Jackie Sue Potts?"

"God only knows. I was a fool, that's all I can say. A damn fool."

"And the worst part, she was one of my customers!"

"I know. I'm sorry."

"Well, you're a man, so I guess some of it is not your fault. You just couldn't control yourself when it came to women, and you're certainly not alone in that department."

"Amen, sister!" thought six other women who were listening in.

"Maybe," said James. "But you think I didn't feel guilty? You don't know how many times I wanted to come home, but I was too ashamed to face you."

Tot heard what he said. But still, she wished he had come back home to her. He didn't know it, of course, but she would have taken him back in a second.

Elner noted that it was always interesting to find out things you didn't know. Although they really liked her, most people thought Tot was tough and bitter. And she could say some pretty cruel things. But bless her heart, the truth was that all along, she had been hopelessly in love with a man who wasn't there. Unrequited love will turn even the sweetest people bitter.

THE NEXT DAY, ELNER and Verbena were talking about how wonderful it was that Tot and James were speaking again. "And he's sober!" said Verbena. "I never thought I'd live to see the day."

While the two old neighbors chatted, a huge flock of crows suddenly landed in the oak tree. Then a few seconds later, the whole flock picked up and took off again. Elner laughed. "Aren't crows funny? I know a lot of people don't like crows, but I always got a big kick out of them. Sonny hated them and tried his best to catch one, but he never did. Poor old Sonny." Then Elner suddenly sang out, "Oh, Sonny boy, the pipes, the pipes are calling, from dust to dawn. Oh, I'll be there in sadness and in sorrow. I love you so, oh Sonny boyyyeee. . . ."

Verbena interrupted her. "You're singing the wrong tune, Elner. That's 'Danny Boy.'"

"Oh, that's right." Then she sang out, "Oh, climb up on my knee, Sonny Boy, though you're only three, Sonny Boyyyeee. . . ."

Will Shimfissle giggled and said to a friend, "Don't her singing sound like twenty bobcats with a belly-ache?"

AFTER SUCH A TROUBLING and rather unhappy life, Tot Whooten found it pleasant out at Still Meadows. As Tot told Ruby one night, "It's so sad now to think how many of these beautiful nights I missed when I was alive. It's just amazing to see all those thousands of little stars just twinkling away. I guess they were always there. Sometimes I'd watch the sun go down with Elner, but then I always went in and watched television until it was time to go to bed. But now I'm really enjoying seeing the night sky, listening to the owls, the frogs, and the crickets. That's what I should have done more of, instead of looking at TV. Every damn night, but I was hooked on watching **Dynasty** and **Big Valley** with Barbara Stanwyck. I always admired her. She looked like she'd just as soon shoot you as look at you. She was my kind of woman."

Lester Shingle, who made it a habit to listen in on his main suspect's conversations, took special note of that last remark. Tot definitely had a violent streak.

Shreveport, Louisiana

2011

LUTHER GRIGGS WAS DRIVING HIS EIGHTEEN-wheeler and daydreaming about hitting the lottery. He had ten tickets in his pocket right now. His dream was to hit it big and buy one of those long, luxurious silver and brown recreational vehicles. And it wasn't a vague dream. He knew the exact model and make. He wanted the Bounder, with all the accessories, the slide-outs, the extra-wide "He-Man" shower, and the awnings outside.

He would quit his job, and he and Bobby Jo would drive it all over America, from one RV park to the next, living the high life. He had read about the Flying Flags RV Park in Buellton, California, that had a pool, a restaurant, bingo every Friday night, and live music and a barbeque on Saturday. What else could you want?

THERE WAS A LIGHT rain falling when he saw the car in his side-view mirror come up behind him. It was a sweet-looking red 1970 Plymouth Duster. He let her pass him, so he could get a good look at it. The lady driving it waved, and he waved back. Yeah, it was a '70, all right. She or her husband had taken really good care of it. It still had its original paint and wheels.

It had been raining off and on for about six hours, and as much as he wanted to get home, he held his speed limit to 55. There were so many oil refineries down here in this part of Louisiana, and this stretch of the interstate could get particularly slickedy in the rain.

He was still behind the red Plymouth Duster, and a few miles up ahead, just as she was coming up to a bridge, an armadillo stepped onto the road right in front of her, and when it did, she did the worst thing she could do. She swerved to try to avoid hitting it, and she swerved too fast. Luther saw her start to lose control, spin sideways, then hit the concrete embankment, and skid down the hill and right into the river. "Oh, man," said Luther. He looked behind him, but no one else was on the road, and nobody was coming the other way, so he slowed down as fast as he could without jackknifing and pulled his truck off to the side of the road. When he had come to a full stop, he grabbed the big heavy wrench he kept in the front seat for protection, jumped out, and ran toward the bridge as fast as he could.

When he got there, he looked down into the river and saw the red car still barely afloat, bobbing up and down in the water, sinking fast. Thankfully, the car was still pretty close to the bank, so he slid the twenty or so feet down the riverbank and into the water. He then waded alongside the car and jumped in a few feet in front of it and managed to grab ahold of the door handle as the car floated by, twisting and turning.

Just as he feared, she had all the windows rolled up, and he could see the lady inside was panicked and struggling to get out of her seatbelt. He had to fight hard to get it undone, because it was under water now, but after about ten tries, he was finally able to smash in the front window, reach in, and release the safety belt. Then with great effort, he got the door to open. He pulled the lady out of the car and pushed her upward as hard as he could. The last thing he saw were her two stocking feet swishing back and forth, headed up toward the surface. Thank God.

Then as he and the car sank farther down toward the bottom, something suddenly occurred to Luther. "Oh, shit . . . I forgot. I don't know how to swim."

When he was five, his daddy had thrown him into the lake, and he had almost drowned. He had been deathly afraid of water ever since.

LUTHER GRIGGS
1964–2011
**No greater love hath man
than to lay down his life for another**

When Ruby's husband, John Robinson, arrived at Still Meadows and was chatting with Elner, he said to her, "Did Luther tell you how he got here?"

"He just said it had been an accident."

"What?" Then John called out, "Luther Griggs, why didn't you tell Elner and everybody how you drowned saving a woman's life?"

Luther mumbled, "Oh, I don't know. I guess I'm kinda embarrassed I didn't know how to swim."

"Well, Luther, you don't have a thing to be embarrassed about. You are a genuine hero. That lady you saved was the mother of three children," said John. "Imagine that. He jumped in a river to save a complete stranger."

After Elner had heard the entire story, she said, "Well, I'm not the least bit surprised. I always knew Luther was a good boy, didn't I, honey?"

"Yes, ma'am. That's what you always said."

THE LADY LUTHER HAD saved did not forget it. She and her husband and children had driven to Elmwood Springs for his funeral. Her youngest girl, who had just turned six, even wrote him a letter and placed it on his grave.

Dear Mr. Griggs,

Thank you for saving my mommy. She is nice and is glad, too. I am sorry you got drownded.

**Love,
Tracy**

Parrot Head

I T WAS A PRETTY T UESDAY, AND D WAYNE J R., stoned as usual, was wearing his "Wasting Away in Margaritaville" T-shirt and taking a break from home. His wife was at work, and the kids were at school. He had walked up to the cemetery with a cold six-pack. He flopped down on his mother's grave, lit a joint, and popped open a cold beer. He looked down across the town and sighed. Now that his mother was dead, the place was such a drag. Tot had always been fun. Mean as hell, but fun. Why did she have to go and die on him? Man, if he hadn't married all those women and had all these kids, he would just take off, head to Key West, and join the other Parrot Heads down in old Margaritaville. He nodded to himself. Yeah, things would be great if he could just get to Key West. Sitting around on the beach, drinking all day. No wife, no ex-wives, no kids to bug him. Man . . . he might even get to meet Jimmy Buffett. How cool would that be? One day, he would do it, too. If he ever got his driver's license back. Oh, hell, he might even hitchhike, if he had to. One day, he just might take off and never come back. Man, how cool would that be? He popped open another beer. "Yeah, just how damn cool would that be?"

After he left, Tot sighed and said to James, "Booze, the gift that just keeps on giving."

"Yep," sighed James.

IT WAS LATER MORNING when everybody up at Still Meadows heard the shrill sounds of ambulances and police sirens come screaming through town, then screeching to a halt. "What had happened?" they wondered. They could tell the ambulance had stopped somewhere in town, but where? Who was hurt? Who was sick?

Tot Whooten piped up. "I hope whoever is getting picked up and taken to the hospital knows how much it's gonna cost them. When I got that needle-nose houndfish stuck in my leg down in Florida, they charged me over five thousand dollars for a six-block ride. I said, 'Hell, I could have called a taxi and saved myself a fortune.' After that, I told everybody, I said, 'If you can get up and walk, do it, but whatever you do, don't let them put you in a damn ambulance.'"

SADLY, THE PERSON FOR WHOM the ambulance had been called, out at the Swensen house, had been unable to walk.

A Ship of a Girl

IN ANY TOWN, THERE ARE ALWAYS SOME PEOPLE who receive a lot of attention, and then there are those who live a quiet life without anyone even noticing.

Norvaleen Whittle had always been a little chubby, just enough to keep the boys away and keep her from being a majorette or a cheerleader.

Now thirty-seven, Norvaleen was a bookkeeper for several businesses in town and, thanks to the Internet, she was able to work at home. Her parents had left her a nice little two-bedroom, one-bath house that she seldom left anymore, except to shop for food or go to the drugstore. Which was fine with her. She had a Yorkshire terrier mix named Mitzi, who was good company and paper-trained.

Then one day, while she was shopping at Walmart, she suddenly noticed that when she walked, she was swaying from side to side like a great big ocean liner. It was the first time Norvaleen realized that she was a big, fat person. It had slowly crept up on her. Her feet were now too fat for her shoes, and she had not been able to wear her rings or watch for a long time. She should have noticed sooner.

The problem was that Norvaleen had been in denial and also in McDonald's, eating the cheeseburger special with fries. Evidently, the Diet Coke had not evened out the calories. What a shock. She had hit the muumuu and flip-flop stage and hadn't seen it coming. Oh, she knew she was a little chubby, but today at her checkup, Dr. Halling had informed her that she had gone way past chubby. According to the fat vs. muscle machine in his office, she had shot straight into obese and was teetering on morbid obesity. He made her an appointment with a diet clinic before she left.

As she drove home, she wondered what she had been thinking. What made her think she could eat like a teenager? That was the trouble. She hadn't been thinking. She had been sitting in front of the television set for the past twenty-two years, eating snacks, and her life had become just one long snack from morning to night. And now she had to keep this appointment because if she didn't, they would tell Dr. Halling.

THE DIET CLINIC WOMAN was extremely cheerful and encouraging. She told Norvaleen that there was a thin person inside her just waiting to jump out.

But Norvaleen knew better. Inside her was a fat woman who didn't have the energy to jump anywhere. Besides, what was the point? Nobody loved her. The one boy she'd loved had married someone else. Why do it? "Do it for yourself," she'd said, but all Norvaleen had to look forward to was something good to eat, playing with Mitzi, and her television shows.

The diet clinic woman said, "Miss Whittle, you don't have a problem with willpower; you are a food addict. You are as addicted to sugar and carbohydrates as a heroin addict is addicted to heroin. The only way to permanently lose the weight is to cut out both sugar and wheat completely."

Okay. Suppose she did sign up for all the appointments, waste all that time and money, go through all that misery to lose weight, then what? She'd just be an unhappy skinny person with probably a lot of loose skin. The doctor had said that if she lost all that fat, she would add another good ten years onto her life.

Norvaleen thought about it, but if she couldn't eat bread and ice cream, she wasn't sure she wanted another ten years. She decided she would rather have dessert, and never went back to the clinic.

IT WAS A FRIDAY morning a few years later when, with great effort, Norvaleen hauled herself out of her car one leg at a time, caught her breath, and headed across the parking lot to the CVS Pharmacy. When she got close to the mall, she heard a lot of commotion coming from inside; people were screaming and falling down on the ground. Someone yelled, "Stop! Stop him!" She looked up just in time to see a man with a gun running out the glass door with the security guard right behind him. Norvaleen didn't have much time to think. She just crossed her arms and stepped in front of him, blocking his path. He ran into her so hard that the gun popped out of his hand, and he fell. She quickly sat down on him and stayed there until the police came. And a good thing, too. As it turned out, the man had just robbed a Kay Jewelers.

People who witnessed it said that no matter how hard that man squirmed and wriggled underneath her, he couldn't get up. The criminal would later claim the woman who had captured him weighed more than six hundred pounds, which wasn't true, but it had taken three firemen and a bystander to pull Norvaleen up to her feet.

After all the excitement was over and the thief had been handcuffed and driven away, the policeman taking down her information suddenly looked up at her in surprise. "Norvaleen? Are you Norvaleen Whittle? We went to school together. Do you remember me? I'm Billy . . . Billy McMichael?"

She turned a strange color of pink. She remembered him. He was the boy she had been in love with.

—

That afternoon, Cathy Calvert interviewed her for the paper and wrote an article that appeared on the front page with the headline:

LOCAL WOMAN RESTRAINS THIEF AT MALL

Norvaleen didn't tell Cathy, but she hadn't restrained him on purpose. She just couldn't get up. Someone with a phone had shot a video of her sitting on the man and posted it on YouTube. And of course, there were the usual jokes made by mean-spirited individuals, mostly teenage boys, but most people were impressed by her bravery. People said, "Maybe Norvaleen couldn't **give** chase . . . but she sure as hell could stop one!"

In appreciation for her bravery, she was given a $100 gift certificate to all the stores at the mall, including every restaurant at the food court. Later, she received a Civilian Hero award from the mayor and was given an honorary Deputy of Police badge by Chief Ralph Childress. For the occasion, Norvaleen bought a new large black dress at Ross Dress for Less and a pair of formal flip-flops with rhinestones.

That night, Billy picked her up in his police car to take her to the ceremony. As he was driving her back home, he asked, "Would you have dinner with me sometime?"

Billy had married one of the pretty girls in high school, but it had not worked out. He was divorced, and for the past three years he'd been living in a bad apartment complex across town.

At first, it was dinner a couple of times a week, then as time went by, Billy started staying overnight. Norvaleen was so happy, and without much effort, a year later, she was back to being only chubby, which was fine with Billy. He found out he really liked a big girl. A year later, Norvaleen used the gift certificate from Kay Jewelers to buy a wedding ring for Billy.

It takes time and a lot of suffering, but sometimes, when you least expect it, life has a strange way of working out. She had been heading to the drugstore to pick up some Cortizone 10 for eczema, and look what happened. She was the last person in the world she thought would have a happy ending.

Norma Has a Close Call

2012

WHEN CATHY CALVERT RAN INTO NORMA AT THE drugstore, she was surprised to see her on crutches.

"Oh, Norma . . . what happened?"

"I broke my foot."

"How?"

"Well, I was out at the mall shopping at the big Macy's. Macky needed some new undershirts, and they had some on sale in the basement. Anyhow, I was headed down there when my cellphone rang, and I went to pull it out of my purse, and I must not have been paying attention, because when I went to step on the first step of the escalator, I missed it and the next thing I knew I was falling . . . rolling and tumbling with my dress over my head all the way down, and there wasn't another person on it to stop my fall."

"Oh, no!"

"Yes, and while I was falling, all I could think about was that when I got to the bottom of that escalator, that thing would grab my dress and pull me in it, and I would be chewed to pieces, so all the way down, I was yelling, 'Turn it off! Turn it off!' Well, thank goodness, some quick-thinking employee at the jewelry counter ran over and at the very last minute, flipped the switch and saved me from being ripped to shreds. But I had landed at the bottom sideways and was stuck upside down and couldn't move. There I was, all cattywampus with my legs up in the air, and at that exact moment, who should walk by but my old school friend Kathy Gilmore, who I hadn't seen in over twelve years, and she looks down at me and says, 'Norma? Is that you?' 'Yes,' I said. 'It's me.' She said, 'Well, what in the world are you doing here?' I said, 'I've just fallen down the escalator, and I'm stuck. Call 911.' So she said, 'I sure will, hon,' and by then, a huge crowd had gathered all around, and me with my dress ripped to shreds. Oh, it was a mess. I was scraped and scratched from top to bottom. I was in the hospital for a week. And do you know what the worst part was? The person who was calling me on the phone that caused me to almost kill myself wasn't even a person. It was a junk call . . . some machine! Can you imagine?"

Cathy said, "Oh my gosh, Norma, you could have been **killed,** falling down those stairs. Remember what happened to poor Hanna Marie."

"Don't think it didn't occur to me. The whole time I was falling, I kept thinking, 'Oh, no, don't tell me I'm going to wind up like Hanna Marie.'"

What Happened

THE HEADLINE READ:

BELOVED CITIZEN FALLS TO HER DEATH

IT WAS THE HOUSEKEEPER who found Hanna Marie at the bottom of the stairs in the morning, when she came to work. The coroner said she had died instantly. When the word spread all over town, everybody was upset and saddened. But later, when they found out that her husband had been in New York on one of his many so-called business trips, they had been infuriated.

As Norma said to Macky, "Imagine, leaving a poor deaf woman alone all night in that big house while you're off somewhere living it up . . . and on her dime, too. I don't know how he can live with himself."

Can You Hear Me Now?

CONSIDERING HER AGE AND THE CONDITION OF HER health, everyone expected Irene Goodnight would be the next of their friends to arrive at Still Meadows. But to their surprise, the very next person was Hanna Marie Swensen.

HANNA MARIE'S DEMISE PRESENTED a problem Lucille Beemer had not faced before. How would she be able to speak to a deaf person?

As she had feared, when she spoke to Hanna Marie, there was no answer. "Oh, dear," she said. "I feel so terrible. I just have no way to communicate with her and let her know where she is."

Verbena said, "Well, Lucille, I don't know what to tell you. We can talk our heads off until the cows come home, and she won't hear a thing. And it's too bad, too. I'd just love to chat with her and find out what she has to say about that no-good, two-timing husband of hers. He's been cheating on her for years with every bimbo in town."

Then, suddenly, a woman's voice said, "I think I can hear."

"Hanna Marie?" asked Lucille.

"Yes, I think so. Is that me I hear talking?"

An amazed Lucille answered, "Yes, it is most certainly you!"

"Am I making real words?"

"Oh, yes."

"And saying them right?"

"Perfectly."

"Am I too loud? I can't tell."

"No, not at all, and you have a beautiful speaking voice. What a delightful surprise. . . . Oh, my dear, just wait until your parents find out." Lucille then called out, "Beatrice! Ander! Say hello to your daughter."

Beatrice spoke first. "Darling, this is Mother. Can you hear me?"

"Oh, yes, Mother, I can!"

Ander said, "Honey, this is your daddy."

"Oh Daddy, I can't believe it."

Verbena Wheeler, who had been listening in, could no longer contain herself and started yelling at the top of her voice, "Oh, my God. It's Hanna Marie and she can talk and hear!"

It was quite a moment. For the first time, Beatrice and Ander could talk with their daughter, and for the first time, she could hear them.

Elner waited for the three of them to talk a little

while, then she said, "Hello, sweetheart. This is your big ol' aunt Elner saying hello."

Hanna Marie said, "Aunt Elner, I'm so happy to hear your voice. Oh, thank you for being so kind to me all my life."

"Well, honey, that's all right. You were always easy to be kind to."

"Hanna Marie, this is your great-aunt Katrina Nordstrom speaking, and I just wanted to say that I know just how you feel. I had gone completly blind, but when I got here I could see."

Suddenly everybody wanted to talk to Hanna Marie and weigh in on the miracle.

HANNA MARIE TALKED ALL DAY long with so many friends and family. At around six o'clock that evening, Old Man Hendersen said, "Good Lord, that girl is a talker. Is she ever going to shut up?"

LATER, AFTER THE SUN had gone down, the Goodnights, as a special welcome, sang a three-part harmony version of "Over the Rainbow."

After it was over, Hanna Marie said, "Oh, thank you so much, ladies. So that's what music sounds like. I always wondered. It's so lovely and soothing. And how wonderful for you ladies to be able to sing so beautifully."

At that moment Hanna Marie's great-aunt Birdie Swensen called out, "For goodness' sake, Elner, don't you dare sing now. Let the poor girl have her illusions a little while longer."

Elner laughed. "I'll try not to, Birdie. I'll give her a couple of days to adjust."

Before she went to sleep, Ruby whispered to Verbena, "Verbena, you shouldn't have said all that stuff earlier about Hanna Marie's husband cheating on her."

Verbena said, "Well, how was I supposed to know she could hear? I just hope to God she wasn't listening."

THE NEXT DAY, when all the excitement had died down a little, Lucille Beemer asked Hanna Marie exactly what had happened.

"When I woke up I started hearing sounds. At first I didn't know what it was."

Lucille said, "No, I mean, what brought you up to Still Meadows?"

"Oh, that. Well, I honestly don't know. But I guess something must have happened, or I wouldn't be here."

"No."

"No. Oh dear, I wonder what it was. I know that Michael was out of town, and the last thing I remember was getting up and heading down to the kitchen . . . then after that, nothing."

"Well, don't worry about it. We'll find out. Somebody will come up and tell us, but in the meantime, everyone is just thrilled you are here."

"Oh, me, too, Miss Beemer. I'm afraid I haven't been very happy lately."

VERBENA WHISPERED TO RUBY, "Did you hear that, Ruby? Hanna Marie said the husband was 'out of town.' She may know more than we thought."

Case Closed

IF LESTER SHINGLE HAD A MUSTACHE, HE WOULD have been twirling it. Irene Goodnight, the last of his murder suspects, had just come up to Still Meadows, and he was finally going to have his day in court. The next morning, he confronted all four in a loud, booming voice. "This is Lester Shingle speaking! I know one of you did it, and whoever it was, you may think you got away with it. But you didn't."

It was true that all four women had threatened to kill him at one time or another.

They had all known he was the notorious Peeping Tom. Ada and Bess Goodnight had told him that if they ever caught him anywhere close to their house they would shoot him. Irene said she'd skin him alive. And Tot Whooten had threatened something even worse involving scissors.

Ada was the first to speak and said, "What are you talking about?"

"You know what I'm talking about. My murder."

"What?"

"One of you hit me in the head with a bowling

ball and killed me in cold blood in the Blue Star Bowling Alley parking lot back in April of 1952, and I intend to find out which one."

Tot couldn't believe what she was hearing. "Are you crazy, Lester? You weren't hit in the head with a bowling ball, you idiot! You slipped on the ice and hit your head on Mildred Ogleby's car. Oh, for God's sake." Then Tot called out, "Hey, Billy!"

"Yeah?"

"It's Tot Whooten."

"Oh, hey, Tot, how's the old left-hander?"

"Just fine. . . . Listen, Billy, I have a question for you. Didn't you see Lester fall and hit his head on Mrs. Ogleby's car, and didn't you call an ambulance?"

"Yeah. Why?"

"The idiot thinks he was hit in the head by a bowling ball."

"What? Nah. He cracked his head open on her headlight—bent the hell out of it as I remember."

Mrs. Ogleby, the owner of the 1946 Buick, joined in. "He's right, Lester, and it cost me an arm and a leg to get it fixed, too."

Tot said, "See? I ain't lying."

After a long pause, Lester said, "Well, shoot. All these years, I thought I had been murdered. . . . Now I feel kinda despondent."

Irene Goodnight weighed in. "Well, if it's any consolation to you, if I had seen you that night, I would have killed you."

"Well, thanks, at least I wasn't too far off. But still, it's a big disappointment. All these years thinking I'd been a victim of a crime, and it wasn't nothing but an accident."

Bess said, "Well, you know what they say, Lester. There are no accidents."

"And people get what's coming to them one way or the other," added Verbena.

"Yeah, I guess so. . . . But now that I'm not a victim, I feel like a big old nobody. . . . Shoot."

So, AS IT TURNED out, poor Lester Shingle had not been murdered after all. But that didn't mean there **hadn't** been a murder in Elmwood Springs. . . .

The Redhead

ALTHOUGH SHE'D BEEN DECEASED FOR QUITE A while now, Verbena Wheeler was still a busybody. Today she was busy staring at the woman who was standing over Hanna Marie Swensen's grave.

Verbena whispered to Ruby, "Hey, who's that redheaded woman over at Hanna Marie's plot?"

Ruby looked over at the woman in the raincoat and whispered back, "I have no idea. She's not from here. . . . Leastways, I don't know her. Maybe she's someone Hanna Marie went to deaf school with."

Whoever the woman was, she stood there for a very long time, just staring down at Hanna Marie's grave. Finally she said, "I'm sorry. I'm so sorry." Then she turned around and left.

After a while, curiosity got the best of Verbena, and she said, "Hanna Marie?"

"Yes?"

"It's Verbena Wheeler here, and Ruby and I were just remarking what a pretty lady your visitor was."

"Yes, she was. Very pretty."

They waited for more information, but none came.

Several days later, Verbena just couldn't stand it one more minute, and just came right out and asked Hanna Marie point-blank who the lady was.

"Well, Verbena, I wish I knew. I have absolutely no idea. I've never seen her before in my life."

"Ah, I see. Well, she **was** pretty."

The whole thing seemed very odd to Verbena. Hanna Marie may not have known her, but that woman had obviously known Hanna Marie. She had stood there for a very long time. And she'd looked absolutely heartbroken. You can't be heartbroken over someone you don't know, she thought. It didn't make any sense. Strangers just didn't show up at another stranger's grave. Unless she was at the wrong grave by mistake . . . and there was no way that could happen. Hanna Marie had a big headstone with her name on it in great big letters. And the woman had been looking right at it.

She wondered if Hanna Marie knew the woman and just wasn't telling her. Either way, there was something fishy going on. And what had that woman been so sorry about? Verbena was determined to get to the bottom of it. She loved a good mystery. She had been a devoted fan of **Murder, She Wrote** with Angela Lansbury.

THERE **HAD** BEEN A MURDER in Elmwood Springs, but sadly, the victim didn't know it. How could she? She was deaf. She had not heard the man come up behind her. She didn't know she had been pushed. The police didn't know it had been a murder. There had been no forced entry. The man hired to do the job had been given a key to the house. Nobody saw him come in or go out.

Overheard at Dinner

2013

PEOPLE DON'T REALIZE THAT SOMETIMES OTHER people do listen in on their private conversations. For instance, on the night the judge and his wife were having dinner, discussing the contents of Hanna Marie's will, their cook, Mrs. Grace, had left the door to the dining room just slightly ajar. She had been very interested in what the judge had to say. She had worked for Mr. and Mrs. Swensen before they'd died.

Although it had taken a while for it to go through the probate process, Hanna Marie's will had just been validated by the judge, and when people heard about what was in it, they would be absolutely astonished. It was almost unbelievable that Hanna Marie would have left all of her relatives and charities completely out of the will. It just wasn't like her. But according to the will, she had left her husband everything. And at the end of the last quarter, company assets were up to about thirty-six million. Even Laverne Thorneycroft, the judge's wife, questioned it that night at dinner. "I don't care what you say, Sam.

There's something rotten going on. She no more left that business to him than the man in the moon."

The judge shook his head. "Laverne, what can I say? All I can do is follow the letter of the law. I have to authorize closing the estate."

"Well, I still don't believe she left everything to him."

"According to the will, she did. Hanna Marie was deaf, but not blind, Laverne. She could read and write. And as long as it's on paper, it's legal." The judge carefully buttered his dinner roll, then added, "But if I were him, I'd be real careful crossing the street in this town from now on."

When word got out about the contents of the will, everybody was upset. They couldn't understand how Hanna Marie would do such a thing.

After the taxes were paid, and the dairy was now officially his, the first thing Michael Vincent did was fire anyone who had been closely associated with the Swensen family. The first person to go was Hanna Marie's cousin Albert Olsen, who had been manager of the company for almost thirty years.

Albert was devastated. He told his wife that Ander would be rolling over in his grave if he knew how Vincent was running the dairy now. "That guy has no idea how to run a dairy. He's fired almost everybody in management, and these new farm workers he's brought in aren't trained to work with cows. He doesn't care about the cows or the quality of the product—just how much and how fast. This used to be a one-company town. Everybody knew every-body. These new workers don't have any roots here. Hell, some of them are still living in their cars. God knows what he's paying them. Mark my words. Before he's through, he's going to run that dairy right into the ground or he could turn around and sell it to some big conglomerate."

Albert's wife sighed. "When I think of how hard Ander worked all those years to build it up, how hard **you** and everybody worked, it just breaks my heart."

The next day, one of Albert's sons told Police Chief Ralph Childress, "I'm telling you in advance, Ralph, after what Vincent did to my dad, if I ever catch him alone, I'm gonna beat the hell out of him."

He was the third person that day to tell Ralph almost the same thing. There wasn't a person in town who didn't entertain thoughts of killing Vincent, or at least maiming him in some way, including Ralph. Even his own wife, Edna, had remarked, "I'd like to poison the rat."

Little Miss Davenport Tells All

WHEN MRS. GRACE, JUDGE THORNEYCROFT'S cook, passed away, and she told her friend Verbena Wheeler about Hanna Marie's will, the news spread like wildfire that the husband had gotten everything lock, stock, and barrel. The people up in Still Meadows were as shocked as the people in town had been. And Hanna Marie was utterly dumbfounded.

She knew what was in her will. Her father had trained her to read documents, and she had read every word before she'd signed it.

Under no circumstances shall the business and properties known as Sweet Clover Dairy be sold or deeded to any individual, other than a Nordstrom, Olsen, or Swensen family member.

Ander was particularly upset. He had promised Lordor on his deathbed that the dairy would always be a family-run business.

Hanna Marie had done exactly as her father had

requested and included in her will the very same clause that had appeared in his, and she had been careful to make sure that all her charity donations would continue after her death. "I don't know how it could have happened," she said. "I'm just at a complete loss."

Little Miss Davenport, over in plot 258, had not wanted to say anything before, but now she felt she just had to speak out. "Hanna Marie?" she said. "It's Dottie Davenport. I used to work for your daddy . . . and then your husband."

"Oh, yes, of course, Miss Davenport. How are you?"

"To tell you the truth, I'm just as mad as hell at myself."

"Oh, no, why?"

"If I hadn't gotten sick and died when I did, I could have stopped that man from stealing all your money."

The cemetery was suddenly all ears.

"You probably don't remember, but I was in the office the day you came in to sign your will. And after you signed it and left, your husband handed me a key and told me to go put the will in the private security box in the file room."

"I remember that."

"Well, he doesn't know it, but on the way to the file room, I read your will, and I know where you wanted your money to go."

"You read it?"

"I wasn't supposed to, but I did. And I'll tell you something else he doesn't know. Before I put it in the box, I stopped and made a quick copy of it, just in case he ever tried to pull something funny."

At this point, Verbena Wheeler was almost beside herself and yelled, "Oh, my God . . . did everybody hear that? Little Miss Davenport made a copy of Hanna Marie's will!"

"And what did you do with that copy, dear?" asked Hanna Marie.

"I hid it."

Verbena yelled again. "She hid it, everybody. Little Miss Davenport hid a copy of the will!"

Ruby said, "Be quiet, Verbena! Let her finish. Go on, Dottie, where did you hide it?"

"Well, I didn't have much time, so on my way back with the key, I folded it up and stuck it behind your daddy's portrait."

Ander spoke up. "The one in the boardroom."

"Yes."

"Did anyone see you do it, Dottie?" he asked.

"I don't think so, but they might have. At that point, people were always spying on one another, trying to get in good with him."

"Do you think the copy's still there?" asked Ander.

"I have no way of knowing, Mr. Swensen."

Hanna Marie said, "But you were so brave to try and protect me. I really appreciate it, more than you know."

"Oh, thank you. But if I only had outlived you,

even by a few months, I would have heard about it and could've stopped him cold. I think he and that woman lawyer got together, pulled a fast one, and changed your will, and I could have proven it."

This news was a surprise to Hanna Marie. "What woman lawyer?"

"The one from New York. She used to come to town every once in a while, supposedly to talk business, but they always looked a little too hanky-panky for my taste."

"I don't remember ever meeting her. What did she look like?"

"Oh, she was pretty, I guess, if you like redheads."

"Did you hear that, Hanna Marie? That woman at your grave that day was his lawyer."

Everybody immediately thought, "And probably his girlfriend as well," but nobody said it.

HEARING THE INFORMATION LITTLE Miss Davenport had just revealed upset all of Hanna Marie's friends and family out at Still Meadows, especially her mother, Beatrice. "He'd seemed like such a nice boy," she said.

HANNA MARIE WAS ABSOLUTELY devastated to have let her father down. She kept saying, "I'm so sorry, Daddy. I'm just so sorry."

Ander said, "That's all right, honey, it's not your

fault. I had a feeling he might try and pull something. That no-good . . ."

Birdie Swensen, Hanna Marie's grandmother, jumped in. "Hanna Marie, this is Grandmother. Don't blame yourself. Nobody is mad at you, isn't that right, Katrina?"

Katrina, her great-aunt, said, "Not one little bit, sweetheart. It's that man we're upset with. He must have done something shady."

Gene Nordstrom, her cousin, called out, "I just wish I could get my hands on that guy."

"Yeah, me, too," said Gustav Tildholme. "I'd give him what for."

Pretty soon, the whole hill was humming about what they would do. Merle Wheeler said, "There are ladies present, or I'd tell what I'd do."

Katrina didn't say it, but she knew that it would have broken Lordor's heart to know that the dairy had gone to a stranger. And the idea that this man was going to get away with it didn't seem fair.

AT THE END OF THE DAY, Elner Shimfissle pretty much summed up the frustration everybody was feeling. "Well, dag-dog it," she said, "this is definitely not one of the perks of being deceased. Here we have pertinent information that could send that no-good crook to jail, and there's not a single thing we can do about it."

The Affair

HER AFFAIR WITH MICHAEL VINCENT HAD STARTED in New York. She had been in the legal department of the advertising agency that handled the dairy account. He said he and his wife were not happy, but she was deaf, and he just didn't feel he could divorce her.

And then to make matters worse, he found out that his wife's last will and testament had left him entirely out. His father-in-law had been a bastard and, besides, he said his wife had not been in her right mind when she had made it out. She had been manipulated by other family members to cut him out of what he deserved. It wasn't fair to Michael. He had worked so hard for so many years and had built the company from scratch, and then to be treated like that. At least, that's what she had been told. And she had been head over heels in love with him. Sometimes a woman in love doesn't see what's right in front of her eyes. Even a woman with a law degree.

—

She had been with him in his hotel room the day he received the call about his wife's accident. Although they had not lived as man and wife for a long time, he seemed terribly upset.

She had changed the will for him, long before the wife had died, long before she had found out what a monster he was and how she had been used. It hadn't been too hard. Remove a clause here, a clause there, reword a few things, change the names of the beneficiaries. Of course, she could have been disbarred for doing it, but at the time, he had been so grateful, and it was, after all, for both of their futures, he had said.

What a fool she had been to believe him. After the wife died, he stopped calling. That's when she started putting two and two together. She had flown in, rented a car, and driven to his office in Elmwood Springs to confront him. When she threatened to go to the authorities and turn him in, he had laughed. "Go ahead. I'll be happy to tell them how you forged my wife's will. You might get out of jail in ten years or so, if you're lucky. So why don't you pack up your little panties and get the hell out of here before I throw you out!"

The lawyer stood there and stared at the man she had never really known until this very moment. "Oh, my God . . . your poor wife. What did you do to her?"

When she said that, something glittered behind his cold blue eyes, something chilling that made her blood run cold and scared her to death. She turned around and left. She got back in the car and drove out of town. But before she did, she'd made one stop at the cemetery.

Another Visit from Dwayne Jr.

ON MOTHER'S DAY, DWAYNE JR. WAS BACK UP AT Tot's grave, drunk again, feeling sorry for himself, crying in his beer, wailing at her tombstone. "You damn crazy old woman. Why did you have to go and die on me, Momma? I loved you, and you didn't leave me nothing. Not one damned cent. Goddamn you. I loved you, you Goddamn crazy old woman. I loved you. You should have bought me that motorcycle. It's your fault I don't have no money. Why'd you die and leave me? I loved you."

Tot was not moved at these drunken confessions of love. When she had been alive, he had done nothing but steal her blind.

She told James that one day she'd come home, and he'd stolen her entire dining room set.

James said, "Damn. He got that from me. I used to steal from you. God and I hate a thief. Thank God I finally got sober. I owe my sanity to AA."

"Good for you. I owe mine to the Pointer Sisters and disco."

"Disco?"

"Yeah, I was way too old for it at the time, but I didn't care. It saved my life. After you left me, I couldn't stand to be alone. I hired a babysitter for Momma and the grandkids, and every Friday and Saturday night, I'd get off from work, put on my makeup, curl my hair, and head on out to Disco City. What a place. They had this big mirrored ball hanging over the dance floor, twirling and sparkling . . . whistles blowing, colored spotlights turning you blue and yellow and pink whirling around. Wow! Me and about twenty gay guys from Joplin, all wearing pink feather boas, dancing to 'She Works Hard for the Money' in our big platform shoes, all decked out in our bell bottoms and false eyelashes. I must have danced a thousand miles that year. It was great. Too bad you missed it."

Norma Growing Older

2014

WHEN SHE WAS THIRTY, NORMA HAD MADE A VOW that when she hit sixty, she would stop dyeing her hair, but, of course, she hadn't. Gray looked pretty good on other people. Macky looked great with it, but she didn't. Her skin was too fair. She just looked old and washed out. She didn't want old-looking teeth either, so she spent a small fortune getting a "smile makeover." She now looked like an older woman with sixteen-year-old teeth.

However, after spending all that money, she really didn't have much to smile about or that many people to smile at. She basically just went to the supermarket and back. And the girls at the checkout counter certainly never noticed her smile makeover. They hardly ever looked up.

Another problem was that all of her life, most of her good friends had been much older than she was. She had read that this was common in only children. But now, most of her friends had passed away.

They say that you should make friends with younger people, and there were a few of Linda's old school friends still in town who would say hello to her if she ran into them, but most of them had moved away years ago. She blamed the Internet. Now that people could work at home, they ran off to other places to live. Some had even moved to other countries like Puerto Rico or Costa Rica or some place called Palo Alto.

Her daughter, Linda, had moved to Seattle, and she almost never called anymore. She preferred texting. But Norma needed to hear the sound of her voice. She really couldn't tell how she was doing by an impersonal text. Besides, she didn't really know how to text. She had never been very good at typing. Macky tried to teach her, but she just couldn't get the hang of it, and she felt so stupid and out of date.

Her six-year-old granddaughter already had a Facebook account. Even Aunt Elner had learned to use a smartphone. Elner and Linda used to text and email back and forth with each other all the time. Norma was sure she must be the only person in America who didn't have an email address. A few of her old friends she used to keep up with never called anymore. Nobody wanted to talk on the phone. Even customer service was done over the Internet now, and if, by chance, you were lucky enough to speak to a live person, they were usually in India, and she couldn't understand them.

She was feeling so lonesome. Lonesome for the sound of old, familiar voices. Lonesome for people to talk to about the good ol' days, to laugh with and sometimes cry with.

Norma had never dreamed that one day, most of her friends would be gone or that she would fall asleep sitting in front of the television set or that she and Macky would sometimes go to bed before nine. Or that she and Macky would reach an age when they were actually talking about moving to a retirement community, looking at brochures showing good-looking, well-dressed gray-haired couples standing around laughing and drinking wine.

"But what can you do?" she thought. You can't push a rewind button and rewind yourself back to when you were young. All you can do is try to grow old as gracefully as you can, keep your mind active, and try not to fall down. Since she had been wearing progressive lenses, she had fallen down the front stairs, and then she had fallen going up the stairs.

And her memory wasn't what it used to be. Last week, she'd gone to the police station and reported to Ralph Childress that her purse had been stolen. Later that afternoon, she had found it in her own refrigerator.

Texting While Driving

When Mr. and Mrs. Arthur Kidd, both automobile accident victims, showed up at Still Meadows, they said that it hadn't been a drunk driver that caused it. They had slowed down to avoid hitting a dog, and some teenage kid who was texting while driving careened right toward them.

The next day, Tiffany Ann Smith, the teenage driver, came up as well, and someone made the mistake of asking her how it had happened.

"Oh, well . . . like, uh . . . I was driving out to meet my girlfriends? At the mall, you know? And I was late? And like . . . uh . . . I, uh . . . looked down just for like . . . uh, a second? To like see, uh . . . like, uh, if it was them texting me? And like . . . uh . . . it said like, 'Where R U?' And, uh, I went to text them back? And I hit, like, this car? And . . . I mean, like . . . I don't . . . like, uh, know whose fault it was . . . or anything? You know? Like . . . I mean . . . like, I don't think . . . like, it's really fair? You know, like, to blame me. Like . . . those people in front of me, like, uh, shouldn't have stopped. Like, it wasn't a stop sign or anything. Like . . . uh . . . how was I supposed to know that there was, like, this dog in the road?"

While Tiffany continued explaining the long and painful saga of how she came to be at Still Meadows at such an early age, Mrs. Carroll in plot 298, a literature major who cared deeply about English language, murmured to her neighbor, "I feel sorry for the young lady, but dear God, if she says 'like' one more time, I may scream."

Surprise Visitors

As it turned out, Gene Nordstrom wasn't the only soldier at Still Meadows to receive a medal.

On Memorial Day 2014, Ada Goodnight looked up, and there stood Fritzi Jurdabralinski and Bea Wallace, two of the women she had served with in the WASPs during World War II. She was stunned. She had not seen them in over thirty years, since her last WASP reunion. What in the world were they doing in Elmwood Springs? And why were her nieces and the mayor with them? And a color guard and Cathy Calvert from the newspaper? Hell, there was a whole crowd gathered behind them.

Fritzi spoke first. "Well, Ada, it took a hell of a long time, but we brought you a little something." She then took it out of a small box and held it up. "It's the Congressional Medal of Honor. Congratulations, pal."

Ada was in a little bit of a shock over the whole thing. She said, "I didn't think anybody would have even remembered us, much less given us a medal."

"Well, Ada," said Verbena, "like I always say, it may take a while, but everybody gets what they deserve eventually."

THAT AFTERNOON, THE GROUP was discussing who their favorite American heroes were and why. Gene said, "I think you would have to start with the men who wrote the Constitution. Without them, there would be no America."

Lucille Beemer said, "Excellent. Elner, who are your heroes?"

Elner thought about it and then said, "Well, I would say that after Jesus Christ, it would have to be Thomas Edison and Walt Disney."

Ida jumped in. "We are only naming important Americans, Elner. Jesus was not an American."

"Oh . . . well, then, Thomas Edison and Walt Disney."

"I agree with Mrs. Shimfissle," said Mr. Bell. "I didn't realize how famous Mickey Mouse and Donald Duck were until I went to Russia. I looked in the window of this shop, and there was a little statue of Mickey Mouse. Old Mickey Mouse made it all the way behind the Iron Curtain."

Soon everybody started jumping in with their favorites.

"How about Babe Ruth?"

"I say Abner Doubleday."

"Who?"

"He invented baseball."

"Oh."

"Franklin Roosevelt. He kept us all together during the Depression."

"Harry Truman. He put a stop to the war."

"Harvey Firestone gave us tires," said Luther Griggs.

"Will Rogers and Bob Hope. They made us laugh."

"Don't forget Andrew Carnegie. He gave us free libraries."

One of the younger boys called out, "Roy Rogers and Gene Autry!"

"J. Edgar Hoover," said another.

Birdie Swensen, who had been with Katrina in 1916 at the St. Louis demonstration for women's votes, said to Katrina, "Did you notice that not one woman was mentioned as being a great American? How about Susan B. Anthony? She helped get the vote for fifty-two percent of all American citizens . . . fifty-two percent!"

"Oh, Lord, once a suffragette, always a suffragette," whispered her husband to his friend.

THE NEXT WEEK, at Birdie and Katrina's request, the ladies were discussing who their favorite American women were, and Elner was ready with her list.

"Ginger Rogers, Dolly Parton, and the Statue of Liberty."

Her sister Ida said, "Oh, Lord, Elner. The Statue of Liberty is not a person."

"Well, she was once, wasn't she?"

"Yes, but she was not an American. Miss Beemer said American women. Now my choice is Mrs. Regina Chalkley."

"Who's that?" asked Elner.

"The national president of the Garden Club of America. That's who."

"Nobody has ever heard of her, Ida," said Gerta.

"Well, I have."

Mrs. Bell suddenly offered a name. "Kate Smith."

"Who?" asked a younger lady.

Elner said, "Kate Smith. She was that heavyset gal singer, used to be on the radio, had that big hit." Then Elner sang out in a loud voice, "Oooh, when the moon comes over the mountain."

"I still don't know who she is," said the lady.

Ada Goodnight said, "Hey, I have one. How about Sally Ride, the astronaut?"

"That's a good one," said Tot.

Verbena said, "Minnie Pearl."

"Who?" asked Birdie.

"She was a comedian on the **Grand Ole Opry**, always wore that funny hat."

Katrina said, "How about Louisa May Alcott?"

Ruby said, "Oh, that's a good one, Katrina."

Elner suddenly made a comment. "Isn't it funny? Kate Smith used to be one of the biggest stars we had, and nobody under seventy knows who she is."

Tiffany Ann, the teenage texter, suddenly joined in the conversation. "Like, uh, nobody's even **mentioned** Lady Gaga."

"Who?" asked about a hundred people.

"Just, like . . . the most famous person . . . like . . . in the whole entire world. Like . . . hello?"

This conversation was so interesting. Lucille Beemer, always on the rove for good discussion questions, thought that next week she might suggest the topic "Fame: Is It Worth the Effort?"

They didn't know it yet, but that was to be their last Thursday afternoon discussion meeting. On Lucille Beemer's next birthday, which was to be her 129th, all of her friends and ex-students, of which there were many, decided to surprise her and sing "Happy Birthday."

On the morning of her birthday, the Goodnight sisters started and then everybody else joined in with a loud and rousing "Happy birthday, Miss Beemer. Happy birthday to you!" After it was over, everyone cheered and yelled, "Speech! Speech!"

They all waited to hear what she was going to say. They waited for a few more minutes. Then Ruby said, "Lucille . . . are you there?"

But there was no answer. Lucille Beemer was gone.

HE'D BEEN A RATHER quiet man and so it wasn't until several weeks later when someone discovered that Gustav Tildholme was gone as well.

Norma

NORMA HAD BEEN SICK FOR ONLY A SHORT TIME, but when she arrived at Still Meadows, she found herself in a state of complete shock. And not so much over the fact that she was there, awake and talking. It was something else.

"All my life, I had been so afraid and scared of dying, and it wasn't scary at all. I just floated on out just as easy as can be, and I can't believe how calm and peaceful I feel."

"I'm so happy for you, honey," said Elner. "I know how you suffered with your nerves."

"Oh, thank you, Aunt Elner. I just hope it lasts."

"Oh, it will, I promise you. If anything, it gets even better. Every morning I wake up and fall in love with the world all over again. I'd had a lot of peaceful moments before I got here, but nothing like this. It really does pass all understanding, doesn't it, Tot?"

Tot Whooten said, "Hey, Norma, glad you're here, hon. It sure does. And it's so nice not to have a thing to do, but sit back and relax and enjoy yourself."

Elner said, "Now, honey, aren't you glad little Macky bought you your plot? If he hadn't, no telling where you might have ended up."

Tot added, "Hey, Norma, it's a good thing I didn't know how much fun being dead was going to be or I would have jumped off the top of a building and gotten here sooner."

Elner laughed. "Well, it's a good thing we don't have any tall buildings in Elmwood Springs."

Tot said, "Well, I could have jumped off the water tower. I didn't think about that. Oh, well, too late now. I got here when I was supposed to, I guess."

"Do you think it's true, Aunt Elner?" asked Norma. "That we died when we were supposed to?"

"Oh, I feel it is, honey." Then Elner added, "In fact, I think you came up at just the right time."

TWO DAYS LATER, ELNER Shimfissle disappeared. It was a huge loss for everyone. First Miss Beemer, now Elner. She would be missed terribly, but Norma was thankful that at least she'd had a chance to speak with her that one last time.

Next Stop, Key West

IT WAS THREE A.M., AND JAMES DWAYNE WHOOTEN, Jr., was rattling around in the kitchen, trying his best not to make any noise. He had looked in her purse, but as usual, his wife, Debbie, had hidden her car keys from him. She worked at Walmart and had just bought herself a new Toyota Camry, and she didn't want him getting drunk and wrecking it. Damn Debbie, she was the cause of all his problems. If she hadn't gotten pregnant, he could have left a long time ago, but he had hung around, taking care of his kids and hers from another marriage. And now he just found out she was having an affair with some dude in the photo department. The kids didn't give him any respect. Just last week, when he had been passed out on the couch, one of her brats had tried to set fire to him, so the hell with all of them. He looked everywhere. In the coffeepot, the microwave oven, in all the drawers, on the shelves, behind the toaster, but no keys. Shit.

Defeated, he went into the living room and flopped down on the plaid La-Z-Boy. Then he had another thought. He got up and went to the drawer where she kept all the information on the kitchen appliances and insurance papers, and sure enough, there it was: the envelope from the Toyota dealership with the car papers, and inside was the extra key. AHA . . . Margaritaville, here I come!

The Pie

Today was Wednesday, and as usual, Edna Childress was over at the senior center. Wednesday was bingo day. Edna never missed bingo day or Texas hold 'em poker.

Ralph Childress was at home, sitting at the kitchen table with his coffee and a piece of apple pie Edna had left out for him, scrolling through his phone. He was looking on eBay at pictures of used recreational vehicles for sale. Luther Griggs, who had been an expert, had told him the best kind to look for.

Edna didn't know it yet, but after his retirement from the police department next month, he was going to buy one and drive her up to the Mall of America and let the old gal shop till she dropped. Ralph was just about to take his first bite of pie when he heard the most god-awful screaming and banging going on at his front door. He jumped up and went to find out what in the hell was going on.

He should have known it. When he opened his door, there stood Debbie, Dwayne Jr.'s fourth or fifth wife—he couldn't remember which—throwing a fit, screaming, and carrying on and on about how that no-good son of a bitch Dwayne Jr. had just stolen her brand-new Toyota Camry. Ralph listened and calmed her down as best he could. He told her he would meet her over at the station in a half hour, and she could fill out a stolen car report. As far as he was concerned, there was no hurry. He knew Dwayne Jr. hadn't gone too far. He was too dumb and stoned to find his way out of town.

When Ralph returned to the kitchen and sat back down to eat his piece of pie, his plate was empty. There wasn't anything left of his pie but a few crumbs and a black feather on the windowsill. "Goddamn it to hell." He wished people wouldn't bother him at home. While he'd been at the door dealing with crazy Debbie, some damn crow had flown in the window and made off with his pie. "Goddamn it." And he'd **wanted** that pie, too. He knew he should have parked his patrol car in the back.

Ralph picked up his phone, stuck his gun in its holster, and slammed out of the house. He was so sick of dealing with the damn Whootens, he didn't know what to do. James Whooten in and out of the drunk tank, Tot's aggravated assault with a cement gnome, the daughter had set fire to one of her boyfriend's trucks, and now Dwayne Jr. again. Lord. There was a bad gene running around in that family.

Dwayne Jr.

THE LAST THING HE REMEMBERED WAS STOPPING AT the Quik Mart for a case of beer for the road. When he woke up three days later, James Dwayne Whooten, Jr., quickly realized he was not in Key West. He was up at Still Meadows in the Whooten family plot, deader than dirt and sober for the first time in thirty-five years.

"Hey, Momma," he said to Tot. "Guess what? I think I just got killed in a car accident."

"Why am I not surprised?"

"You ain't surprised I'm here?"

"No. I'm just surprised you didn't come sooner. What I want to know is where did you get a car? I thought they had taken your license away for good."

Dwayne Jr. opened his mouth to lie (always his first instinct), but strangely enough, he suddenly found himself telling the truth. "I stole Debbie's car."

"Oh, Lord . . . poor Debbie. You didn't kill anybody else, did you?"

"No, just me. It was a single-car accident. I think I hit a tree."

"That was just pure luck. I'm sure you were drunk as a coot."

"Yeah, I guess I was."

"Well, I hate to say I told you so, but I told you so."

"Hello, son," said James, jumping into the conversation.

"Oh . . . hey, Dad, did you hear what happened to me?"

"Yes, I did."

"What a bummer, huh?"

"Well, son, as bad as it sounds, it might have been the only way to get you sober."

A MONTH LATER, DWAYNE JR. said, "Momma, I'm sorry I stole all that stuff from you and called you them ugly names."

"I appreciate you telling me that, son."

"I didn't mean none of it."

"I know you didn't, honey, and just remember, no matter what, I love you, and you will always be my little boy."

Hearing that one sentence gave Dwayne Jr. a better high than any drug or booze ever had. He'd had to drive himself into a tree to get here, but at last, he was at a place where he felt happy, joyous, and free and stone-cold sober. How cool was that?

—

LATER, WHEN NORMA WAS CHATTING with her mother, she said, "Mother, you just sound so relaxed."

"Oh, I am," Ida said. "Ask your father."

Herbert said, "She's right, honey. It took a while, but she's finally calmed down."

"You know, Norma, I always thought if I wasn't running and doing all day and night, I might miss something, but now, just watching the world twirl by without me is so enjoyable. I wish I had known it sooner."

"Me, too."

"Honey?"

"Yes?" said Norma.

"Thank you for the roses every Mother's Day."

"Oh, you're so welcome, Mother."

"By the way . . . who is that little Chinese person Linda brought out to see me?"

"Oh, that's Apple. Your great-granddaughter."

There was a slight pause. "Has Linda married a Communist?"

"No, Mother. She adopted a little girl from China."

"Oh . . . I see."

"And the Chinese aren't Communists anymore."

"**Really?** Well, that's good to know. . . . There were too many of them."

The Tip

T<small>HE RULE OF THUMB IS THAT WHEN A CRIME IS</small>
committed, there is usually someone out there who
knows who did it. And no matter how long it takes,
either out of guilt or sometimes just plain revenge,
they will suddenly decide to tell what they know.

And that is exactly what happened in the Hanna
Marie Swensen will-tampering case. One day, out of
the blue, Chief of Police Ralph Childress had a
strange message on his phone that read **Look behind
A.S. portrait at dairy.**

Ralph had no idea what it meant; the only A.S. he
knew was Ander Swensen. There was a painting of
the old man down at the dairy. But it could be just
some kid playing a prank. He'd gotten a lot of that
lately, but he decided to drive over and check it out
anyway.

W<small>HEN HE GOT THERE,</small> the young man working in
the front office was not a lot of help.

"No, sir," he said. "I've been working here six years, and I've never seen any portrait of anybody out here."

"I see."

"I'd be happy to show you around."

"No, that's okay. Thanks anyway."

Ralph went back to the car and suddenly remembered that Mildred Flowers, a gal he had gone to high school with, had worked at the dairy right after Little Miss Davenport died. He decided to give her a call.

"Hey, Mildred, Ralph Childress."

"Well, hey there. How are you? We haven't seen you for a while. You okay? Is Edna still feeding you all those pies?"

"Oh, yeah. Ah, listen, let me ask you something. Didn't there used to be a portrait of Mr. Swensen down at the dairy?"

"Yeah, it was hanging in the boardroom with all the other awards and things."

"Whatever happened to it, do you know?"

"Sure. After poor Hanna Marie died, His Royal Horse's Assness ordered us to take it all down and throw it all out. Why?"

"Did you?"

"Well, hell no . . . I took them down, but I didn't get rid of them. I knew the Swensens. That man worked hard to build that business and win those awards. I wasn't going to sling them all out in the dumpster just because **he** said so."

"So what did you do with them?"

"I stuck them in a big box and took 'em home and put it in the garage. Why?"

"Do you still have them?"

"Well, yeah, as far as I know, I do, unless Carl threw them out. But I doubt it."

"Do you mind if I come over and take a look?"

"No, but it might take a while to find it. That garage is packed full of forty years of Carl's crap. He don't believe in throwing anything out. He's still got his daddy's old shoes."

Ralph took a couple of young deputies with him, and after two hours of hot, sweaty work pulling down boxes, they found the one they were looking for. And by God, there was something wedged in the wood frame in the back of that painting. Ralph opened the envelope and saw what it was. He wasn't quite sure why it would be important, but he took it over to the judge.

SHORTLY AFTER RALPH CHILDRESS located the copy of Hanna Marie's original will and presented it to Judge Thorneycroft, two arrests were made. They located the woman lawyer, and she took a plea deal for a lesser sentence in exchange for a written confession explaining in detail how she and Michael Vincent had falsified the will. The lawyer got two years for fraud. He got ten, with no time off for good behavior. As one juror said after his trial, "That man wouldn't know what good behavior was if it walked up and bit him in the ass."

Another man said, "It just goes to show you, the old saying is true."

"Which one?"

" 'Hell hath no fury like a woman scorned,' particularly a redhead. She laid that bastard out to filth, and I think she enjoyed doing it, too."

The headline read:

Dairy Owner
Michael Vincent Convicted

The Off-the-Grid
Goat Farm

2015

HER FATHER HAD STARTED THE ELMWOOD SPRINGS News in 1949. This morning, Cathy Calvert sat down at her desk and looked around the office, the same one she had worked in all her adult life. It was a mess—papers everywhere, things stuck up on the wall. She had vowed for years to clean it up one of these days, but she never had. And now the newspaper was closing.

The town had lost population, her subscriptions were down, and she couldn't compete with the Internet. She'd come to hate the thing. With so many tweets and instant news, she couldn't keep up. She was exhausted at the end of the day, just trying to answer all of her emails. Now every kid with a camera was a reporter and could get a story on Facebook within seconds.

For the past thirty-five years, she had written a weekly editorial under the byline "Chatty Cathy," and she found that lately, she really didn't have much left to say that she hadn't said already. It was time to go. She was retiring from the newspaper business and starting a new one. She had been saving her money for a long time and had bought a large piece of land and a farmhouse and planned to raise goats.

It would be a big departure from what she had been doing, but she had always loved baby goats, ever since she was a child and had played with them out at Elner Shimfissle's farm. So now she was typing out her very last "Chatty Cathy" column.

Dear Reader,

As you know, I will be leaving Elmwood Springs and closing down the paper. Sadly, this will be our last issue.

I find that after all these years of being your "girl reporter," it is very hard to say goodbye. I have learned so much from all of you: The true meaning of family and friendship and what it means to be a good neighbor. I have known most of you all my life, and I have been especially honored that you entrusted me with the job of writing your obituaries. It's a sad thing to lose loved ones or contemplate our own mortality, not knowing what will happen after we leave this world for another.

But what I can say for sure is having known all of you, I leave here with a very high opinion of human beings. I bid you a fond farewell until we meet again.

Cathy Calvert

P.S. You may write to me in care of the Off-the-Grid Goat Farm, P.O. Box 326, Two Sisters, Oregon, 94459.

Who Done It?

A COUPLE OF YEARS LATER, WHEN RALPH CHILDRESS arrived at Still Meadows, people were very eager to talk to him.

Merle Wheeler said, "Hey, Ralph, we heard about you finding that copy of Hanna Marie's will. How'd you do it?"

"Yeah," added Verbena. "How'd you figure it out?"

Ralph chuckled. "Well, I'm kinda embarrassed to tell you, but it sure wasn't no fancy police work on my part. Somebody told me to go look behind the portrait, so I did."

"Who?"

"Well, that's the thing. I don't know. It was an anonymous tip. One day, I was flipping through my phone on my things-to-do list, and there it was, written right in my calendar."

"And you don't know who put it there?"

"No, and it wasn't Edna. She said she'd never seen it before. All we can figure is whoever did it must have hacked into my phone."

Ruby said, "Well, personally, I think it was somebody who must have seen Little Miss Davenport hide it there that did it."

Tot agreed. "Yeah, or else was told about it by someone who had seen her."

Verbena said, "I sure would love to know who it was . . . and why they waited so long to speak up."

Merle said, "I think it was the redhead."

"Maybe so," said Ralph. "But we'll never know now."

Macky Is Worried

NORMA HAD BEEN GONE FOR MORE THAN THREE years, and Macky was just hanging around the house. Their daughter, Linda, had begged him to come and live with them in Seattle, but he wouldn't go. He needed to be in Elmwood Springs, where Norma was.

He took care of her grave, made sure it was kept up. Even though he missed her so much, he was glad she had gone first. She'd been so scared at the end, and if he hadn't been there with her, it would have been terrible for her.

Today was the Fourth of July, but he didn't feel like going to the parade. The kid to whom he had sold the hardware store had asked him to ride with him, but he had no interest in seeing it. The way the world was going, Macky knew that the old guys marching in the parade today in their VFW hats would look foolish to the young people watching them go by. And maybe a lot of them **were** foolish old men trying to hang on to their glory days. But they had been young men once, ready to fight and die for their country. And where would America be today if it hadn't been for a lot of foolish young men?

He was worried about his country. Something was rotting from the inside—a slow decay of what was right and wrong. It was as if hundreds of cynical little rats were chewing at its very fiber, gnawing away year by year, until it was collapsing into a vat of gray slime and self-loathing. It had oozed under the doors of the classrooms, the newscasts, and in the movies and television shows and had slowly changed the national dialogue until it was now a travesty to be proud of your country, foolish to be patriotic, and insensitive to even suggest that people take care of themselves.

History was being rewritten by the hour, heroes pulled down to please the political correctors. We were living in a country where there was freedom of speech for some, but not all. What was it going to take to get America back on track? Would everything they had fought for be forgotten? He was so glad he and Norma had grown up when they had. They had come of age in such an innocent time, when people wanted to work and better themselves. Now the land of the free meant an entirely different thing. Each generation had become a weaker version of the last, until we were fast becoming a nation of whiners and people looking for a free ride—even expecting it. Hell, kids wouldn't even leave home anymore. He felt like everything was going downhill.

Up at Still Meadows, not everyone felt that way. Mrs. Lindquist's great-granddaughter had just arrived and was saying something else about her generation. "Oh," she said. "So many wonderful things are happening now. They are finding new cures for things every day. And people are so much more tolerant and accepting of everything now: different races, different religions, different lifestyles. Life is so much easier than when you were growing up, and women are just doing everything, and now with the Internet, well . . . the whole world has changed. Honestly, I have to say I grew up in the very best time possible."

Hello, Macky!

WHEN MACKY WARREN FINALLY WENT TO HIS REward, as they say, and landed up on the hill, the first voice he heard was Norma's shouting, "Surprise!"

"Good God, woman, you nearly scared me half to death."

Norma laughed. "Think again, Macky. You are dead, silly. Oh, Macky, I'm so glad you're here. I have so much to tell you. Aunt Elner was right. She told me I'd be glad you bought us these plots, and am I ever. You are going to just love it out here, honey."

LATER, AFTER MACKY HAD recovered from the state of shock of Norma shouting at him, he began to realize that this new state of being was a relief. He had always been casting about in his mind: What was life all about? What the hell was his purpose? What was he supposed to be doing?

But now, everything made sense. He had lived and died; it was as simple as that. He hadn't needed a purpose. The fact that he was born was all the purpose he had ever needed. He was meant to be his parents' child, his wife's husband, his daughter's father, and on and on. Despite all his grand schemes and ambitions to set the world on fire, to be someone special, he was just another little link in the chain of life, inching forward from generation to generation. The only thing he had to do was relax and enjoy where he was. This was exactly where he was meant to be right now. He had to agree with Norma. He didn't think he had ever been happier in his entire life.

As the years went by, all the old gang—Tot, Ruby, Verbena, and Merle—had all disappeared. One by one. And it seemed they were all leaving much sooner than they used to. And people were talking.

Dwayne Jr. said to Gene Nordstrom, "Hey, did you hear? We lost three more people last night."

"Damn, that's not good," replied Gene.

"You don't think those people are going to hell, do you?"

"No, I don't think so. If that were the case, I think they would have gone there right away."

"Yeah," said Dwayne Jr. "You're probably right, and for all we know, they could be headed off into another dimension or to some real cool parallel universe."

"To where?"

Winding Down

2016

MACKY WARREN WAS THE LAST PERSON TO BE LAID to rest at Still Meadows, and since there weren't any more new people coming in, almost nobody came to visit anymore.

As the years went by, it seemed that Still Meadows had just become a place for people to jog, ride their bike, walk the dog, teach their kids how to drive, drink beer, smoke pot, or make out with your girlfriend.

One morning, Old Man Hendersen woke up furious. The day before, some kid had knocked over his headstone, along with four others, when he'd put his car in reverse instead of drive. "And they won't fix it," he said. "This place is going to hell in a handbasket—weeds everywhere—and has anybody noticed that we have an infestation of gophers out here? All night, I hear them digging. Scratch, scratch, scratch."

Ida Jenkins turned to her husband. "He's right. The way they have let this place go is disgraceful. I don't understand where the Garden Club is. This would not have happened on my watch, I can tell you."

Three days later, Eustus Percy Hendersen was gone. And as odd as it sounds, people missed him. As Gene said, "He was crabby as hell . . . but I liked the old goat."

BY THE YEAR 2020, the town of Elmwood Springs was almost nonexistent. The old mall had shut down, and a factory outlet mall with an IMAX theater had been built on the other side of the dairy, where a new community had formed. The WELCOME TO ELMWOOD SPRINGS sign put up by the Lions Club that once stood on the turnoff had fallen down. There was almost nothing left but a few of the old houses, a trailer park, and a row of storage units. Linda used to send flowers to her parents on Easter, but she eventually stopped. She didn't really believe her parents were there, anyway. She was right, of course. By then, both were gone.

As the years went by, there would be nobody left at Still Meadows. Nothing remained but a lonely hill full of overgrown weeds and grass covering broken headstones.

In the grand scheme of things, their time at Still Meadows had been a short time, but it had been a good time.

Epilogue

2021

IT WAS GETTING LATE, AND THE SOUND OF THE traffic was growing fainter by the moment.

The old crow in the tree lifted herself up, shuffled her shiny black feathers in place with one long iridescent ripple, then hunched back down for the night. She watched the last of the couples scurrying home through the park. After a moment, the old crow blinked her eyes and sighed. "I just loved being a human being, didn't you?"

The gray mourning dove that sat beside her shook her head. "I couldn't say, Elner. Never been one."

"Ahh . . . well, you have a lot to look forward to. It's a lot of fun," said the old crow. "But then, I enjoy being a crow, too. I know a lot of people don't care for crows, but personally, I always got a big kick out of them. Every morning, my husband, Will, and I used to sit on our back porch and watch them flying around way up in the sky. And now, I'm one of them, doing the same thing, and it's just glorious to be able to fly."

A gray squirrel who was curled up in his nest above chimed in. "I was a turtle for over sixty-four years."

"Oh my, what was that like?"

"Very restful," said the squirrel.

"Isn't it wonderful? We just keep going. . . . Who would have believed it?"

A small four-leaf clover under a bench laughed. "Not me. I always figured when your time was up, that was it, and it's sure a lot of fun going from one thing to another."

The dove said, "I agree. Whoever or whatever set this life thing in motion certainly knew what they were doing."

"That's for sure," said the squirrel. "But I just wonder where we will go after we have been every living thing on earth."

"I wouldn't worry about it too much," said the four-leaf clover (who used to be a science teacher in Akron, Ohio). "That process will take trillions of years, and . . . there are over eight million species of fish alone, not to mention all the insects."

"I was a flea once," offered a small grub passing by.

The gray squirrel bit into a walnut, spit out a piece of shell, and said, "But, still, it is something to think about. Who knows? Someday we could all end up on another planet, in an entirely new universe, and start all over again."

"Ah, sweet mystery of life," sang the old crow. The moon smiled and went behind a cloud, and pretty soon they all settled down for the night, looking forward to another day.

Meanwhile, outside of Oxnard, California, Luther Griggs (now a small green weed that had popped up in a crack in the cement out on the 101 freeway) was so enjoying watching all the different makes of trucks and RVs passing by.

Mr. Evander J. Chapman (presently a snail in Woodsboro, Maryland) was still at it, and as snails are among the slowest-moving creatures in the world, he pretty much had a captive audience. As the group leisurely slid along, headed for another leaf, he continued, "Yes, sir. There we wuz, just me and ol' Andrew Jackson. Ol' Hickory hisself. Why, we musta been surrounded by ten thousand Seminole Injuns, and they's all mad. . . . So there we wuz, back to back . . . and we fit them off right smartly, tilt we run clean out of ammunition. Next thing I knowed, I sawed a hole in the woods and hollered, 'Run!' Well, sir, I runned one way, and he runned the other. . . . The next time I seed him, he says, 'Evander, you done saved my life, boy!' So I says . . ."

Though snails are usually slow moving, a little-known fact is that, if provoked, they do have the ability to pick up their shells and gallop away. And after listening to Mr. Chapman for a while, some did.

And somewhere in South America, two beautiful

yellow-and-black butterflies were fluttering together in the bright sunshine—one named Gustav and the other Lucille.

And even though she was now a crow, Elner still had her memories and a few secrets. And if crows could laugh (which they can't), she would have. Nobody knew it, but she had been the one who had flown into the kitchen window and pecked out that message into Ralph's phone. Eating Ralph's pie had been an afterthought. It was downright thievery, she knew. But then, she never could resist Edna's apple pie. That gal could bake!

A short time after the arrests had been made, Hanna Marie's original will was reinstated, and all the properties, including the dairy, went back to Albert Olsen and all of Hanna Marie's nieces and nephews. And the Missouri School for the Deaf received an anonymous donation of $5 million for their scholarship fund. All compliments of Little Miss Davenport and one old crow.

SADLY, MICHAEL VINCENT WAS not serving time for the murder of Hanna Marie, like he should have been. However, while he was in prison, a fellow inmate had suddenly, and without any provocation, stabbed him straight through the heart with a knitting needle. How that knitting needle made its way inside of an all-men's penitentiary remains a mystery.

Maybe it's like Verbena Wheeler always said, "It may take a while, but everybody gets what they deserve, eventually."

Of course, both Hanna Marie's grandmother, Birdie Swensen, and her great-aunt Katrina Nordstrom had been quite the knitters in their day.

AND SO IT ENDS . . .

Or maybe not . . .

What do you think?

Acknowledgments

―――

THE AUTHOR WISHES TO EXPRESS HER SINCERE gratitude to the wonderful people at Random House publishing for all their invaluable help and support throughout the years. Thank you from the bottom of my heart.

About the Author

FANNIE FLAGG's career started in the fifth grade when she wrote, directed, and starred in her first play, titled **The Whoopee Girls,** and she has not stopped since. At age nineteen she began writing and producing television specials, and later wrote for and appeared on **Candid Camera.** She then went on to distinguish herself as an actress and a writer in television, films, and the theater. She is the bestselling author of **Daisy Fay and the Miracle Man; Fried Green Tomatoes at the Whistle Stop Cafe; Welcome to the World, Baby Girl!; Standing in the Rainbow; A Redbird Christmas; Can't Wait to Get to Heaven; I Still Dream About You; The All-Girl Filling Station's Last Reunion;** and **The Whole Town's Talking.** Flagg's script for the movie **Fried Green Tomatoes** was nominated for an Academy Award and the Writers Guild of America Award, and won the highly regarded Scripter Award for best screenplay of the year. Fannie Flagg is also a winner of the Harper Lee Prize. She lives happily in California and Alabama.